PRAISE FOR

THE REST OF THE EARTH

"An epic tale masterfully told. An astonishing novel. Related with extraordinary precision. There are pages of descriptions of the kind that entranced 19th-century readers that all but disappeared from fiction after the coming of movies and television. The period detail is exact and convincing. So are the many descriptions of ever-changing yet unchanging nature, the hills, lakes, vegetation, and wildlife. Henderson has been in these places, seen, smelled, heard, and felt the imprint of all these things."
—*Boston Globe*

"A torrent of sensuous, elliptical prose . . . lyrical, evocative, beautiful . . . flows unrestrainedly across the page like the Wind River in space." —*Cleveland Plain Dealer*

WILLIAM HAYWOOD HENDERSON has taught creative writing at Harvard and Brown and is a former Wallace Stegner Fellow in Creative Writing at Stanford. He grew up in Colorado and Wyoming and now lives in San Francisco.

"Henderson's greatest strength as a writer is in his prose, steeped in detail and hypnotic in rhythm. Whitmanesque sensuality infuses every word. Henderson's almost mythical bond with the natural world makes *Walden* look like a walk through a city park." —*San Francisco Bay Guardian*

"Plot details can't start to convey the hypnotic attractions of place in this walkabout through the wilderness that transforms near-random events into a mysterious evocation of human longing at its most extreme."
—*Kirkus Reviews*

"Henderson's novel is set in a wilderness that staggers the imagination. Mesmerizing and beautiful . . . as mysterious in its portrayal of character as it is in terms of rocks and stars." —*Providence Journal Bulletin*

"Masterful . . . beautifully written."
—*Rocky Mountain News*

"Meticulous and magical." —*Oakland Tribune*

"Rich, remarkable." —*Seattle Post-Intelligencer*

"Truly stunning." —*Publishers Weekly*

By the same author

Native

THE REST OF THE EARTH

WILLIAM HAYWOOD HENDERSON

A PLUME BOOK

The author wishes to express his gratitude to Bob Lowney, Paul Davis, the Corporation of Yaddo, the Wallace Stegner Fellowship, Malaga Baldi, Deirdre Mullane, Mary Egan, and Rita Gabis.

PLUME
Published by the Penguin Group
Penguin Putnam Inc., 375 Hudson Street, New York, New York 10014, U.S.A.
Penguin Books Ltd, 27 Wrights Lane, London W8 5TZ, England
Penguin Books Australia Ltd, Ringwood, Victoria, Australia
Penguin Books Canada Ltd, 10 Alcorn Avenue, Toronto, Ontario, Canada M4V 3B2
Penguin Books (N.Z.) Ltd, 182–190 Wairau Road, Auckland 10, New Zealand

Penguin Books Ltd, Registered Offices: Harmondsworth, Middlesex, England

Published by Plume, an imprint of Dutton NAL, a member of Penguin Putnam Inc.
Previously published in a Dutton edition.

First Plume Printing, August, 1998
10 9 8 7 6 5 4 3 2 1

Ⓟ REGISTERED TRADEMARK—MARCA REGISTRADA

The Library of Congress catalogued the Dutton edition as follows:
Henderson, William Haywood.
    The rest of the Earth / William Haywood Henderson.
        p.   cm.
    ISBN 0-525-93981-4 (hc.)
    ISBN 0-452-27416-8 (pbk.)
    1. Fiction.   I. Title.
PS3558.E4944R47   1997
813'.54—dc21   97–12759
                                                CIP

Original hardcover design by Leonard Telesca
Printed in the United States of America

To my mother and father

The whole of this immense area was inclosed by an outer range of shadowy peaks, some of them faintly marked on the horizon, which seemed to wall it in from the rest of the earth.

—Washington Irving,
*The Adventures of
Captain Bonneville, U.S.A.*

Walker Avary crouched in the lee of boulders, in the violet bloom of thistles. Through the long cold morning and on past noon, fog reached flat across San Francisco Bay, the water jade in the breeze. He ate wild strawberries. Far below, an acre of tents with their even spacing, their sameness, seemed a plot of graves in the crosshatch of buildings. To the south, in a forest of ruined masts, the old ship Rockwell, with its sides finally given way and its rigging gone, had settled onto the bay's sediment. Four years ago, Captain Avary had abandoned the Rockwell, taken a new ship, and continued west on the Japan route, sailing on from this city with barely a pause, leaving Walker behind.

And through his first winters in the city, when a storm set the waterfront into rhythm, Walker would climb out from one of those ships to the next, find a family in a deckhouse, laundry in the rigging, dark pools in the holds, rank flotsam. On the Rockwell, the farthest ship out from solid ground, he would balance at the stern, above the chop, safe in his oilskin, his face chilled, his ears deafened by the rustle of his hood and the pop of rain. Out there was Yerba Buena Island, the rush of tide mixing salt and less salt, and the far shore, the hills corralling whatever clouds couldn't rise. He knew of desert beyond the hills, of mountains, he knew of the destination of the train he saw moving against the distance, the smoke and steam, the luxurious speed. The train had broken all the way through, east to west to east, and been spiked at Promontory, and now there was nothing to keep the land from filling. He would force his way into the Rockwell's captain's quarters, sit through the evening, and listen for rats in the hold. The glass still kept out the wind, the hull still tight enough, then, to suspend all that dark weight in the swaying storm. Shut into that space, with the silk rotted, with the brass and crystal gone, pried off and carried away, Walker would sleep.

He finished the last of the strawberries, made the descent through the thistles, along the creek, and entered among the buildings. After a long ramble with the buildings rising taller, the ornate shadows of cornices and false fronts swinging slowly with the sun, he turned onto Montgomery Street, to number 121, in through the door. The clerks were all busy muttering and shuffling about in the closing-time doldrums. From a table he picked up a pale blue tourist pamphlet and waved to young Mr. Stanwood, the slick-haired clerk who had chatted him up about graded inclines, chasms and trestles, and the elegance of the Pullman Palace car. *Comfort, Luxury, and Safety Combined. Sleeping on the Pioneer Route.* He stepped back onto the street, sheltered himself in a doorway, and opened the pamphlet, folding out the map to a narrow slice of the continent from Boston to San Francisco, with the web of rails to the east, and to the west the vast squares and angles of open pastel cut only by the single rail line and a few spurs and stage routes and lonely roads. Wyoming Territory, the clean pink square, with hardly a town but along the rail, hardly a road, and the great clusters of mountains, the geysers, Indian country. *Shoshonees and Bannacks. Sweet Water. Heart Mt. Stinking R. Diamond Field. Wind River.* From his back pocket he pulled his old copy of the pamphlet, dropped it on the ground, and replaced it with the new.

He crossed Montgomery, on toward Market, then west to Atkinson Mercantile, around to the alley and the thick metal door. Working his key in the lock, he was into the stock room, shelves rising with bolts of wool, plates, silk, enamel bowls, powder, bottles of scent. He slipped past a door and its opening toward patrons and windows, moved beyond the light, ran his fingers until he felt a stack of tins—oysters in smoky oil. He palmed three tins and slid them into his pockets.

Along a quick aisle back toward the door, he paused, crouched where he could look through the shelves and into Mr. Atkinson's office. Atkinson was at his desk in his long black suit, his eyes blue in that white untouched face, not a hint of ruddy, the beard black and clipped, the hair black and oiled. Beyond him, pushing her mass of coffee curls back from her brow, Miss Haugen laughed, the lamp warming the side of her face, her shoulder. Walker had met that young woman last week at a party at Atkinson's house, an anniversary celebration—twenty years ago Atkinson had made his first killing, selling ten crates of cookware from the back of a wagon at the wharves, and got himself started from almost nothing, with the city barely settled. And now he'd constructed that house of his, the number etched in glass, and the lamps all lit for the party, hot white overhead and on the walls. The young ladies watched Atkinson talk, watched him tip a couple into the first steps of a waltz. Walker had tried that night to think himself into Atkinson's stance, the bulk of chest and thighs in the black evening wool. A sideboard held platters of great round rolls dusted with flour, pastries glazed with yellow sugar, pink beef, a long fish with its serrated mouth gapped in an almost-grin, its eye blue. Beside the food, Atkinson took Walker by the elbow and drew him round to face the girl, saying, "Miss Teresa Haugen, this is Walker Avary. He is a young man you might want to know someday. Works my merc as if wages were the least of it. For the love of the work? Is that it, Walker?" The girl laughed, her mouth an exquisite crooked rose and delicate teeth, and she reached and pressed fingers to Walker's neck as if testing his tendons, and he said, "I work for you, Mr. Atkinson. Yes, sir," and he moved beyond them, out the glass doors to the terrace, the iron railing, darkness. Turning, he watched the dance slowly gather each guest until only the servants held themselves off the rhythm, and then even the servants were caught by the nearest swirl or grasp and drawn in. The music played on. Walker let himself back in and ate a roll, took a sweet bite of flaky crust, berry, pocketed the fish server, the long-handled sterling like a heavenly trowel, palm fronds hammered along its surface, and he found the front door, out, and down the stone steps.

Walker rose from his crouch in the stock room, left Mr. Atkinson and Miss Haugen, and he was outside, into the alley, the metal door solid again in its jamb. He threw his key high in that gap of brick walls, and the key lost its shape against early evening, rattled on the roof of the laundry behind, slid into the rain gutter, and remained there twenty feet above the muddy drainage.

Gray had blown in. Taking to the deeper streets where the buildings might block the cold, where the horses raised their heads and glared white-eyed, stamped against the tension of the reins, he hurried toward the Mission, finally saw the squat white church ahead in the fog, and entered through those thick walls. It was almost dark but for the votives at the rear, almost silent. He came forward in the narrow space. The beams far above, the design hatched out in fading dye, the Dolores altar with its faces invisible but for the uneasy glint of eyes or a bit of ungrounded gold, a staff raised. The high yellow windows filtered the rush of cloud, leaving him no sense of the floor. He thought he might reel, the building adrift, but he continued, and then he touched the altar, steadied himself. He found the wood cool and almost soft, as if it had dried there a thousand years and lost its core—but it was no older than the country. He remembered the face of the Lord on a locked panel—he made out the eyes, pushed at what he guessed to be the bearded chin, and heard the lock rattle. With his pocket knife, he forced the lock, heard the faintest squeal of hinges, and he placed a tin in that black space and closed the door again, knowing he could not lock it. "Walker Avary," he said, repeated, and then listened for movement, for anyone he might have missed in the dimness.

Nothing. Turning, he saw the candles far at the back, their heat trifling with the darkness beneath the choir loft. He came down through the space, found a cache of unlit candles, and took a few. His heart still raced from the ground he'd covered that afternoon, and he hurried from the Mission, accelerating until his pace matched his pulse again.

Beyond open stretches, uneven blocks of housing, he came to a row of storefronts that leaned toward the puddles. He clattered along the sidewalk, in through a door, into a crowd. Forcing himself among the taller men at the bar, he gave his order, felt the heat of them all against the backs of his hands, felt the sudden pain of noise in the curves of his chilled ears, waited in the smell of damp wool.

Even with the railroad, still these men had almost all come round by way of the sea—French, Irish, German, Russian— the whole range, and they all spoke at once. A great Spaniard tossed back a drink, and the drops that escaped his lips ate clean trails through the grime on his chin. Walker knew them all. He had seen these men bathe, nearly bathed with them, in an establishment a few blocks away. In the wood-slat room with the boilers, they each stripped and waited, stepped into the tubs of water gray with soap and heat. One after another. With Walker waiting until the crowd cleared, until no one opened the door to the entry hall, and then he stripped and submerged himself to the neck, the leavings of someone else so close to his mouth—the grime collected in crevices, soil of the city, sweat, flecks of wood and stone and brick, the smear of love. He looked down through the water, slowly ran his fingers over his limbs and under, where the week's work had settled, watched new men come in through the door, watched them so casually drop their shirts, trousers, tatters of long johns, and step through the steam, submerge, laugh, move on. He might wait a long while until he was alone in that room again, and then he slid deeper into the tub, allowed the water to cover him completely, his head back, his hair a loose wavy flow, and he opened his eyes, opened his mouth, swallowed a gulp, came up with his eyes stinging, his mouth sour and intense. He dried himself. He entered back onto the street. For hours, he tasted the ridges and joints of the men, the slab of haunches, heat of straining muscle, direction, precision. For days, he felt the fine coating on his skin, smelled it, knew it kept him safe.

Most evenings, he was with them all in that saloon. The men ate and drank together, might as well have been trapped together on a nighttime voyage for all the time they spent outside those walls. Through the windows onto the street there were never more than specks of light passing. What must the place seem to these men—the plank tables, the yellow walls burnished brown with smoke, the sound of rain on the stovepipe above, plates of hot food, whiskey, a back room with bunks to let. Someone sang, mournful and struggling, words of a vessel, a storm, and finally the voice was lost and someone demanded the proprietor buy a piano. Someone slept in a corner, his coat still buttoned up to his throat. Someone stepped into the darkness of the back hall. They came in from the city, they took their way out into the city again, followed the streets in long looping rambles toward their return. Walker saw a woman come in from the alley, lean there at the door to the back stoop with her skirts up, late at night, and a man had his way, and then another man. As Walker paused before stepping out into the night and across the alley to his own place, he heard from the bunk room, more than once, when there weren't any women, sounds that had little to do with sleep. The building had a strong smell of humid forest, the building was shabby, unsteady, might fall in a few years to be replaced with finer construction, sharper details, the building was completely without foundation, but it locked them together, locked them away from something.

Walker drank his whiskey in tiny sips, holding it beneath his tongue, burning away the day's great tour, the ground he had covered, unfinished yet. The rowdy laughter, held in this box of heat. He spun a coin across the bar, fought his way toward the back, into the kitchen.

"Frank," he said. A tall young Chinese looked up from the stove, from the skillet of eggs. Walker handed him a tin from his pocket, hoisted himself onto the counter near the sizzling fat. "I got time to eat one more of your meals. Make it enough to keep me going."

"Avary," Frank said. "Green River City. I'll tell you again you have the right idea." He slid the tin beneath his apron, handed Walker a cup of coffee, a plate of ham and molasses. "Smart boy. I'll follow you soon, if I got a brain."

"Your brothers expect me, right?"

"I wrote them three times to tell them when you come and what you need."

"Yes. They'll know what I need."

"They know what any man needs in a place like that. All desert, mountains, hostiles. They tell me buffalo and hot stinking springs. Such a big land. They are ready to get you started."

"You didn't tell anyone round here, Frank, that today is it for me?"

"Tell who? I told my girl and she said Frank I want us to go, too, and I say tomorrow, or a week, or next year, and then we see my brothers in Green River City."

"Not a week or next year, not for me." Walker finished the meal, slid down from the counter and gave Frank a sharp sideways hug—the bony angles of the boy, the rich film of cooking, his short black hair bristling against Walker's temple. "Find me if you want, Frank, but I don't know how."

On out the back, he leapt across the alley, beneath an arch, through a brief musty almost-tunnel, and into his room. He'd already swept the bare floor, already cleaned the high window. The evening light was falling west into the ocean. He lit the candle stub on top of the stove. He rolled his mattress off the four crates it lay upon, shifted his shadow around the candlelight, opened a crate, and wedged the last tin and the Mission candles among the other goods, and with a pencil he added them to the list folded on top. He lay down on the crates, watched the sky through the window, the last pink streaks of sun rushing through the clouds.

A long while and someone knocked at the door. He awoke to a square of black sky, a streak of illuminated cloud falling through. The candle had burned away. He opened the door. He saw the darker shapes of two large men against the darkness of the buried walkway. "Here," he said, and they came in past him as if they could see. "Those. There's a manifest for each." They hefted a crate and already they were out the door. He followed. They slid the crate into the back of an enclosed van, returned for the others, loaded them, then stepped up into the van, closed the door behind, and soon a light brightened the tiny side window and Walker heard shuffling and low voices. One of the pine lids dropped.

He left them there, headed beneath the arch and back into his room, stood at the center, listened to the wind rattle the casement. He found his leather case, turned it on its side, and sat on it, waiting. After a while, he thought he heard voices from above, from beyond the walls, the saloon across the alley muffled and shut off from the cold. If he filled his lungs, he could taste the city's fumes—gasses, paint, standing water, and beyond it all, the ocean. He could hear people passing on the street at the head of the alley, he could almost hear bricks stacked, the grass on the hills ready to brown toward summer. And he heard the horse breathing, waiting to lurch that van through the ruts, off into the street.

Unhooking his jacket from the back of the door, he came out, setting the lock. The building was dark above him. No one watching. He stood there at the edge of the alley, gripped his leather case against his chest, waited for the men to emerge from their work. They were attaching a value to each item. He had no idea what sum they would come out with— there were the new items with nothing but his own touch to mar their clarity, and then the items he had acquired, balanced on his palm, examined to see if the owner had left a trace of oil from the fingertip, a blush of powder, sheen of perfume, a sense of what it had meant, what silhouette its absence would leave in the owner's memory.

Sterling silver fish server, candlesticks, tea tray, sugar bowl. Other odd silver—spoons, butter knives. Pearl necklace. Stack of cook pots. Scarves. Five leather-bound Bibles. Muffin tins. Ivory comb. Black lacquer and mother-of-pearl picture frame with its

etching of a fat-faced girl on a lace pillow. Tins and jars of olives,
oysters, caviar, snuff, opium. On and on.

Not an easy task, all those four years in the city, to collect
four crates of worthy goods, to adjust and discard gradually
to improve the value. Some of the merchandise was easy,
lifted from a shelf, drawn from a blanket on the beach, but a
special item might be a week or more in the getting. The hills
were stacked with lit windows, some of them open squares,
some draped and shuttered until only obscure patterns of
light gave out. It was toward these darker windows that he
had made his way. Perhaps he'd first spotted the window
from the crest of another hill. He would try to memorize the
pattern of buildings that surrounded it, to imagine the view
that that window itself opened onto. He shifted slowly
through the streets until that view took shape and he knew
that through the next alley that world would rise. It did. He
was below the window, saw the shuttered pattern illuminated
with the light it constrained. He leaned there, ear against the
clapboard, and listened. He heard nothing but the sounds of
the city—wagon wheels, the hiss of guttered water—until he
placed his palm against his outer ear. Then, in the barest
increments, the interior emerged.

The men came out from the van. Walker would take whatever they offered—their reputation was too dark for an argu-
ment—he hoped they would be fair. "Very good, sir," one
of them said, and he handed Walker a roll of bills. "There
are many useful beauties in your collection. We thank you."
They returned to the van, climbed up front, took the reins,
and the wagon rattled into motion.

Walker followed, turned another direction, away through
the streets, across the hills. Lights in the windows, lace shadows, flames in glass globes, and the black void of the bay
spreading below, beyond, strings of faint light girding the
nothing. He came to the waterfront and caught the last ferry
to Oakland.

From the stern he watched San Francisco recede. Beneath
his feet, through his hands on the rail, the engine's throb
increased. The whistle blew, and with the echo the square

ranks of windows on the hills seemed to dim for a brief flicker. Already the pathways between those buildings seemed impossible—years of diving through those deepening canyons as if he knew the place, but now it would continue without him, continue toward stranger complexities.

Before the city faded to a faintly glowing strip, he saw the grave of the old boats. Four years since he'd sailed round by the Strait of Magellan, ten months on that ship tarred with age and streaked with the whiteness of salt and sun. The ship had seemed hardly seaworthy, but it had kept on lurching toward the next crest.

Walker could have come round by way of the Isthmus of Panama, could have ridden an oxcart through the jungle, but he'd heard tales of crumbling bungalows lined with the sick. The heat wraps a man till he's ready to peel his skin away. Malarial fever. Cholera. At night, the lushness of the rotting green takes down even the stars in the weight of its noise.

The strait had been a safer risk than Panama, so in his nineteenth year he had come out from the forest to the Boston waterfront and boarded the Rockwell for the ocean voyage round the tip. They made ports in Carolina and Rio, and then on south through open sea. The air seemed to draw ice from their lungs as they neared the strait, the waves took them into their troughs and nearly flipped them back out, the birds seemed high and buffeted in their gray passage. And then they cut in from the open, and the dark green land guided them, protected them as much as any mound of rock could protect a ship from the untold rage of ice to the south.

The Strait of Magellan was cold and incomprehensible— islands, mountains, blind gaps. The dark Fuegians pursued the ship in their canoes, shouting "Yammerschooner" and begging for scraps. At night, by the moon, the ship sailed on through the narrows, no sound of bird or animal. A storm set them to anchor in a cove, and along with the lines of sleet came the occasional arrow from the trees—a stone point, lodged in a plank, was gathered the next morning as a souvenir. A small steamer passed, west to east, rocking and unsteady with its paddle wheels, heading for somewhere, its smoke fogging the channel, its whistle full and clear. The oystercatchers startled from the shore. The otters rolled. The condors hung black against the fast underside of the clouds. And then Cape Pillar and the Pacific. Walker stood in the lee of the deckhouse and watched that rocky end-place recede— the strait was nothing but a scattered puzzle, flooded by sea and storm, a moment of hushed steepness at the end of the world.

The Rockwell went skylarking, the ranks of square sails set straight to the royal, out to the stunsails. The passengers crowded on deck, shifted from sunlight to bellowed shade. Albatross. Driftwood. In the hold, weighing the ship steady, were cheese, shovels, dark bottles of champagne. Even whale oil.

Captain Avary called Walker into his quarters. Whichever way the sun wheeled beyond the glass, the captain's bulk was a shadow against the white walls. He was a tall man, broad and soft, a strong man, his face red and heated. They looked over the charts laid out on the table. Walker pointed to the islands lost in the blue and white, and the captain found a name for each, explained how you aim for a speck a thousand miles away, how you slowly reel that land in until you're in danger of busting your keel on its sharpest edge. "Such a joy when you've arrived," he said. "Such a pleasure of scents. It is what you've anticipated, but you didn't know you'd anticipated it."

"Someone has found each of these places?"

"Wouldn't be on the map otherwise. But some places have been more found than others. That's what makes the journey worth the danger—eventually you'll travel far enough to find yourself alone." He sat Walker on the red pleated-silk settee, said, "You're good company," and rummaged for treats in a cabinet.

Walker accepted the hard maple candies and sardines. "How long you planning to stay in San Francisco, sir?"

"I can't say. I might tighten this ship up, or I might get another. There's value in this cargo. I might keep going to the Orient."

"I could go with you. I could sign on, if you want."

"Oh, I don't know—you're no good in the rigging, and you wouldn't want wages for chores around my cabin or following passengers with a bucket. You're a young man, Walker."

"I guess you'll find a lot of money in the Orient. These quarters won't be nothing next to what you'll have. I'd like to see that."

"Yes, I'll do all right, but you're set for something else. Get some muscle on these skinny bones." He sat beside Walker, pinched his arms. "You'll do better than locking yourself in a little hold like this. I'm sure."

Walker inhaled the captain's brandy breath, held it in his lungs, let it hiss away. He watched the captain's eyes swirl with the window light, those eyes black and without focus, deep beneath the brow, the thatch of graying hair above the sheen of his forehead, nearly sun-stroked.

The captain was right—Walker was almost always unbalanced and aching from the sea. But, still, he wanted the sensation of moving on, of arriving at a sheltered place after months or years of approach through the empty. In the captain's quarters, he found maps of North America, and he folded them, slid them into his shirt, felt them a slight, nearly weightless irritation until he could bring them out, flatten them, trace them under candlelight, alone for a moment or two. The longer he stared, the more clearly the routes emerged, and from where the routes ended he began to guess at the trails, or the lack of trails, and the shape of the horizon, and the number of years it would take for that space to fill, finally.

From an anchorage off a safe, deserted shore, the crew rowed in, landed, and began rolling water barrels up a creek. The ladies stepped into the last foaming edge of the breakers, up toward the dry sand, shook out their hems, and started this way and that, leisurely along the white, looking for shells or a place to sit and watch the men. Walker followed the line of fresh running water across the beach, through the dunes, for a gradual mile of stiff grass and windblown husks of reed, onto the first rocky steepness. The creek carved beneath the lay of the slope, the sound of cool among the flat boulders. He looked for a path but found none. Was this place too hot for men? Not much but cactus, nothing quite green enough to eat. Turning back a moment he saw his shadow stretch far below him, a gray unformed line cut by the black creek. The land reached on toward the ship, the three black masts and yards and booms and furled canvas like a clutch of stanzas afloat in that near blue, a song he'd almost lost in the heat, on solid ground.

He stepped away. The dirt had been packed hard by the sun. Then he was over a lip and faced a wall of rock, water dripping from the seams into a pool as square and stone-lined as if it had been constructed, admired, abandoned a millennium ago, all decoration scoured away by wind and heat. Near the pool was a stretch of tangled green—berry and date. And above, the broken brown hills held the sky from descending and washing the day as white as the white sun.

He undressed and stood at the water's edge, stepped off, submerged, and found the bottom—cobbles of slick round stone. Holding himself beneath the surface, he drifted between earth and air, the sun cooled by the dense water. He kicked, breathed, swam away from his body's salt, the sea's salt. The rock wall sheened with water, channeled by the crevices, dribbling small disturbances. If the water fed this pool, this brief bit of vegetation, it might feed richer hollows farther in. Perhaps this trickle had been a river, its power captured by lakes, by chilled caves, by the windings and dead ends of those sharp hills. That's where men would live— farther in. If he paused long enough, he might find a way to survive here, might find that the cobbles beneath his feet were not stones but turtles. He climbed from the pool. The sun left the hills. The light reflected and waved across his white-ness.

Valuable cargo, he thought. Gain an advantage toward

something. He was small, he knew, and not overly strong, but he could get some muscle, get some cargo. He pinched at his shoulders, arms, ankles.

He stepped into the undergrowth. A spine pierced his sole. Gathering blood on a fingertip, he traced the word Avary down his abdomen, painted a stripe down the sunburned limp of his sex and felt it stir a bit, painful. He dove again, left his blood behind, and as he climbed out and started dressing he watched his blood drift on the surface of the water, slowly toward the outlet, over the edge. He followed down the slope. How fast was the water? If the crew was still filling a final barrel, would they take on board a bit of his blood, serve it with the next soup or coffee, swallowed by the captain, held inside?

As the ship moved on with the wind, he found the dark corner of a hold, peeled away his clothes again, and let the cool air soothe his burn. The heat was centered in his gut, in his groin. Leaning against the damp planks, he tried to hold himself still, to see where he was headed. Long after dark, when there was nothing left of the voices from above, he came up through the passages to the captain's door, let himself in, heard the rumble of Avary's breath as he slept in that soft white berth carved and trimmed and ideally placed in the curve of the wall. There was only darkness. He stood at the small thick squares of the window, hoping the glass would magnify the light of the stars, but the white specks swayed and lurched, leaden. If he stared long enough, he might make out the crests of the swells, but they would be unbearably steep, unbearably the same. There—the moon was rising, broad and red—he saw crest after crest cutting across the bark's progress. He turned in that blood light and looked through his own shadow. The room clinked with crystal, richer and tighter than any room he'd known. And the captain—stripped in the heat, his chest heavy, hairy, and the arms like great careless constructions of strength. Walker claimed no surname, so on that day he took the captain's— Avary, of French lineage. He balanced his way across the room, came to the berth's embellished rail, hoisted himself up, and without seeming to stir from his dreams, the captain took him under his arm, let him sleep there without trouble, and then the sun came round again through the waves, and the captain awoke and sent him to fetch breakfast.

They sailed in through the Golden Gate, through a wall of fog that had come up of a sudden and robbed the sight of the headlands and the sunlight beyond. They heard the ocean tear at the rocks, the sea lions cry, and then they were free of those lazy clouds. The hills were green, the settlement scattered across the knobs, hidden away from the endless Pacific.

Walker slept in the Oakland station and boarded the train in the morning. They headed east through California, through a long day of nothing but dust and oaks and rivers and the mountains in a hot blue haze. Finally they rose, quick away from sunset, high and into snow. In the darkness, the white rushed in jagged cuts among the peaks, and then the trees again, the descent, a lake like a gate to another sky, colder stars. Reno lights came and went. A river in a moonlight canyon. With dawn they moved through a land burned dry, salt leached on the flats where water had stood and evaporated among the half-dead scrub.

A young lady sat across from him, introduced herself—Miss Greta Mueller, from Kentucky—and asked his name. He muttered, took her small hand and shook it, dropped it. She watched him, her face round and pitted and almost pretty, her hair in thick, oily curls. She couldn't have been more than eighteen. She offered a portion of her lunch. "You need to eat more," she said.

He took the boiled egg, the slice of bread. "I forgot to eat," he said, and he leaned his forehead against the glass again, watched the flatland blur, watched the solid slowness of the mountains. "I'm trying to see whatever can be seen at this speed."

"You didn't sleep last night."

"No."

"I watched you."

"You didn't sleep either?"

"Who could sleep," she said, "knowing this was coming? All this nothing. When I came west last month I couldn't bear to look at it. I asked the conductor, 'What is all this we're passing through?' He told me it was the Great Basin. Great! The thought of such a word attached to such a slice of Hades. Here. Eat a tomato."

He took the soft red fruit. "I've never seen a stretch like this," he said. "Endless."

She smiled at him, shook her head, slowly peeled the shell from an egg. The blueness of her eyes, something vaguely stupid in the whiteness of her grin. "I'm going home to trees. Do you think, Mr. Avary, that you could live a day in country like this?"

"I think that if you sit anywhere long enough, you'll finally get up and start figuring things out. Even this place. What choice?"

She took a bite of the egg, chewed, and swallowed dryly. "There are plenty of places where everything's already been figured out."

"Then what's left to do?"

"I couldn't even begin to tell you, I suspect."

They passed through towns, a few buildings waiting for the shadows of those serrated peaks to sweep across, the day's heat gone to the sky. Miss Mueller left him to join her mother in their berths. He dozed a bit and awoke to find she'd returned and sat watching him.

"I can't sleep," she said.

"If it frightens you, why do you travel?"

"I go where my mother goes."

"Always?"

"It can be quite pleasant. It's only intolerable when she travels someplace like this. What is your destination, Mr. Avary?"

"Green River City. Then up into Wyoming Territory."

He pulled out his tourist pamphlet, spread the map open on his lap.

She leaned close in the dim light, watched as he traced east with his finger, following the broad line of the main rail that cut like a river across mountains, plains, and entered finally the mass of tributaries. Slowly his finger drifted west again, pausing at landmarks, familiar cities, gradually across the tiny lettering of the strange places, Laramie, Howell, Coopers Lake, Lookout, Misel, Rock Cr., Wilcox, Como, Medicine Bow, Carbon, Simpson, Percy, on to Summit, Separation, Fillmore, Creston, Latham, Washakie, Red Desert, his nail making the minute shift from stop to stop, through towns that might have lived only a few weeks or months as they fed the construction, that might now be nothing but a water tower, a litter of painted boards, broken springs, and then he found Green River City and headed north. Mazes of thatched ranges, and W Y O M I N G fell across in a grand curve, devouring fifty miles with each letter. He caught the towns, South Pass, Atlantic City, Camp Stambaugh, Miners Delight, Camp Brown, what might be no more than an old building on a trail, and then on north to where nothing but rivers carved through the narrow spaces of that pastel pink square. Tribes. Wind River.

She reached and brushed the density of elevation with her fingertips, laid her palm on the fine crinkle of the paper, buried it all beneath her white hand. "Please. I wish you would come on to Kentucky with me," she said. "Or anyplace." She took his hand and led him back through the coach, out to the gap between the cars. They stood there with the dry cold wind around them. "Do you smell that?" she said, releasing him to steady herself.

"What?"

"It smells like death. It smells like a body when it starts to lose its fluids."

She took his hand again, and he kept them both steady against the sway. He listened beyond the racket of the rails, thought he heard the distance the sound traveled before it ricocheted. What could move through such darkness? Animals, of course, and men with an unearthly sense for what they could feel or hear. Stars streaked the sky like the leavings of old clouds. He smelled the lack of rain, smelled no sign of rot, no sign of anything but sandy soil and dry roots. "It smells clean," he said.

"Do you believe that?"

"Sure I do."

"You're sweet, to lie to me." She backed them into the lee of the forward car, and they held themselves there for a long while. Behind their progress, along the tracks, pale light from the windows wavered along the embankments, brushed the edge of a boulder or sage or stretch of stiff grass, crusted ditch. To the north, the puffs of steam and smoke shredded against the black, blown by the wind, and slowly those puffs swung back around and passed directly overhead. They smelled the harsh edge of the smoke, felt it rob the ease of their breath. The stars caught in the gaps between the mountains, skimmed and disappeared and emerged green where they touched the earth. Then the moon rose—its glow infused the puffing steam long before its clean round whiteness climbed into sight above the train. Now the land was edged in sharp shadow. The plains seemed to have washed from the gaps in the precipitous peaks, flowing out in great fans that folded one against the next, every inch of land a product of the destruction of elevation. The train rose across the face of a range, struggled through a canyon where trees stood on the slopes, pines too lonely to guess at the idea of forest, and a creek gathered chill along its shores and broadened into a pool with the moon at its center. The canyon's echoes sparked their ears. Then the train braked toward another plain.

With a dull smooth clanking the train slowed, came to a stop, and they leaned around the edge of the car and looked forward. Lamps on poles. A water tank to quench the locomotive. A child came up from the sage and stood watching that serpent with its stripe of dim windows. Beyond the child rose a few trees that caught the lamplight and seemed stark and huge and nearly blinding against the moonlight world.

Out there, a building of some kind sat pale and crooked. The train moved on.

Greta Mueller took Walker Avary's hands and pressed them to her bodice, took his fingers and worked them to pinch her pearl buttons, trace the piping. "This is fine work," she said, her face against his shoulder. "My mother has a woman who sews my dresses for me." Rising onto her toes, she pushed the top of her head against his chin. "Smell," she said. The scent of dead hair, and, beneath, he smelled rose, lavender, honeysuckle. "There is nothing you could want."

She whispered tales of Kentucky and its riverbottoms awash with constant flood and the pollen green against the blue sky and the great flocks passing north and south and the horses so deeply muscled they quivered with breathing, barely able to contain themselves against the prospect of the fields reaching toward the shadowed forest. Her father had a farm, the loose-slatted tobacco barns, the pond where they stuck bullfrogs with sharpened sticks. Bridges crossed the rivers. The roads were graded and smooth. For years there had been lines of troops, she said, flowing in the summer green, in the winter. There were fires that ate for days without attention, the smoke against the sky as red as the leaves falling through, no voices on the air. And in those days, under a sun that seemed smaller, colder, uncertain, as if the earth had begun to drift, she walked to the far boundary of the property and looked beyond the fence to the cut in the woods where the creek sank slowly into the soil, not enough power to the flow to drain anything away, and turning she looked back into the heart of her daddy's world and saw, beyond the muddy fields left fallow, the white square box of pillared house that kept out the rain.

She guided Walker's hands to her neck and said, "Feel my pulse. Does it seem delicate?"

"No. It's strong."

"I could go anywhere if I had to. I'm not scared. I've seen enough in my life. My cousin lost an eye. My brother lost a leg. But why go if you don't have to?"

"I don't have to."

"But you will."

"Yes."

"You're a fool."

"Probably."

"If you're unhappy, you just wait, and it passes. Or you leave for a while and return."

"That's what *you* do."

"Yes, I do."

In the gray of dawn, they came back through the car, sat together in the silence before the other passengers stirred. The train rushed beside a body of purple water, whole ranges of shattered peaks rising from that dark choppy stench of salt. They watched the magnificent pelicans, the white sharp points of wings in their cruising over that landlocked sea.

"This is not a place for you to live, Mr. Avary. You'll get yourself killed by something you can't even imagine. Do you have the means to protect yourself?"

"Yes," he said. "I have means."

"Well, you will need more than that." She took his hand and held it in her lap until the sun rose white and gave that sea its full, endless reach toward a dead horizon. "This train can't move fast enough, whichever way it goes." She left him there.

All day at the window, he watched the passage. Miss Mueller didn't return. The track rose through layers of the earth, red and brown and crumbled, and stretches of pine forest thick or cut and abandoned. The mountains melted with the altitude until the train seemed to traverse the top of some great uprising.

That evening, as darkness came up ahead and closed in behind, his nose bled, from the dry, from the elevation, and he sopped the blood with a white towel from the washroom, watched the red quickly darken to muddy brown. Such a flow, such an ache across the bridge between his eyes. He hadn't known that blood could taste so sweet or be so hard to wash from your senses. A gentleman offered a silver flask, and Walker took a long swig.

———

Nearly midnight. Green River City—*6,200 feet above the sea*. Walker stood on the platform, heard his name, and he saw Miss Mueller far at a window of a forward car. He came along, stood below her. "Get back on the train, will you?" she said, and she gave him a dull white smile.

Behind her stood a small woman, dark hair piled in a mass about her sharp face—an ax in a storm cloud. She elbowed her daughter aside and said, "Greta tells me you're in danger, Mr. Avary. She thought you might come with us, work for us. I think not. It's best for you to stay here." She held her fist out the window, opened her fingers, and a few dollars fluttered down. She shut the window, pulled the blind, and the train started to move, stirring that fall of cash. He walked back along the platform. The locomotive whistled as the caboose passed him, and quickly the chugging rattle was swallowed by the next ridge.

There was no one left on the platform. He listened. He heard the Green River, its wide rush. He heard, he thought, the air stirring far up toward the moon, the rolling of the earth. He guessed at the scents—plants too dry to hold anything but silver-green oil in their leaves. Moonlight on the bluffs, the hills across the valley, moonlight on the town, pressing the buildings flat beneath the stars. He thought he heard music, a banjo, from somewhere across that town. Not enough light to make sense.

Taking up his case, he gripped the handle, tested the weight—the case was all he could be sure of now, and it wouldn't get him a week into this world. Frank Chin's brothers to be found in the morning. He stepped from the platform, into the street.

The town was old enough already to have left a few abandoned buildings—mud brick walls washing away, casements stripped of their glass—but mostly things seemed solid. Tall wooden facades, a lit cleanliness of window, horses tied, a hotel, shuttered cafe, the stable. No one was about. Walker stepped into the hotel, to the desk, and a boy looked up from the register. "Sir?" the boy said.

"You got a bed?".

"The train filled us up."

"I was on the train."

"You shoulda come right over. No one waits for anything around here."

"You know where else I could go?"

"I'd go that way." He waved vaguely toward the far hills, the river. "The Circassian girl is in the tent."

"Who?"

"You've heard of her."

"I haven't heard of nothing."

Back into the night, on toward the hills. Houses here. Some barns. The air chilling quickly. He walked on, heard dogs barking, a circling howl somewhere past a line of cottonwoods. The road slid from beneath his feet, descending through gravel and boulders, and he left the buildings behind, onto a path, with the trees suddenly above him, the dark clouds of starless leaves against the sky, the clouds of moonlight in the breeze, sound of wind and water. He saw a long grayish glow ahead, and he stopped. He heard the banjo, shouts, and then he jumped back into the lee of a cottonwood trunk—someone approached—he'd seen the form against that glow—someone moving slowly, a low hum rattling his teeth, and as the man passed, Walker smelled the old filth of him, the human oil. That man had been out there for a long time, wandering. Waiting against the cottonwood, Walker thought he felt the dampness exhaled by the leaves, gathered in the air. How dry was the land beyond the river? A territory nearly empty.

On through the trees, he heard the river more strongly—the path seemed to be draining away from anything he needed—and that gray glow took on a shape, points and slopes, a tent. The music was clearer now, frantic notes of a banjo, and the voices male and female, and one voice louder—"One more couple to make the set." Walker approached. There was grass here in thick bunches, and veins of river rock carved through the smooth sediment, the damp clay, with willow shrubs scattered tall and half dead, masses of leaf. He wedged his case into a willow, walked on to the tent, pushed aside the flap, and stepped in.

The space traveled into darkness in each direction. From the twin center poles, bright lanterns hung, sharp-cut shadows across the dirt floor. The master of ceremonies must have found his final couple—in the clearing at the center a dozen pairs stood poised. On the small stage at one end, against the burgundy velvet curtain, the banjo plucked into rhythm again. They all started to move, the men holding themselves straight, glancing, thinking of cutting loose, and the ladies a sorry lot of sows in silk. The dirt stirred with the patterned steps.

Walker moved along the edge, tasted the dirt in his lungs—metallic, old. Here there were some wooden tables, green felt, and games of Faro, Black and White, others. The men stared at their cards, at the table, slow smiles all around. Walker pulled a coin from his pocket and bought himself a whiskey, held the glass up against the weak light—sediment settled in a gradual swirl, fingerprints on the glass as clear as if etched, the white print of someone's lower lip on the edge. He placed his lip on that other lip and downed the whiskey, handed the glass back to the barman.

"You got your ticket?" the man said, looking at Walker's hands.

"Ticket?"

"For the show."

"No, sir."

"Give me two more coins and you got yourself another drink and the show."

Walker looked at the man's neck, broad and ringed with grime, looked back toward the center of the tent. There didn't seem to be much anticipation percolating, the dance grinding along, but he dug into his pocket, came up with the coins, and drank the whiskey.

The music stopped, the dancers cleared, the men wandering off among the tables, the women in a clump onto the stage, out through a gap in the curtain. Walker moved along,

stood beyond the last man, in the farthest light, and watched
the clearing. Those lanterns shined down into the footprints,
the craters of heel marks. He saw how the lantern smoke
gathered in a layer toward the twin canvas peaks, how the
shadows of the poles cut blank swirls in the gray. A spark
escaped its glass and fizzled, alive, rising from its own white-
smoke tail, then dying and falling.

Walker felt the whiskey like a warm lump in his gut, felt
that he needed to find a place to sit, now, but as he focused
among the men, as he watched the shoulders hunched, the
scruffy chins, he saw that they had taken every seat, shifted
as a group to face the stage, and they talked fast and soft to
each other as if they had all arrived together. Walker came
up behind them, leaned right and left, stood on his toes to
see the stage, waited.

The master of ceremonies dragged a stool out toward the
center poles and climbed up, brightened each lantern—the
flames wavered, more smoke rising. The man pulled his coat
square on his shoulders and dragged the stool away, a glance
at the crowd, an exaggerated nod. The men fell silent. In the
new light the space toward the peaks above had opened, a
tight draping of stretched canvas and black streaks and smoke
in slow eddies. The banjo started a wandering scale, minor
or out of tune. Someone clapped once, then held himself still.
Someone let out a long, airy whistle.

The curtain gapped and the Circassian girl came to the
forward edge of the stage. A small girl. Oval face. Dark eyes.
Her black hair slicked back and tied with an ivory silk ribbon.
She came down to the ground, to the first pole, leaned in
its shadow, her white hands gripped around the old wood.
She raised and shook a foot to the side, then to the other side,
as if settling the black leather boots more squarely against her
heels. The crowd leaned this way and that. Her dress, long
and heavy and dark blue with black brocade, high collar,
sleeves with tiny buttons, seemed far outside the construction
of movement contained within. She stepped around the pole
and came forward again, stopped at the center of the clearing,
lights and shadows and footprints alive around her sudden

stillness. She glanced at the banjo, it fell silent, and she began to sing.

The Circassian girl from beside the Black Sea. What dreams behind those flat black eyes? A sad song in a foreign tongue. She worked through the notes deliberately, formal, her soprano held tightly to the words, her vibrato a delicate vibration, a blink's hesitation before one word or another, one sound or another, as sad as made no difference. She looked at the trampled ground before her. She looked beyond the light, far beyond the men gathered there. They might have turned to see what she saw, but they could not look away from her tensed throat, the lips that formed the sounds. One song ended and another began.

The girl's voice. Walker didn't know the words, but he heard the sounds, followed them across a stretch of beach, gray sand, tracks of sea birds above the water's reach, cold water that swells toward the clouds, a street curving up through a village, a progression of facades white and win-dowed and stained by rain, guttered rain slicking the cob-bles, the light deep and yellow behind each window, and the woodsmoke gray around one final dwelling where the village ends and the forest rises on toward granite canyons, ravens perched on the stones, rivers, wind.

Smoke came down across her. She raised her hands, her voice descending to a warble, to silence, her arms carving gaps in the smoke, swirls that churned beautifully as she turned and looked up, stopped altogether.

Sparks from a lamp had ignited the tarred seam of the canvas, and a line of white flame wicked in each direction, splitting the bright grayness open to the black night and an edge of the whiter moon. The girl made for the stage, the flames following, and the curtain took fire, the girl was gone, a lady came through the gap with fire in her hair. The men all rose together, they turned to the nearest wall of the tent, Walker turned with them, they grabbed the hem of the can-vas, lifted, and they were all outside.

"Buckets?" someone said.

"Cut it down."

"Where's the ladies?"

Walker backed away, found his case in the willow, continued to the cottonwoods and watched. The flames strung along, bright as a decoration, peaking at the two high points. People ran to the river. Someone screamed and screamed, a woman's voice, and then went silent or was buried beneath the other shouts. A man threw tables and chairs out from an opening, and they splintered and took flame. Voices without words, rising with the smoke, muffled by the starkness of that white light. The canvas shredded and the whole draped form began to billow and cave. Along the seams, charged by the bellows of the collapse, the fire burned whiter in the uprush of air, and the poles emerged, lit at the top like torches set in the floodplain, set for some new entertainment, surrounded now by the fallen canvas. Those high flames were all that was left of the night sounds—the crackling rush of heat as loud and complete as the bright moonlight. The men ran in groups. Someone toed through the smoldering heap of furniture. Someone pissed against a boulder. The ladies fussed at the back of a wagon.

Walker tipped up his case and sat on the edge, beside a tree. He saw a girl wander against the fire. She kicked at stones, paused to pick a leaf and crush it between her palms, held it to her nose, touched it with her tongue, and gradually she approached him until he saw that it was the Circassian girl, stripped now of her stiff blue dress and wearing only a white shirt too large, too meager for the cold, and a pair of dark trousers and boots. He sank back against the tree, thought he was dark there beneath the mass of leaf, thought she would pass, but she looked right at him as if in daylight, came on straight, and he looked down at his arms and shoulders and saw that the firelight was so bright on him that it might have been warm.

She bumped him over with her hip and balanced beside him on the case. There were streaks in the powder that had paled her face—perhaps she had been crying. She watched the fire, leaned forward and held her knees, and her hair caught in her collar, fell over her ears. He couldn't tell if she was frightened or lonely or bored.

When he was this girl's age, whatever age, quite young, years ago, he had sat near someone, anyone, and watched the movement of troops against the light of windows, moonlight, a bonfire, anything that clarified the chill. To sit near someone had seemed better than to sit alone or to sit beside someone and talk. Better to watch, to see that that other person also watched, better to remain silent and listen to the rattle of equipment, wagons, boots on the road. He had known enough to know the shape of each man's wound without seeing it again—the waxy whiteness of a stump, the sometime under-shadow of purple as if pain were painted there, a face caved into blue. They might have been old men, but they were young, long years on the road, to and from. Would they find their home passed on to some other family? Walker didn't wait on his own doorstep. He waited where others waited for others.

"Tell me, miss," he said, and he touched the girl's knobby head silked with that black hair. "How far have you come?"

She turned beneath his fingers. Her eyes were dry, edged in firelight, but her skin was hardened and streaked, blacked with soot around her nostrils. "We came on the wagon," she said, her accent deep and thick but the words clear, as if the accent were applied, a strange make-up. "Not on the train. Last week we were in the town of Rawlin's Springs. There is nothing in these places. We were going soon to the Mormon Desert, but then this fire. I suppose we will go anyway. Do you know a woman is dead?"

"I think I saw her."

"She is the woman who brought me here. She is dead, and I knew her for no more than two years."

"Where is your home?"

"This is Wyoming Territory. Can you tell me about this place?"

"I don't know it at all. Tell me. Where do you come from?"

"This is where I live." She twisted, held to his collar, pulled herself up onto his leg, knees to his crotch, pressed her lips to his mouth. If he shrugged, she would fall away. She tasted of whatever leaf she'd crushed and touched to her tongue, bitter. She withdrew her lips, rested her chin on his shoulder, spoke close against his neck, at first just air whistling her teeth, warming his skin, and then her sounds eased so finely into language that he wasn't sure that it was English. But he listened, closed his eyes.

She was a woman of very great beauty, the woman who is just now dead. I was singing, as she had first ordered me to sing, and you were listening, as men are somehow ordered to listen. She dressed me. From the very first I dressed in the same place with her, with a lantern with clouded glass on a triangle of her mama's lace on a round table with legs like a running dog's in a room of white suspended sheets with the almost invisible embroidery of the American wildflower columbine so pale purple that it might be no more than a reflection of forgotten chill or storm. We took the room with us. Sometimes it was a room inside another room. Sometimes it was a room that rippled in the wind from a thousand-mile plain, and only the lantern light let us make the stars a ceiling, let us be together without looking up. She was the first woman I had been with without clothes—this is not true, there were some women on a ship—she was the first woman who moved around me and I around her as if we were clothed. Her breasts were blue with watery veins and heavy and beautiful and she let me touch them as I touched my own, as if I could draw a grown woman out of myself with that touch. My two legs were not equal to one of hers—mine are not long, not full with soft flesh. Now her white skin is blistered. Now her hair comes away from her skull. I will not be dressed. That's all burned.

She barely held to him. Her voice tasted of the air. She was cold. Walker settled them down on the leaves, pulled a few warmer things from his case and draped them together, curled deeper, watched the firelight take shadows off across the river, up a hillside speckled with sage, into the sky.

"Tell me what you heard me sing," she said.

"You sang about your home."

I sing songs I know from when I was a child, she told him. I heard each song through walls, through windows, from down an alley where tall houses meet, and the voice could come from anywhere, from the sky, impossible to locate, but the voice was sad and it almost sang with itself when the echoes caught up and repeated. I sit in the limbs of a tree and the sky is raked with cloud and fall has taken the green and the last of the harvest is being gathered far across the hills and the sun is gone from the waves far out on the sea and the air is full of cold salt and I come down from the tree holding to the hard solid heavy limbs with their smooth bark and their wrinkles like elephants' legs and I am on the road with its cobbles rolled into mud but I keep to the edge where the dead grass gives me footing and I follow the men who come back in through the evening and each is locked away beyond a wall or behind a door and here is a square of glass where I see a woman no stronger than a stick laid on a sofa of green as dark as fir and she is pink where she spreads herself and holds herself open very still with her eyes closed and her knuckles going white with the clench as the man undresses slowly with the buttons each released from their holes and the shirt peeled back from the shoulders and the trousers shaken down the legs to the floor and then the whiteness of that man with the darkness of his member as if it came from another creature's skin full out and awkward and then he holds it still in his hand as he hunches there and begins to move and the woman's hands finally come out from behind the man and stretch slightly as if she is waking or reaching and the night goes on down toward the shore where the waves draw white slashes in the black and a ferry cruises its lights far out and always you think of how quickly in a storm a vessel is taken down into cold.

"You see. It is not about my home that I sing," she said.

"I heard you."

"I don't think you heard much," she said, "but maybe you did. Tell me where you are going."

He pulled from his pocket the blue tourist pamphlet, let her hold it. She turned it over, folded out the map, held it up against the sky, into the fading firelight. The rails were dense black in the East, frail and direct in the West. Slowly, in precise detail, as if she wouldn't understand, he took her along the road he'd imagined. He built for her a horizon, the smell of a coming storm, a river deep black in a valley, a mountain ranging beyond, the composition of granite, the habits of the animals, and then four walls, two windows, two doors, fire on the hearth, a table surrounded.

"You got this idea from this map?" she said. "This is a very small map."

"From this map I only know where I'm going."

"That is good for you," she said, and she pressed her lips to his ear, and gently she edged his trousers and he felt her fingers at his pocket, at his money, disturbing the warmth that had gathered between them. He took her wrists, held her against that strange ground, and when she shrugged and seemed to smile and touched her bitter tongue to his throat he released her.

The night was still. Sparks rose, drifted, and glowed for lazy minutes before falling cold.

For a long time before dawn he lay still, alone in the warmth of his wrappings, watching the gray light on the back of his hand, on ice crystals in the dew, on the veins of the fallen leaves. He thought only a moment of Greta Mueller and how far the train would have reached through the night, gaining speed toward the plains. Her pitted face pressed with the creases of pillows. Her mother trailing paper money down the corridor toward the dining car. The elder spreading white butter on the toast of the younger.

But when had the Circassian girl left him? He checked his money, found it intact. The clothes he had tucked around them still held a bit of her shape. He rubbed his face, touched his fingers to his nose, couldn't separate his own smell from hers or from the ground. The remnants of smoke. He thought of her voice, the songs and the music of her accent when she spoke. He couldn't separate this world from whatever world she had created. But he knew that she had fit his limbs as if they were the same person peeled in half, that she was right to say that men were ordered to listen to her, as he had been ordered without knowing it. Her teeth were small. Her ears tiny. Her eyes black as the sea. She had lost that woman. She was traveling alone now, in with the others.

Rising onto his elbows, he looked off through the cotton-woods to the charred poles still rising from the canvas. Beyond, a mist hung where the river carved. A flock of magpies came dipping along, steadily above the water, off toward the hills, swallowed from sight. He heard voices, someone talking, an echo, a clang of metal, then the crackle of a fire.

He might have lain there for hours, afraid to let his captured heat slip away, but he roused himself in one stiff movement and pulled on an extra shirt and his jacket. There were men all around him, as close as ten feet, curled among the roots, eyes shut tight. Their hands and faces were blackened from the effort of fighting that small disaster.

He walked down toward the Green River and saw the campfire at the top of a steep cutbank. The ladies, dressed in trousers, their hair wrapped in cloth, crouched beside the flames, poked at some trout browning in a pan, and a ways farther along someone tended to a body laid out beneath a length of black silk. Walker sat on his case in the grass, ate a bit of bread and salami from the pocket of his jacket. One of the ladies waved him over, but he stayed put. He heard a shout from up along the river, heard the thump of hooves against boulders, and there he saw the Circassian girl up on the back of a gold draft horse too big by far, and a man chased her until she was gone into the willows. She could handle that horse, it seemed.

He thought of an image she had left him—the woman bathed her, ran a sea sponge warm with soap over her limbs and between her legs, the roughness of that dead sea creature, the thought of how deep the water, how dark the night, what silver fish might have brushed past it in its slumber, cruising and unseen, the slickness of passage and the sudden darkness

alone with the gentle swirls in the wake, the memory, but
what does a sea sponge hold but dark water in its thousand
salty chambers, and the woman patted her dry, powdered
her, laced gold on her wrists, led her forward through a curtain, and she was alone with the lights far overhead, filtered
and obscure, and the faces deep across a wide open space
with only her voice to soften them, and she sang, and she
was led away, outside, where the night was cooler, and for a
moment she watched the sky and judged the distance, and
then the woman led her forward again to be taken in the back
of the wagon, in a hotel, against a blanket, the bodies she
remembered only by touch and the scent that lingered in her
hair, the heft of each, the moment when the softest under-
parts retracted and protected themselves with bristles, the
scars like wax, the teeth like stones, the lips like paper, and
the woman took her back, they slept coiled deep in the sag
of a feather mattress with the girl's hand on the woman's
breast until the sun was high and the light was clear. And
Walker remembered his own men, lined up to bathe, smelled
them on his skin, and he lined with them, his own smell on
his own skin and the smell of the Circassian girl, and the men
would line far across the territory, far up the river, he knew
each of them, what they brought with them, their veins and
the blood they carried.

After a while the men roused beneath the trees and came
to the fire. Coffee was passed. A few stood at the edge of the
bank sipping and looking down at the deep rush of nearly
black water, broad and fast and bubbled with tiny whirlpools.
The sun hadn't cleared the bluff, the air was still icy, but
across the way the sun lit the upside of the hills so bright they
shimmered, and the sky, cloudless, was so blue it seemed
solid, heavy, ready to tip, waiting to settle the sun toward its
center. And as the ladies flaked off bits of that pale sweet
trout flesh and passed it around, the sun topped the bluff,
heat fell directly, and the men ate, stripped away a layer or
two, and headed out.

He walked back down along the river, saw some men
clearing away the tent, saw the angles of the town beyond the

cottonwoods. The air was warm and dry and absolutely still. Sounds carried straight and echoed.

There were flecks of ash along the river. After a while he heard voices, men's voices, or thought he heard them. As he moved along, the voices came clearer, he heard a sloshing of water, and here were a dozen men out in the river, stark and fooling and scrubbing away soot. They looked his way and waved and went back to their business, quiet now. He dropped his case, stripped off in a break of willows, and when the men floated away a bit he teetered over the river stone, into the water. It was nearly ice, though warmer than he'd expected, the bottom sandy and firm. They all kept toward the edge, to the slow pools, away from the rush at the center. Walker dunked himself, tasted the earth in the water—that crumbled soil, those rusty rocks—and came up, clearing the sting from his eyes. He was surrounded. The men stood up from the water—broad hairy chests or skinny—and floated again. "Where are you all from?" he asked. They bobbed about, silent and smiling. These could be the men from the tent, floating in a bit of memory, or they could be others— hard to tell through that slicked nakedness, that taut edge of muscle, eyes gazing here at the bluffs, there at the sky, up- river. "What's the farthest you been in the territory?" he asked. "Where do the trails run out?" They laughed, stood around him, took hold of his skinny ankles and wrists and swung him out into the heart of the channel. He drifted. They waved. The hills rose more steeply as he gained momentum, and he felt the power of that flood draining the pastel emp- tiness of Wyoming, and he felt the rapid distance he was carried from the men, guessed at the rocky barefoot hobble back to his clothes, and paddled for shore.

M*ule. Pack. Harness. Rifle. Revolver. Ammunition. Fishing tackle. Tarpaulin. Wool blankets. Water bottle. Skillet. Kettle. Copper pail. Plates. Cups. Knife. Flour. Tins of baking powder. Bacon. Beans. Dried fruit. Tins of vegetables. Salt. Pepper. Sugar. Ax. Hatchet. Saw. Hammer. Mallet. Chisel. Shovel. Rope. Box of hinges, latches, and nails. Whiskey. Bear dog.*

Walker stood with the Chin brothers in the stable, beside the pile of goods and the tall black mule. "Can the mule carry all this?" Walker said.

"I seen him carry a bull elk. Could carry two," a brother said.

Walker pointed at the gray mutt that slept against the pack frame, curled on the panniers. "What's a bear dog?"

"Jay Dubb there'll back a grizzly up against a tree till the bear is on two feet, stretched out tall, and then you shoot, O.K.? Shoot the bear."

It was mid-morning when the Chins sent him across the bridge. Jay Dubb harassed the mule's heels. Walker followed the road north, like a prospector aiming for the Sweetwater Mines, but that rush had already risen and died.

Even in the first edge of summer, the cottonwoods were still fresh green, still cool shade. Long stretches of the road were flat and direct, the ruts caked with a sheened skin of dry mud, and Walker made good time. His eyes focused close on the river, on the trees, on Jay Dubb zigzagging ahead, and beyond his focus the hills flowed past, a wash of speckled gray-green, and the occasional white cliff cut in against the river. Birds screamed and echoed and dove. He saw the rope in his palm, his skin already chafed red, saw his boots crumble the road, the mule's small black hooves keep pace. There were tracks on the road, wheels and animal, north and south, but he was unsure of how to judge the age. Here, for a brief stretch, the marks of someone's boots, and he matched his stride to the impressions, the short steps, lost the prints, and moved on.

Gradually the sun drifted to the horizon, and in the yellow light Walker looked north, focused on the distance, on whatever he was walking into. The river far ahead funneled through white rapids. And then, as he rose to the edge of the floodplain and lost the road to a fresh slice of erosion, as he was forced to head far out from the river to gain easy passage, he found himself in the last red cooling breeze of sunset, and he saw how unobstructed that breeze was, flowing direct from the giant rippling sun, saw how the plain was immersed beneath the advancing shadows of hills, gullies, steep troughs, shadows of a million sagebrush, and the vast stretches of salt or sand flashed pink and then suddenly gray as the sun sank.

The sky changed, losing its high solid arc and opening out to cold. That sky wasn't anything he didn't know—he'd sailed beneath skies cut adrift, skies rising from an unsettled surface. He tried to taste the air. Certainly the animals that crossed this plain would have a scent, but he caught nothing beneath the sage. The breeze died away, started again—he felt it enter through the seams of his clothes, tighten his skin, and he wished that he'd laid on a layer of fat against the unrelenting open. On the Rockwell, in the cabin tight with windowpanes, he would crouch beside the captain's stove. In the city, at the saloon, with the distance sealed by fog, he would listen to the warm basso soup of language.

He found his way back from that view, back down in toward the river, and looked for a place to camp. He stopped in a ring of tall cottonwoods and fallen trunks that had caught and tangled into lengths of almost-fence, and he unpacked the mule, watered him, picketed him in a sunken meadow beyond the trees. Jay Dubb returned from wherever he'd strayed, and he sniffed at the edge of the river, scaring up a few ducks. "You stay close," Walker shouted, and the dog looked at him, looked away at the distance as if watching for an echo, and then he came along, pausing to take sticks in his mouth and give them a chew before dropping them. "You'll have to find yourself something better than that."

Walker rummaged through the panniers, came up with some biscuits and an apple the Chins had packed, ate them quickly, said "All right," and tossed the apple core toward the dog. Jay Dubb came forward, head low—the hunter in him—took the core with a dainty nip of his teeth, and ran off, quickly lost to sight.

On the shingle of rock beside the river Walker found a fire ring, a slush of old cinders. He gathered fuel and got a fire going, returned to the pile of his goods in the last light and brought along the box of hardware, the whiskey, and laid himself out beside the flames. The day's final heat had drifted away. He forced off his boots and warmed his feet, took a swallow of whiskey and capped the flask.

When the liquor had settled the tight seam of his gut, he roused and took out the hardware, laid each piece on the river rock, arranged a pattern—hinges and latches for the doors, hinges for the shutters. He lay there with the heat of the fire blowing across his face, with the squeal of a hinge working in his hand.

He awoke. He heard the rush of water, heard it above him, around him, felt the cold damp on the air, and sat up. Not sails but cottonwoods taking the force of the breeze, not sea but river. His fire was dead, the moon not yet risen. He pulled on his boots and walked up from the river, kicked at the blackness, but he couldn't find the panniers. No flint or matches. No candle. No rifle. No blankets.

The trees were full against the stars, the river loud and constant—no sound of anything but endless movement, endless direction. Walker found his way out from the trees, over the fallen logs, away from the river, and climbed a slope, stopped when he felt the distance overwhelm the noise at his back. He stood there waiting to see anything but stars, to see something of the shape of the world, but all he saw, eventually, was the faint clouds combing across the constellations, disrupting the guideposts and myths. Then, for a moment, he thought he saw, far to the north on the plain, a speck of light as if a star had fallen, gone quickly as if it had burned through the flat earth and smothered itself in sediment, doused in the cold of old winters. He moved a bit, but he couldn't resurrect that light, and then he thought that he must have confused the earth with the sky, or that his tired eyes were sparking phantom bonfires and lanterns.

Years ago, he had followed no more than a shard of light through leafy forest, never more than a fleck of window or a sliver of lantern to pull him through the breaks of alder and elm and the god-awful bramble and thorny tangle. Then he was at a fence or clearing and he could hear whoever attended that light—a widow, perhaps, or a waiting girl—could see through the glass the cleanliness of surfaces, the polish of brass, or he saw someone down toward the barn, the lantern slung at the end of an arm held out from the skirts, and the face would turn a bit to the side, give light to the sharp white chin as the creak of the barn door joined the pulse of insects and the light was swallowed, expelled through knotholes and slats, the light shifting along with the sound of chores. Then Walker was quick in through the door of that woman's house or cabin or shed, and for five minutes he was the only man, though he was still a boy, only man that place had seen for weeks or months or even years. He smelled the lilacs in the basin, tasted shortbread from a jar, wished for liquor but rarely found a drop, and he collected the items that might have belonged to him—snuff box, watch, knife, coin—and he took them all with him, out of the forest, one day, to buy his way round by the strait.

Walker turned back toward the river, slid down through sage until he found the grass again, sensed the cottonwoods above him, knew only that he was somewhere close to his camp. He found the trunk of a tree and held to it. The river seemed quieter now, the air less riotous in the leaves. As he worked his way gradually around that thick, rooted trunk, he tried to hear the distance in each direction, to gauge the slopes and approaches, but nothing matched his last memory of the place at twilight. How long, he thought, before he'd be able to walk through such darkness, to gain some other sense. Perhaps someone or some animal—an owl, a coyote, wolf, grizzly, Indian—watched him now. To something that could see in darkness, would his eyes be as bright and open as lit windows?

He moved on, found his way over fallen trees, and finally, after turning and turning and catching himself on roots, falling, making himself dizzy enough to lose sense of the ground, he found another tree and held on. "Jay Dubb," he said, quietly. The river continued, pulling sound away. So he screamed the dog's name, and as soon as he heard the shrieking foolishness of his voice he would have stifled the sound, buried it before it came back. Somewhere, the mule let out a tired groan and shook itself. No sound of the dog. Walker slid down the tree and sat among the roots.

When he next awoke, the moon had risen. The river sparkled. The mule grazed in the meadow. The panniers lay in a heap at the edge of the camp. He stood and looked out from the trees, the unholy distances half lit as if painted on the back of thick glass.

Walker held the Chins' map at arm's length, reconciled it with the horizon, replaced it with the railroad pamphlet. He continued, studying the distance for the Colorado Desert, Pilot Butte, no idea if they would match his thoughts. No doubt but the Wind River Range would rise up out of the blue haze, that day or the next, or perhaps he saw those peaks already and they were too cloudlike for him to grasp.

No sign of Jay Dubb. The dog's tracks came into the road

every now and then, crossed into sage, always north, and then
he lost them completely—that mutt had a map of his own.
Walker didn't think of grizzlies—those monsters wandered
somewhere else—he thought only of the money. What else
could he have purchased for the price of a bear dog? The
animal was sniffing down coyotes, looking to plant its disloyal
seed, or it was digging out rabbits, following wolves, stealing
carrion, looping south toward home. No trusting a friend you
pay for—he should have tied the dog up.

He came along to where a trail led up out of a broad ford
of the river, and the trail crossed his road and continued west.
His map labeled the trail the Overland Mail Route, and the
Chins had drawn in telegraph lines, but there were no poles
and wires. The Chins hadn't been this way, had only sent
others. There was a fringe of trash caught in the sage and
willows—paper, cloth, tin. Walker led the mule down to the
water, let him drink, looked east. Messages had flowed from
that eastern horizon toward the western territories, letters lost
in box canyons, love notes, news of bad fortune. The trail
was a white line in the scrub, might not have been followed
for years. That dry land would leave a trail bare—it could be
a decade or a hundred years until the sagebrush swallowed
the passage.

He watched the river, squatted beside the mule and drank,
cupping water to his mouth, held the water to his forehead
and let it run into his eyes, held it to the back of his neck.
The early sun shone red through his closed lids, and then he
opened to the morning and saw wet tracks leading up from
the river, directly across the ford, clear on the gray soil. Even
from across the wide river he could see that it had been shod
hooves. He stood and looked east along the trail again. Far
out there, a horse stood, backlit, without a rider. He hadn't
seen it. Maybe it hadn't been there, maybe it had been hidden
beneath a fold. He waited while the horse moved in and out
of sight, while the sun inched over, and he saw, he was sure,
that it was the gold draft horse, saddled, bridled, alone. It
moved on and didn't come into view again.

He looked each way along the trail, brought the mule up

from the river and looked north and south along the road. Nothing for miles, nothing that he could see. He checked the tracks underfoot. He had no talent for clues. Already he was unsure of what he'd seen to the east. The tracks across the ford had dried, but they were still deep, round gouges. He whistled once, long and loud, and then listened for a full minute, watched the mule's ears casually pivot and then droop back, nothing heard, nothing pinpointed.

He walked on north toward the fork at Big Sandy Creek, and now he studied each mark on the road closely. The tiny sharp points of antelope—he saw them out on the flats, pacing him, dun and white, turning away. The dog prints of coyotes. Hooves and wagon wheels. Rabbits. He paused and looked back at his own tracks—the line of scuffing boots woven with the precise little hooves of the black mule, weighted and steady and straight. He thought of how far he might have traveled on the gold horse's back. He thought of the impossibility of hiding a horse that size if he had caught it, taken it, if someone came looking. He thought of the Circassian girl.

She was someplace else, invisible in a hundred square miles. She knew where she was. She knew where the gold horse was. Anyone could follow those hoofprints. Anyone could follow a river, north or south. His maps weren't magic—they could lead him only where he was headed. Even if he had turned onto that trail, even if he had succeeded in crossing the river, if he had searched with his mule clanking along behind, what good was he at catching anything?

As he walked, he watched again the hand of Mr. Atkinson on the arm of Miss Haugen. Mr. Atkinson's hand was long and scrubbed and hairy at the knuckles, his nails pink and trim. His arm was casually jointed beneath the stiff fabric of his coat. His shoulders turned at an angle from the young woman, and her shoulders also turned at an angle from him —one moved, the other moved, never quite in line. It was only his touch on her arm that brought her around, his fingers extended and pressing through the layers of dress and blouse, red and gold stripes and pure white, his eyes on another guest, his smile in another direction, and she was turning to face him, her chin tilted slightly away, her eyes on his fingertips. And then he replaced that hand with the other hand, he was behind her, holding her at the joint of her elbow, her hand rising and falling loosely in a graceful casual flutter, as if his pressure made it work, and his head tilted to her neck, must have brushed her skin with his words as he released her, took to another guest, and she came around again, near him. He was tall and oiled and entirely constructed of desire.

To the north, deep across late afternoon, through the miles of air sliced by the low angle of the sun, Walker thought he saw a black mass moving, what could have been a mirage drawing down something unseen, painting it for the eye, what could have been buffalo or elk or even humans on some forced migration. That shape drifted to the northeast, gradually colored, and swallowed itself in haze.

With nightfall, he settled in against the river, in a stand of trees, and banked his fire high, watched the sparks feed into the wind and gutter into cold. Some of the plants around him, he was sure, could be eaten—leaves steamed, roots dug and roasted—but he wouldn't risk experimenting until he reached someplace permanent where he could sleep off a sour stomach. He stewed a handful of dried fruit.

Two days on the road and he'd passed no one, and now wolves beyond the firelight—he heard their scrambling, their moans, saw an edge of them sleeking along the far bank of the river. He picketed the mule closer, gathered his goods beside the fire, added fresh branches until the flames stood nearly as tall as his shoulder, and nestled himself against the panniers. He held the pistol in his lap, oiling the metal with the worry of his fingers.

He tried to listen beyond his camp, out along the road. At first he heard only the river's rush through his mind, the flow of air through his lungs. Then he heard sand skim the road's twin tracks, rattle the sagebrush, nothing else. He thought for a moment that no one else would pass this way, that perhaps no one ever had, that the road was scratched as a trail on a map is scratched, a mere approximation of direction across a flat idea, that the tracks and footprints were tricks of light and memory. Nothing moved on the road but the surface pushed along by the wind. Only the surface traveled, only the river flowed, the errant shift of erosion. Deep beneath the plain the bedrock waited to be exposed.

He knew how to construct a building, had seen it done a hundred times in more and more distant forest, had let himself be enlisted for the wage of a meal. He would square a joint. He would fit a latch. Mix mortar from the materials at hand. He would slice through a felled tree with a saw. He would chip shingles with an ax. The building took for itself a volume of the wilderness and held it against the season. And darkness was contained within the walls, what would have been darkness alive with the whispers of distance, the flow of sap, roots into rock, the burrowing of night, sounds uncertain from too far a reach, voices human and inhuman, the scattering of intelligence. And then the lantern illuminated, and the soundless sound of the flame eating fuel consumed the sounds of open darkness. Here was a table bare but for a plate, a cup, a spoon. Here was a shelf with green bottles and clear glass jars. Here was a window frame sealed and shuttered. Even though the building was solidly anchored, the lantern flame flickered shadows through it all, and the play of light made the place fluid, restless, so that a man would have to wait for daylight to assure himself that he had not been cut adrift, that he was not locked in a cloud of his own making, permanently alone.

Out across the plain the Circassian girl might huddle without a fire. Perhaps she had caught that horse, and she heard his snuffling as he grazed nearby, his bulk a blot against the stars. Perhaps she had dug herself into the lee of a ridge of sagebrush, curled among boulders stirred up by the wanderings of outwash. Her scent settled about her, taken in with the buffalo grass, the shed skin of rattlesnakes, husks of seed, fluff of cottonwood carried far from the river on the western wind. The wolves followed those ridges, knew the settled areas of antelope and their unearthly fawns, so brilliantly small

and fast, knew the diversions of the land, the flows of intermittent water, the pools, the swales of thick green. The
wolves paused only briefly when the horse came up against
the darkness—the vast and sudden alertness of that horse,
the shuddering thud of its hooves, the clatter and slap of its
saddle and bridle—the wolves moved on. They paused not
at all as they coursed a trail just above the Circassian girl,
and the soil that kicked in their wake rained on her hands
and eyelids.

Within an illuminated space the Circassian girl moves, dis-
solving the darkness, the distance, the plain leading toward
the mountains, the plain washing from those same mountains, the sound of the wolves' pads pressing and releasing
the surface of the plain, the sound of the river carrying coldness from the peaks toward the far ocean, the unmitigated
barren of salt flats, and she allows Walker to settle her in a
tub of water gone silver-green with crushed sagebrush leaves,
steam making that sage a soothing spice and not just the scent
of dry, the scent of absence, the scent of great distance without bearing, and she floats there for him, he touches her
shoulder and she tilts to one side, drifts back to the other, he
circles and finally lifts her from her rest, she is alive with heat
and light in beads running her ribs, her legs, the ridge of her
spine, she follows him through the room, her passage pooling
behind her, they circle his table, they carry their shadows
across his walls, they hear nothing but the light they carve
and shape. He would allow her to come to his side, and he
would take her elbow in his hand.

He held his hand toward the fire. His hand was delicate
and raw and burned by the sun. The wolves had moved on,
or they waited for his fire to die. He piled on fuel. The light
reached to the river and raised white ripples, reached up
through the cottonwoods and lent heat to their shivers. What
part of the visible world had he contained there, with the
firelight? What other, unseen, waited for him?

An hour before dawn, with the air gone white with cold and the coming sun, Walker sat up in his blankets. His fire had fallen to coals, his pan was crusted with charred sugar, his mule stood asleep at the full extension of its lead. The river rolled stones deep in its bed, the horizon grayed into hills. He stood and dropped the blankets, felt the fear still tight in his joints, laid a few sticks on the coals and fanned them into flame, hunched there for long minutes as bark curled away from the heartwood. At the edge of the river he pushed his fingers down through the water, felt the slick stones and the pull of melted winter. He cupped water to his face, wincing, inhaled and coughed. Clearing his eyes, he stood and slapped at his arms and legs to start some heat. No tracks but his own in the wet sand.

He looked back at his fire. The smoke lined straight. And then he saw that the mule, roused and taut, was intent on something back along the road. Walker came up from the water, up to the road, and looked south. Someone approached on horseback, too distant to be more than a shape, the light still too slack for clarity. Walker thought of the sound of hooves on the road and how that sound would reach his ears and register and wondered whether he would bolt for his rifle or simply wait, and then he heard the steady thumps and he didn't move, he felt the morning chill, and he anticipated the heat of his fire and the sizzle of breakfast and the sun rising and lashing the distance with quick light, because he saw now it was the Circassian girl on that magnificent heavy horse, her form tiny in her oversize white shirt, her legs gripped high in the stirrups. She urged the horse into a trot, and then she was above Walker, past him, already receding, but with an invisible gesture she turned the horse sharply, leapt down the bank, and brought him up near Walker's fire. She slid far down to the ground and waited there. Walker came along, forcing himself to take slow steps, and she handed him the reins and said, "Water my horse. I lost him yesterday when he spooked from a snake. I have no food. I need something to eat." She crouched at his panniers.

Walker took the reins and led the horse to the river, stood with him as he drank. He felt the heat of the horse, smelled the depth of its muscle, the long neck frothy with sweat. Leading him deeper, he cupped water and smoothed him clean. The horse could probably go for days without a pause, hooves large as boulders. Up out of the river, beneath the trees, Walker picketed him in the grass, removed the saddle, pad, bridle. Surely the horse was missed. Walker leaned into its chest, reached up around its neck, his hand in the rough white mane, and the horse's neck ran the whole length of Walker's body from his shoulder to the grass underfoot. The horse breathed and shook and moved forward. Who were the men who might look for this horse? They were tall, Walker remembered, and slick with showmanship, and they were blunt, and one had shouted after the girl as she flattened the river brush and sailed north.

Coming out from the trees, he approached the fire and sat across from her. She had bacon in the skillet, the last of the biscuits on a plate, coffee in the kettle. She had gone through the last two nights with nothing but a shirt and trousers. Now a blanket draped her shoulders, moved with her movements, a loose shadow grazing the flames. She settled everything around the heat, nudged the bacon with a twig, and sat back, removed her boots and socks. On the ball of each foot, a small

gold coin had impressed its relief, and as she curled her toes
the coins fell. Taking them up from the dirt, she rubbed them
clean on her sleeve and placed them on the flattest stone of
the fire circle. Grease spattered, sheening the winged figures
with oil.

"I thought we were going to come to something by now,"
she said, "but there's nothing." She served out the bacon and
biscuits, poured the coffee. They ate. Dragging a biscuit
through grease, carefully cleaning the surface of her plate, she
said, "Ride with me on my horse, and lead your mule."

He looked at the gold coins, at her small feet upturned
with the round red marks still bright on her soles, the whiteness of her ankles beneath the road dust. He said, "I'm not
sure if I'm up to riding a stolen horse."

"I told them that I will ride to the Mormon Desert and
wait for them. That is west. This is north. Anyway, maybe
they think I'm dead now. Fallen in the river. Eaten by something. Starved. Gone crazy."

"You'll be dead for sure if they catch you. You can't just
take a horse."

"I live with those people. The horse is mine. I didn't steal
it."

"The horse is not yours."

"It pulled me from Kansas. I watered it and brushed it. It
is mine."

She finished her meal, downed her coffee, reached for his
dishes, and cleaned them and the skillet and his sugared pot
with a handful of sand, rinsed them all in the river, returned.
She worked everything back into the panniers, pulled on her
socks and boots, picked up the coins, and pushed the rocks
in on the fire, crushing the flames. She held the coins down
to him. "For the breakfast and whatever else I eat," she said.
He didn't move, just looked at her hand. She knelt in front
of him, opened his hand, placed the coins there.

The coins were heavy and warm. He might keep them.
He might send her south, see her quickly swallowed by the
plain at sunrise. He tucked the coins into her pocket and said,
"If you're in any trouble, I'll hang you myself. Or I'll send

you back to your friends where they have food and a bed for you."

She looked at the horse. "You ride behind me. We will go fast. Pack your mule."

In the smooth saddle, Walker sat behind the Circassian girl and held the mule's lead. Hot air lay on the distance like a flood. A mile and they left the Green River behind, headed northeast. The hills rolled, sagebrush on the gray soil, rabbits panting in the tangles of shade. He asked her to stop, and he went back to the mule, got out the rifle, climbed back up. They continued. Balancing himself, he took his time to load and shoot three times. The horse took no notice, just kept on with its heavy strides. He hit nothing, checked the rifle's sights, wondered about the quality of the bore.

"You have to kill something some day," she said.

"I can hit something if it's necessary."

"Don't throw your bullets at the dirt." She reached around, took the rifle from him, loaded it, held it to her shoulder and sighted. "Here," she said, "you hold your breath and pull, like this." The gun recoiled, and a rock skipped up from the ground. She loaded again, reined the horse to a stop, climbed down, sat cross-legged in the middle of the road, held the rifle, scanned the brush, and shot. She jogged away and returned with a rabbit. She placed the rifle back in the pack, handed Walker the rabbit and a knife, and climbed up again. "Gut it for me," she said.

"Good shot."

"I have had time to learn some things that I can use." She heeled the horse, and they continued.

The hills finally lost even the sage and rose in washed-out folds, knife edges, crumbling crenellations to peaks and boulders and slabs of red rock half broken, half slid away. And then those hopeless hills ended and they rode into a flatness that seemed beyond gravity. Even the Big Sandy, on the plain north of the road, seemed to stand still, seemed a wet snake napping on a tray of sand, no ripple to its sky-blue skin. Walker might have dozed, might have dreamed—the horse kept right along, Walker's grip stayed tight on the mule's lead—and in the dream Walker thought he heard a thousand steps pacing them along that road, thought he tasted the sulphur he breathed, that coated his lungs, and when he awoke to that unrelenting afternoon from what might have been a second or an hour he found that the girl had reined the horse to a stop, or the horse had stopped on its own. The backs of his hands were red from the sun, the land about him molten, ungrounded in the uprush of heat. She was hot against him.

"Are you awake?" he said. She nodded toward the north. The mountains had risen, high and light as clouds, the Wind River Range reflected against the far curve of the sky. Granite as thin as watercolor, glaciers translucent as steam. No entry to such a place, it seemed. She urged the horse on. The mountains paced them across the plain. The sun burned away shadows.

Hours later, Walker saw a mass hovering directly ahead. He would have thought it was nothing—an echo of that huge shape he'd seen moving the day before—but the horse also saw something and walked on quickly. The mule trotted up beside. Walker tried to squint the distance clear, and eventually he lost that massive shape—it settled beneath the angle of the sun—but green came clear, and what in any other world would have been a fringe of desert seemed to bloom with rich grasses. They rushed into that green, the trees half leafy, half shattered and bleached, and the horse nearly pitched them off as he jerked his head to graze. They slid down and left the animals there to feed, the mule's rope tied to the saddle.

Among the trees they found a burned-out building—a way station, perhaps, a stage station—and they crouched in a corner where two walls still linked together. Walker found cinders in the grass, a pot handle, a sliver of bubbled glass. He held the glass up against the view, each direction, but not enough of the walls remained to tell which way the window had faced, if there had been a window. From how far had they brought these logs, from what pine forest? He studied the mountains. The peaks, separate from their mundane foothills, were whole other creatures entire, an endless shattered wall somehow behind the sky, immersed in a blue that had leached gray through the depth. He wondered who might have manned this station, placed as it was in a hole in this lower world, at the edge of nothing, wondered who might have sat each day waiting for travelers, sending wagons on with barrels of fresh water and a list of warnings. To sit here, day after day, with such a challenge looming like a storm, would be almost too much to bear—either turn away from those mountains or go into them.

The girl had leaned back against the charred logs, her face up toward the sky. She was asleep. He left her there in the shade, came out from the ruin, walked through the hollow to the edge of the Big Sandy. That clear water poured on through, soon to be nearly swallowed on the plain. Kneeling, he felt the coolness the water carried from higher elevations.

From up along the creek he heard an animal exhale and stamp. Standing, he looked to see where the horse and mule had gotten to, edged through a bank of wild rose, pink blooms among the dark green leaves, fine thorns like needles. He stopped.

He had seen etchings of buffalo in newspapers. At an exhibition he had viewed a huge painting of the beasts stirring the earth against a flat horizon, a train caught in the black sea, rifles spiking from the windows. And here, a bull watched him, pausing from his scratch against a broken tree. Strings of his winter coat hung like mange from his hump. Walker didn't move. The bull went back to rubbing, bits of bark falling against his bulk, an animal larger than Walker had ever hoped to see, the dense wool, black horns, beard, and the rich brown smoothness of his flanks. So it must have been a herd of buffalo Walker had seen moving, perhaps heading for grounds where only Indians would pursue them, where they knew their enemy. Walker backed away a step, and the bull heaved himself around and loped upstream, out of sight. Walker followed to the edge of the hollow, and there he saw the bull far out in the sage and rabbitbrush and grass and prickly clumps of cactus, the land continuing toward evening in long inclines and soft shoulders.

He took his time back down along the Big Sandy. With a stick, he dug through the soil, found bulbs that smelled of onion, brushed them clean and carried them along. He came back to the ruin, found that the girl had unpacked the animals and set them to graze. She squatted beside a fire, mixing flour and water in the can. The rabbit, a pink stretch of meat, was spitted above the flames. He handed her the bulbs, sat in the shade and waited. The girl rolled the dough into a long snake between her palms, braided it around the end of a stick, planted the stick at an angle above the heat. She pinched the green from the bulbs, smelled them, pushed them down into the coals at the edge of the flames. Slowly the meat became glossy, and she snatched it back, placed it on a bed of fresh grass she'd laid out. When the bread had browned, she split it from the stick, placed it with the meat, dug out the onions and arranged them with the rest, scooped up the bed of grass, and brought it over to Walker. She sat beside him, and they ate the meat, the hot bread, peeled the crinkly scorched layer from the onions and ate the soft white.

"Over there," he said, "I saw a bull buffalo."

"Don't tell me stories."

"No. I been seeing a herd, far ahead, for two days now."

"You got the brain of a buffalo."

Evening set in, sunset between the trees. She built up the fire, rummaged in the panniers, padded two spaces with grass, laid out the blankets. They watched the stars come over, felt the day's heat cool by slow degree. It was still hot.

"I am going to sit in that creek," she said, and she rose, off past the fire, her shadow across the willows and then gone.

He followed into the darkness, heard the creek, pushed his way to the bank, stood there a long while trying to separate the flow of water from any movement she might make, any disturbance of the surface. Then he heard her beside him, she was not in the water, he felt her bare side brush against the back of his hand, and she stepped down into the water, the heavy slosh of her legs against the current. She continued, the sound of her body louder as she went deeper, and then with a splash she was nearly silent, only her slender neck, perhaps, carving a wake, her hair muffling the disturbance. He stripped off and stepped in. The water, cold as late night, surrounded them, suspended them, moved on. The creek was shallow, fast, and he settled on the washes of soft rock, slid across a stretch of slick sand, held himself against the flow, tipped himself up with elbows and heels and let himself be moved. He found her, tangled his feet with hers, and she pushed away.

He dipped a bit, took in a mouthful of water, swallowed the cold without taste. "This creek makes an ocean, south a thousand miles," he said.

"Every creek makes an ocean."

"There isn't any salt in this water, not that I can tell." He took another swallow, but it tasted only of pure cold. He knew it must flow over tens of miles at least, that it must carry with it a soup of everything they hadn't yet traveled into, the fields and sand and roots and animals that ventured near—perhaps the taste was simply frozen.

"The mountains are close," he said. "Do you think the snow ever melts on those peaks?"

"I would not think so."

"When travelers pass through here in the summer heat, what would they think of those peaks?"

"They would not believe them. And I don't believe them. But I hope the peaks are on the way to what you told me. A valley. A river."

"Wind River. I'll build a lodge."

"Walls would be nice. Yes. I have slept too much where the night air blows right through."

He heard her climb from the water on the far bank, heard her teeth chatter. He followed, thought he knew where she had stepped, but he didn't find her, heard only the patter of water falling from his fingers to the leaves. Turning back to-

ward the creek he saw, far across, the tiny light of the fire
and the space it formed—a globe of leaves and trunks and a
corner of the burned building—and it might have floated,
might have risen into the stars or sunken away, for all the
certainty it engendered.

He turned from the fire and the creek and felt his way.
Here was a tree, the creases of the bark rough and deep, the
density a challenge to his soft nails. Sand beneath his feet
swallowed his momentum, the grit scoured his skin. Leaves
with their pliable freshness ribbed with veins, serrated edges
so innocent they couldn't cut the air or the darkness.

She was with him. The Circassian girl. He touched his
tongue to her neck, beneath her arm, her spine, to judge her
salt—black salt, black sea, bitter and lost in the mineral of his
own saliva. Leaves had pressed to her back, to her legs, sand
to her feet, her palms, and he found that he also was encrusted. Each leaf, as it peeled away, left an impression of
cool on his skin, left a flush of damp on the girl's skin. The
sand dried and fell away with movement, leaving a dust of
that world ground infinitely more fine than sand, so fine it
might enter their pores, flavor their blood. He did not know
what he rolled onto—his own ankle or the knob of a root,
dust or sand or smooth gravel or knuckles, a hummock of
grass and leaves or the hollow of his back, crease of buttocks,
gap of limbs. She touched her tongue to his neck. He found
his hands on her body in a mirror of her hands on his body.
As he moved, as he breathed with her, he worked to listen to
voices he had heard, to watch the men he had known, see
their limbs, mirror the memory, the turns they took.

The man who thinks he is alone in the heat of steam, his
voice hissing a woman's name, a formal name, a fancy. The
man stands and holds himself, bites his own shoulder and
releases—a whiteness of pressure, a slow split of the skin, a
welling of blood that runs and dissipates with the running
of water across his chest, into the long crevice of his arm
clenched at his side, channeled to his fist. Redness with the
redness of the heat of his skin, redness with the string of white

he expels. He submerges to his neck, eyes closed in a sudden, brutal sleep. The woman's name hissed again as if in unconscious exhalation. The coagulation of syllables.

And the man who slides from a chair in the saloon, the room dim, and stops long enough to listen, the city stifled by the hour and the cold of the whole winter ocean blown through. The man sees what he thinks is a room of sleeping men—they are propped in corners, heads on the bar, pillows of crossed arms on the table. He steps into the corridor where, at the back door, another man has just stepped away from a woman. She had hiked her skirts to allow access to that juncture of thighs and grace. The man unbuckles and his trousers descend with his advance until he is completely hobbled and hunched and nearly falls against her, against the jamb. His testicles are alive beneath the vault of his thighs—a bull in flight. Her feet lift from the floor, she is spread and afloat as if she falls down through a well—the depth of the corridor—and the man falls with her. They grapple with the plunge and the impending wreck. There, the testicles grip and the man blurts an ungodly mix of language and rolls from her. Now, backs against the door, it is as if they lie side by side. She turns her head away and reaches down into herself, her skirt draping her arm, and seems to be searching for something he might have left. And he watches the arch of his prick—it is wet and fat and unwilling to yield—what else could it possibly crave? He shrugs and weighs it gently on his palm.

And the man years ago, at the inn on the square of an Eastern village, the man who had succumbed to his wounds, a young man who had languished in hospital and is now home, laid out on a sheet on a table in the dining hall. Mother is down from her room and the guests are exiled from the inn for that hour. She should be turning the linen. She should be chasing a young watcher from the window. Should be cutting lilacs for the sitting room, seeing to the evening meal, the stew of chicken, carrots, the pies and biscuits to be thought of. And the whole structure around her—the white clapboard, shutters black and ready for storm, each fireplace

tall and shallow, each floor a lining of knotted boards to be
swept. And here the pewter, here the silver, here the copper
pans, cleavers, spikes, ladles, china bowls, thimbles, snuffers,
shears, wax, lye, baskets. And at the center of the room to
the left of center of the whole inn the young man is attended.
She dips the cloth in water, wrings it, folds it into a warm,
neat square. She contemplates him a moment. The limbs are
in need of alignment, legs akimbo, and as she smoothes the
cloth down a leg her other hand runs underneath, shifting the
weight, the same with the other leg and with the arms, so that
he is straight and slightly sheened with moisture, a yellow
underglow to the thick pallor of his skin. She oils his hair, the
black cap of his skull. She trims his moustache, the black
frown that shadows his mouth. She traces each eyebrow with
the wet tip of a finger. He is her son, after all. He has her
lines, the slender nose, the narrow lips, slight cleft of the chin,
but on him it is all quiet and solid and always has been. She
studies him. Gravity gives rise to ribs across a chest that
should have been muscle, one nipple a blood-red bud, the
other gone with a blue scar that hasn't healed, that seems to
enter the cavity of his lungs, his heart, a raw entry. She
touches that opening, lays her palm across it, stands there a
long while, until evening takes hold in the trees and the guests
murmur on the porch. Then she is quick about her business,
taking the uniform from its rest on the sideboard, tipping the
boy to one side to work the sleeves up his arms, and in that
last light before the lanterns are lit the manly weight of that
yet-unloved boy shifts in its black cloud of dry hair, and the
mother takes no notice, sealing him away in the stiff thickness
of blue wool. And the boy is folded in the sheet and carried
away, and the tables are scrubbed and set, and the guests are
admitted, and the meal is served. Walker finds the seat, places
his bowl before him, spoons the stew, thinks that here, where
his cup rests, rested the hip of the young man. The glow and
heat of lantern and hearth have sealed them all against night.
And where one was ministered, they all are ministered. It
might rain. The windows are bright with reflection.

Walker held the girl's arms spread beneath the spread of

his arms, his hands at her wrists. They were aligned—toes, lips—but for the slight softness of her chest they might have been the same person. He found them locked, his little hook set. He said nothing, no great motion, found his thoughts separate from the soft cool of the night, found his way.

These are the same stars, she told him, her voice deep inside the drift of the creek, their backs on the leaves. I've seen this sky, I remember seeing it from the square of dirt behind my home, from the stone shingle beside the sea, from the deck of the ship that brought us—the man and me—west across the Atlantic Ocean. He was my family, before the people you saw found me—and then I left them too. He was a man with white skin, and the dry hair on his body crackled when I touched it. I saw the moles and gold flecks in the shadow of that hair, the angles of each cluster. The stars fell into the west, far ahead of me. The stars are uncertain, their light cannot hold steady against the faintest breath of air, and clouds pass through, clouds that sometimes bring rain or, in winter, high drifts of snow that block the paths. I would have to break through, fight my way into the village, find what I'd been sent for, and return to him.

The ship was small, the voyage hot and unsteady. I was often sick. I slept with the women in a dark room, berths up into the curve of the walls. They hung sheets and blankets to close in their spaces. I tacked a line of white handkerchiefs across the front of my berth, leaned back in against the hull, imagined I could push through the thick planks and fall through the water. The ocean is green. I thought of the serpents that swim through its depths, thought of how their scales might be bright, might be as colored and sharp as gems, but no one would see them or know them, so deep, so far from the surface. The serpent would find you, take you into its gullet before you knew you had been devoured, and you'd find yourself in the warm sack of the stomach, lodged against the knobs of the monster's spine. I held my hands against the cool planks, pushed, listened for the water, for the brush of some creature against the hull, but then I heard the women's laughter. I had not heard so many women's voices in my life. They spoke in a dozen languages. I tried to pick out the English, tried to repeat it in my head, hold it for when I would need it. I stood in the darkness at the door to the room where the men slept. Far in there, in the weak circle of a lantern, the men sat stripped to the waist, their skin red and dark and streaked. I smelled the salt of them. A man pissed in a bucket. A man pushed a man against a pillar, chest to chest, and they spoke against each other and pushed off.

We came to New York City, where people move the snow for you, where they step out of your way and say nothing as you pass. A new man and a woman waited for me when I returned to our room—all that was left was the furniture and a broken case with my clothes in it, and even some of my clothes were gone—I lost the lace that I believe had been my mother's, the fur cuffs, the long red muffler. The new man and the woman took me with them. They displayed me to rooms full of men. They had me sing the songs I remembered. We traveled on a wagon. We gathered others, set up a tent. The forests gave way, and the sky opened out.

In the morning, the heat started again. They packed and saddled, mounted, caught up to the road, continued among the hills, almost directly into the low sun. Skirting the dry ranges thrown against the northern horizon, they lost sight of the Wind Rivers. They crossed the Little Sandy and came along toward the Dry Sandy. In a depression near a gully they found a well covered with a thatch of sticks and grass. They pushed aside the cover, lowered their bucket far down on a string and brought up that cold water densely flavored with minerals. It had filtered through years of sediment. It left their mouths sour and numb.

Another mile and they saw something ahead, just off the road—an animal feeding. They came near, and Walker said, "That's my bear dog." The girl brought them up, reined the horse to a stop. Jay Dubb gnawed on a freshly dead, dusty calf, letting his eyes strain halfway up the horse's legs as he pulled at the calf's cheek and tore it open. The mule, testing the air, made a nervous sidestep forward, brought himself

around, pack lurching, and threw a sharp kick toward the
dog, hit instead the calf's skull with a hollow thump. The dog
backed away, snarling, the horse pranced about, the mule
tried for a better position, and with the girl working to bring
the horse steady, with the mule stumbling across the calf, the
dog took off toward the next ridge. Walker shouted, "Jay
Dubb," but the dog didn't look back, and the girl, in a final
grasp for control, urged the horse into a trot, back onto the
road, and the mule fell in, wheezing against the lead.

"That was a longhorn calf," the girl said. "Are you sure
it was a buffalo you saw yesterday?"

"It was a buffalo. A bull. You can't mistake a bull buffalo."

"So this calf just took a walk way out here and fell over
dead."

"Could be."

"Your dog does not mind you. Are you sure you are not
mistaken about him, too?"

"He don't know me. I just own him."

They came along through the green fields of Pacific
Springs. Here they saw clearly how the land was trampled,
the scattering of cow flops. Beyond the hills, the Wind Rivers
came up again, a clear-edged holding of snow. The dust they
stirred hung around them, seemed to travel forward with their
steps. Into the valley of the Sweetwater River, the road cut
through the thick willow bushes, wet across fields of long
grass, and without slowing a step they passed dead Jay Dubb
stretched on the grass with a bullet hole clean through his
neck, black crows hopping the grass around him. "That is
some bear dog," the girl said.

Ahead, on a slip of flat ground, a cook wagon sat beside
a fire ring, a few canvas tents flapped loosely in the afternoon breeze, and, beyond, a good-size herd dotted the slopes,
deep in feed. No men in sight. They rode into the camp,
dismounted, stood there stretching their legs, slapping the
dust from their trousers. From a tent a man stepped, saw
them, reached back for his pants, pulled them on, buttoned
his shirt, tried to get his fingers through his hair. "Ma'am,"
he said, and he came forward.

Walker handed the girl the mule's lead, took a step to meet the man. "You shot my dog."

The man nodded. "That's the rule. Any loose dog is done off with before it can harass the herd. Couldn't know it was yours."

"You want to pay me for him?"

"Not particularly. I'll give you something to eat." He came past Walker, took the leads from the girl. "Set down, ma'am. I'll water your animals."

He took the horse and mule into the willows, and Walker and the girl sat in the shade of the wagon. Soon the man returned and tied the animals to the wagon, rummaged a bit, came out with two tin cups of cold beans, spoons, handed one to the girl, one to Walker. They ate. Out in the sun the man sat on his heels, squinted toward the girl—his face was creased and focused. Finally he leaned a bit forward, caught his balance, and said, "Where you from, young lady?"

"The Black Sea," Walker said. "This is the Circassian girl."

"Ah. I heard of her. Some dudes passed us a week ago, said she was something beautiful. They didn't get close, ma'am."

"Right," she said.

"You her manager?" he said, touching the brim of his hat toward Walker.

"I'm not managing her. Not even halfway. We're traveling together."

"Oh." He sat on his butt in the dirt, looked to the road, the sky. "Where you headed?"

"Wind River Valley."

"Is that right? Us, too. We brought this herd down around from Montana. Why don't you ride with us? You'd be most welcome. We've gotten full up with each other."

Walker leaned back against the wagon wheel, felt the spokes press his spine. From the hills, the sounds of cattle, the smell of the tall grass. The girl also leaned back. She hooked her hair behind an ear, left her hand gently cupped there as if she listened to the afternoon, the birds chattering in the brush.

Walker thought of taking up with the drive, thought of the men riding on ahead, tending the herd, circling back to have a word with the girl. She would sit there in the V of Walker's legs, give each man a nod, a bit of talk. This man was tall, long neck, shoulders and arms like wings of muscle. He was handsome and dusty and ready to laugh. Who knew how sure the other men were, how casual in their handling of their mounts, of this country. She'd lie with one or another, most likely, before long. But if Walker and the girl rode on alone, caught the Wind River, headed up toward the divide, they could take to the meadows, to the trees, and the men would arrive in their own time and settle and come looking for the girl. She was bright with reflected sun. She reached and took his cup, scooped gritty dirt into it and began to scrub.

"I think we'll go on alone," Walker said. The girl kept working her fingers round the cup and didn't look at him. "Are we going to have any grizzly trouble, now that you've shot my bear dog?"

"I don't know about grizzlies. Could be trouble with Indians, I hear. Stay clear if you see one. They'd like your animals and whatever else you got."

As they mounted up, Walker looked down at the man looking up at them, and said, "My name's Avary. Find me when you get up there. I'll have a lodge started."

"All right."

Walker heeled into the horse's flanks, the girl gave the reins a shake, and they started away. There were men on the slopes, on foot or on horseback or lying deep in the grass, asleep.

"Why did you tell him that?" the girl said.

"Tell him what?"

"Your name. It won't help him find you. Who else will be in the Wind River Valley?"

They passed the last of the herd, came on through late afternoon, up a long incline and into sage again. Finally they came to a ridge and saw South Pass City below, a sudden

jumble of squares on a cross of two streets, an odd, constructed shock after days of distance and flat.

"Do they have telegraph up here?" the girl said.

"Don't know. You see any wires?" So much brown and
green, a creek running through, the long shadows striping
everything. "Is someone looking to leave you a message?"

"Not that I know."

They sat on the horse and watched awhile. A child ran
from a cabin to the dense fuzz of willows along the creek.
A goat scratched its neck against a hitching post. A few of
the false fronts had ripped loose and leaned dangerously.
Roofs had gapped to the air. There were piles of dirt on the
slopes—who knew what minerals had been extracted, where
the money had been carried off to.

Coming out from the white hotel, a man walked down the
center of the street, held his arms out as if airing himself, like
a black-dressed vulture gathering the last of the day's heat,
and slowly he turned as he progressed, and when he came
around toward them he stopped, stood still, looked to them
on the ridge above. He removed his hat and held it to his
chest. He shaded his eyes. Came on a few steps. Stopped
again. Waved the hat at them. They didn't move. He replaced
his hat, turned, and walked quickly among the buildings. A
voice echoed.

The girl gave that gold horse a sharp kick, and they were
fast toward the aspen and pine of the southernmost tip of the
Winds, they caught the shadows of the first trees, the sound
of the mule and pack as loud as shouting, and they wove up
across the slope, into denser woods, through gullies thick with
undergrowth, skirted the meadows, saw evening come over
in the surface of beaver ponds. As darkness caught them up,
as the mule pulled harder against the strain, the girl reined
them short, slid down, leaned in against the horse's thick
chest and stood a long minute in his lee.

"You say this horse ain't stolen," Walker said, taking the
reins, finally looking back. The forest was solid behind them.

"It is not stolen. I said that already."

"That's what you said."

"I did not want to stop in South Pass City."

"No. Me neither."

Night without a fire. He listened to each move the horse and mule made, each thump of hoof against stone, each exhalation, and tried to follow the sound out, to guess how far it would travel before bouncing back to them huddled there. The stars circled through the pine branches.

"What have you got us into?" he said.

"Nothing."

"Then why are we hiding?"

"We are not. I just did not want to talk to anyone. That man looked as if he wanted us—"

"Wanted *you.*"

"—and we cannot build a fire if there are Indians."

He reached again for the rifle in its rest on the pack, hefted it, replaced it. "I don't know if we need to be scared of Indians," he said.

"Have you seen an Indian before?"

"In pictures. And from the deck of a ship with them falling back. Savage, I guess. But they didn't frighten me."

"Once an Indian wanted to dance with me. He talked to the master in the tent a long time. I saw his arms black with designs, full bare from his vest. Terrible. But the master made him go away."

"That man in South Pass City wasn't an Indian."

"I know."

He felt her lean against his arm, and he pulled at the blankets, brought them together, tried to get comfortable against the panniers and frame, against the emptiness of his stomach. She lay there without moving.

Clouds came over, dissipated. The moon would be late. The breeze moved nothing, the pines were still against the slow creep of the stars, a chill on the ground's bare surface. He listened. Perhaps he heard lichen pry its dry roots into granite, flecks of stone take a tumble. Perhaps the gray jays dreamt of cones on a trail of sap, a lake bright as a cloud far in the wall of a mountain.

"What does an Indian think?" she said.

"I suspect he thinks of how to get on through this country."

She tugged the blanket across his throat, pressed her face against his arm. Her teeth caught his shirt, pinched his flesh, released him. "I tell you what I know," she said. "I don't know nothing. What do you know?"

He knew that he had been this close to her now for almost two days. Longer than he could remember being close to anyone for a good ten years or more. Even with Captain Avary they were always shifting around that warm cabin, off to various posts, Walker alone watching evening come down across the waves and the sea birds glide through the scud tossed from each swell, the ship creaking around him as if a good roll of thunder would render it tarred sticks and sinking gear. The albatross floated in the gray sky before night so smoothly, so steadily, it might have been floating in still water, only its sharp beak black against its gray rigid form, the wings spread wider than Walker's full measure, two feet wider, the bird whistling, banking, carried solid on that unobstructed wind and the foam the wind broke and shredded back into the sea, the bird waiting for stars, the bird waiting for cuttlefish to draw the moonlight at the green surface, the bird waiting for sleep and the long steady rise on the air until nestled up against the stars, feeling warmth deep in the eyes, memory of stark brightness without end, feeling the prick of each feather as it held to the currents, the heart pulsing deep beneath the down, until the earth turned, the tide rolled, the sun woke him and he saw in the early light the long shadows of land on every side, land rolling far into green, high into snow.

He had not known his mother—she had bled when he was born, and they couldn't stop her from draining away—so much blood, they told him, that a basin on the floor beside the bed floated toward the door, caught on the lip of an island, a raised knot on the floorboards. He had not known his uncles, aunts, cousins—they remained unnamed, moved on, dead. He had not known his father but by name, by sight—

his father had worked a farm in the next town west and
Walker had lived with a man and woman with many children
and a bakery that smelled of dark rye. Rounds of bread dense
as stone. They sliced those loaves into eighths, sopped cups
of broth. He stood in line with the children, waited to bathe,
the tub steaming with the kettle water, the lot of them naked
and clutching themselves, silent, stepping forward, and he
was always the smallest, smaller even than the tiniest girl, and
he was the whitest, his skin so pure you might have seen the
working of his heart in the fine wire cage of ribs. He would
press his palm to his chest, feel for his pulse, but often he
felt nothing, held his breath, clamped his ears shut, but still
found himself silent, cold, until the thought of that silence
started him shaking, and his heart pumped warmth to the
balls of his feet.

There was the war. Walker took to the woods, toward the
next town, and along the way paused when the view opened
toward the road. He watched for the men moving in lines,
on wagons, watched for the uniform step, the blue, the sun
on something burnished, but he saw no one he recognized,
no one with his own gait. He came to the town, came to the
table in the shadow of the steeple and said his father's name.
You are far too young, the man said. No, Walker said, see if
you got him on your list. We ain't got him here in these
names, the man said, but I know the man—he's been gone
for weeks. At the farm, Walker found the main house and
said his father's name. You are his son all right, the man said,
you got the same little eyes. Your daddy said he's going to
sign on, but I don't know where.

Walker didn't return to the man and woman and the
children—he still smelled those children on his skin, the
musty spoiled flour scent, the yeast of stained trousers. He
waited for a while near his father's shed, but eventually a
family moved in. He waited near the church in the town, but
the men had left, and after a time the men started returning.
He took again to the woods, to the towns east, south, north,
west, said his father's name, and on occasion he would hear
it repeated, hear that, yes, his father had come through, hear

that his father had taken money one way or another and then gone on to sign up for the war in some other town, somewhere else. And finally Walker came to a town, said his father's name, and the people took him by the ear, angry, inspected his resemblance. Walker turned back, didn't mention his father's name again.

He lay on his shoulder, on the shoulder of the Wind River Range, shouldered against the Circassian girl. With another hundred miles they would turn up into the canyons, toward the granite spine and the sheets of eternal ice. His lodge would grow from a stand of spruce and pine, the beams drawn overhead with the power of the girl's horse. He sees her there. He hears the song she sings in his lodge, hears the silence of those who listen, those who lean forward in the light of a dozen lanterns suspended in the rafters. In the moon's flat silver light, that lodge is a massive moonlight shadow, and if Walker stood in that shadow a long while, if his eyes slowly learned to see through the filtered, reflected, dead cold light, he would see the hillsides grow with cabins, houses, a mercantile, a church. That new town is abandoned for the evening—the Circassian girl sings, her voice locked with the lantern light in the thick walls and peaked ceiling of Walker Avary's lodge.

Down through a canyon streaked with huge, red cliffs, they rode on, north and west along the northern wall of the range, through the rocky ridges, into great slumped sagebrush plains that spread halfway up the foothills. They saw no one, stayed clear of the road, if there was a road—perhaps it was an animal trail in intermittent pale threads along a distant gully, across a bank, into a cup of tall grass. They wandered up a river that dove into a cave, bubbled silently from a pool, fed swirls of trout heavy from whatever magic the water had accumulated in its brief, dark journey. The grass burned away in the white sun, and then they came to where the grass was thick again. Long hummocks of willow along the creeks, cottonwoods tall and light green. A burned-out cabin—scraps of curtain, square nails rusted, a pile of animal bones—someone had been, lived, gone. Pools of black oil on ground as barren as ash.

They knew they should eventually come to Camp Brown, but they missed it. They knew they should not light a fire, not yet, not for another fifty miles of Indian territory, but they lit a few sticks each night, kept the flame clean, wood dry, smoke light, and cooked whatever—bread, hotcakes, meat, coffee. They knew they would run short of rations— the Chin brothers had provided enough for only one man— so they shot a rabbit, a duck, fished trout from fast water.

They saw a field of white tents far in an open valley, too distant to make out as tipi or army canvas. They heard gunfire at night, but they couldn't place it, and at first light they came out of the brush where they'd slept, looked toward sunrise, saw nothing, even when the sun had risen and sent shadows stretching, shrinking, the heat burning away the night's moisture.

After miles of high, parched grassland, they turned up into the Wind River Valley, took to the lushness of the riverbanks, followed the cold flow through the willows, fields of grass high as their dangling feet. The river wove past a butte, huge and wonderfully flat above its ruined sides. To the north, another range—the map gave it no name, obscured it behind SHOSHONEES—beyond forbidding erosions of purple, red, and white, the range seemed to rise in another country altogether. From the south, the foothills of the Winds slowly verged in to meet them, great yellow cliffs and dark forests.

They camped for days beneath cottonwoods, beside a field of grass, and the river took a long wide curve around them, cooling them against the dry upland heat. The center of the river was too cold for bathing, the water drawn too recently from the peaks, but they found shallow pools where they could lie on sand, half in, half out of the tepid water, with the sun hot on their bellies.

"I could sleep in this water," she said. "I do not believe this summer heat will ever end. This is beautiful heat."

———

At first light they caught the animals, saddled and packed, and headed upriver. It had been five days since they'd been out in the open. They watched the distance, watched antelope scare up out of draws, away into the sage so fast that nothing could catch them—the black hooks of the horns. Magpies along the river. Crows in the gray of dead trees. Each new roll of the earth took them higher. The northern range came down, the Winds came up, and against the morning blue they thought they could spot elk or some other dark creatures on the highest green meadows of the Winds. The girl took the horse along the edge of the floodplain, clear of the swampy tangles below.

"We will reach the end of this," she said, "if these mountains keep coming in."

"That's good. We'll get to where the water starts."

"It will be a cold place, I think."

She turned in his arms, looked back into the sun, down along the river. He also looked. The mule came along, shaking flies from its neck, and the butte rose in the clear early air like a ruined monument, holding in its shadow a thousand years of passage, memory.

"There," she said. "I thought I heard something. There."

He watched the softened earth, the creases, the sagebrush, the stripe of the river. From the fast shadows of clouds, the rising heat, he caught three figures on horseback, on the far edge of the floodplain, a few miles back. They seemed to be coming along.

"This valley is getting popular fast," he said.

"Bad luck."

She urged the horse on. The mule pulled back against the lead. They covered a lot of territory.

The sun had come high enough to shine straight down into her collar before she looked back again. The figures had gained ground, still on the far side. She flicked the reins, took off into the sage, a slow angle away from the river. Toward the Winds, the ground rose for miles.

"There's nothing out here," she said.

"You looking for anything in particular?"

"Anything."

She angled back toward the floodplain, turned a bit as if glancing at the sun. He looked. They were men, not half a mile back—what looked to be two Indians and a white on small, plump horses. She took her way down a slope, toward the river. Eagles stood in the grass, started up as they approached, seven white heads, silent, huge wings catching slow scoops of air, riding the heat higher in wide spirals. She urged the horse into a trot, and he churned the soft ground, threw clods back at the mule. The cottonwoods came up around them, and she hurried on into thick willows. The branches whipped at their legs, the mule fought the lead, nearly jerked Walker from the saddle, the pack forcing through the narrow gaps.

"What the hell are you doing?" Walker said, and he took his free hand from her waist and grasped her hands and the reins and pulled them up short.

"All right," she said. "Here."

She slid from the saddle, and he followed her. The animals stood with them, slowly calming. She looked at the sky, at the ground. Birds startled in the branches, unseen flutters in the deep green.

"Listen," she said.

The river flowed past, out of sight, an almost silent rumble. She turned and looked at him, her face round, eyes nearly closed, and touched a finger to her ear. The animals' heads drooped. Flies buzzed. There was a dampness to the heat.

Walker looked up at the clouds—they seemed to rise directly from him, smearing to nothing in the blue. Above the willows, the cottonwood leaves glimmered in a breeze, but the air was dead on the ground.

She led the horse forward a few steps. Walker waited with the mule—the pack would snap the willow branches.

Clearly the sound of hooves. No voices. He looked toward the river. Above the green, on a slice of dry grass and open soil and sage, directly across and close, the three men moved. The Indians were young and very dark, the white man older and nearly fat. They were lightly provisioned, each with a small roll behind the saddle, a rifle in a scabbard. They seemed to keep going, quick out of view, then the thump of hoof on rock, the slosh of water.

The girl was suddenly up on the horse, her black hair sharp in the blue, nearly taller than those willows, and she looked back as she strung the reins through her fingers, said, "Wait right there," and kicked. The horse jumped, the willows crashed, bluebirds and a huge flicker came low and fast over the leaves, and she'd gotten herself free—the clean sound of the horse at full gallop.

Walker left the mule and came forward to where she'd stood. He saw her take the lip of the plain, a moment of clarity, and then a few strides into sage and she was gone.

Sound of air moving, river, birds circling round again.

The three men, at a full gallop, took the same lip, into sage, also gone.

Walker pulled the rifle from the pack, loaded it and held it to his shoulder, tested along the sight, lowered it and held it against his side, pinched under his arm. He came on through the willows, across the ground freshly turned, followed the girl's trail until it met with the prints of the men's horses, and he continued up the slope. The mule followed him without the lead. He left the deep grass, stepped around cactus, through sage, and the distance opened. No one in sight. He stood there. The mule came up, passed him, grazed the short grass. The white clouds puffed along, thicker above the peaks, north and south. Then he saw, beneath a far ridge of the foothills, the huge gold horse lunge into sight, a few strides and it took the crest—silent, the distance, with the breeze buzzing faintly in the sage—and the Circassian girl held low to the neck, and the horse cut from sight. Walker watched, counted, ten, eleven, twelve, up to eighty before those three men—they were still together, hadn't split up, hadn't circled back—all came up against that ridge, their horses floundering, digging into the slope, onto the crest, and down from sight.

Walker waited another count—two hundred, three hundred—but saw nothing else, nothing farther along. He tried to pull from the contours of those foothills an idea of the canyons, streams, cliffs that guided the chase. With nothing but that tiny girl in the saddle, the gold horse would take anything.

He came up to the mule, took the lead, and got them back down out of sight, down to a spot along the river where the floodplain was wide and he could look out from the willows to the whole stretch of foothills. Sitting in the shade, he watched. He balanced the rifle on his crossed legs.

Walker was caught with an image.

Her arms reached far along the horse's neck, hands held the reins in a clutch of mane. The ground rose, the atmosphere thinned, and the horse slashed its forelegs on brush and slips of gravel. On the horse's neck, across the heavy chest, sweat gathered, matted the hide, foamed white until the strike of hoof broke it free, shredded it back against the girl—the foam clung to her arms, caught in her collar, fizzed at her ears. She tasted the fluids of that horse. On her tongue she held the distillation of river water, of grain snipped from buffalo grass, bunch grass, deer grass, the dust of the horse's lungs, roads from Kansas, salt licked from white soil, the edge of poison from mosquito and black fly. The foam drifted on her brow, whipped against the thickness of her black hair, filled the hollows of her eyes, caves of her nostrils, smoothed the line of her lips held tight. She saw nothing of what lay ahead. Her thighs tensed high in the scudding white.

He knew her face was round, eyes dark, body frail. He tried to shape her again.

She had only those trousers too long, that white shirt. He had everything else. Everything but the horse.

He waited three nights, watched through the days, thought once that he saw smoke to the southeast along the Winds, but as hc watched that gray line it diffused into the haze and he couldn't know if it had been more than a thread of sun caught in the heat. On the third morning, he packed the mule, checked the rifle and propped it on his shoulder, took the mule's lead, and started toward the foothills. A half mile along, he intersected the hoofprints and followed them through the sage. He continued across the gradual incline, the soft rise toward the foothills, passed down into a steep swale where water stood in elbows of creekbed—here the hoofprints dug deep, left chunks of mud scattered and dried on the grass—and then the ground steepened. He looked back toward the river, tried to see the spot where he'd waited—it was hidden by a rise, and when it came clear again he was traversing the ridge where the girl had climbed and disappeared. The hoofprints here were wild and gouged and long. Walker used the deepest prints as footholds on the steep face, the mule complained and teetered with each step, and then they gained the top and looked on into what had been hidden—a long valley that rose direct to the first dark edge of forest.

Walker angled from the ridge, lost the tracks, found them

again at the center of a dry, sandy creekbed that split the valley, that scraped among boulders and a few stunted cottonwoods. He led the mule through the sand. The mountains seemed incredibly high above the heat of that centered crease. The Wind River, far below, carved through the brown land.

Finally he entered the dry woods, the pitchy shade. A jay screamed and swooped among the treetops. The hoofprints gapped across drifts of needles, cut through gravel, gave out finally in a broad depression of undergrowth. Walker circled that low brush, examined the ground to every side, but found nothing more.

He led the mule through the trees, came to a place where he saw cliffs steep across a canyon, saw the edge of peaks above. That land went on, no clear access or sense to it. Sunlight on upthrust, sunlight on shoulders slumped into rockfall, sunlight on the surface of woods girded with shadow. He watched the flows of light. Brightness pooled along exposures, leaked across fissures. Darkness moved through, clouds detached and trailing their likeness up and down the defiles. And the birds—the square wings of a drifting, steady eagle, the momentary unshaped fist of a diving red-tailed hawk. What might have been trails he saw were gouges where water and avalanche had scoured the rock. What might have been a flat, broad ridge that drove toward the peaks he saw was no more than a sliding wall, a dozen ridges, each ridge blocked before it could take hold. What might have been squares and angles of bellowed canvas were holds of dirty snow.

He sat against a spruce, and the mule stayed near. "You tell me what you hear," Walker said, and he watched the animal, but the mule was standing stiff beneath the strapped puff of the pack, eyes closed against the afternoon.

Walker listened. He heard the tree above him, the needles catching the air, shredding it into sound. He heard the structure of the trunk conform to the breeze, the slow creak and sway, the sap drawing through, the bitter yellow pliability of the wood. He opened his shirt and held his palms to the bones of his chest. He shook from the uncertain rush of his organs, the sudden intake of air, the chill of his palms, the tightening of his skin. He looked down at himself, watched his hands quiver with the thump of his heart, heard that thump as if it rose through the ground, as if it approached. His trousers draped the points of his hips, his hips as smooth as hers, his navel as shallow and clean, rimmed with colorless down. What would shield him against that world—how dense was his spine, how thick was his skin? He rolled onto his face. The needles pierced his belly. He slept. Awoke to his own dry whistling intake of breath, as if the sound had echoed and returned a great distance to rouse him.

He caught the mule and moved quickly down from the trees, out from the close sound of his own movement. He angled to catch the Wind River far up its flow.

Across the river, on the yellow, gray, violet badlands, mountain sheep with heavy curled horns trailed along, watched him pass. He came to massive red cliffs overhanging the river, blocks of stone the size of railroad cars fallen, broken. He saw through a gap in the red a slice of burned-dry desert and the mountains in cloud. With no bank left to follow, he had to step into the river to skirt the cliffs. The water came to his chest, seemed to squeeze his lungs, and the mule threatened to wash away, to be dragged under by the weight of the pack. Walker pulled, cajoled, and they came up past the cliffs, into grass again.

Another day. An old trail, lightly traveled, wended up the valley, and he followed it where he could, saw the old fire rings. There might have been wheel marks, hoofprints, bootprints, bare feet, but it had all been muddied or erased by rain and snow and the trailing antelope and the occasional coyote or dog. The badlands on the far side of the river rose steeper now, red and deeply carved, black shadows in the folds. Crows sat high on the knife edges. From the Winds a fast creek flowed and joined the river in a swamp of mosquitoes and willows. Walker stopped and looked up that fork, but still the range seemed too steep, the approach too dry across those mounded, bouldered foothills, so close above. He crossed the fork.

In a stand of dead cottonwoods abandoned by a new curve of the river, something had been left. The stunted trees had never been much, trunks too thick for their meager height, branches gnarled. It seemed that animals had been wedged into the joints, but then he saw the poles suspended from branch to branch. Walker left the mule and approached. There were five bundles in the trees, wrappings of what looked like buffalo hide, bits of the fur scattering the ground and caught on the cactus spines. Strips of gut twined and secured each bundle. He took to the tree with the sharpest lean, climbed up the trunk and crouched there. No scent on the air but water, sage, grass. He hooked a finger beneath a strip of gut, tugged, and the gut gave way, the hide shifted. He pulled it aside and found a hand so dark it might have been burned, skin thick against the desiccation beneath, the forearm leading toward the bulk of the man's or woman's body hidden, an edge of smooth yellow deerskin, a pattern of decoration, what might have been bark or straw dyed and woven onto the hide, evenly spaced lines, fine work. Walker pulled the hide closed, slid back down to the ground, took the mule and hurried along. Looking back, he saw magpies swarm up from the badlands, and the birds took to the high branches of those funeral trees. The birds swayed, unbalanced, thrusting their long black tails, trying to catch center and steady themselves.

The next day, the badlands opened to the north, another valley with a noisy creek, and he saw the land that creek drained—distant peaks widely scattered, massive blocks of stone ornately carved, buttressed with their own leavings, with forest so thick it might have been black, and one peak above them all, a horn, its height as sharp as the leading point of a mountain sheep's curl.

He followed the trail. No sign of recent travel or settlement. The badlands wandered and banked and stepped to the north, and the forest of the Winds slowly came down.

Finally he entered among tall spruce, where the branches, heavy with cone, hung far out over the water. He found a fire ring in a clearing, slept there through the afternoon, awoke and listened to the river, to the birds, the air moving high above him. Clouds spilled from the peaks, rained in straight lines. He was dry beneath the trees.

A mile upriver, another valley opened to the north, lush with ponds and rich feed, a slow creek meandering, and at the head of the valley the sharp-horned peak again, and Walker saw that the peak was only the highest rise in a long wall of cliffs that cut off the north completely. He watched the sun shift across that valley, watched the specks of animals wander far toward that battlement, and then he turned away. Up from the Wind River, up from the trail and the spruces, across the round foothills, into woods, finally straight on into the Wind River Range.

He heard flowing water, came to a creek he had crossed once already down where it joined the river. The air was cool in the shade beside the creek. He cupped water to his mouth, tasted nothing but cold, let the mule drink, then continued up the bank. Boulders large as houses jutted above the water and clogged the wooded drainage. Fallen trees, spiked and impassable, bridged the banks. Jays harassed from every side. For a mile or more, as he fought to lead the mule along safe footing, he saw nothing but steepness to each side, the boulders giving way to brief, sheer walls among the slopes. The air moved the trees against those gray walls, and Walker was not always sure if it was the sky or stone he saw through the branches. And then quick fields, red spikes of wildflower, and the land flattened a bit. Sound seemed to travel more freely, and the sky settled closer to the treetops.

He was through a knot of shoulder-high willows and boulders, he left the trees behind, the creek pooled in deep pockets and ran white through steepness, and he looked up beyond the sound at his feet and saw to the left a line of silver cliffs that cut high above scree slopes, to the right meadows that stretched to aspen, evergreen, and he sensed that these two flying runs against the blue sky centered something immense, and coming out from the willows, up a last steep slope, he saw a lake, its surface chopped white in its clean dish of sky, a mile at least toward the waterfall at its head. The cliffs, slopes, white lines of aspen, fur of evergreen, seemed the barest fringe or lip or promise of what lay beneath the lake's unruly surface—the lake might descend miles to some exquisite, monstrous depth.

In the evening, as the night sky settled across the lake, Walker stood on the promontory above the lake's outlet. Nighthawks took the air around him. He had not seen their approach—their slim wings were sudden knives, their voices like a chill buzz, an electric pulse across a wire. They dove around him, toyed with his hearing, sent him spinning, dodging, and he dropped to his haunches, looked directly up, and saw them ascend, braiding themselves into the first stars.

He slept in the open, on stone, beneath his blankets, with the mule wandering near. The fickle stars in the sky, those same stars adrift in the lake. The miles and canyons and peaks and mountain air all swung wide, tilted and swirled toward the next day's sun. He knew the rumble that took the hollow of his ribs, the ache where the tendon sprung his heel, the burn of sun on his neck, the heat of thirst. He knew something of the distance he had traveled, the continents circled, the scent of the earth's salts. He knew that he could be tracked, that he had left signs that only a long, hard rain would erase. He knew that his map had drawn him along, that someone had drawn an idea of this world and that he had entered it and devoured it and that now he had drawn his own map, a blank square of white with a definite snake of passage, a definite corridor of hills and towns and views and lost canyons, and along the border of that square he etched Captain Avary's shoulders with their veins like roots, and men at the end of a journey gathered in the sound of their own voices, and a young man rolled dimly in a sheet in a white clapboard inn, and rain beyond the glass, and his own thin limbs and a buffalo, and the Circassian girl asleep in the Wind River's shallows. He dug his fingers into his own crev-

ices, beneath his arms, behind his knees, felt the things he
carried with him—breath, heart, hair, skin. He was where he
wanted to be. Alone. Starting. He wrapped a blanket around
his head to shut out the mountains, and then he listened to
the thin whine of his thoughts and tried to amplify those
thoughts into clear-drawn plans—empty valley, heat, muscle.

In the morning he took the full circuit of the lake, far up to
the waterfall, and he gauged the views and the animal trails.
Trying to guess at the depth of the water, he climbed the
slopes in the hope he might penetrate the surface and see
the submerged contours of the valley, but all he saw were the
brown, murky shallows that stretched briefly from the grassy
slopes, and the rocky shallows that stretched even more
briefly from the scree slopes. The center of the lake, for all
he could tell, might have dropped forever, and deep, far from
the sun's light, a trout the size of a man might sleep. Walker
saw the gills as broad and curved and etched as fine china
plates, the hooked jaw like a crook of bronze, the tail as ribbed
and strong and pliable as a corset. That fish slept in whatever
had washed from those mountains through a thousand years.
   He wondered what might be missing from the valley.
There were no flat fields, but the slopes were thick with grass
and wildflowers, and across the outlet the brief meadows
could hold a barn, a few cabins, and fallen from the cliffs was
plenty of broken granite for a foundation, and there were
miles of untouched forest with trees thick enough to brace a
palace.

He worked for a month or more, lost track of the days. Down
in the woods, hidden from the sky and the wind, he built a
shelter of thin poles peeled and jointed and stacked, a roof of
boughs and moss—a tight structure that smelled more of
woods than of man—and he fashioned a bed from canvas
and sweet grass. Across the lake's outlet, along the edge of
the woods, he fenced a corral with dead-fall trees dragged
and woven, and the mule spent its nights in that square, a
trickle of water running through to quench it, and its days

the mule spent picketed in one fresh space or another. Such a stout mule. Walker found bear tracks in the soil around the corral, cougar tracks, but each morning the mule seemed undisturbed, its tail switching at flies, its hard hooves black and glossy.

On the promontory he paced out the dimensions of his lodge—a room with a high peaked ceiling, and space on every side for the structure to grow. With the mule and the panniers he spent days hauling stones from the scree slopes, and he piled them beside his imaginings, slowly started to fit them into a shallow trench he'd dug, mortared them with a paste of the clay and minerals he found, puzzled them into a square foundation.

He ate through most of his provisions. He ate berries— bitter red. He ate fat trout pulled from the lake, trout nearly as long as his leg, he gorged himself on the pale meat, but he couldn't keep pace with his hunger. He should have ridden the mule back down into the Wind River Valley to see if the cattlemen had arrived. He should have spent his days setting up winter provisions. But he built that foundation all the way around, back to where he'd started.

He awoke, deep in his mattress, the blanket holding his warmth. If the moon was out above the trees, it gave no light through the branches, through his roof, through the seams of his walls. He felt the itchy wool against his shoulder, chest, across the sharp bevel of his hip. Pushing aside the blanket, he felt for his clothes, found his shirt and pulled it on, left it unbuttoned, stepped barefoot from his shelter.

He listened. The trees creaked, the air moved above, it all wavered, paused, continued, on through the darkness.

He took to the path he'd followed each day, slowly up the slope on the balls of his feet, and beyond the tree trunks there was a slight lightening toward gray. Gradually, he left the sounds of the woods behind, he was out from the eaves, small at the edge of the valley.

The lines of the ridges cut the stars. He came toward the promontory, felt the stiff grass, the stones, the dry lichen, and then the trampled ground of his work space. He stepped over his foundation, through the room that he would eventually close, and then over the far line of the foundation, to the edge of the promontory. He thought he could almost feel the bulk of the finished lodge at his back, as if it already rose in fresh pitchy darkness, as if it gathered the sounds of the valley in its shadow, making the lodge the center and all else something else. But the lodge wasn't built. The sounds curled unimpeded through the valley, skimmed the surface of the long lake—the sound of the falls at the fringe of upper forest, the water frothing white into the lake, the rings of disturbance growing.

He shouted his name. Nothing returned.

The filthy whiteness of his shirt puffed around his torso. He let the shirt fall back from his shoulders, onto the ground, and left it there. Stepping forward, he made his way down the slope to the water's edge, balanced on the boulders above the plash and plunk of the minor swells against the shore. He lowered one foot and laid it flat on the water's surface, felt the cold caress of movement. Then he plunged the foot straight in to the bottom, got his balance on the slick, rounded stones, stepped in with his other foot, and started out. The lake dove quickly from the promontory, and Walker was soon to his neck, soon floating with the water at his ears, at his chin, and his body tight and small in the lake's grip.

There was no warm layer at the surface, as there would be under the midday sun. There was no distinguishing the night air from the water, black from black. Only the center of gravity and his tight breath kept him swimming at the median between above and below. The stars came all the way around. The Milky Way snaked. He didn't know if his movements took him farther from the shore, or if he remained stationary. He didn't know how far below him the earth descended, or how high above the valley the peaks finally rose. He did know that now, even with all his cold effort to keep his head steady at the surface, he seemed to hear each significant movement within the valley, as if the sounds accumulated in a layer just at the water's surface—the mule snipped at the grass in a near slumber, a bear dug roots far up through a stand of aspen, pikas gathered warmth into their dens on the scree slopes, birds asleep in the branches, frogs in the mud—and engulfing it all, the constant waterfall, a sound that had been with him every moment since his arrival, a sound that penetrated the woods, his shelter, through each night. He always thought he heard a bit of the Circassian girl's voice carried with that rush of water, perhaps just the sound of her lungs steadily filling and emptying. He was sure that if there was a sound of her from anywhere in those mountains, the sound would have echoed and channeled and found its way through the canyons to him. But how to separate the sound of that girl from the sound of the waterfall? That water spilling into the lake and catching in his mouth, stinging his eyes, flowed from the peaks, far in. He could pull himself from the cold water, follow the trail of the valley, listen again for the Circassian girl, assure himself that it was not her voice he heard each moment of night and day.

After sunrise, with the long day ahead and the air clear and alive, he wrapped a bundle and tied it behind the blanket on the mule's back. Mounting up, taking the reins, he rode along the lakeshore, passed the waterfall, paused to look back. His foundation was a small line on that point above the water. As soon as the walls rose, the reflection of the building would set squarely in the mirror below.

He ranged up the valley, through the meadows. The woods closed in, the slopes thick and somber. The ridges slowly lowered, breaking into granite veins. The animal trails were too intermittent to hint at any real intelligence. An Indian might follow a trail through this valley, or he might weave a new path each time, catching fresh scents. A trapper might have followed up along the water's flow, or he might have crossed the ridges from drainage to drainage, dipping into the valley only long enough to set the trap, to return and take the pelt. Walker saw ashes in piles of charred stones. He saw peeled sticks scattered in a muddy rut, white bones scattered without the skull for identification—the sticks and

bones might have led him to beaver or cougar, might have
led him to something else entire.

At noon Walker stopped to let the mule graze. In an elbow
where the creek flattened, where the water was so slow and
clear that the bed seemed covered by nothing more than cold
air, a long trout held itself from the sun in the shadow of the
cutbank. There had been moose through here recently. There
had been birds tracking the clay and sand. In winter the snow
might weigh so heavily that the tracks would smooth from
the ground, leaving no trace for the new year.

Walker mounted up and continued. He couldn't pull
enough air into his lungs. The trees around him slowly
thinned and grew tougher, and little by little, with the altitude,
they shrank to spiked blankets of evergreen. The mule's
hooves clipped at the rocky ground, the air raked faintly
through the boughs, an eagle screamed somewhere beyond,
rodents fought in the scrub, in the trees, the chattering black-
rosy birds flew on ahead. He followed past the last of the real
trees, moved on among the boulders huge and broken on the
thickset green flowered mats. Shadows of white clouds rippled through a vast, carved, cliffed upheaval of granite.
Threads of white water drew down from the high cups of
snow. And in all that he noticed something that seemed
constructed—an odd squareness in the overwhelming jagged.
He thought again of the Circassian girl and the straight line
of her shoulders in the swirled shallows of the Wind River.
He approached across the ground spongy with strange ferns
and flowers and hard grass. He stopped and dismounted.

It was a structure of piled rocks, so like the piles of rocks
to each side that it might have been overlooked but for its
roof of long pine beams. He ducked in through the entrance
and squatted there on the littered floor, in the dimness, waiting for the room to come clear. Sunlight pierced the gaps on
all sides and speckled his arms. The breeze played the building—a sad, broken instrument, its unsteady whistles and
groans liable to fall silent without attention. And here he
found a stack of broken ram skulls, the thick curls, and shards
of bone, a pile of black hooves, shreds of tawny fur, the nub-

bed beginnings of young horns. Quickly he was outside again.

He turned away from that dwelling, knowing that someone could live in this place, knowing that someone might still live in this place. He picketed the mule and left him, walked on, listening. He almost couldn't look at the cliffs, the spikes of mountain peak—the afternoon was so bright that even the clouds with their crazy trailing darkness couldn't dampen the caroming sunlight, as if this dead-end valley, this stone vessel, were held up directly to the sun's boldest angle. Here was a lake, dark blue against the hazing of cliffs, and he passed along its safest shore, up the ridge behind, and here was another lake, paler, the shore bare of scrub, and he made his way along the water, over scree, up another ridge, to a lake paler still, smaller as the cliffs came in, the water more white than blue, the far end taking into its whiteness a thick slab of snow and ice, and he came around, crossed the snow, looked up at the head of the valley above him, all around him. The sun had nearly tipped away now, he had left his provisions behind, but there was water channeling through the shatters of those cliffs, water flowing from above, so he continued. Up the wall, his boots prying stones loose from beneath him, he followed the water. Nothing but lichen, and moss in shadows, spider webs, and those black-rosy birds darting away. And then he was over the edge, his palms bloody, and he stopped there, dazed by the sun's last brightness square in the center of a lake so white it might have been milk, the light intensified by the funnel of cliffs that still rose through sheets of snow. He listened. He thought he heard a voice. Or water. The sun fell away, its bright rays angling suddenly from the ridge, capping this flute of high evening. Then he saw what he had heard.

She moved at the far side of the water. A brisk hobble across the stones, and she crouched, her dark body naked against the snow and ice. There was nothing else in that granite-shattered space. She must have seen him, but she turned away, reached among the stones, busy at something, and he heard strings of sound lifting and sliding—sounds that might have been sad, clearly music, sounds that might form words, but he couldn't draw enough to make a picture or even a fragment. All he saw was that glacial lake, the stone, the ice, the girl. She kept on. A brittle insect skimmed the water's surface.

He looked back over the ledge. The lakes grew larger, deeper blue, and the forest came in, and this range ended and another began, peaks into peaks until it all turned down into the horizon. No sign of anything out there, no smoke, no pale cut of a road. He felt his empty stomach beneath his ribs, felt for his pulse in his neck. He felt his brain press behind his eyes, his temples throb. And he heard her voice continue, whoever she was, her voice woven into that place, that flow of water. So he turned toward her, started around the shore of that tiny white lake. She was steady at her work.

He stood behind her—her sharp shoulders, black hair long and nearly gray with dust, her skin dark and streaked. Her fingers sifted through a midden that filled the spaces among the stones.

Fish bones, rainbow scales. Crushed sticks, peeled twigs, flecks of charred bark. Black and blood-red stones, their edges worked to cut, points and blades and scrapers. Bowls shaped from soapstone. Bruised roots and leaves. A bow of the strangest translucent material. A tunic of fine quill work—Walker had seen the design before, lashed in the funeral tree. And before her, balanced at even intervals on the rocks, a dozen clean and yellow skulls of bighorn sheep, teeth still strong in the jaw, great weighty curls of the horns still lustrous and fresh—the sockets, with their fine bone edges, watched her.

He touched the bony seam of her shoulder blade. She leaned forward, rolled over, looked up at him from her nestle there. She was silent now, her face oval and burned by the sun. Indian. Black eyes. Perhaps thirteen. Perhaps sixteen. Breasts no more than a vague softness below her knobby sternum. And her sex, black hair, and the underside curved down into the gravel. He waited for her to make that noise again so he could watch the shape of her lips, the set of her tongue, but she only grimaced, squinting. Her hands were empty. Her lips parched. The skulls behind her. Walker in front.

He tried to see her at the center of a room, his room. Tried to see how men would see her. Her voice alone in its soft idiot wandering, or her voice pressed into the lyrics of a ballad. *The Factory Girl. The Maid of Green Hollow. My Love In Lace.* The men would know her, or know of her, this mountain girl, supine, this girl from the snow, from the sky.

He pulled off his shirt and boots and trousers. Her eyes scanned his body. Her grimace slackened. He reached and took her hand. She stood up, teetered a moment on the sharp rocks, and their shoulders touched, their knees touched. Releasing her, he backed into the water—he might have been stepping into deepest winter. The rocks cut his feet. She watched him. He fell back, floated, and the cold pulled his limbs to center, hunched him around his heart and gut, but he kept himself afloat.

She followed him, dove, wallowed beside him. On the water, a slick expanded from her shape. Quickly they splashed to the center and returned to the shore. Out on the rocks, they jumped together, slapped at their arms and legs, and he saw that she was smooth and fine.

Hurrying as the sky began to gray, he put his shirt on her, and he pulled on his trousers and boots. He took her hand, led her to her mass of litter, pointed at one thing and another. "Do you want to take this?" he said. "This?" She gathered a stone blade and the bow. She lifted a skull and he took it from her, surprised by its unbalanced weight, and shook his head, "No," and threw it into the lake. It bubbled, sank, and rested in the white shallows. She offered him the tunic—he held his arms behind, wrists close together, and she slid the tunic up those white arms, fit it to his shoulders, the tunic banded with quills, his chest banded with ribs.

Through the fall, the girl would leave him at his work on the foundation, his work at the first logs, and wander away around the lake, and he would look up and see her moving there in the distance, a dark spot in the green heat slowly fading. Snow fell and evaporated. She returned each time loaded with goods, and she described with her hands her journey up over the passes, along the waters, to the caches left behind. Finely tanned skins, blankets woven from strips of rabbit with the white tails in crazy tufts of pattern, bowls hollowed from stone, baskets of woven sage bark, arrows straight and sharp to arm the bow. She showed him how the bow had been fashioned from the heart of a ram's horn, how great the strength of that bow was, how it could propel an arrow deep into a tree or clean through the chest of an antelope, deer, elk. With the trails of her fingers in the air, with the movement of her eyes, she told of her people in blinds or traps, waiting for the bighorn. She named her people— Tukudeka—Sheepeater—and showed how they had died, a spotted sickness, the bodies fading into the granite dust, and the more hearty had fled, and she had waited, thinking they would return, but no one had traveled these canyons and defiles until Walker climbed to find her in the sky. She described a story for him.

On an island in the center of a great pale body of water, a young woman lived with her mother. No tribes. No men to bring life to tribes. The mother found her daughter at the edge of the water, and they stood together there, watching their shadows ripple with the soft advance and retreat of the waves. The mother took her daughter back to the fire, fed her a meal of berries, fresh meat, herbs, until the girl was full and awake and eager to move, and then the mother took her daughter from beside the fire, and as dawn lit the shore she pushed the girl out across the world to find a husband. She went round the shore and found no one. She went up across the hills and found no one. Finally in a burrow in a shadow of scrub she found Coyote. He was sleek along the ground, following her footsteps. He was brave with her scent, running on ahead. He was wonderfully howling when she brought him home and took him as her husband. In the cool of late night, with the starlight in the cone of the old wickiup, he lay with her, tried to take her, but he found that she was sharp between her legs. She laughed and held herself in the grip of her small hands. He left her, brought from the riverbed a soft round stone, and dulled her sharpness. Soon she gave birth to a thousand babies, each the size of a grain of sand. She took the babies up and placed them in a stone bowl, and when the bowl brimmed she gave it to Coyote and told him to scatter the children to each direction of the wind. He did as he was told. Finally, when nearly all were gone, he held the bowl high and poured the last of the babies into the sky. They lit upon the clouds, rose against the wall of the mountains, and rained onto the peaks.

The Sheepeater girl knew how to stalk prey, knew her way in and out of each valley carved into the Wind Rivers. She led Walker across the ridges, showed him the scratchings on the rocks—animals, males, speckled monsters with limbs like tendrils. She showed him the chipping grounds where points had been struck from black stone. She led him so close to deer and elk and bighorn that he couldn't miss bringing them down with one wobbly rifle shot. She roasted or dried the meat. She tanned the hides, softening them with a smear of brains from the broken skull. She dressed herself and this white man in ever thicker layers as the air cooled. She brought him moccasins of tough badger for his soft feet, leggings of coyote.

She secured his shelter in the woods, tightened the roof with fresh branches, and built beside it a wickiup of aspen poles thatched with spruce, connected it to his shelter with a crouched tunnel of woven wood. She gave order to the new and old provisions, buried stores in holes stone-lined against marauders. She gathered roots, herbs, berries, fish, stacks of firewood tall as a man and banked around the shelter, leaves for bedding, bits of lichen and dry moss and needles for kindling a spark. She cut grass for the mule, cured it, piled it high beside the corral.

With the first deep snow, she stood Walker before the shelter, stripped him in the cold, brought out a shirt of elk lined with rabbit and pulled its softness around him. Trousers of antelope, also lined. Earmuffs of coyote sewn to his cap. And she brought out snowshoes framed of that beautiful smooth translucence of sheep horn.

As the snow fell in layers so thick that the leavings of a single storm would have been worth an entire normal winter, she led him occasionally down from their valley toward the Wind River. On the foothills, or near the river, or across the river and on into the valley that angled toward the northern range, they found their prey weakened by hardship, killed it, dressed it where it fell, and trekked toward home. Once, on one of these excursions, the clouds lowered and caught them in white, and they paused for a day, wove themselves beneath the lower branches of an old spruce, chewed on strips of frozen meat in the silence of the blasting wind, and finally they dug themselves free and continued, the girl in the lead and moving on as if she had never stopped.

When the storms allowed, they worked the wooded slopes. It was a painstaking process, cutting down tree after tree, stripping them of branches, sharpening the ax again and again, attaching ropes to the logs, skidding them through the snow behind the mule, down the slope, to the building site.

Slowly, Walker and the Indian girl accumulated a stack of straight spruce and lodgepole pine. The snow kept falling, the stack kept drifting over, the foundation was buried, the sky was a constant bitter gray, and the two worked until Walker had counted out enough logs to raise the walls and beam the roof.

But, other than these hours out in the snow, the winter was a long, shut-in darkness. A dish of coals barely glowed at the center of the shelter. They sat together at the back, against the ground, and watched the smoke hole in the ceiling shift from gray to black and then finally brighten again, rarely enough light to see, and they explored surfaces with their scarred fingertips. They crawled through the tunnel to the wickiup, where they could stand a while and stretch their legs, and then they crawled back to the fire. The shelter would drift over, the trapped smoke would burn their lungs, and then they'd climb out and sweep the snow away with a pine bough. On one of those long nights, he named the girl Mary, the name of a woman he had known in the East, a woman who had taught him to read and fed him scrapple and eggs with double yolks.

Together there in that smoky hole, Walker and Mary heard the wind pushing eddies through the clouds. They heard the distance of the lake, its vast unprotected stretch of black ice beyond the trees. And they heard the trees themselves, weighed and lurching as if to fall. The accumulation of the steady flakes, the race of those flakes across icy crust, into newly stirred clouds of soft fall, into banks, settling, compressing the layers of snow far beneath. The rush of air across the smoke hole in the ceiling, the air playing the shelter, drawing out the faintest deep note, like the welling of a dirge. The hiss of flakes caught in the smoke of the updraft, the crystal gone to mist. The smoke itself gathering in corners, drifting toward escape. The heat of the coals as they worked their way through fresh fuel. The snap of branches in Mary's hands, the shuffle of the wood into a pile, the fingers judging each length, taking hold of a straight stick, laying it gently across the coals. The settling slosh of snow in the tin can at the edge of the coals. The rustle of one strip of meat peeled from another. The slow grind of teeth, gathering of saliva, and a dry swallow.

Reaching into the darkness, together there, Walker and Mary felt the smooth dirt floor. They felt the poles and tight chinking of the walls, the hides hung to blanket the cold. And they felt the stacks and piles of their goods all around them, cold smooth bowls and the scratch of baskets. The blankets and hides slowly stiffening with the grime of skin and smoke. The hides stitched and those yet unstitched. The ribs of Mary's fine quilled tunic. The buttons of Walker's old shirts and trousers. The softness of the fur in against his chest. Tendons in wrists. The thick mats of their hair. The build-up of soot in the channels of their ears, in their raw nostrils. The torn skin of their lips. The curve of Mary's jaw to its hinge with her delicate skull. The construction of her bones and his, their limbs nearly the same length, their muscle as taut, their joints warm with strain and cramped rest.

Mary spoke on and on, and Walker came to know some of the phrases, the ones she repeated—the sound of something old, like the guttural of granite split by cold, the sound of something open, like the wind over a bank of tundra, the sound of something sharp, like the crack of curl-horned brows and the echo equally sharp, as if it might bring down a million years of gray rock wall. She sang, and still he made no sense of it beyond sad. He sang, and she caught his words, glued the end of one word to the beginning of the next, and slowly the words separated and the phrases came clear and she sang songs of places and people she had never seen or imagined. Her voice was soft. He tried to make his own voice as soft so that his words would fit more gently on her tongue.

Walker thought sometimes that Mary was as frail and strong as the Circassian girl. That Mary's fingers were capable of the most intricate work. That Mary, ahead in the snow, her snowshoes leaving great dragged holes in the clean surface, was leading him somewhere, but they always seemed to be heading directly into the center of a fast-moving cloud.

That the snow would not stop falling, and the trees would splinter under the weight, and with the forest flattened, all hint of spruce and pine would disappear beneath the white, and the valley would fill, and he would not be able to swim up to the air. That if spring came, the heat of the high country sun would wash a great flood through the valley, busting the lake free, scouring the soil clear down to stone, the valley a bare V as polished as a silver mirror with veins of light and dark deep beneath the surface, an endless reflection of wall and sky continuing far into each side, perhaps on through the range and into another world.

Walker dreamed that Mary wandered that scoured range, and he followed, no tree left to shelter them or give soft sound to the wind, with the sun a hot point through the cloudless days, with the moon a cold echo through the starry nights. Mary traced the spine of the range, the top of the world, pausing to scan the horizon, but the gray horizon had bled into the underside of the pale hazy sky until the whole distance circled back on itself, granite below and blue above, and only Mary was there, turning to take his hand. He knew her hand. It had taken hold of him before. It had stripped him, settled him. But it was the Circassian girl who turned toward him. He had not seen her for more days than he could count. She did not take his hand. She turned away again, wandered, and he followed. She led him to where she had waited for him. It was a crevice of shadow in a rock wall. Deep inside, she slept within the white cage of the gold horse's ribs.

At night, as the sky opened to stars and the day's meager degrees rose into the black, the lake ice expanded slowly, the pressure edged itself this way and that in the confines of shore and stone, and then great fissures raced across the surface, and the lake boomed. Walker opened his eyes. In the glow of coals he saw Mary's hand spread above the heat, the smoke sieving through her fingers as if the hand constantly lowered but never reached the fire beneath. He spoke to her—"Mary, Tukudeka, come here, you're frightened." He knew she wasn't frightened, knew that she had lived in and through these mountains as he never could, but still he raised his blankets and brought her in with him and spoke against her ear—"Mary, hush, the sounds you hear are just the world settling." She rolled into him, her knee forcing his knees apart, and then they were woven together. He found his fingers in her mouth, his mouth on the flesh that just barely pillowed the bones beneath.

On a day when the wind was not so strong, she led him up the valley. She broke the trail, and following was easy. She led him beyond the lake to a reach of open snow where the earth at the center appeared to smoke. He thought of fire, of the woods in flame, but fire would be smothered, and as they approached he smelled not ash but sulphur. A large rock hole gaped. He followed her, passed her, and stepped to the edge. Far below, on the surface of a pool, the sky hovered, clouded, uneasy in the drift of steam. He couldn't lean far enough out to see himself against that lower sky, and as he held to his balance, as the steam wet his skin and tightened his lungs with the distilled taste of earth, he thought he felt for a moment the rush of his body down through that rising steam, into water that bubbled away his clothing, through passages soft and dark and lined with the smoothest accumulation, until he lodged in a fissure, moved not another inch, the stone contained him, the heat fizzed at his nostrils. Unhooking first his snowshoes and then her own, she led him down over the edge, balanced them on the sliver of beach, stripped away their clothes, and led him into the warm water. He floated, she held him, and she wouldn't let him drift to where the pool descended into darkness. He watched the sky above in the circle of rock, the rushing gray and spitting snow. She held a palm of water above his forehead, turned her hand, let the water pour across his eyes, into his mouth. He tasted the earth, the depth and layers that propped the mountains.

Finally the snow slackened. He stood on the promontory above the lake and watched the winter begin to melt. His footsteps pooled with water. His foundation freed itself, and the pile of logs grew more massive, the snow melted clear down to the flattened grass. He worked at measuring, notching, and listened to water drawing down from everywhere, gathering, overflowing, pulling away the flaked surface of the valley, listened to the echo of his own work, the wood splitting and chipping away, his work multiplied and ricocheted and blended with the flowing water. And then Mary came along the edge of the lake—he saw her far up toward the waterfall. She came along the south-facing slopes, where the snow remained in streaked patches and the grass was already greening, and she walked sometimes in the water, the slosh of her steps lost in the rest of the afternoon, and sometimes up along the shore, leaving smeared etchings of her feet in the mud, on the sand, leaving white lines in the dirty snow she crossed. He kept at his work, watched the saw eat the yellow wood, watched the dust coat his moccasins, looked up and she had rounded half the lake, looked up again and she had come almost below the promontory, had to step out where a boulder blocked her path, and her dark skin submerged in the dark water, she bent and trailed her fingers through that dark cold, raised her hands and held the cold to her face, stepped again and turned suddenly toward him and dropped herself straight back into the water, her eyes on him far above. She floated. He turned the log, scraped at the bark, heard the slosh of the water. She stood, the sunlight bright on the drops that drew down from the weight of her hair. She climbed from the water, scaled the promontory, and when she came up beside him he saw that she was already dry, that the crease behind her knee and the pooch of her belly and the line of her brow were all clear brown. He had never thought—she was young and unmarked and her hair was a black tangle— never thought when he first saw her that she would ever look like a woman to him. He turned and looked for her clothes as if they lay somewhere back toward the edge of the woods. Already she was loosening the ties of his shirt.

She talked to him as he worked, she talked a steady stream, testing her new language, and she held what needed to be

held, took her end of a log and hoisted, seemed not to notice
the wonderful fit Walker had engineered. She said, "You sail
a ship like a mountain with white hides in the wind. You
come here across flat ground and you are not leaving. You
tell me—heaven when I die." They completed the walls, four
square, with gaps for a door and window above the lake, gaps
for a door and window on the opposite wall, a gap for the
fireplace, and the roof beams held the blue sky. She said, "My
sad fate. Tie my bones." With round stones from the creekbed, he built a fireplace and chimney, and she mixed the
mortar from the parts of the earth he showed her. The stones
were round and black and white and gray, like a pile of ancient eggs. Deep into the opening he placed some kindling
and struck a spark. The smoke drew up. She said, "Sheep
trail near the edge of the fall so they can see the world below.
Antelope will wander close if they see something strange.
Moose will sleep in the willows if the day is hot." They raised
the roof by raising the earth. On a lattice of poles and crude
shingles they placed long strips of sod cut from the slopes,
and suddenly, on the roof, wildflowers bloomed. She swept
the dirt floor smooth with a bundle of sticks. He constructed
a long table, fashioned benches, stacked bunks up into the
beams, and she fashioned mattresses. She said, "A white man
brought the sickness. They all went off to die. Bones in the
roots. Bones in the water. Bones in the coyote den."

And he would answer her, phrase for phrase. He said,
"This is the way you construct a sill. This is the way you
attach a hinge. This is how you latch the shutters against the
night." They stood at the center of the lodge. A fire burned
on the hearth. The light moved around their feet, across the
walls. He took her hand and held it high, he circled her waist,
and she sang with his words as they danced. She was willing
to flow with his step-step-turn, and if his brow tightened and
he struggled with the movements and he lost the words, she
sang alone until he regained the pattern. He said, "Your hair
should be pulled this way. Let me tie it. Your face is best
when the light strikes it from the side. I have never seen such
a brow. I think you could think your way through granite."

He laid out whatever he had, but it wasn't much. He had no candles, no whiskey, no glass for the windows. He had the meat they had dried. He had the view of the lake. He said, "Men will want to see your face. These are the things we need: flour, dishes, money, glass, whiskey, oil, butter—" In the shelter in the woods, where they had added to their walls with logs, a sod roof, and the wickiup had been broken down and burned, they gathered the hides, bundled them, stacked them, gathered the snowshoes, the baskets, pair after pair of moccasins drawn from caches throughout the valleys. He said, "These are for trade."

He left Mary. She would listen until she heard nothing of him, and then she would wait in the lodge through the days, sleep in the shelter through the nights, hear the valley and its plain echoes. He had explained—he would be gone a few days, maybe a week.

He led the mule down from the lake, into the woods. The trees closed in. The animal trail descended along the creek. The mule balked at the rougher of the fallen logs and had to be coaxed or led another way. For any real traffic, the trail would have to be cleared, but for now it was passable, opening through the occasional meadow.

Walker saw the distance clearly—green ridges and far slabs of badland and northern peaks. He watched that distance a long while. Listened. The mule exhaled. The birds screamed. The breeze advanced and departed. No sign or sound of human movement. He could not be sure that anything remained of the world. Perhaps the snow had frozen out the last living soul. Perhaps he would walk for days, weeks, years, sail to the horizon, and never find a trace, history taking some untold turn without him. And there would be Mary, alone in the valley. If he could find his way back.

He continued. Soon he came to where he could see the Wind River below, its dark rush, and there was the river trail

freed from winter, dusty for stretches and then wet and pud-
dled in the depressions. Down the rounded grassy slopes he
led the mule, and then they were through the spruces and
onto the trail. Beneath his feet, he found tracks—human,
horse, wheel. Surprised at his luck—to think that people
passed so close without a lure—he looked up the valley,
looked downriver, tried to listen beyond the flow. Nothing.
But he smelled smoke on the air, judged the direction of the
travel, and turned upriver, tugging hard at the lead rope.

Not a mile and he saw the camp beside the river, a wagon
with spars askew and stripped of canvas, a single horse picketed in deep grass. He stopped and watched. There were
three men that he could see, out in the water, chasing something they had corralled in the shallows, probably a trout.
They shouted and stumbled and seemed to see no humor in
their flailing. Walker whispered—"Greetings, welcome, gentlemen"—to test his words, but he couldn't be sure of the
sense of his language—maybe it had lost its syllables, de-
volved to strings of gibberish. He came forward slowly, the
mule in step at his side, and, as one of the men stood up
from the water with a long fish in his hands, the three of them
all at once turned toward Walker and stopped. Walker also
stopped. He heard their voices. "Jesus." "Get there."
"Damn, hell, here we are." The men jumped onto the bank,
headed for the wagon in the trees, dodged around in the
shadows. They were gone. Walker smiled, felt the fuzz on his
chin, saw the sinew of his arms, smelled for the first time the
animal must of his deerskin clothes. He continued, seeing
himself dark with sun and filth and knowing that the rifle
angled clearly up from the top bundles, but there was nothing
to do about that, no foolish moves, nothing to worry. And
then the men were coming out around the trees with arms
almost casual at their sides—two pistols, a rifle—and they
waited, and he heard a voice again, though he didn't see who
spoke. "Nothing. No moves till." Walker kept on, and he saw
that the man with the rifle was older, maybe fifty, and that
the others were young, not yet twenty, and clearly the man's
sons, the weight of the pistols uneasy in their fingers. All three

had the same small ears flat back against the narrow skull, pale eyes beneath the knobby shelf of the brow. Walker wanted to take their hands, pull them around in a circle, watch their lips as they spoke, but he walked on almost as if he hadn't seen them, stepped into their camp, dropped the lead rope, left the mule to graze, and came to an unwavering stop, hands at his sides. "I'm Walker Avary. Welcome."

"To what?" The man let the rifle swing forward a bit till it pointed at Walker's feet.

"To the valley."

"Shit damn, a welcome," the older boy said, and he tipped his pistol to the sky beyond Walker. The younger boy watched his brother, watched his father.

Walker said, "Are you stopping here?"

"We have stopped. Yes, sir. And you'll be going on?"

"I'm no one to worry about."

"We'll judge that." The man nodded to the older boy, and he took the rifle from Walker's goods and tossed it into the back of the wagon.

They all had the look of men who'd gone through long miles without a good dream. Walker sat on a stone beside the fire pit. He saw the fresh fish in the dirt, beyond the smoldering cinders. The fish was still moving, chewing the air. "Don't let me keep you, if you was going to eat. I got some elk steaks if that would do."

"That would."

Quickly, in silence, the boys got the fire built up, and they all watched Walker as he tended to the mule, all relaxed a bit when he returned with the meat. Soon the dark red was dripping fat into the flames, and the trout was browning in a skillet. Walker sat back against a tree and watched the meal, refusing whatever they offered—coffee, the meat, slices of hard bread. Each broke a chunk of the orange flesh of the fish straight from the skillet, chewed, and spit the bones into the fire. Each sliced with a knife a strip of elk, seemed to swallow it nearly whole. The bread crumbled, leaving white dust on their hands. Then they all sat on the ground beside the wagon and watched Walker.

He watched them back. Saw the metal of their belt buckles. The shift of their shirts as they breathed. The cool energy
of men resting, on edge.

Across the river, the northern peaks flowed in and out of
cloud, and slowly they were obscured in white, and the white
darkened, and the sky went stormy. It started to rain. "Here,"
the man said, and he stood, and Walker and the young men
followed him off beyond the wagon, to a tarp strung between
trees, among wild rose. They sat there on the ground, with
the rain tapping the tarp and rustling the undergrowth. The
fresh scent of rain slowly cleansed the woodsmoke from the
afternoon. And then the clouds opened and the air went gray
with the rush of water. "That mule could use a bath," Walker
said, and the three glared at him and nodded. He ran to unpack the mule, threw his bundles under the wagon, and returned to the tarp. He pulled his wet shirt out from his skin,
settled back and looked up through the translucent tarp and
the shadow of water channeling away just above his reach.
He wanted to hear their voices, all three at once. "So, tell
me," he said, "are you following this trail?"

"We think we are, yes."

"And all you got is that one horse?"

"That's all."

"Where does the trail come out, that way?"

"Union Pass. Over into Jackson's Hole."

One of the boys propped himself on his elbows. "We
heard there might be a road started over Togwotee Pass, but
I don't think there's a damn bit of luck about that, from the
looks of it."

"Where'd you hear that, about the road?"

"From some ranchmen downriver," the man said. "Some
troops or trappers or someone told them."

Walker raised his head and looked off downriver. Ranchmen. Army. "That's good," he said. "A road would be good.
But why are you going over Union Pass, when there's got to
be easier ways. I been through South Pass, and it ain't no
trouble at all."

"We don't want to go this way," the younger boy said,

"but we got funneled and now we ain't got the power to get anywhere. Damn this shit trail." He didn't speak with anger, but more in a whisper. "Curse this hell territory."

They had lived on a farm in the center of Illinois, the man said, he and his wife and two sons. No other relations—all dead in the war or dead from disease or never born in the first place. They didn't own the land, didn't see that they ever would, didn't want to waste whatever they'd saved on building a stronger house on someone else's spread. They watched the rivers rise with flood, watched the crops green and die. So the father sold everything but the wagon, decided that the road would cost them only time and save them the cost of the train, and they had a final meal of roast and corn before they gave their house over to the new tenants and headed out, two oxen pulling the wagon, a horse for someone to ride on ahead to the horizon and then loop on back. They came across the plain, and those they saw were usually traveling only a short distance or were too far off to see clearly, kicking dust into sunlight and wind.

Slowly the plain carved more steeply with hill and gully, and they left the bulk of settlement behind. They found that the winter snows had soaked deep into the crust, leaving long stretches of the wagon road in mire. But they were fresh, the air was cool, they came up out of Nebraska along the Platte, into Wyoming, and passed Ft. Laramie, the peaks in snow like clouds beyond the horizon. On north and west past Ft. Fetterman, with warnings of Oglalas and Brulés farther north, but they had planned to turn soon toward the south, through the Rattlesnake Hills, toward Independence Rock, so they continued, the fort's chimney smoke forgotten.

And then they were alone on the road. Into the Platte River flowed R. de la Prete, the Boisee River, Deer Creek, so their map indicated, and other unnamed and rushing muddy tributaries, each more difficult to ford than the last, with the wagon wheels submerged and the oxen wide-eyed and slashing for good footing. Along the course of the river were deep grass and cottonwood, but just beyond the lip of the floodplain the earth was sparse, clearly drying toward desert. What they first thought to be eagles soaring turned out to be turkey vultures tagged stiffly to thermals. What might have been fields of game were boulders scattered, as if tossed from the sky. The antelope were too far off for them to bother giving chase. The elk were high on the hills, beyond range. No buffalo. Only jackrabbits to be taken.

At night, the cold wind came down from the north, from the elevations to each side. Burning white, their sagebrush fire threw sparks and seemed to carry oil in its smoke. They had heard wolves before, the voices far in the flat black distance, but that night the wolves' voices seemed to move right through the camp with the wind, and they sat by the fire and barely breathed for fear they would inhale a yelp and find it tearing their lungs, deep inside. Green eyes down along the river, a dozen of those gray hounds at least, all half-starved from a terrible winter. The sky lowered, and although there had already been little light from the scattered stars, the night seemed to reach even into their fire and dull its flames, and then it was raining, great lines of sleet, and the fire doused completely, and the wind tore the canvas of their wagon, and the ground ran with a slurry of mud and rocks that seemed likely to break them all and force them into the river. They sparked their single lantern, a small flame. Lightning opened up the reach of road in each direction. No choice but to break camp and move fast from that flood.

And that was when they lost the road. The oxen bolted before they could be secured, and somewhere out with their heavy panic the wolves merged and took them down—they heard the brief, blind attack. So with great shouting all around and pistols shot into the storm, they brought the horse up, made the harness fit, though it pinched and stabbed the poor animal, and they all climbed into the wagon, and with sheets of lightning advancing from the west, mountain ranges rising and dying in quick greenish flickers, they moved on. But the wolves were still there. The horse, despite the wagon's weight, tore at the ground, flailed against the reins, and they were fast along the road, heard to their horror a bridge pass beneath them, a torrent of river, and as their goods tum-

bled behind they rushed on into the frozen rain, no road under them now and no hope of control until the horse broke
down or the earth gave way. And then they stopped.

The horse's breathing rasped like a scream, as if its breast
were split. The sleet bit them all. Mother had gashed her
head, and blood washed away as quickly as it welled. They
wrapped her in whatever was left. The eldest boy went forward with the lantern, waited until the horse stopped shaking,
then took the reins and led them on through the sage, around
the sudden ditches, hour after hour, toward something they
couldn't imagine.

They were far in the wrong direction, into a sage-choked
valley, and the early sun brightened a road at the center.
Looking back they saw where the Platte must flow, far against
the red buttes, saw their tracks dragged through the brush.
They weren't going back that way. They came down through
a ditch, onto the road. Their map placed them to the north
of the Rattlesnake Hills, coming to Poison Spring, and then
into the open, with the Big Horns to bring them along. And
once they were out on the plain, the huge oblong space of
white at the center of the etched filigree of ranges, they knew
they would stick to the road, to the north of that space, par-
alleling Bad Water Creek, beside the foothills that held the
promise of cool and forest above. At night they banked their
fire, turned in from the declivities and sharp buttes and endless waves of dead world, from the southern and western
snow-capped peaks that might never be reached.

The mother didn't hold up. She had bled too much, and
the chill of that sleet never left her. She was buried in soft
earth near the confluence of the Big Horn and Bad Water,
the grave piled with river rock to keep wolves and coyotes
from digging—the husband and sons wouldn't allow for the
image of bones carried into dens, dropped along trails, the
tiniest bones woven into a packrat's midden.

The man's voice went on, quick through the Shoshone
land, up the Wind River, the bare beginnings of a ranch,
cattle in the fields, ranchmen taking them in. Walker knew
the ranchmen, he was sure they were the same he'd passed

nearly a year ago, knew exactly the surface they'd traveled since that time, knew almost the smell of them, knew the winter they'd spent. And he was with them for a moment, in their winter shelters, not twenty or thirty miles from his valley, all those snowbound months, all the noise he had given up for silence. How well had they protected themselves from the snow, the men all coming in from their winter work? They had built shelves to hold whatever they'd carried with them—blankets, pots, maybe a book or Bible, guns, belts, heavy coats. They would sleep in the howl of wind, think the howl was an animal looking to take their cattle, think the howl was the dream of the man in the next bed, or the next, and someone added wood to the stove, and someone came in with a blast of the cold, and someone soaked his feet in a pan of heated snow-water. The man Walker knew, the man who'd shot the bear dog, he slept through an afternoon, the snow too deep and the cold too strong to venture out, slept and slowly awoke to voices, rolled onto his back and watched the ceiling and the vague haze of escaped smoke, reached beneath the blankets and tested the muscle that still linked his ribs and strapped his gut, felt the hinges of his hip joints, the idle scratch, the casual tracing of the surface of his skin, across the ridges of clavicle, hollow at the base of the throat, the faint fur in the plain of the solar plexus centering the rise of muscle to each side, the river of barest tension down the belly, the lightness of his touch pulling blind sparks from the backs of his thighs, the bones of his wrists, the slack muddle of his crotch, until one voice among the ongoing voices of deep winter finally broke through with the distinction of meaning, and he was drawn from his body, his body now an unsettled warmth without focus, lightning on a shrouded plain, and he listened to each voice stray and range the outer world—

In a square room with the white ceiling twelve feet above, a woman sits at a table, her fingers woven loosely. Her dress is so dark blue it might be black if the day fades another minute toward evening. Her collar is high against her neck and linked with a double clasp of four silver roses. Within her collar, an edge of frail white lace circles. Outside the collar, settled high about her shoulders, are strings of red beads, twisted and dense. Her jaw is a solid shapely curve, her lips tight and full, her nose faintly blushed, her eyes a spectacular deep brown beneath her brow, her hair a dangerous black, serious and curled.

On a beach, on the shore, two boys dry their skin on white squares of cotton, the sea a foaming green in the pools and upsweeps of tide, the sea violet where it clings to the horizon, the twin bellowed sails of a ship thinly tracing that distant line. One of the boys balances on his toes above the blunt and worn stones of mottled red, green like jade, stones as translucent as sugar candy, maple sugar, pitch. The late sun is nearly pink. His friend sits on the rocks drying the back of a leg. They follow the ship's slow progress as it hunts for something, or it carries cargo, or it transports people—they can't tell in the setting sun. They buff the salt from their hair, from their arms, each boy's hands and face and neck browned by the summer, the rest of their cooling bodies as white as cloud, as colored as those high clouds with the reflections of evening. They turn. They cover themselves with trousers, boots, white shirt, black sweater. With the sea-salt dampness of their towels slung around their necks they make for the path, up through the rocks, the sumac with its dry-blood spikes of flower. The surging basso waves follow them across the field toward the pines, the scent of woodsmoke, the first square lines of rooftop and barn, the first human voices calling, each to each.

On a prow of desert rock a man sits with a sketchpad on his crossed legs, a pencil in his fist, creating the lengthening shadows. It is as if the rock moves out onto the plain, and he rides above the details he creates. The starkness of open ground. The trails white in the tan soil. Far out, the hills ring the plain. A canyon cuts deep below sunset, as if that giant rock crevice has already filled with night. There are strings of oily trees where water flows. The last heat of the day comes up across him, bellows his pad, tears the corner—he smoothes it with his palm. He must find his way back down in starlight. Long before he sees the fire he hears the voices, the clink of gear, the mules in a ruckus.

From a small boat on the sand walks a young man in white trousers rolled to his knees, blue jacket buttoned high, gray cap, and he balances on his shoulder the poles and canvas. He steps along. Behind him, at the edge of the water, the boat sits, a tangle of net and kelp in the stern, oars angled up and out, silver fish piled on the sand. On the edge of the boat a young woman sits upright, arms to the side to hold herself square, and beside her a young man drapes himself along that same edge, propped up on an elbow, his head inclined toward her knees. The young woman wears a dark full skirt flecked with white petals, an apron equally full, pale green blouse puffed around her chest and arms, a rose scarf loose at her neck, her thick hair pulled back from her sad face. The young man wears long black trousers, a brown shirt with sleeves rolled to his elbows, a speckled neckerchief, his dark hair cropped short, lips in an open pucker as if he waits to speak something yet unimagined. Beyond them, in the last light, a dinghy oars toward the ships at anchor, men working to lower the canvas. A lantern illuminates a round window and streaks the surface of the water with a yellow line. A ship, under full sail, inches beyond the point.

Darkness and the same stars again. A man draws the shutters, douses the lantern. His wife has ensconced herself in a curl of the blankets, and he follows the folds until he finds her ankle, her thigh.

The ranchmen spoke of all this, and of a woman in black who gathers a sprig of autumn leaves and places that burst of orange in a mason jar, of brick walls and echoes, of seventeen miles of lush bottom land, of black walnut trees, of the afternoon sun on a lemon tree slender and gray and weighted nearly to the ground, of the aftertaste of whiskey in coffee, of a woman's full waist. Walker thought of the voices and the accents and how the pauses caught them all off guard, and someone would inhale deeply and slowly exhale a laugh.

Continue. I insist.

Why'd you laugh? There's nothing funny here.

I'm nervous. I want to know what you remember. Please.

The rain continued to funnel away beyond Walker's reach. The river carried the rain. The woods caught the lower clouds. Perhaps it was snowing on the peaks. And the man and his sons and Walker, in their tight-packed angles, were close and protected beneath the tarp.

The man and his sons had slept nights on the plain with the Big Horns in the stars. Then the loss of the mother. They might have stopped where Walker and the Circassian girl had lingered. They might have used the same fire circle, listened to the same blend of river sound and wind through that same conglomeration of cottonwood and willow. How would those memories light their minds? The man's voice could have gone back to the Illinois plain, could have set that distance again and again, and still Walker wouldn't know. He rolled a bit toward the others, watched the man's face contort around the words, the boys' eyes closed. He closed his own eyes, tried to see what they saw. He saw a dim black blur with the after-shapes of the boys drifting through. He looked again. The man had fallen silent, his eyes open toward the rain.

"I have a lodge for travelers," Walker said. "Up that creek a mile back."

"We don't need a lodge," the man said.

"We just need to sleep," the older boy said.

"We're fine here," the younger boy said. "We have the river."

"I'll have food," Walker said.

"We have enough food," the man said. "We can hunt. There's plenty of game. We have the time."

"I have a girl to dance. A girl from the mountains. From the snow. She's something you haven't seen."

Walker Avary opened his case, ran his hands over the starched whiteness of his shirt, the cloth so stiff it might not have been cloth at all, might have been pure paper. Unfolding the shirt, he drew it on, buttoned it straight up to the neck, tied the black string tie, fastened the cuffs with gold links, tucked the tail into his silky trousers. From the bottom of the case he cradled out a black wool evening jacket, shook it, slapped it, knocked loose the creases, and pulled it on. Mary had washed him, oiled his hair, scented him with elephant's head and fireweed.

The guests had already arrived—he'd seen them come up along the creek, spoken a few words—Owen from his ranch, with five of his ranchhands, Ab and J.K. among them, and the brothers from Illinois, their father left to sit their camp. Walker came out from his shelter, onto the trail, up through the woods. There were steers among the trees, lent to him for summer grazing, to help him secure the homestead. Owen's ranch was already a growing set-up of crooked buildings in the fields along a creek north of the Wind River. Walker had spent a night with the Illinois family, then spent a day trailing down toward the ranch, and the men had come out from the doorways at dusk to watch him approach. "We thought you were dead." "We looked around for you when we arrived." "Thought you had got lost. Or killed." "Thought the hostiles got you—they just about didn't let us pass, not without the army's persuasion." They helped Walker unpack the mule, and they found the moccasins a wonderful novelty, the hides and rabbit blankets a necessary luxury after a winter that had taken half the herd and three of the men. Walker had come away with more than Owen could spare—candles, a lantern, a large cook pot, keg of whiskey, plates, cups, and, most unexpected, glass for his two small windows. No way to tell who the trade favored, but there would be years for it all to reach balance.

And now there was woodsmoke on the air, brightness beyond the trees. He stopped and listened. Music. The man with the fiddle had started. Walker looked straight up through the branches to the sky, expected to see the notes drift like ash, but all he saw was the sun's final strength, the rays laid horizontal across the range, and a great weight of cloudless blue.

Out from the trees, he moved into his valley, approached his lodge. From the open door the flow of music took the valley, up across the cliffs struck hot with sunset, out across the lake deep with reflection, and the music dove right down through the lake's surface and into that nether evening, an evening of still air, cold sky, forest rising, white falls drawing the memory of winter from granite. Everything seemed to wait for stars. The lodge was a solid box on the promontory. Smoke gathered in a thin layer above the chimney. Now Walker could see the window, the shutters pinned back, and the window on the far side was a gray backlight. The men moved in there, lit between the panes.

Walker stepped up, paused on the jamb between grass and the dirt floor. In the fireplace a stack of fuel drew into heat, and the cook pot bubbled with elk, deer, roots, herbs. On the table a stone bowl brimmed with dried berries, dense and sweet. The whiskey had been tapped. On the corner of a bunk a man perched with a fiddle clenched to his jaw. Up toward the beams a wheel of light was suspended, a circle of steady flames. A voice said, "It's our Mr. Avary, dressed to break a heart," and Walker felt his face heat, stepped from the jamb, into the room, stopped at the fire, his back to them all. He held his hands toward the flames, watched the light paint a bright edge around his slender, short fingers. They came up behind him in a mass, he felt them there, and they all talked to him.

"This lake here. Who would've thought?"

"I'm glad for a reason to drink whiskey."

"This lodge is good work. We could've used your help on our buildings."

Someone touched him on the elbow, and he turned. They all faced him, leaned in at him, smiling. He said, "I'm very pleased you all could make it this evening." They looked at him for a few seconds, and then they all laughed and jostled each other.

"We're pleased you're pleased, Mr. Avary, esteemed proprietor," J.K. said.

"This valley is a treat," Owen said. "You've got great sense or luck to have found it. No doubt but you'll build it into something worthy of a visit, once the people head this way. Get some cabins started. Some horses. No doubt. Beyond compare."

"People can't come soon enough," another said. "I ain't never seen such empty land as this territory."

"Don't let on about the winters, or no one will come."

"Can't all winters be that bad."

"Something was trying to tell us to keep moving."

"Or telling us to stay put. Freezing us in place."

"Tell me, Avary, how'd you get through the winter, what with both you and that girl you say you got. You had two mouths to feed."

"Alone in all that suffocation."

"A feat."

"We were just about dead and buried on our ranch."

Walker came forward, and they parted around him, closed in behind him. He took a handful of berries and ate one, chewing slowly. "You stay in a place long enough," he said, "and you figure out what to do."

"We could have used some better figuring, I guess."

The Illinois boys stood one to each side of him. "And where is this girl of yours?"

"Is that the Circassian girl?" Ab said. "I've got a dream going about her. I've been thinking of her ever since I saw her on that horse with you. I've been telling them."

Walker smiled and shook his head slowly, reached to touch the men softly on the arm. "It ain't even her, gentlemen. Don't you worry who she is. I want you all to enjoy. I want you to forget that damn deep winter. You know this song?"

A breakdown had sent the fiddler's bow flying on the strings, the broken horse hairs loose and flowing. Walker took a few bouncing steps, looking up at the faces, pushed the men into rhythm, and when they'd all started to move, turning around and in on themselves, he found his way through them, back to the fire, and watched. They danced alone or in pairs. They took their whiskey with them. He smiled when they looked his way. He nodded and flopped his hands about to indicate that they should all continue. And they did. Continue. The closeness of the room kept them tight and friendly and almost fighting for a space in which to kick up their boots, play funny and goosey with their arms, and the table in the center kept them all circulating, trying to gain advantage where the floor opened slightly toward Walker and the hearth. They stirred up the dirt, and maybe it fell into the stew, maybe it clouded their whiskey, but it didn't matter— the dirt was on their tongues, and they'd taste it for days, wouldn't forget it.

They were all tall, all gangly, half starved, poorly shaven, newly bathed, faces red with heat and sunburn, brows as pure white as snow from the daily, brimmed shade of their hats, as white as if those brows had never contained a dark thought. Under new or changing light he might read that whiteness, he might begin to see the topography of pores and worry. If he stood behind them, if he watched with them, if the girl stepped in and sang her song, a sad gibberish or an approximation of a familiar tune, would he move closer, see the rise of hair on their necks, move around them, see their focus, smell a shift in the scent of them, know what they heard, remembered? Would they hover after she left, would they remain silent, would they turn to him for direction, for the next step, would they speak to him, their lives?

They took him in. He was spun by Owen, caught by Torrey, he stomped through a line with the young men, tangled his boots with theirs, and he felt the stiffness of his shirt crack away and the rhythm chafe through his socks. Someone peeled his jacket from his shoulders, and he let it fall, let it be tossed onto an upper bunk, where the empty black sleeves hung over the edge. His hands were small in their hands. They passed him beneath their linked arms. He looked up into the nostrils flared with the intake of air, up into their lidded eyes. They had bared their teeth. They howled and whistled and banged into the table, tipped a bench. They were ready for something.

And then the girl was at the door—Mary—the name he'd given her. The men stopped. She was dark, her black hair pulled back stiffly from her face. She was a hostile, Walker thought, smiling. An Indian. Sheepeater. She was dainty as a child, not tiny, held herself steady, as tall as Walker, actually. She stepped from the doorway, onto the floor, nothing furtive about her movements, nothing cunning, just focused on him, moving toward him. The music went on, a sudden lament— the fiddler sang of a string of young rangers crossing a plain, the lances of the enemy, the boys left unburied. Walker met her, took her by the elbow, hooked her into a quick pirouette, and as she came around she took the gaze of each man but she didn't return it—her eyes were on Walker—the dumb wonder of her eyes, the sad smallness of her features. Her hair was blacker than Walker's, her skin darker than his dark eyes, her hand a stain in his. Red flowers on the midnight hide of her skirt. The pale pliable amber of her shirt. And above that shirt, about her breast, around her shoulders, she wore her tunic—quilled, dyed, decorated, balanced.

Walker took a half step back, and Mary waited for him to catch the music and lead her on. He swayed, he held out his arms, she moved into his embrace. He closed around her. They moved together in the pitchy space of that lodge. She looked up at the ceiling, higher than any ceiling she could have known or imagined. She looked at the stone edifice of the fireplace, such a solid and permanent construction. The table. The metal pots. The windowpanes, with night beyond, and all their shapes captured and rippling. There was smoke in her hair, sulphur on her skin. Her quilled tunic pressed through Walker's shirt, the quills like lines of delicate new ribs.

They all danced again, all the ranchmen and the Illinois boys. Walker entered the flow with the Sheepeater girl in his grasp. The men turned more slowly as they came around to face her. They reached. They took her. Walker's hand slid from her waist. No resistance. She went along. She had been told—the men will want to dance.

The pattern began to weave. She was threaded and spun.

Perhaps summer had not yet begun. Through the open doors a cool breeze drifted, but the fire was still high, built up with fresh logs, and the crowd of bodies almost steamed the air.

They dragged the table to the side, they ate great sloppy plates of the stew, they shouted when a candle sputtered, demanding that it be replaced with a fresh, they drank full cups of lake water, clear as ice, and full cups of whiskey. The fiddler hunched at his music in front of the fire, sending frenzied, chopping shadows across the ceiling, and the notes came faster. Walker kept them dancing, nearly dancing himself, bumping his knee at a man's leg to restart a fallen rhythm. A roar, it seemed, was contained there, as if the darkness beyond the open doors was nothing, dead, vacant, would not absorb sound, only reflect it—door to door the voices multiplied, window to window the men divided and paired. The Illinois boys danced in a corner, clung to each other in a serious demonstration of forgotten choreography. Four of the ranchmen wrestled and sang. Walker added to the whiskey in each cup, tried to hold to each string of words. Owen had Mary close to his chest, and she might have slept there, her face shut down.

The Illinois boys sprawled deep in a lower bunk, and Walker perched on the edge, the ceiling of the upper bunk just above. "We started too early," they said. "We got mired. Ambushed. Pursued. We buried our mother. Look at us." They were tangled and flushed, trying to straighten themselves and speak. "We're too young."

"Too young for what?" Walker said, and he saw their hands cut and scabbed, their chins mottled with patchy stubble, their gaze roving back and forth, on each other, on Walker, on the others in the cloud of dust and heat.

"Too young to be buried in this territory. That's no trail we're following. It's half washed out. Hasn't been followed. Where will we get?"

Walker placed their faces against his memory of their father's, eliminated the father's influence, and was left with a certain fullness to the lower lips, a slenderness to their necks. "Where will you get what?" he said.

"Anything," they said. "We don't sleep. Our bones are pushing through our skin. Our hands bleed just from feeding ourselves. Our lungs are stuffed with that shit sagebrush. And this," they said, looking out into the room, "and this. So far from anything. You've got that girl, and she's hardly a girl at all."

She was trying the whiskey she'd been offered, wincing as if it burned her lips.

"Tell me what you remember," Walker said.

Walker touched a man on the shoulder. Touched another on the back. They scooted out of his way with a little bow, smiling, and then resumed their shuffle. Their feet left long gouges in the dirt, their trousers quivered over their calves, their hips made a square wooden shift from one side to the other, their heads lolled and rolled as if poorly attached, their ears burned bright red. The cook pot was coated with black gravy and strings of meat. The berries were gone. The fiddler seemed to be playing scales, gradually working his way higher, as if he would eventually reach beyond hearing. Walker drank water, felt its cold descent into his stomach. He followed it with whiskey. He was damp, overheated, chilled. He made his way among the others, retrieved his coat, pulled it on, smoothed it against his torso. Beside Mary, he paused to tip her from her partner, move her on to someone else.

Walker sat with Owen on a bench. Only two candles still burned. The fire had flattened to coals. Beyond the window the moon seemed to waver at the center of the valley, as if it might fall into itself in the lake, and the light it sent in through the lodge was cold, metallic, quick and sharp. "You tell me," Walker said, "what moons you have seen," and then he watched for the words, their emergence from those lips screwed crooked, watched the inclination of the shoulders, the twitch of the eyes, and he would have placed his hand on Owen's belly, placed his other hand on his own belly, waited for the depth of the voice to filter to the gut.

"I've seen an orange moon on the Snake River," Owen said. "And years ago, a moon caught in palmetto. And I think of a moon beside a church spire—I thought of that often through the winter. I've seen moonlight swallowed by a lava bed, miles back in Idaho."

A vein throbbed slowly on Owen's temple, a blue line on the white. Walker reached a finger, pressed at the source of that vein, but it didn't subside.

Owen brushed Walker's hand away. "Like a mosquito," Owen said. "Persistent."

The light was gone. Only moonlight. Walker roused from his lean against the wall. He stared a long while, and slowly the silver light filled the room nearly to the beams. There were men in the bunks. Silence. No snapping or faint hiss from the fire. He stepped to the center of the room and tried to count the bodies. They were inseparable shadows. He came closer and listened. No spark of thought or dream. Drowned deep in late night.

On the promontory he stood with the cold wrapped fully around him, and he held his coat closed at the throat. The cliffs were lit with the westering moon, the lake a surface without bearing. Directly below him, on the sand at the edge of the water, two men were at something. He studied their whiteness, their sameness, their hunch and spring, the unsteady arc of their pricks, the skinny length of limb so fervid, as if they swam through cold, trying to reach a warmer layer, but then one or the other was down again. The Illinois boys. They might have been at the bottom of a hole, there, with Walker far above, but as he watched he finally saw a pattern. The Sheepeater girl was on the sand beneath them.

Walker spoke from the promontory. He was sure he heard his own voice, the syllables small and flaring. He thought he said her name, the boys' names, something else. Still the movement continued. He waited.

He wondered if a voice is dampened by the cross-current of moonlight. What else is dissolved and carried in that stream? Perhaps the light brought with it some dead essence of lunar distance, some fragment of ancient erosion and the lifeless ticking of months and the regular swallowing into darkness and the regular birthing of mottled brightness, the particles of revolution thick on the air, interfering with the particles of sound. Perhaps his voice couldn't penetrate that wash of illumination. The boys and Mary were deep behind the light, submerged.

But then the boys grabbed their clothes, broke from the shore, angled almost straight at Walker as if they hadn't seen or heard him, or as if they would take him down in their passage, and Walker waited for them, felt the tension at the back of his thighs, ready for something, but the girl was up and off in the other direction, and he turned and followed her. On the shore she ran, he was above, and as they neared the lake's outlet he had to weave down through a graveyard of boulders, and he lost sight of her. Spanning the creek, he climbed back up to the shore, ran along the narrow meadow, and saw, far ahead, her shadow. Fast and naked and silent, she was already onto the scree slope. By the time he reached the scree, his steps twisting in the jagged rocks, she was half-way up the lake, no more than a shift of gray against gray, and then he lost her. He stopped. He stood there a long while, heard nothing but the waterfall.

He balanced his way over the rocks and sat beside the water. He tasted blood on his breath, from deep inside the bones of his skull. He had sweated through his shirt—it clung to him—and through the blood he could smell his minerals coating him.

Then he moved on along the shore, stopped, sat, tried to nestle among the rocks, to let his heat pool around him. Where the stones sliced his silky trousers, cold leaked in. His evening coat still held to his torso, but for all the coat's serious stitching it was a frivolous costume, useless against real night—the cold pockets, the slick lining, the buttons too widely spaced to create a tight seal. An edge of rock gouged at the back of his neck. Lichen crumbled beneath his finger-tips. How long since the valley had been one solid block of granite, with only a few deep fissures to convey water down from the creeks far above? How long since the pressure of sunlight and the dilution of moonlight had loosed that scree from the skin of the cliffs? The moon looked puny in its descent—the slice of sky above the high ridges of his valley seemed incredibly slender. He thought of the distance of the moon and of how quickly it rose and fell here, how long it shone before it cleared the cliffs, how long it continued to shine after it had been taken by the western ridge, on its way to a farther horizon. The moon was falling away, its bright-ness contained for these moments in his sky. He wanted to feel that light on his skin, if he could feel it.

Unbuttoning his evening coat, he held it open to let in the moonlight, but the light only glared against his shirt. He slipped the coat back off his shoulders, held it by the collar, and flung it out onto the water. It lay skewed on the surface, the black wool slowly went glossy, and it sank. He thought he saw it fall through the water, the sleeves wavering, and then it landed on the rocks and stirred a haze of sediment. He followed the coat with his trousers. Those four black limbs draped on the lake bed. He dropped his white shirt at his feet.

Leaning out over the water, he saw himself in half-light, the image extending from the loose black of his hair to the dark of his nipples. He held his arms out, studied the shadow beneath each arm and the stretch of skin across his limbs. Maybe the moonlight shone around him and not on him— there was nothing clear about the light, not enough power to draw him completely from the smooth darkness of the water. He thought of winter and how at night the snow generates its own light. In the coming winters he might draw curtains shut in his cabin, feed a woodstove, sit on a bed in darkness and watch the storm's own light leak in around the curtains. He imagined a young man sitting beside that shrouded window, the light settling on his bony shoulders, on the mild plump of biceps, on the brush of hair, on the moons of chest, the light a solid mass about the form. Beneath the light, does the young man speak, is the face a face Walker knows, will he rise and step toward him, will he name himself, will the storm thicken and finally extinguish the light? The sky is full of snow, full of weight, vacant.

Walker closed his eyes into darkness. The sky was unencumbered. No clouds. He heard wind—it moved through the miles above him, nothing to catch it, hold it, slow it, its cold density pressing on his drums, tautening, dampening, until he heard nothing at all but the slow dull bubbling of blood through the folds of his brain. He opened his eyes to his reflection.

His close-set gaze. His long nose. His shoulders slightly rounded. His countenance had not yet fully formed when he'd last seen his father, and now he searched for his father's features, for whatever history he wore on his skin. He might be molded directly from his father. Or he might be a marred reflection of his mother. He studied his chest, the moonlight

on muscle and rib, but the light couldn't bring any answers.
Would he recognize his own traits on someone else? The East
must move with men at least vaguely in his image—there
would be his father, and others, perhaps, with an imprint of
his blood in their veins. They were surely up to something,
those relations—someone observed a shopkeeper, someone
bit down on a chicken bone, someone scratched himself
slowly across the underside of his belly—but what was the
worst of it? Had his father only stolen money? His father
might, at that moment, wander through that far night, searching for a scent on the air, anticipating—what?

The drape of trousers on a wooden hook. The afterglow
of a dead lantern, the remnant light and smoke lingering in
the corners. A woman, her long thick oily hair spread like a
frond on the pillowcase. And then his father climbs in, his
shoulder tenting the blanket. "What is it?"

Through the New Hampshire forest, the trees rose up and
reached over. Walker would step into the leaves, each leaf as
large as both his hands spread side by side. The leaves layered
in great thickness underfoot, each leaf in its own stage of
decay, some of them red and pliable, some reduced to a skein
of tough veins, and some no more than an imprint on an
imprint in a slab of damp matter. He pushed through erup-
tions of fern and sapling. He found a stream deep in shade,
the banks of black soil embedded with round rocks. Above
the edge of lime froth where the water slowed, exposed roots
drew moisture from currents of humidity. He heard a tiny
insect buzz at his ear, felt its wings fold as it found its way
down the canal to his eardrum, and it buzzed there, beyond
reach, trapped. On his fingers he found lines of white bumps,
and when he scratched them, they oozed a clear, sour oil.

Walker continued through those woods, miles from the
last town, found a road, found a lane with a sign and gate—
a boys' farm—wayward youth, abandoned youth. He turned
onto that lane, up through the woods until the view opened
to neat fields. A white mansion anchored a cluster of barns

and bungalows, and groups of boys worked, regimented. It was almost military, almost more military than the military he'd seen. It was all crisp and maintained.

Through a week of rain, Walker circled the farm, followed the shadows of the eaves, listened and watched. The boys were sheltered for a half hour in the dining hall of that mansion, and then they were marched back out into the wet blast. Sometimes they would head to the fields or the barn, but on a day when the wind brought the rain straight along the ground the boys were locked into the bungalows for the afternoon. Twin lines of boys stretched on twin lines of cots in a dry oblong box, the green daylight soaking from window to window, the damp forced through the casements by a burst of wind, by the rush of fluid.

In the dining hall, the boys pulled chairs to round tables, draped their legs beneath the white tablecloths, and served themselves a lunch of sausage, potato, corn-on-the-cob blackened with pepper. The boys had been scrubbed—hundreds of crescents of clean fingernail. With their hair too short to show much color, they had only plump or pale to set them apart, or the bulk of knuckles in the grip and shift of a fork and a knife, those hands struggling to get the motion of the cut correct. Walker hadn't learned the boys' names, hadn't attached whatever shouts he'd overheard to whatever lay beneath each black jacket, pair of tan trousers, brown leather boots. Each boy, until you got close enough, could be any boy, could be Walker himself. Such short hair was nearly invisible. Knots of bone at the temple, knobs on the crown, a kiss of birthmark where the neck took hold. At the far end of the hall, at the fireplace, the men stood with their shoulders against the mantel, and they watched, pointed at a slouch or spill, absorbed warmth and sent shadows. The men stood as if they had built the place, as if they would squeeze a wrist tight enough to crack bones just to keep the lines straight.

Walker ran through the yard in the evening gloom, onto the vacant gravel tracks, down to a bungalow. Against the wet red boards he pressed himself, pulled a hand back to see if the color transferred—his palm was clean, red only with chill. The pummel of guttered and free-fall water was too loud for voices. Along the wall the wind held him flat, and he came to a split between vertical boards, dug his fingers into the opening, leaned close, lips on splinters of paint as he tilted to bring both eyes into line with the narrow slit. The boys moved upright through hot water, a fist of soap jammed under an arm, down a leg to heel, a quick scrubbing at anything out there. A boy shouldered another aside, a boy twisted a towel around another's neck, a boy smacked another's back and left a broad red handprint that seemed to coddle the spine, a boy pulled another by the ear until the victim bent and hobbled in pursuit of the pain, a boy took another by the genitals in a soft little wrestler's grasp that almost went unnoticed as they all broke toward the men far in the steam. Some of the boys had the heft of men, some the undisturbed alabaster of a child, and they all hunched in a long line, they all hopped first on the left foot, then on the right, as they pulled on their trousers. They stood straight. Their skin was still damp—water seeped through their clothes, raising the lines of shoulders, the foremost curve of a thigh, the high shelf of a chest if it filled the cloth. They were jostling, a series of partial shadows and hints.

What had they done to get themselves grouped there? Did they love the grand whiteness of the mansion? Were they bold? Soft? Orphaned? There must be a list of crimes with a name attached to each, all numbered and ordered and set down in a ledger. Perhaps a boy had lifted a pewter spoon, or tangled gold thread, or tested his tongue against a cameo carved from shell, the cameo's lovely white woman's face shadowed by the pink mid-coat layer. Perhaps a boy had arced a rock toward a bank of windows, the house itself hugely shadowed in brick rising and slate gables above, and he'd felt the sudden violin and piano, the glissando, drain out through the shards of glass. But which body, which crime?

On the final day, Walker forced himself in through the shrubs, against the mansion wall, and the thorns lifted his pant legs, tugged his coat against his throat, punctured the sleeves, drew blood at his elbows. He slept there through the afternoon, awoke to find that the rain had stopped. He stretched his legs, flattening the nearest border of flowers, the humps of violet and marigold all battered and misshapen. He watched a hummingbird shift among the blossoms, tipping in, moving on, watched until he caught his weight forward and tried to steady that darting into focus, tried to see iridescent feathers on what was now clearly not bird but insect—the fuzzy sections of tubular body, the stiff spread of antennae, pairs of legs—a moth feeding on those crowded moons of color.

That night he stole bread and a slice of ham from the kitchen, ate alone at a table in the vaulted hall, the moonlight setting those round white-draped tables floating in the darkness. He entered a bungalow, undressed in the linen closet, buttoned a plain, clean nightshirt. He found the last cot—he knew it was empty—straightened his legs beneath the blanket. If they had taken him in, would they have locked him in shackles? Would they have shorn him and doused him with lye soap? A man entered through the far door. Walker lay still. The man carried a lantern, and in that cloud of light he seemed thick and ungrounded, his shadow hovering around and above him, trailing him as he paced a few feet from the door, and then he stopped, his hand cupped the globe, he bent to extinguish the flame, and for a second his face was steady—a face as flat as a pan, the lump of the nose, the large eyes an odd, pale non-color. He cut the light and backed out the door. Walker's wrists ached—a pain as dull and constant and worrisome as the ache of growing bones. He rolled the blanket away and moved from cot to cot. Slowly the windows brightened with the night, and shapes floated up around him—shoulders, hips. The boys didn't rouse as he hovered. What did you do? he said, his voice no more than a thought. What did you think? Did you feel the flutter of tendons as your hand took hold? He waited until, in the late-night silence, their dreams came clear—in the basin of each skull, a slow tangle of light, a blood sunset—and his thoughts entered their bodies—their muscle burning the last meal, their muscle hardened through the repetition of maintenance, sowing, cut-

ting (the beautiful softness of his own limbs not yet as beautiful, not yet controlled), the skin so scrubbed it seemed liable
to assume the shade of the flesh beneath, all that blood motion directed across all those rich fields, all that motion
trained into an ease of movement about the grounds, as if the
place was usual, as if they had earned it, as if it was theirs.
At the center stood the mansion, grounded and vertical.

When the first light grayed the clouds, Walker dropped
the nightshirt on the floor—a boy would be punished for it
—and he found his own clothes, got dressed, and left the
bungalow. The rain was falling again. He ran, climbed to the
top of a white fence, to the top of the next, swung his weight
forward, stirred a mob of sodden sheep. The ground rose
beyond cultivation into thistle and trees, the black slick trunks
and the yellow-white skew of broken limbs. He was back into
the woods and their green exhalation, and he slid along banks
of leaves, made the miles quickly, leapt the roar of run-off
where it burst the ditches.

He found a house, a room with shelves to the ceiling, walls
of books. He slid a book out, read the first page, returned it,
slid out another and another. He found his name in a cap-
tion—"Walker believed the birds to be lost"—beneath a fine-
lined etching of a boy deep in bramble, reaching to grasp the
top rail of a ruined fence, looking through a gap in the trees,
and the distance grew from a vague wash to a valley divided
by farms, lopsided acres, a village distinct with church spire,
another village no more than a hint of gathered boxes, and
the mountains narrowed, and the sun hovered, the clouds
evaporated. Walker tore the page slowly from the binding,
listened to the damp rending of the heavy paper, folded it
and slid it into his shirt, closed the book and held the ridges
and deep letters of its binding to his face, ran it along his
skin, replaced the book on the shelf.

And at the seashore, far south during his last summer east,
he wandered past the white wooden buildings, the black roofs
and awnings, the windows blank squares of sunrise, and he
came finally to where the dunes opened to a lawn of spiked
grass, a gray stucco building, tile roof, dark green shutters.

There were men in there, moving about the lawn in their black robes, tending to flowers in urns, carrying trays of cups, bowls, tall pitchers of milk. At a grouping of iron chairs and tables on the veranda, the men seated themselves, clasped hands, and bowed heads. Walker came up from the water toward that lawn, turned and continued to the next line of dunes, up onto a face of sand anchored by tough shrubs and reeds. He laid out a blanket, removed his shirt, his trousers, and lay down in the light. He slept while the sun warmed, and waited for the first real heat to wake him again.

He dreamed of the sand sliding away, drawing him down, and the waves catching at his feet, the brine sting of the water. He was alone. The white plumes, gray plumes, black slashes, yellow razor beaks of the birds circled up from their inland sanctuary, passed overhead, stabbed at the waves and sand and drew out flapping silver, nuts of muscle. Cold salt. The sun was high now.

Up on his elbows, he looked back toward the gap in the dunes, toward the lawn. The men walked out from the building to the beach. On the sand they dropped their robes, and then they waded into the green water, submerged, floated and turned and surged with the swells, let lines of tumbling white force their shoulders under. Sheets of water rose beyond them, brighter green and brown with the sun's back-glow, each sheet speckled with small masses of shadow—jellyfish drawn from a safe current and pulled toward the beach. The men moved in a knot, stood tall from the water for a chilled second and scanned the incoming wash, and then they all pointed toward something and bounced away. Whole lines of waves turned at once, all down the shore, the green torn to muddy white, and there was a voice caught in the crash, and a man ran from the water, paused beyond reach, dabbed at the welt on his arm, the sting red as a kiss, and then the men surrounded him, all moving as he moved, all dabbing at their own arms. The men hurried toward the building, they dove into the doorway, and an hour later they emerged dry and calm in their black robes, and they settled on chairs about the lawn. Which man had been injured?

The sun fell west, and Walker gathered his clothes and blanket, headed across the dunes to the road, stopped at the long gray stucco wall at the front of the retreat—the tall bunches of sea grass, green shutters, tile roof. He waited at the far corner of the wall, waited for the blank door to open, for the men to head out. What would they wear? Which way would they turn? Would they blend right into the world and pass unnoticed through the next town and the next?

The sun would soon cast a final orange line across the lagoon. Birds flew up from seaward, caught the crest of breeze above the tile roof, hovered, gave a swallowed squawk, and fell toward the road, catching speed with a thrust of wings, heading inland. Walker climbed onto the wall and looked west. The land was flat, with specks of birds dropping into whorls of cross-cut salt outlets, an open stretch of reed fanning toward black pines, and here a clearing of sand mixed with discarded shell and leaf and bark, and here a wall of plant so tall it seemed liable to surge and break in a wave of smooth curved thorns and waxed leaves and branches wound to branches against gravity and nests spilling.

And now—moonlight on the Illinois boys as they ran the line of the creek toward the Wind River. Moon in the branches, moon lighting the gray of the fallen logs, the creek white where it broke against rocks. The boys caught light in their passage through the brief meadows. Whites of eyes, white slash of teeth with the intake of breath, white of shirts on white skin. If Walker were beneath one of those boys, if the moon were above, if the boy descended, if the moonlight brought the boy's hair out full and wild around his skull, a gnarled nimbus, if the boy's hands extended as if to grasp, light curving between the long fingers, if the weight were on him, if the light on his own white body shone up onto the body so close, if Walker saw then the hollow beneath the ribs banded with lean muscle, the hinge of thigh with the box of pelvis, the weight of that weighty apparatus centering, if the pressure against him drove out his own thoughts, and he felt only the structure of long bones arched around him, his own limbs meager and pinned, if the small intensity of the moon brought down on him the boy's thoughts so that he heard them as his own, *the village lights far in the trees, the dread silence of the owls' wing, the voice of the mother, the moan of the wolf, the trail gouged by erosion and lined with bones, the dead heavy chill of the lake, the whiskey's sharp heat like coals falling through, the air thinning the passages through the brain, the touch suddenly of skin and the heat no longer soft in the gut but a straight dark line foundering,* if he felt then the boy's ribs fitting into his own ribs as if to grind and lock, if he were discovered and split, would he lie still? And the Sheepeater girl was not as strong as he was, although he and the girl were nearly identical in size, and she had not seen another human for who knew how many years, no human other than Walker, fine little man that he was, builder of great buildings, teacher of language, host to tall lanky handsome men, host to men as far from home as himself, host to a vile bit of suffocating pleasure—not pleasure. She felt them on her, felt them inside her, felt the heat of her blood, and maybe she saw Walker's face, maybe she held still for him, felt his hips on her hips, his ankles at her ankles, his wrists at her wrists, and his gentle hook holding them together. She wouldn't fight. How could she know to fight? He had handed her off. Handed her back out into those mountains.

He stood there in the dry cold beside the lake. The moon fell, and before it caught in the trees along the ridge it shot a white line directly across the water, so bright that he squinted, shading his eyes. Then darkness, with the stars brightening from the eastern sky, finally filling out the full range of constellations. He looked deep behind the brightest stars, through the moonlight that still shone above the valley, deep into the spaces where the flecks of heat gathered and swirled. He was far. Alone. The sky slowly expanded.

He saw again the alley in San Francisco, and he came out from his doorway, smelled the water dank in pools, and a woman came out from the back of the saloon. She brushed at the flow of her skirts as she hurried up to the street and turned. He followed. They moved quickly down toward the bay, came to a row of brick fronts, along a stretch of boardwalk, the unsteady boards, and she kicked into a gap between buildings. With the lit windows high above, she entered through a side door, and in that moment, beyond the block of her shoulders, he saw gas flames, the pressed reflections of the tin ceiling, the etched glass in sliding panels separating one chamber from the next, the carpet heavy with huge blossoms, mirrors multiplying the women standing about, hands on hips, white as the flames, and the men in black with half-smiles.

And Miss Haugen in the smoky gold light of Atkinson's office. She removed her jacket and squared it on the back of his chair. She unbuttoned her blouse and slipped it from her arms, rolled it into a silk ball, placed it on his desk. She ran her fingers along the broad waistband of her skirt, smoothing it, adjusting it. She wore a chemise with short sleeves, white embroidery around the collar and down the front with the line of small, glossy buttons. She stood tall. She turned her head slightly to the side. Reaching with one arm, she squinted vaguely, her lips full and slightly pursed, as if she were running through words in her head. What words? The sleeves were gathered by a dense line of finishing stitch. The light gave shape to the triangle of tendon and hollow at the base of her throat. Her skin was shadowed beneath her eyes. The lace of her further undergarments and the thin shoulder straps were visible against the gauzed, buried hue of her skin. Atkinson pushed aside her outstretched hand. He found the top button of his vest. She spoke then, but Walker did not catch the words. All he saw was her mouth and the way it shifted and stretched through a series of red shapes.

And Greta Mueller in the rush of night between the railroad cars. The moon came over and caught her there, her dark hair paled by the cold light, her pale face dark in downturned shadow. "I am a young woman," she said, her whisper muffled beneath the clank of machine. "I know things. I know what a man wants. I have seen my father. He has a smile that creases his face clear out to his ears. He wears a hat to keep the sun from his skin. Only the backs of his hands are spoiled by the sun. He should wear gloves, but gloves in summer heat are worse than chiggers. In the shade, along the creek, past the pond where we stick bullfrogs, I have seen how white his skin is. It is good that he stays to the shade, or he would take a painful sunburn. I have seen how his body is smooth white, with only the rough brown wrinkles of his elbows and the blue creases behind his knees and the winks of his nipples. And he has a man's weight there, long and hooded. I held to the leaves where I watched him. I know the leaves of every plant in that state. These leaves were dark green and shaped like a teardrop with a spike at the end—they could draw blood. You know, Mr. Avary, I am as lovely a young woman as you could want. My eyes are a beautiful blue. Men want to stare at my eyes. Even women want to stare at my eyes. Kentucky is not perfect. I can make it perfect."

And the Circassian girl beside the morning fire. She held her boots in her lap. She reached into the fry pan with a rag and sopped some grease, spread it on the leather. Slowly she glossed the boots, until they were rich as wet soil. She pulled them on. They were man's boots. Much too large. Her feet were raw from travel.

He tried to see Mary. She worked in the close space of the shelter, with the coals red. She separated a heavy, curled horn from a sheep skull, and she soaked the horn in a soapstone bowl of steaming water. She removed the horn from the water, tested it for softness, cut at it with Walker's knife, placed it back into the water, repeated it all. Eventually she carved and pried two long strips from the center of the horn—the material was as milky and swirled as marble. She flattened and secured each strip against a straight stick. When the material was dry, with the night storming and the shelter in bright heat, she scraped and whittled each piece, smoothing the straightness, perfecting the elegant curve at the end. She boiled horn shavings with hide shavings, and she used the glue to secure the two halves of the bow, and she strengthened the join with two sections of elk antler, and she sealed it all with heated strips of elk sinew. A sinew string held the bow's tension.

She selected two thin, flat cakes of dried tobacco-root. She palmed a few pine nuts. From a cached container she drew a handful of root flour, and she sprinkled it into a steaming vessel of chokecherry soup, stirred it with a stick until it thickened into a dark, sweet pudding. Two strips of venison grilled on the coals. When Walker came in from the snow, his joints still limber within the warmth of the hides she had cut and stitched for him, the clothes she had drawn from the mountains, she undressed him, wrapped him in a wolf-skin blanket—the silver-black lushness of the soft heat—and laid out the meal between them.

Walker turned on the shore, looked toward his lodge, saw only a hint of the beautiful squareness, no movement, no smoke on the air. He took up his shirt and ran back along the lake, the dangerous way through the rocks, crossed the creek, up to the lodge and inside. The room was cool, the ashes dead. Beside the bunks where the ranchmen all slept, he crouched and waited. He heard breathing from the head and foot of each bunk. The men were lolled around each other, crowded and twisted and hugging themselves for warmth. The men were still, as if they would never move again, their weight heavy into the hard stuff of the mattresses.

"I need your help," Walker said, and then he said it again, giving volume and an edge to his voice.

A man spoke from the upper bunk—it could have been Owen. "What's that?"

"I need some men to come with me."

Still no movement. Someone else spoke from the lower bunk. "I think we're sleeping here."

Then silence. Nothing, it seemed, inside or outside the lodge, and Walker slowly wrung his hands, the slim bundles of his fingers. "Those Illinois boys took the girl."

"Took her where?"

"They attacked her."

"Harassed her, did they?"

"No. They took her. Raped her."

"How could they?"

"They did. Down by the lake."

"Wasn't you watching out for her? Wasn't she yours? Wasn't she *for* that? Can a man rape a girl like that?"

Walker was on his feet, out the door and on down into the woods to his shelter—no one there, nothing beneath his fingers but the hides, the bowls, the tension of the bow. He found the clothing stacked where she'd left it, dressed, took his rifle, ran through the woods to the corral. The mule seemed alert to his approach, and he soon had the animal bridled and was up on his back and following the creek down through the woods. The mule found the way. Walker held close to the mule's neck to avoid the scrape of low branches, and he heard the animal breathe and grunt, heard the hooves on the shifting surface of the ground, heard nothing else but the rush of water. He looked up once and saw that the moon had not set finally in the west, and the northern mountains rose clearly in that dull light. He watched for spaces in the darkness, thinking he might see what the mule saw, but where he would have turned left to avoid a tree the mule passed right into that space and Walker felt branches to each side.

Then they were out of the woods, into the moonlight again, and he saw the trees fall back. The mule hurried into the advantage of openness, the grassy slopes taking them fast. If the mule had caught a hole or boulder he could have snapped a leg, but he was sure in that moonlight.

They reached the trail along the river, and the mule stopped dead-center in the nearly invisible line. Walker finally had reason to give guidance, and he tugged violently to the left and they headed upriver at a trot. And then Walker saw the fire—it seemed to spread straight across the distance— and when he came to where he should have faced the Illinois camp, he saw the whole stretch in flame. Sparks had jumped the river, and already the northern valley swept bright with a line of yellow flames pushed by the wind, and as the fire ate through the sage, ate the dried leavings of the grass, it left a deeper blackness in its wake. Walker urged the mule forward, and they came to the camp. The fire circle roared with logs piled on, the ground toward the river was charred, the trees above were in fire. No sign of the man or the boys, their wagon gone, everything gone.

Walker gave a kick, and the mule leapt. They continued upriver, slower now. The moon fell into the western peaks. Walker peered ahead into darkness, the ghosts of flame still confused at the backs of his eyes. The mule seemed to be following something, no way to tell if it was the correct trail, even if there was a trail. But this would be the way for those boys and their father—they weren't going back to anything.

After a mile or more, hard to judge, with the ground rising sharply and the mule struggling, Walker began to hear sounds from ahead. Something mechanical or thumping. Voices now, and clearly the rattling of a wagon.

"Don't light that lantern, I said."

"This is too dark."

"We're going over an edge somewhere if we can't see what's under us."

"Trust the animal."

"He's gotten us out of more than this."

"No one's gonna follow."

"You boys is dumb as wood."

"Ain't nothing happened to her."

Walker raised his rifle, pulled back the hammer, and with the sound the voices stopped. The rattling stopped. He pulled the mule up short and sat a full minute, trying to place the wagon in the dark. He held the rifle to his cheek. Finally he heard a whisper. *There. There.* Walker held his breath, pulled the trigger, and the rifle blasted.

He saw the white flash of their barrels. He heard their bullets in the ground around him.

The mule turned on its own, quick out of there, and Walker was back toward the fire, past it, to the creek, back up to his valley with the fire left behind, the flames still sweeping far toward the sharp horn of the northern peak.

Walker perched at the edge of the lake. Far up the valley, just below the reach of the aspens' shade, the mule wandered, reins dragging. The sun had cleared the cliffs, and in the undiluted clarity of the growing heat Walker ran his fingers over the surface of the shore. There were black flecks in scalloped lines on the sand, left by the lapping of the water. He pinched a bit of the black and examined it—it could have been charred wood, could have been bark, but it had definitely once been alive—with its minuscule veins it could have been a fragment of leaf or some material floated from the depths of the lake, perhaps a hundred years in its destruction, the gore leached away and replaced with this raw black. And there were prints on the sand, what seemed gaping hollows in the bed of tiny grains. The print of a boot with the heel half worn away. The print of a foot dug deeper at the grip of the toes. And there were indecipherable prints—sharp cups, lopsided gouges.

He heard voices now, from behind him at the top of the promontory, voices that flew high into the still space above the lake.

"He's back?"

"He's down there."

"He's been off running somewhere."

"The boy don't look good."

"You looked at your own self?"

"I got hit with a hammer."

"Same hammer got us all."

"I tell you, this day is too bright."

"Looks like the sun is in the water there, don't it?"

"It looks like it's under him."

"You think he's gonna jump in?"

"Into the sun?"

"Well, one or the other. You got the sun. You got the ice water."

"That's the choice?"

"These mountains got a sun like nothing I seen before."

"Like the sky got a hole burned through it."

"The dark blue."

"No sign of those Illinois boys."

"They'd have clear traveling on a day like this."

"Clear blue."

"Shame about the girl."

"You seen her?"

"Yes, sir. I seen her. Sure did."

"No. You seen her today?"

"I ain't seen her. I woke up looking."

"Looking. Sure. Shit."

"Enough of this. Someone get a breakfast fire going. We've got a mess to clean up from this damn social."

The voices receded toward the lodge. Walker smelled smoke and heard the dull knocking of form against form.

The sun swung higher, the day heated through a breeze, a rising of storm, a quick shower, and the following cleanliness of small white clouds. The ranchmen came down to the edge of the lake and looked Walker over. He was a sorry mess. They stripped him off, made him soap himself and dunk in the lake. They handed him dry clothes from his shelter and brought him up from the shore. The lodge had been put back in order, with the benches righted, the floor swept, the pots and dishes scrubbed and stacked. The man with the fiddle played mountain ballads as Walker ate the lunch they'd fixed. And then they brought their horses around, mounted up, and against the sun Owen said to Walker, "We're sorry for your trouble, Mr. Avary. You've got a good start on this place. You find that girl. Charlie here will watch the cattle." They turned and were quickly into the trees, sliced into shadow, and gone. Down along the creek, Charlie was already setting up a camp for himself.

The Sheepeater girl did not return. Walker trailed around the lake. Water flowed through gullies and ditches, bubbled from the rocks, filled the creek. He found prints beside each flow or pool of water, laid his hand flat on the cold impressions—some were larger than his span, some were tiny scratches no bigger than the join of creases on his palm. He pressed a finger down into a mountain lion print, felt the cat's grip in the soil, felt the dig and slow spring of the leg, judged the cat's path up from the valley—no doubt these ridges were a shallow flow beneath such muscle, the Wind River Range mapped not by steepness but by shelter and prey and desire. He found bear prints, the broad weight and the straight-cut lines of the claws, and he remembered the sight of a bear's muffled waddle and the almost careless swipe that uprooted a sapling and brought a feast of grubs. He found a layering of wolf prints, each print nearly filled with the kicked leavings of the next print. Abandoning old thoughts of gravity and night, the wolves must have flown, pursuing scents drawn like blue sparks through the center of the air, until prey was illuminated in a mesh of its own vulnerability. He found the spiked prints of birds that had paused briefly from the sky, quick to rise again—beneath the birds' flight a creek shrinks to a thread of reflection, and then the range dwindles to a gray flatness gilded with ice and forests and small accumulations of sky.

From the lake Walker made his way up along each tributary, caught what trails he could, bushwhacked to the next flow and the next. There were elk asleep in the sun, their legs pulled tight beneath their bulk. A line of mountain sheep, ewes and lambs, followed a seam across a granite face.

Walker slept in a knot of aspen, leaned his spine against the cool solidity of a trunk, the smooth white bark marred by a hundred black scars. Or he slept deep in grass, and he smelled the crush of living shoots and the mulch of slough and the leavings of insect. Or he slept in the lap of a boulder. He tried to hear the night as the girl would hear it, but the sounds of mountain and wood were mixed and indistinguishable in a soup of empty.

A week passed. Walker sat above the waterfall and watched foam rush over into mist. He saw movement at the far end of the lake, around the lodge—a crowd of men and horses. He walked all the way down the shore, crossed the outlet, came up thinking that someone had found his trail, that he would need to hunt some game, get some whiskey, work out the numbers, but it was Owen and some of the others. They sat on the rocks watching the valley, and they stood as he approached.

Owen stepped forward. "I've got a proposition, Mr. Avary. I'm taking you and my son—that's Henry there—to the land office in Cheyenne. Gather your things."

"How can I leave?"

"You have to leave. We both need to secure our claims, me and you. We both need a witness."

"But I've got this lodge."

"There doesn't seem to be much traffic through these parts just yet."

"No. Not yet."

"Charlie will watch your lodge and watch for the girl. He'll keep her for you if he finds her. You don't need to think about it no more. We'll pay for your time. It's almost a favor you're doing."

Walker looked up the valley to the waterfall shredding the surface. There were clouds mixed into the water, and the sun burned. He remembered the close red space of the coals as Mary lifted a sharpened stone and brought it down on the brow of a white skull. The bone splintered, and she brushed the slivers into the fire, where they grayed and disappeared into their own flames. She brought down the stone again, and the horn was free. It was ridged, like a strangely twisted idea of the inside of a tree or a root. He ran his fingers from the heft of the horn's base to the sharp taper. The horn could be all bluster, or blunt force, or echo against the altitude. Imagine if the thought behind that horn still drove it—imagine the animal heaving itself tall on its hind legs, then driving his whole force down and forward, and then the crack of contact. Walker had cut into the sheep they had felled. There was more muscle in a quarter of that animal than in Walker's whole being. He had held the bow sprung from that horn. With that bow he'd driven an arrow nearly clean through a bull elk. Surprising power. Mary had dug the obsidian arrow points from caches, or perhaps she had chipped them herself. In the chipping grounds, high in late summer, she had flaked bits of mountain from a black vein. What odd accumulations of world and sky and star had heated and flowed into that vein? She held the thinnest flakes up against the sun for Walker to see the dirty brown translucence. Like burned glass. She held her hand close to his face. The splintered stone had cut her fingertips—tiny slices crossed the swirls of her prints. He saw how the faint specks of blood swelled and took a channel against gravity and darkened almost immediately, frozen with coagulation in the dry heat. Mary ducked into the shelter before him, turning to clear the way so they wouldn't stumble together in the dark. Mary floated him in warm water, kept him from sinking into sediment. Mary mixed her traces with the traces of rain and lichen, root and ice, paddle and wing, ash and swamp laurel, and he wouldn't find her if she wouldn't be found.

Walker said, "I'll go," and he turned and hurried down from the view, into the woods, toward his shelter. The men mounted up and followed, and when Walker came out through his door with his roll of traveling gear, they were all waiting a ways off in the trees. Owen held his hand down, and Walker swung far up and settled behind the cantle, cradling his roll. They found the trail and descended.

"That-a-boy," Owen said. "It's a quiet afternoon. You

hold on. This is what we need to do. You want to own a valley like this. Don't want to take a bad turn and lose it. I could sit there a whole life and watch that lake. Listen to the waterfall."

Walker leaned in against Owen's back, felt the slickness of Owen's leather vest, the bone and muscle beneath, smelled the buffed sheen of the hide. The sun heated them and sent a dull charge through the dust, and then, in the deep shade, the only heat seemed to be generated by the horses and the men. The huge blocks of boulder to each side were nothing but scrap on the immense weight of the mountain. Walker knew each granite block, knew its settle on the ground, the way the years had cracked the bulk and allowed entry to sheets of lichen, roots, shrubs, and the long streaks of water stain, and the trees grown and died and leaned there against the stone. But another winter, a storm, a flood, a shift of sunlight might color the land in another direction. He looked back. How had those sights entered his mind?

Owen and his son sat hip-to-hip at the front of the wagon, and Walker sat in back, propped among the gear. The ranchmen all stood still from their work, watching the wagon as if trying to see the long trail and the crowds at the end, trying to get a sense of that other world almost beyond memory and sound. The men paused in the shade, or out in the morning sun, along the lines of new buck-and-pole fence, along the irrigation ditches starting to stretch across the lower fields. A man on horseback waited beside the barn, that weaving of split logs beneath a roof of sticks and a hump of molding hay. Perhaps the man planned to head up the valley to scare out strays. Or perhaps he had already ridden twenty miles since before dawn, and now he would slide down from the saddle and find himself a meal. But he waited there, unmoving, the horse's head lolling till it nearly nuzzled the close-cropped, trampled grass. No smoke rose from the cabins that leaned among the trees, with the day blowing through the walls.

Slowly the wagon started into motion, the two horses urged on by a shout and a slap of the reins. With the wheels groaning, the wagon splashed through the creek, then ascended a draw, over the ridge, and lurched on across the bench. The crush of sagebrush was constant and fragrant.

Walker looked back to the wall of the range, saw it shift perspective with their progress, looked far up to where his valley tucked into the slopes, but he couldn't pull the details of entry from those contoured shadows. He wondered what had first taken him up there, wondered if he would remember the scent and stone.

They cut over to the East Fork, circled through badlands, and came down to the Wind River past the red cliffs, into Indian territory. Clouds built high and dark above the Wind River Range, and blots of shadow flowed down the foothills and out across the sage. Owen and Henry, a grown man himself, talked on and on, almost a drone, as if the rocking of the wagon and the slow modulations of the horizon brought from them musical responses without thought.

Henry held the brim of his hat down against the sun. "—the cabin on the river in Montana with the mountains so steep they seemed they would tip under the weight of the snow or a strong wind."

"That river, sure, the long curve in the gravel."

"Through the evening, the geese came up fast over the willows, right over my head, and I thought they was stones with wings, they looked so heavy like they shouldn't be able to fly, but they was strong, with their necks out straight in front and the white slash beneath the fat cheeks and the black eyes and the whistling of their muscle and feathers. They circled off to someplace else, like they could tell one stretch of icy water from the next, or like they knew where to hide."

"And the swans."

"Yes. Huge and white. They got a span of seven feet easy, and the black bill, and the voice like a cold horn."

"Those wings rasping."

"That sound overhead with the first stars at sunset, the swans taking their sound with them."

"Mornings in the cabin, the sunrise made it so you couldn't hardly see out those filthy windows. All I saw was the shape of the spruces along the river, and I heard the birds' chatter, and I heard the horses rumble the rocks at the edge of the river."

"Mother in her wool coat at the stove, trying to pry the biscuits from the pan."

"Yes. Your mother in her wool coat at the stove, her hair high on her head in that loose bundle, like always, and her ears white with the cold."

"She'll be coming to this territory."

"Soon as I tell her to. Soon as we're ready."

Their clothes were nearly worn away, their shirts bare threads at the elbow, belts slashed and scarred, trousers secured with heavy stitches. Walker saw how, beneath their hats, their hair swirled at their necks, the patterns moving clockwise in identical dark wisps. Their ears, pinned beneath the hat brims, were small and delicate, but Owen's were fuzzed with transparent hair. The skin of their necks was creased with sun and dust. And their voices, both with the long soft drawl and the occasional sharp catch of a consonant or curse.

They stopped a night not far from where Walker had waited for the Circassian girl. With the horses loose in feed and a fire circle formed and a pile of dry wood gathered, they pulled off their boots and wandered the bank of the river, stepping out into the shallows where the sand was soft and the water almost warm. Henry moved a few paces ahead, with Owen following, and then Walker. When Henry glanced off to the undergrowth, Owen also glanced. When Henry mumbled something, almost a whisper, Owen nodded in response as if Henry had turned back to look at him. The two had walked together often, Walker thought, with the son ahead and the father following. Walker stopped and let them continue. They zigzagged from wet to dry, their footprints on the stones. Years back, a young Henry might have followed Owen, might have taken the chance to run on along, listening all the time for the sound of his father's footsteps through water, the crack of a branch, the crush of gravel beneath his father's soles, watching for the stretch of shadow to come up from behind him and grow beyond him, the shadow details of shoulders and neck and bulk of head or halo of hat brim, his father's elongated spindly fingers moving through Henry's own small shadow, through his gut, up his spine, out the top of his head, with father moving on.

The surface of the water ran with the darkening trees. Here, from Walker's vantage on the smooth, gravel bank, the sky opened just beyond the floodplain, no cliffs or ridges to hold the light and sound. The world was awash with evening, unfettered to the horizon, to the clouds. If he shouted, his voice might carry without echo, the words absorbed into the distance. With the low angle of the sun, the mountain range far to the north and the Winds closer to the south seemed to have withdrawn, retreated, until they were nothing now but the barest rim of a vast open. A black bird flapped unsteadily from the cottonwoods across the river, headed north, and Walker thought he might see that bird's flight continue forever, thought that the world might tilt and spin and keep the river and that flight always at the center of the dry plain. The bird would continue to carve the evening. The river would continue to pass below.

Upriver, the shallows were full of trout, their dorsal fins etching brief ripples of light on the gray water. Henry and Owen stopped, backed away from the water to the nearest willows, stripped off and hung their clothes in the branches. They were both stark white, sullied only by a few streaks of grime and the hair in shadows and the yellowing of the sinking sun, and they teetered over the rocks as if in losing their clothes they had lost their sense of balance. They could have been any age, those two men—they could have been the same age—and when they submerged in the water and came up dripping and tight with cold, they could have been the same man. They moved slowly into the shallows, herding the trout, which frothed in panic, leaping through the surface, and the men reached a point where they could crouch in the water and scoop up fish after fish. They flung them to the shore, where they flopped and writhed on the rocks. One of the men looked back over his shoulder and shouted something at Walker, pointing at the beached fish, but the voice was caught in the flow of the river. Walker came up along the bank and stopped among the fish—seven fat trout. The men stood up,

smiling broadly and smoothing the water from their arms and
legs.

"Why don't you grab those fish, Mr. Avary, before they
find their way back into the river?"

Walker took a good stone in hand and stunned each fish,
and when they had all settled, he strung them on a willow
branch and carried them back to the camp. With his knife he
slit each belly, pushed through the slit with his thumb, forced
out the guts—the pink tangles, the whitish globes, the bloody
strings, all darkened on the dirt. As he rinsed the fish in the
river, he studied each hollowed body, the ribs and spine and
flesh, with the rainbow scales and membranes obscuring and
containing it all.

Silent along the bank, Owen and Henry returned. They
were clean and dressed and back to work. While Owen
started a fire, Henry found the cooking utensils. The trout
browned in a skillet. It was dark when the three of them finally sat around the fire, drinking cold water from tin cups,
each with a plate piled with that sweet orange flesh. Walker
picked bones from his teeth, chewed bits of the charred skin,
dug the nugget of meat from the cheek of a sharp-toothed
skull. They had nothing else to cook—most of the provisions
long gone in the winter, the salt pork consumed, the flour
exhausted, the remainder left with the ranch hands—but
these fish were enough.

Walker took the skillet down by the water, sat with it between his legs, and scrubbed it with sand. Henry came down
beside him and sloshed the utensils and plates slowly through
the river's flow.

"Do you remember a whole meal?" Walker said.

"Sure," Henry said, "but I don't remember a meal that
ever made me so ready for sleep as I am now. I guess that
cold river soaked the day right out of me."

"Tell me what your mama would fix after you'd been
working all day."

Henry shook the water from the plates and forks, and then
he stood. His shadow flickered out across the river. "I don't
know. She'd just fill our plates." He raised his arms and

waved, and his shadow swayed and stretched. "I ain't sure I can pick out the particulars—just the soft sound of hot water pouring, or something stewing."

Walker leaned over the edge and lowered the pan into the current, trying to hold it steady against the pressure. "If I came by, what do you think she'd feed me?"

"You'd get a meal, like anyone."

They headed back toward the fire. Owen had gone off somewhere into the willows. Walker stood beside the wagon as Henry placed the utensils back in the box, and he handed him the skillet when he was ready. Then they sat beside the fire and warmed the icy stiffness from their hands.

"We're in Indian territory," Henry said. "I don't guess you're bothered by that."

"Why not?"

"You got that Indian girl. I heard you lived with her and all. I wouldn't think a hostile could put much fear into you."

"I'm smart enough to keep my eyes open."

"If the tribes around here ain't tamed yet, you could get us out of scrapes, couldn't you? How much of their language do you have?"

"I've got a few of their words, but mostly for things like rocks and water. I don't know hardly anything about Indians."

"Shit. Don't hold out. That girl of yours must've taught you about the way they deal with each other or the way they deal with a white man."

"I never saw her with her own kind. I just saw her with me, so maybe she was just doing what I wanted, just to please me."

"Did she?" Henry said.

Walker poked at the coals, shifted the logs, got some brighter flames going.

"Did she please you?" Henry said.

"We were working all the time."

"Sure. I heard you kept her fed all winter. That's enough work in itself, I'd guess. But then you got that lodge built. Dug yourself out of the snow. I don't know about you, but I thought I was buried for sure. I thought I'd gone to blue meat, like I ain't lived yet and wasn't going to. You're a lucky man."

"I don't think I'm all that lucky."

"Lucky enough to find yourself that girl." He jostled Walker's knee, looked Walker directly in the face, and leaned closer. "I wasn't at your social. I was listening to our creek and watching the fields in moonlight. All I got was the stories later. Tell me about her. I ain't seen any kind of woman for more miles than I can remember. For a while, in that snow, I didn't think I'd ever see another. I know I gotta wait for the fort or Cheyenne, probably, but I always want things sooner than later. What does she look like?"

Walker saw the fire bright on Henry's skin, on his eyes, burning away the contours of his face until he was flat, the eyes centered, the lips pale as the skin, the chin with stubble like flecks of ash. With that face close and open, Walker couldn't rearrange the features, couldn't bring Mary clear. He saw only the young man's nostrils, the lashes like spikes around his eyes, the texture of his brow like a delicate, bleached orange. So he tried to draw from that heated flatness a sense of how Henry might dream the Sheepeater girl.

She is young and round, far in a doorway. There is heat in the room, and the sound of rain or ice against the window. She does not seem ready to move. She is just a silhouette, with the glow of yellow flame from beyond her, from down the hall, her hair an ornate creation on her head, the curls held with some sort of ribbons and combs, her features hidden but for the small curve of an ear and the line of her jaw. Her arms are loosely folded, her elbows jut. Her bare hip angles with her lean against the jamb. Henry rises from the chair and steps to the bed. He removes his evening coat and lays it out flat. He removes his tie. Watching Mary, he feels his way down the front of his shirt, freeing the buttons, reaches his waist and unbuckles his belt, opens his trousers. His clothes are now loose around him, softly brushing him, liable to fall away if he were to move too quickly. His boots slide off—the heat of the damp, soft leather. He thumbs off his socks, releases his cuff links. And then he shakes free his

clothes and his underclothes and lays them out on the bed
with the jacket. Even in the dimness there is a fine sheen to
the cloth. He climbs onto the bed, onto the pillows, up against
the headboard. Now Mary is framed by the spindly bedposts.
He pulls his knees up, rests his chin, feels the pressure between his legs, thinks it is something he might control if he
remains still. A stretch of lightning freshens the light, a flash
without thunder—it must be summer—and then the walls
and ceiling sink away again. He studies the fall of light that
leaks around her shape and into the room, and he finds blocks
of furniture, rows of brass handles, a mirror half filled with
reflection of the windowpanes, half filled with reflection of
the tied-back drape and the sheers and lace hem. She watches
him there—he is deep in against the wall, a hunched shadow,
with his clothes a distinct black human shape flat and straight
on the white spread. She comes forward. She has left the
clarity of the yellow light behind, and she moves into the dim
afterthought of light. She hears her feet compress the pattern
of the burgundy rug, an odd, stiff sound that seems nearly
contained beneath her soles. She hears the rain. She hears
horses on a hard road, as if the road is made of stone. The
man hasn't moved. At the foot of the bed she reaches and
takes his clothes, holds each item against her skin, smells
each—scent of flower, scent of oil, scent of powder and
roasted meat, charred aftertaste, and the scents she can't
place, the dry harshness of something like metal, the must of
something kept locked from the light. She lets the clothes
slide to the floor, where they pool, black and white about her
feet. Like a cloud, her own shadow obscures the man in
shadow. She moves around to the side of the bed, reaches,
takes hold of his ankle, pulls him, and he slides down from
the pillows, flat on the spread. She waits for the lamplight to
echo from the hall and accumulate in the room, to illuminate
his shape. This is a young man, his ears small. Like ice thick
on blue petals, his skin is strangely white. There is a looseness
to his arms, to his legs, as if they cannot quite yet control the
weight of muscle. Across his chest, black hair forms an unfocused cross. His navel is distinct, like the opening to a well

in a desert. She climbs onto the bed. Spindles and lighted doorway. Rain. Warmth. Her hand takes him, holds him. She seems to study him, to wait. He is controlled, frozen for more than a moment. As if the lighted hallway reflects on his whiteness and reflects up onto her, he sees now the shape of her breasts, the darkness of her skin, her black eyes, and he thinks she might cut him, but she is gentle. He thinks she will not understand if he speaks to her, if he orders her—what can he say to pale this girl, or to blush her with his own memory? What are her thoughts? Is he a man like the men she knows? Is she surprised by the size of him, one way or the other, by the shape of him, by the way he lies and waits? Perhaps he should roll her beneath him, hold her with his weight, but now he can no longer imagine the motion. All he sees is her eyes watching him, and then he begins to see smoke behind those eyes, he sees coals in a circle of stones, and he smells the unwashed heat of hides, and he sees the stars far above through the apex of a leaning cone, and he hears voices talking against night, men in another language at fires circling out toward silence and distance, and he feels the black scratch of her hair, and he knows he can take her, and he knows nothing of what she will understand, and he wants something else entire, and he removes himself from her grasp.

"I can't tell you anything about that girl," Walker said.

"Don't hold out."

"It's not a good story. I'll tell it wrong."

"I don't care. Just tell it."

But they heard movement in the willows, and Owen walked up behind them. "Come on, boys. We've got ground to cover in the morning."

"Do you know how to get us where we're going, Daddy?"

"I've got the direction pretty much settled." He pointed vaguely southeast, into the darkness. "I need the sun. You don't trust me?"

"I just don't want to take any extra miles, that's all."

"We're going as far as need be, and then we'll get ourselves home properly."

Owen laid out blankets beneath the wagon, got the boys

to their feet, got them into the bedding, tossed a few sticks on the fire, then climbed in beside Henry. The wind kicked up. It heated the fire, consumed the sticks, and quickly the firelight hissed away. And then the wind faded, as if it had had no desire but to douse those flames. Only the blackness was left, the huge rush of the river, the sounds of branch and animal, and the stars remote and cold. And beneath the wagon, beneath the ceiling of planed boards and hardware, the sounds of the men were held close—the whistle of dry breath, the shifting about for comfort, a bit of a word uttered and swallowed in a cough. Walker tried to catch the words, to place vision against sound, to set his breathing in time with Henry's or with Owen's—no separation of man from man in their closeness there, no distinction between dream and intent. He pushed his hand out from the blanket, reached for Henry, felt Henry's shoulder, felt the tent of blanket that sheltered his belly, felt his chin, his head, the bristle of his hair. He withdrew his hand, cupped it under his own head, used it as a pillow, felt his own heat and the chilled ground.

"You awake?" Henry said, so softly it might not have been a voice at all.

"Yes."

"You all right?"

"Sure I'm all right."

"O.K."

A few minutes of silence, and then Walker felt Henry close, felt his breath, heard words coming along in a bare whisper, as if Henry had been talking and Walker's ears had only just become accustomed. "You know, we got that ranch started," Henry said. "That's all. We got the creek coming down through the canyon from those big soft peaks in the northern Absarokas, and we got no final idea of where that water comes from. I been up that creek no more than twenty miles—you know, you follow the creek north from the Wind, through all that feed and the old spruces lined tall along the flow and the snake of red-striped badlands, and you find our ranch in the cottonwoods and move on. Then you got the woods, and you got the stone cliffs starting. I found shells in the rocks—I cracked open the layers of crumbly gray stone and got the shells like little clams and something like snails. The view drops way past a thousand miles toward anything like an ocean where those shells might have lived. That view is nothing but stone and snow and red stripes. You go on north and the creek cuts in with those cliffs and then you got a mile of marsh and grass so thick it'd swallow you and your horse, you got aspen with their white trunks up in the forest edge, you got ponds clogged with weed and rimmed with the big slashed grizzly prints, you got trees raked yellow and pitchy from those bears, you got trout big as logs lazing at the surface of an elbow, you got eagles far up and ravens huge and just overhead, you got trails cutting in and out, you got a split in the creek with equal flows coming in from one peak and another, the peaks so huge you'd think they'd sink with their own weight, you got a final look far down into another valley blocked by cliffs that go on and on and show no splits or passage in the long afternoon shadows. I guess I'll hike into that someday, when I have the time. Back down the creek, you know, you find our ranch. In early morning, you could stop and see the cabins in the cottonwoods with the woodsmoke mixing with the steam from the creek, and already we got a road worn down to dirt and gravel, and the herd in the fields. You might think we been there awhile—nighttime you look out the window and see the other cabin windows yellow—but I'm thinking that spot is maybe just barely holding on against a downward slide, with the peaks floating around in the night. I think I heard the boom of those elevations colliding."

Walker awoke to the dead fire. Cold air pooled on the plain, straight from the peaks far against the stars. With his blanket wrapping his shoulders, he wandered down through the cottonwoods and willows, smelled the dampness settled there, felt the dampness in his lungs, the cold ache, almost afraid to inhale too deeply—that ache might sink so far into his lungs that the next day's heat wouldn't burn it out.

He heard wolves making a tangled music, ungrounded on

the plain to the north. He climbed to the lip of the floodplain and looked off toward the wolves. Each sound focused his eyes first here, then there—he might as well have been trying to pull focus from the faintest star. He stood there through the darkness, might have slept standing, and when the first edge of morning began to give distance to the land he thought he saw the black shapes of buffalo or horses moving toward the west. When the light reached a full, cold gray, he saw nothing to the north but open and mountains, and then he heard Owen and Henry talking, he smelled smoke, and he returned to the camp.

They found the going easy just above the edge of the floodplain. Only the occasional gully slowed them. To the left, they watched the river curve and swing through its strand of cottonwoods. To the right, they scanned the dry plain rising toward the foothills and the entry to woods farther in.

"I would say this soil could support potatoes and yams and beets and maybe corn," Owen said.

"With a diversion of water," Henry said. "Where those scrub trees start in the foothills, you could have a ranch, and then you got this spread of fields as far as you could ride in a day or a week."

Walker looked deep into those foothill trees. He guessed at the meager creekbed. Through most of the summer, the creek was likely to be dry. A man might dig in the creekbed and find moisture buried in the clay, nestled among the round stones. How far down did the moisture work itself? Through what strata did it travel before welling up and taking leaf? In the hills above, and on into the canyons, were the most delicate pools, the spikes of heavy purple flower, the trees tall and stiff and sublime, saplings bedded in blankets of dropped needles, fungus in hooded white lines. But here in the low country, beneath the wagon wheels, there were spined paddles of prickly pear with their waxy yellow blooms, and sagebrush with half its branches bare and bleached, and swords of yucca, and rabbitbrush, and the scattered lace of Indian rice grass, and desert wheat grass, and the rare little green-leafed lily on its own barren hump of dirt, and ants marching.

"Yes," Owen said, "with a good diversion of water, you'll have ranch after ranch. You'll never be out of sight, all the way across this territory."

"What about the Indians?" Henry said.

"Once you get enough whites in here, you'll get towns, you'll get bricks and telegraph."

When they left the river, they took to the hills, found a road southeast along the range. For a stretch of miles, the hills were striped with greenish stone, blocks of the stone broken and fallen in heaps. Twice they lost the road, trailing after dusty scratches in the wrong direction. They saw, east through gaps in the hills, red formations swept by the wind —gnarled posts and temples.

The day was cool. Owen climbed down into the back and pulled a blanket over his face, settled into the sun. Walker climbed up front and sat with Henry.

The road was vague but flat, cutting across the soft decline of outwash. The peaks, sharp with snow, didn't seem to shift at all with the miles. The horses' ears circled, searching for anything but the sound of the wagon and their own steps. With Owen asleep, the boys might have been alone there, the horses drawing the wagon along without guidance.

They had seen no game since they left the river, but now they caught sight of a band of antelope down through a draw. Henry tapped Walker on the knee, and Walker pulled the wagon up short. They slid down, left the wheels blocked with stones, left Owen asleep, took their rifles and loaded them, and headed down the draw. The antelope were already gone from sight. Henry went ahead, and Walker followed, weaving among the sagebrush, down into the dry, sandy gully for a stretch, but when Walker thought that another few steps would bring the antelope back into view, he touched Henry's elbow and Henry let him pass. A slow stride or two, a careful step over cactus, and the lip of the draw opened out, and Walker saw the miles of flat, the sky streaked high with thin cloud, and, not fifty yards distant, a buck snipping at the grass. Walker raised his rifle and shot. The buck dropped

straight on its legs. The rest of the band blurred and disappeared.

They walked to the kill. The antelope's legs were twisted
beneath. Eyes open.

"I'd say you been hunting these bucks all your life," Henry
said.

Walker took hold of a leg and flipped the animal onto its
back. He drew his knife and pounded it through the chest,
slit the buck down the belly, opened to that heated smell of
blood and viscera. A few slices and Walker pulled out the
heart and lungs. "You want the heart?" he said.

"We'll get by without it. There's plenty of meat here."

Henry got onto the other side of the animal. Both men
rolled up their sleeves, then pulled the slit wider, worked the
edges with their knives, reached in and took hold of the guts
and scooped them out. That steaming mass of white and red
seemed almost alive as it settled, soaking the dirt. They
cleaned the cavity, the bone and muscle like a ribbed bowl.

Henry dug around the spine with the tip of his knife and
found the bullet. "Good hit," he said.

"If he'd moved, I wouldn't have got him. Nothing runs as
fast as these brutes. I'm not a steady shot."

"Well, something leveled your sight. You already said you
ain't lucky. And you're as short in this territory as any of us."

"I guess I picked up some skill. Must be on the air."

"You gotta hunt with me, Walker."

"We can hunt all the way to Cheyenne. Not like we got a
choice."

"No. Hunt with me in the valley. If we get that bad snow
again, I ain't going to scavenge for winter kill. I ain't going
to be froze for fresh meat. I want some heat in the blood."

"You don't know your way with a rifle?"

"Just hunt with me." Henry looked down at his hands,
turned them over. Both he and Walker were bloody to the
elbow. "Let's get out of this mess."

With Henry following, Walker headed downhill, tracked
through the gully, felt the stones through the soles of his
boots. Then they entered among sagebrush taller than a man,

and the bed of the gully was suddenly damp, and in among the deepest sage they found water bubbling, sheening the bank, swallowed into a muddy pool no larger than a good-size trough. The break of sage blocked the chill breeze, and the sun shone through the white horsetails streaking high, moving eastward. Small birds scared down the draw with a flutter and a sharp note.

Henry carefully loosened his shirt and let it drop off his arms, caught it up from the ground with the toe of his boot and kicked it into the sage. Walker, too, removed his shirt and tossed it to the dry ground.

Walker saw the thin wire of Henry's chest, the ribs shadowed beneath the warm yellow sun, the sparse black hair spread like blown cuttings. Henry looked down at his chest, pushed at himself with his fingers, leaving red prints, saying, "Guess I'm pretty much ganted up. I'm looking like the least part of our sorry herd."

"I don't know about that. Your herd is putting on muscle all right."

"And I'm not. I know. Hey, our bean master went loco."

They laughed, a brief burst, and crouched together at the water, reached down in, bathed their hands, worked the water up their arms. The muddy water darkened. Even on that tiny pool, a bug skimmed on spindly legs, holding its fleck of a body tense above the unreflecting surface. The scent of blood. The scent of iron-red clay.

They came up to the wagon with the antelope buck slung between them. Owen squatted against a wheel, drinking from his canteen, rubbing dust or sleep from his eyes. They hefted the buck and dropped it into the wagon. Owen climbed up front, and Henry joined him. Walker cleared the stones from beneath the wheels and climbed into the back. They started again.

"Good," Owen said. "It looks like you two will care for me just fine."

Miles along the road, they found themselves in an abrupt canyon, unloaded their gear and carried it up, led the horses, the wagon rattling, the horses struggling to gain their footing as the dirt slid away. At the top, they loaded their gear again, pushed the antelope in under the seat, and headed on into a cold afternoon wind.

Clouds blocked the heights and descended from the peaks, filling toward the plain, bringing the featheredge of a storm. The first snowflakes drifted in flimsy spirals. The snow kept on, shifting between soft white and raw sleet. The clouds seemed to scrape along the low ridges, and the men could hear the movement of that gray mass, the shiver of sagebrush taking the brunt of the ice.

"Summer in Wyoming," Owen said, and he tipped his hat down against the wind, reached for his coat and pulled it on. "You boys get under cover. There's no use in all of us getting drenched."

Back against the tailgate, Henry and Walker wrapped themselves in a tarpaulin. Henry's hands worked inside, folding the canvas in on itself, sealing out the cold, and then he settled, his hand linked around Walker's calf, the two of them reefed together. Their hat brims dripped. Pools filled and overflowed the creases of the canvas. The wind swung around, and they ducked their chins until only the strip of their eyes was exposed. They breathed inside their gathered warmth.

Owen drove them along. They rocked and jostled. With Henry's heat at his side, Walker listened to the clatter of the wagon, watched the snow and ice accumulate on Owen's shoulders. Blind shadows flowed across the miles.

"Tomorrow," Henry said, "we'll drive on into something, judging from what the army told us—there's Fort Washakie, now, on the Little Wind River, to keep the Indians."

"There wasn't anything down here last year," Walker said, "or not that I got close enough to see. I kept my distance."

"Why'd you come into this territory, anyway?"

"I got a map. This country looked empty."

"Sure. Being first is all the difference. But we just about got ourselves froze." He pushed his hands up from the canvas, held them out flat in the sleet and snow, and turned them over. Three fingertips were scarred, the skin darkened. "Frostbite. On my toes, too. You got any damage?"

Walker looked at those scars, remembered the cold, felt again the cocoon of fur—the badger and coyote and wolf. He remembered the ice nearly freezing his eyes shut, crusting his lashes. He remembered Mary leading him to a bowl of snow beneath a tree, and they sank there together in the white, and they were slowly drifted over, and he saw nothing but the splay of branches girding the trunk in a dense thatch, the sharp blue needles, the oval of Mary's eyes, and he heard nothing but snow and the rush of his own breathing inside the wrap of fur, and he felt nothing but the weight of the storm and the strength of Mary's patience. Walker looked again at Henry's scars, the gouged ridges of the fingerprints. "No. I wasn't damaged."

"Lucky." Henry pulled his hands in and sealed the edges. "It's good you got those mountains figured. If I'd known you was there, I would've gone up for a visit and learned some things. You're a good sign. That Indian girl of yours ain't the same girl we seen you riding with in Pacific Springs, is she?"

"That wasn't the Indian girl—she was a white girl."

"I seen her from the ridge, you and her on that big horse you was riding. She was sweet, I think. I got a look at the shape of her. Where'd she go?"

"She split off. I haven't seen her."

"That's a shame. You'd want a girl like that up here."

Walker listened to the sleet pop against the canvas, to the wheels splash through the thin layer of mud. The sun was folded deep in the clouds, a dull brightness through the thinner layers, illuminating mazy fissures in the storm's darkness.

"How long till we get a town started so we don't go crazy?" Henry said. "With the luck I've had, I'm afraid I'll be wolf meat before I'm twenty. How long till I get roostered? How long till we got a real place with music and a calico queen?"

Walker tried to remember the sound of the fiddle in his lodge. He remembered instead the breeze raking the trees, the buzz of the nighthawks, the water gurgling at the shore.

And he heard, beneath where the music should have been, Mary's feet moving through a pattern on the dirt floor, pressing flat prints, dragging long slashes and swirls.

Walker looked at Henry. The boy was almost too close to focus on. His hat was soaked, the brim chewed by pack rats or worn ragged with age, the band woven with a few shed feathers and strands of grass, a spike of scarlet globe mallow, ruined gumweed. In the gloom beneath the brim, his eyes were half closed, rimmed dark as if daubed with ocher. Black pores on his flared nose. Walker leaned forward to gap the canvas from Henry's face. Henry's mouth was set crooked, a seam down the center of the lower lip as if it had once been cut—a fine slice—and his chin was unshaven, the beard starting in forlorn patches.

Since he last saw his own face clearly in the lavatory mirror on the train, Walker had seen no more than a rippled reflection moving with moonlight, sunlight, white clouds or clouds of spruce. What age or earth had darkened his own eyes? He thought he remembered that his nose had a cleft at the tip— he ran his finger down from the bridge, felt the straight line, almost frail, and found the cleft. Had his lips been scarred by the constant winter smoke?

He ducked deeper into the canvas. He smelled Henry's sweat and oil, the congealed miles and months worn through his blue shirt. He watched Owen's back, his steady hunch against the wagon's progress through the snow, the white fringe crusting his coat. Owen drew them along the overlap of one alluvial plain after another.

From off toward the foothills, a dark shape approached, and then, slowly gaining clarity, it separated into two birds, one after the other in the white. The one ahead—sharp wings in rapid strokes, blunt into the snow, with its tail long and trailing. The one behind—much smaller, almost buffeted in the wake, fighting through a few short wingbeats, then a moment of unbalanced sailing, then the beats brought it up again in pursuit. They flew straight toward the wagon's progress, slowly the sound of those wings fighting through the snow, and then they were directly overhead, so close that Walker could have stood, could have raised his arm and let his fingers brush their sleek undersides. The one ahead—the size of a raven but mottled sandy, with a black V in the pit of each wing—a falcon—the hook of its beak, the grip of its talons along its underside, the slick power of the unthinking strokes. The one behind—a black V across its yellow breast, the short tail flashing white in the brown—no more than a meadow-lark—fighting to gain. They moved on, down east through the snow, and their voices returned—the key-key-key of the falcon as keen as ice, and the small gutter-note of the lark.

A stolen egg? A confusion of territory?

They could fly on, skimming between white and white, as far as the plain stretched. And as the storm continued, that long flat world would fall into evening, with the vague shadows finally as flat as the plain, and the snow lifting from the ground as fast as it fell, and the clouds turning their heads down against the earth, until the birds found themselves above, with the surface of the clouds alive and flowing, eroding in the currents of wind, and the stars circling up, and the voices again, carried off with the spin of the globe.

Walker looked at Henry, at the tracery of the ear that caught the whip of wind, the eyes tearing in the cold. He moved his foot, circled it behind Henry's, barely pushed against Henry's calf. He imagined Henry's feet on cobblestones, on brick pavement, on sand, stepping back from the highest lap of the waves with their hollow black scraps of reed afloat, Henry's legs splayed from his seat on a stool, heels hooking the rungs, strings of letters carved on the bar top, one word crossing another, Henry's chest in a mirror, the bones buried in a new layer or an old layer of muscle, the skin stark and powdered, and beyond him, far in lamplight in the mirror, the bucket of coal and the scoop, the stove to be fed, the jacket hung on its peg, the window squared high in the wall, and, beyond the window, the streets as steep as stairs, the views as sheer as free-fall, and a thousand faces unformed through a thousand miles, groves of alder and ash, salt marshes, islands white with shit, the tide drawing out a flooded river, a bull elk rubbing velvet from its spikes, wolves cutting calves from a herd, moon on a glacier, on a lake, on a cascade, the Milky Way rivering through cloud, and the smoke of gathered walls. Henry turned toward him, and Walker looked at him full on. Henry's skin was so whitened by the cold that the grime seemed to hover above it, and the features were singular, or maybe Walker had seen that face before, on a hundred men, familiar, but he couldn't remember.

"Tell me, Henry, what do you see in that town you expect on the Wind River?"

Henry leaned in against Walker, worked the canvas tighter, tipped his head forward until his hat cut him off completely from the day. "We're so high into Wyoming Territory, we'd be lucky with some shacks and five or ten neighborly humans, at least for some years to come." His voice was buried in the canvas. "Then you got a few false fronts, square along a street. You got the men you know and already the new men you might never know. You got a church at some point, with the cross up high in a stand of spruce or cottonwood. You got the sound of early morning, with the working of hinges and the thump of ax on firewood. You got that view coming in when you ride down along the creek—the rooftops straight in the trees and, beyond and above, the mountain range steep and dark with forest. Then you ride in from the trail, turn onto the road, and the town is lined up, the windows facing each other. You dismount, tie your horse, go into the establishment where your business is, and close the door behind you. Whatever you want or need is right there, crowded all around you. But after years of this wide open, maybe I won't want nothing to do with it. I think I might be spoiled for easing into town life, for getting myself into anything more than just a visit for supplies."

"I don't know about that. It seems to me you'll probably end up wanting the town named for you."

"If it was named for me, it sure wouldn't be much of a town."

"But you'll want a hand in it, won't you?"

"Maybe. Or not. I don't want to think about it, like I won't be able to wait for it all to come, or it won't come at all, or what I been waiting for ain't nothing any man should want. I only been to a few towns in my life. I been out here in this kind of open territory, never less than twenty miles to the nearest neighbor. Tell me where you've been, Walker. Tell me about a place I don't know."

Walker told Henry of passing through streets. He listed the name of each establishment, the gold letters painted on windows, the gables, the shutters turned back, and then the end of town, and the sounds left behind—voices in a strange music—and the fields opening, the trees far toward the hills, the inlets to be skirted, and finally the mild salt of the water on the afternoon air. He sat on the shore where the grass came down across the dunes, and there was driftwood, glass, a corner of a sail washed up. He sat at one end of a board, felt how smooth, almost soft, it had become in the catch of tides, the travels, the days and nights—he thought he might push his fingers right through the wood, separate the grain, and rub it all to dust. Across the bay, the hills rose and fell, dark with trees, and the far shore was scattered with white buildings. At the center of the water, a skiff moved under sail—it was bright, as if the only sun that hour had found it and followed it. But the rest of the sky was black, and the undersides of the clouds dipped toward the water and swirled back up into themselves. The water was equally black. And then Walker saw a man in the middle distance rowing a green dinghy, saw him rowing where before he had seen nothing, as if the man had rowed himself right up from beneath the black water. The man was struggling, fighting with the chop of the water and the wind, and nearly half his strokes foundered without taking full purchase. Walker ought to have been able to hear the groan of the oarlocks and the skip of the oars against the water, but he heard nothing. Then the clouds took the far shore in the shifting, slanting gray of heavy rain, and the gray advanced, and the skiff fought with its sail as the gray came over, and the man in the dinghy rowed and was overtaken, and Walker watched the surface of the water stir and churn, and then he heard the roar, and the cold rain fell around him, soaking him, digging craters in the sand. The rain lasted a few minutes, and then it moved on. Out there, the skiff continued, its sail full, and it still seemed bright, still seemed to be followed by light. The far hills were tall behind the white buildings. And the dinghy was gone.

Henry brought his face so close that their brims overlapped. He whispered. "And you found help, to look for the man in the dinghy."

"I didn't. I just watched the water."

"You're sure you saw him."

"Of course."

"Tell me who he was."

"I can't."

"What did you see of him?"

"White shirt. White hat."

"Was he old or young?"

"No way to know."

"That skiff didn't turn back and search for him?"

"No. It kept on sailing past the point, till I couldn't see it."

Henry retreated a little, turned and looked back between them, back along the twin lines of the wheels and the muddy digs of the hooves. "There's always storms coming through, ain't there?" He squared himself forward and shut down, quiet for a mile. Then he spoke again.

Henry didn't know anything about sailing or salt water, he told Walker, but he had followed rivers through valleys orange with bare willows, through canyons where the trail passed across crumbling slopes, up to gates in impassable ranges. When his horse lost its footing in a wash of panicked steers, he nearly drowned, and beneath the water, with the horse and saddle still clutched in his thighs, he felt the blocked shapes around him, saw the sun doused and drifting, felt the slime of stones worn smooth, thought he tasted blood and granite. He spoke of a river broken by tumbled boulders, the holes deep and glassy, the trout drifting through brown shade, an egret white at the shallow edge. He'd seen a river slow across a plain, reflecting only its fringe of short grass and the final sliver of moon, with the preceeding day's reflection of lodgepole and columbine abandoned. He'd seen a river spread thin across a downslope of gray stone, so that it seemed not a river at all—it was as if the surface of the stone had dissolved, had come alive. He'd drunk from the water bubbling from a beaver dam and thought he tasted the animal's musk. He'd smelled the water sinking through skunk cabbage roots. He'd seen water break a line of insects carrying white eggs.

He told Walker of a winter years ago when each new storm held to the tail of the last, and only a few moments of open sky passed over, an icy blue or frozen black. In their cabin, he and his mother and Owen laid sticks onto the blazing coals, shut the stove, sat tight in the snapping, roaring heat. The river beyond their walls hissed as constant as the wind, and at dawn, as he sank the bucket into the flow, he watched the ice pass, he watched the green strings of slime wavering on the bottom rocks, he saw water bugs crawling beneath their own densely rolling sky, and he let his hand stray into the water, saw the grime and soot blacken into a cloud around his skin, the soot torn atom from atom as it washed away. The view downriver cut quickly into banks of fir, and there the passage of his leavings would be shadowed from the early sun, then carried on through to the soft meanders of the marshy reaches, miles below.

That winter, his mother expected a baby. She slowed as the winter deepened, her hands stiff and clumsy. Soon, in the corner of the cabin, she propped herself in bed throughout the days and nights, her hair against the curve of the logs. With the nearest woman thirty miles across a snowbound pass, she depended on Henry and Owen. They fed her, the large spoon dipped into broth, the bread sliced thin and warmed on the stove top. They bathed her, dabbed at her cold white skin, steamed her with pine scent, flower scent, scent of winter wheat. They wrapped her in layers of wool.

Late at night, when the lamp had guttered through the last of its oil, Henry waited for the night's light to silver the windows. Nothing brightened. The stove settled toward cool, the metal groaned, contracting. He should have pulled on his boots, hurried outside, gathered an armload of fuel from the woodpile, pushed back inside with the force of the wind, opened the stove, felt the dry glow, and fed wood onto the coals. He should have found the bottle of oil on the shelves, unscrewed the slick stopper, and replenished the lamp's reservoir. He should have buried himself in blankets and slept, no dream more dangerous than a bit of frost or a glimmer of heat lightning. But he listened to his mother's breath, to the slow rustle of cover. She was on her back. From that corner she would see only darkness—the night had retained nothing of the day—and she would hear the last of the heat escaping from the stove, hear the coals consume themselves and settle, light as paper, hear Owen beside her, lost in a dream of cattle kicking through ice, hear Henry holding himself silent. In the darkness she might feel herself adrift, the sound of the wind as thick as the sound of water, and she is boxed in, held to her spot there against the wall by the force of the cabin caught in a swirl, an eddy, and the jolt as they spring free and continue. But she is still, with the blankets around her, the sweat cooling her brow, the clench of her bowels, the thick useless tension of her fingers. She pushes her hand toward Owen, feels the slump of his shoulder, the muscle of his chest, feels the line of his jaw slack with sleep (and Henry hears the scratch of her nails across his father's stubble). But she catches at the wall for balance—she thinks the cabin (or perhaps it is just the bed or just her heavy body) is lost in a downward flood—now, certainly, there is no mistaking the lurch against the cutbank, the acceleration through narrows, the shiver of the riverbed sandy and contained and channeled with passage. She thinks she sees the splay of branches far above, dark against dark, and the sway of breeze, and then the fringe of marsh grass, the reeds choking in, and she anticipates the decay of slow stagnation.

Henry heard her voice. He was on his feet, and then he and Owen lit candles, fired the lantern, the wavering shadows and smoke circling them as they moved, as they brought her near the stove, heated water in a pail, tried to separate words from her sounds. She was gripping at whatever she could reach. Her face was streaked with red.

"Get it out," she said. "Cut me. Get it out of me."

It was breech. It was delicate. They had skills only for larger animals.

Henry held the boy—wet and heavy and slick. The air in the cabin was too dry. He tested the water in the bucket—it was as warm as skin. He lowered the body into the water—the perfect curl and settle of limbs down through the gentle steam. He carried the bucket out into the night.

A few hours toward evening, the snowflakes were larger and slower. Owen said, "Enough of this," and he pulled the wagon up at the edge of a swale where water pooled. Then the clouds broke, the distance opened, the storm moved east, and the late sun reddened a soft white world, the drape of erosion.

They set a fire going. From the antelope they cut a dozen steaks, and they grilled them, watching the fat sizzle.

It was a cold night, with the breeze trying to break back into summer. The stars wavered in a perfect dome. The horses, sloshing at the water's edge, were easy keepers, and they dug out enough grass to keep themselves going. The men cleared a spot beneath the wagon, rigged a canvas windbreak, and climbed in together. The canvas shivered and luffed. The wagon creaked, shifting against the wind. Walker looked out into the night. Shrouded white rolled toward the plain. The snow was too wet and heavy for the wind to kick up any scud.

Beside Henry, Walker pushed his hand through the covers, felt the boy's shoulder, and now he laid his hand on Henry's skull, let his fingers conform to the curve, and left his hand there a minute, as if he might sense the shape of his thoughts. He felt down along Henry's chin, felt the stubble sparse and airy. He felt the tattered ridges of Henry's long-johns, the folding of his limbs to maintain warmth, the pulse in his neck. Walker moved closer, and in an echo of Henry

he brought his limbs in tight, lay there against Henry, felt his
breath dampen the skin just behind Henry's ear. Henry didn't
move. Walker shouldered tighter against him, pushed his arm
over and around, laid his hand flat on Henry's hand. Henry
was taller than he was, all sinew and length—the youth in
him had frozen away. Walker brought his breath into time
with Henry's breath, and with each inhalation his chest and
belly forced against Henry's spine, the space between them
gone, and then he exhaled with a chilled separation, and then
inhaled to the heat again. He thought of nothing but gaining
the young man's shape, the exact curl of his body in the
pocket of warmth they shared. His breath condensed into
droplets, gathered in the channels of Henry's ear. Henry
didn't struggle, didn't move within Walker's arms, remained
still, his heart steady, as if waiting for Walker to gain his
repose, to settle completely against him, so close he nearly
settled through him, spine pushing past spine, ribs interlock-
ing. These were Henry's bones and tendons. These were the
palms calloused from the rub of reins. These were the thighs
sprung with muscle from miles of rough passage. And it was
all shaped into Owen's shadow. And the dead brother—what
other shadow would that child have been? Walker pressed a
leg between Henry's legs, and, with Walker's shin as the ful-
crum, Henry's pulse was borne across bone. Walker felt that
beat through his veins, felt it pass through his heart.

Walker found comfort there, he heard the night sounds
return, the wind and the rattle of sage, with Henry warm in
the curl of blankets. Owen's slow snore seemed far away in
the enclosure. The cold was held off by the scent of the wool
blankets. Even the slightest shift would destroy Walker's
comfort—his hip and shoulder and knee had found in this
spot of ground the perfect cradle—but with great care he
loosened the buttons of Henry's longjohns down from the
neck, reached into the gap, held his hand flat against the sternum, and found the deep, direct workings of the heart constant and buried beneath that skin.

He traced the miles down from his lodge to Henry's ranch.
Maybe it was twenty miles, but it could have been fewer.

From the lake he would follow the sound of the creek as it cut through the woods, and then the world opened onto the slopes, and on a good night he might see the whole trek laid out below him in silver and gray—the Wind River flowing miles down through its valley snaked with badlands, and then the creek coming in through its valley that cut toward the northern range, those distant peaks as blocked as a string of drifting crates. And through all those miles, along the trail to the ranch, he would hear the sagebrush drag against his legs, the grind of gravel and branch beneath his soles, the softest crush of grass and stem and petal, the water deep through the rocks, the wings of owls, the wind.

He had approached that ranch twice, and he'd been only mildly surprised by the structures after all the unfocused miles. It had been almost a year since he'd seen a real gathering of men, and that had been the quick sight of South Pass and the Sweetwater Mines. Two days ago, he had gone into those ranch buildings only briefly. They'd fed him a sad meal, Owen had offered a few words about the trip to Cheyenne, and then they'd sent him with a blanket to sleep beneath the cottonwoods. "Too nice a night to lock yourself into our rotten cabins," Owen said. So Walker watched the windows darken, and then he heard the creek, the cattle in the lower fields, and the great weight of silence looming with the Winds.

He might have entered those buildings in the late night. He knew the steps—he would force a door with a constant, silent pressure, and then he'd find his way to the wall or shelf where he knew the goods were stored or secreted or delicately displayed, and he'd wait for moonlight to find the windows, to find the things he could lay his hands on. There wasn't much in those cabins, not much more than he himself had, and most all of it was of poor quality, store-bought and ruined, worn out—clothing, dented cups, rope. Henry might have saved a few items in a box or a can—a coin, perhaps, or a tooth, a pin—but they were nothing a man could take. Through their months in the high country, Walker and Henry had shared only the moonrise, only the storms stagnating in the valley, and the sky centered on the Wind River, the scent of pitch and sage. And they had both kicked through snowbanks deeper than a man.

With a vague stretch, Henry rolled within Walker's arms until his face nestled beneath Walker's face, his brow against Walker's shoulder, their legs tangled and shifting until the knobs of their knees were cushioned by muscle, his arm now under Walker's arm, his hand coddling Walker's back. "All these miles," Henry said, his voice soft. "The cold."

"Yes."

"The same few men to see and talk to over all that time. A long winter."

"Seemed like years. Seemed like we got buried right down into another world."

"It got so I couldn't even talk to those men. We was quiet for days. But they were there, they were bumping into me or pointing me toward my work, and sometimes I knew they'd be looking to follow me, to harass me."

"Are you an easy mark?"

"I'm strong enough. I got a bit of fight in me, if I have to."

"Then why?"

"Just 'cause there wasn't anyone else to harass." He tightened his hold around Walker. "You know something strange? Sometimes I can't count back into those months and come up with any particular days, just a bunch of different thoughts stirred around. Someone died. We ate no supper. I found a steer frozen right into the creek, like it had been cut in half by the ice. Ravens followed me. I never got enough layers of clothes." Henry freed the rest of the buttons down the front of his longjohns, opened the cloth, opened the laces of Walker's shirt, and pressed chest-to-chest with the faint crackle of hair. "I was alone. My daddy asleep, or off after something." He brought a hand between them, pressed at the softness of Walker's belly, the thin layer of skin over the silent guts.

Walker felt the pressure of each fingertip, and he could almost feel the darkened scars where Henry's nerves had died, where the spark wouldn't transfer. "I thought of you sleeping," Walker said.

"You did? What did you see?"

"I couldn't see anything clearly, not at all."

"What did you want?"

"To see another man."

"Did you know me?"

"Maybe it wasn't you. I thought of all of you sleeping. Or anyone."

"Yes. Of course."

"I thought I might be alone forever, with the world gone."

"I thought that, too."

"Easy enough to believe it, even now."

"When I think of you in your shelter through winter, all I think is that I'd lose my sense after only a week, alone like that. You gotta have things you been wanting to tell, things that only another white man could know. What did you tell that girl of yours?"

"I told her how to follow me, how to help me."

"And what didn't you tell her? Tell me something that you wouldn't tell her."

Walker found Henry's fingers loose at his mouth, as if trying to catch his sounds.

"I'll tell you this," Walker said.

He told Henry of a cove where the ship had anchored for a few hours only, Captain Avary had promised, just to pick wild fruit from the forest beyond the dunes, just to repair the rigging. None of the passengers complained—they lolled on deck, watched the men high up the masts like birds hopping for a perch, watched the boats row to shore through the soft rollers, felt the calm of it all, with no canvas aloft to fight the wind. And then, after a lazy, timeless stretch, a woman pointed to the shore, and they all came to the rail, rare for them to stand together, but they crowded, squinting against the early sun. A young man was crossing the dunes from the forest. He was no one they had seen, clearly not of the crew. He reached the shore, the dark, wet sand. He wore only a pale cloth around his waist, and he dropped it, carried a net with him, entered the water. His brown hair slicked against his head, flowed against his neck. He swam naked through the rollers, his feet kicking up behind as each wave washed across him, and then he was free, the water pale and clear. He struck with his arms, pulled forward. They watched his body, white in the blue shadows. They saw his eyes black and scanning away from the ship, as if he hadn't seen it, but how could he have missed such a thronged vessel? He entered among the black rocks where the eddies surged and foamed. As he disappeared for long moments, they held silent, and when he emerged gasping and paddling, they laughed and talked of his skill. He dove again. There, someone said, I can see him enter a cave. No, another said, he sinks straight, he holds to the sea fans. They tracked the swirls of the tide, they called to him although they couldn't see him, they cursed the surging water and the sharpness of the rocks.

And then he was gone too long. At first they laughed again at his skill—he was hardly human. But then they saw him against the rocks, rising, rolling, near to dashing there on the edge. They ran along the rail, they directed a boat, they called with each stroke of the oars. The young man was pulled from the water, carried back to the side of the ship, where they looked down on him in that small boat, watching for him to move. He was unbruised. He was stretched out straight, arms above his head, ankles crossed, draped back over a coiled rope. Bring him up, they said, and the men carried the young man up the netting, passed him over the rail, and a dozen hands laid him flat in the sun, on the fresh-swabbed deck. No one reached to cover him. No one turned away. They watched his ribs, his belly. They watched the sea water dry from his hair, and the strands loosed themselves and blew across his brow. His skin dried, leaving a faint dull layer of salt. The ship swung slowly, and a mast came across the sun, setting the young man in shadow. They saw that he was not pale, as he had seemed—he was white only with the intensity of the tropic sun—in the shade he was colored a smooth brown, his eyes were narrow and fine, his nose with a slightly royal Roman hook. He could be my sweet cousin, a girl said.

He could be a clerk I met in Charleston, a man said. He is well made, a woman said, and I think he will be missed.

The crew arrived from the trek into the edge of the forest, laden with baskets of nuts and soft yellow fruit. What did you see in there? the passengers asked. The crew had found nothing but trees—even the birds were too high, only their calls falling through the leaves. The passengers sent men back to the beach, back to the trees, to look for a trail or a village. Through the afternoon, the men shouted into the trees, scoured the ground, but found nothing.

The passengers called on Captain Avary. We don't want to leave him on the sand, they said. He'll be destroyed. We don't want to bury him, they said. Animals will dig him up. He'll leave a sad mystery on that beach. Let's take him with us. Let's put him to rest. The captain agreed.

The passengers sent the men back to the beach one last time to fetch a basket of stones. Then the sails were raised, and the canvas filled without shaking. They sat with the young man into evening. One by one the passengers retreated and returned with an item of clothing. They dressed him in white trousers, a smooth blue shirt, black leather shoes. They decorated him with silver pins, slips of ribbon, a cameo. They oiled his hair smooth to his scalp, gathered the long strands back against his neck. The stars came up. The lanterns were lit.

Before dawn, they sewed him into a length of dark silk, sewed the stones in with him. The ladies brought out a large square of lace, and they wrapped it around the silk and stitched a seam—through each delicate hole in the lace, the silk gleamed.

The sun tipped up from the horizon. The coast had been lost.

They lowered him to the water, and then they followed along the rail as the ship moved on. They passed around the deckhouse. They gathered above the captain's quarters. Perhaps the captain, too, watched the ship's wake from his window. They leaned at the transom.

The body didn't sink. At first it seemed almost to keep

pace with the ship, drifting only slightly to the stern, slowly turning in the wake, clearly at the surface. It should have sunk directly. Perhaps the silk couldn't hold the weight of the stones, and the seam had split. The birds that had caught up with the ship as it left the cove, the brilliant white-and-gray gulls, the rusty brown sukas, the sooty shearwaters—they all held back, circling above the body as it traveled through the ship's glassy trail. The column of birds seemed to grow as it receded. It was tall and churning. The distance hazed, until that column sank away beneath the blazing horizon.

The horses, picketed together, slogged through the sagebrush. The night had calmed. The canvas was silent.

"Waxy," Henry said. "My dead brother. The long black cord. The bones just beneath the surface. It was like a good shake would bring him apart."

"I'm sorry."

"I don't know the ocean. What does it taste like?"

"Here." Walker brought Henry's mouth against his shoulder, felt the quick point of Henry's tongue. "This."

"That might be the ocean, I guess—just the salt part, anyway. But any man has salt. Each man has his own taste, I think, his own scent, beyond the salt."

"What's my scent?"

"You're deerskin."

"That's just what's on me—that's just my shirt. What else is there?"

"That's all there is, I think. I've been close enough to others to judge what else is underneath."

The men harassed him, Henry said. Once, on an afternoon in the barn, when he waited too long, afraid to step out, the storm too thick, afraid of losing himself, afraid of freezing somewhere in the yard not halfway to the cabin. Once, on a night along the creek, when he only wanted to drink fresh water. Once, in a cabin where he had gone to look for a lantern. Once, on the first spring afternoon, when the snow had melted to slush and receded from the sun, when the matted leaves mouldered and steamed, when the branches were budding in only the most protected groves.

A man's chin, cut by cold wind and raw with the scraping of a dull blade, smelled of iron—but that man also smelled of whiskey, of maple sugar candy. The back of a man's hand, strapped and scarred by leather, the hair singed away by flames, smelled of willow smoke—but that man also smelled of apples in a pan, blue calico singed by a flatiron. A man's ear, burned by frost, the black skin dense with congealed blood, smelled of tallow—but that man also smelled of lacquer on oak, lemon oil on pine. The knobs of a man's spine, worn purplish from a month in a sickbed, smelled of shaggy wool—but that man also smelled of boots heavy with spring mud, of straw blue with mold and drying in the sun.

Henry remembered a man laying his head on a horse blanket, and the white snowlight drifting in with the storm through the slatted weave of the barn walls, and the amber drops at the corner of the man's mouth, the chapped skin and lips flaked and peeling in red sheets, so that the liquor must have stung more than it soothed.

He remembered a man pulling from the fire the last of a meaty rib blackened by the flame, and the man's hand seemed to smoke as much as the rib he'd rescued, and he held it toward Henry, the blackness of his skin and the thick scent of beef and the way that scent hollowed Henry's gut. But Henry turned, out into the night, up to where the water flowed beyond the cattle's messing, and he cupped water, felt down in through the cold to the stones. He heard someone coming along the trail, and he caught the scent on the breeze, felt that hollow, crouched to pressure his gut against his thighs.

He remembered his own hand in the dim rife funk of a cabin, reaching for a lantern, taking the wire loop and lifting, letting it sway, listening to the fuel shallow in the reservoir, thinking of the hours that fuel might burn. Then the door opened and a man came in, hopped and danced toward what was left of the fire, tipped off his hat and let it fall, unwound a long soiled rag from his head, dabbed at his damaged ear.

He remembered finding his own footprints left from the

day before, his soles shaped in compressed ice, with the rest of the snow melted away from around those murky tracks. And there, a man he hadn't expected, a man shut in so long that they had expected never to see him in daylight again except at the bottom of a hole. But he was stripped, finding scraps of ice, dripping handfuls of slush, and rubbing his skin, turning himself from blue to pink.

And over the winter there were three men dead. The young one, Henry's age, went first, found dead in early fall, when the snow started, far up the northern valley in the spruce forest. Then Finn was found dead in his bunk at the end of a day on which the sky was so thick and low that no one had moved outdoors, the windows shuttered, the snow dusting through the seams. And then Mulford, kicked dead by a bull in a blizzard. Each man was laid out on a table, cleaned, prepared for burial. And, even so soon after death, with the heat in the room, the dead were already starting to lose whatever they had held inside their veins—the scent of lilac heavy with rain, of sumac with its spiked flowers as deep as dry blood, of cellar tins rusting, of whitetop bitter and tough, of sulphur pools and thermals, the scent of whatever ground they'd traveled, the beds of lava, the wheat, the black delta loam.

"I'm not thinking too good about getting to Fort Washakie tomorrow," Henry said. "Too many faces. I ain't ready to know nobody. What do I know of strangers? Maybe I don't know anymore how to know somebody I ain't lived with right through winter."

"You know me. We been through the same winter. The same sky. We traveled this same plain, a year ago."

"No. Not the same. I told you. You're deerskin."

Henry rolled in the blankets, curled away, but he let Walker follow, let him form against his back. Walker tried not to breathe, tried to settle, to let the air lie across him, let the last remnants of their voices sink into the ground and die. He felt the first of the next day's heat settling in with the night, moving over from the west.

"Listen to me," Walker would have said, but Henry was asleep. "This is what I see. Or remember." But he didn't know where he'd seen this. Or if he'd dreamed it.

The surface of the water steamed, the steam and the water as pale green as milky jade. Across the water, black rocks rose like islands, curved like atolls, and then the black shore cut with inroads of the green. There, below Walker's vantage, a man floated in the green, as if the color held him at the surface, as if there were no depth beneath him, no shadow around him. He was straight, his legs together, his face flat to the sky, arms slightly spread and stretched with the line of his body, palms up, his face in the crux of his unmoving form. No shift of his hands, no kick of his legs. For there to be such steam, the air must have been cold, the water warm.

Walker sat up in the space beneath the wagon. The east had grayed. There was smoke already. He looked for his trousers and boots among the empty blankets.

He saw the fire, the flames as high as Owen's waist, the skillet laid across the hot-burning sage. Owen carved what remained of the buck, and he tossed the scraps far into the brush—the skull with its hooked horns, the spine, the forelegs, a sheet of hide. Then the slips of meat hit the pan, and a hiss rose with a brown shot of steam and smoke.

Down by the stagnant pool, Henry worked at the horses with a brush, following the path of the bristles with his other hand, palm flat, smoothing and smoothing. He murmured, he leaned in against a horse's chest, he scratched their ears. Without turning from the animals, he said, in no more than a whisper in tune with his soothing notes, "Don't you burn that up, Daddy," and in that swale, with the ground chilled and the air warming, his voice was young and clear.

"I don't intend to."

Walker stood up from the wagon and pulled on his trousers, tried to keep his feet free from snow until he slipped into his boots. The snow had thickened and compressed to a layer of less than an inch. Each sagebrush was a lumpy white dome. He took a blanket around his shoulders and headed uphill to piss. He kept walking a ways until he gained the ridge. The peaks were high white, beginning to go pink with sunrise, and then his shadow started slim and scant across the snow, seemed no more than the natural gradation of the desert, the snow soaking in, and then the shadow sharpened, he felt the light against his back, he felt the heat, and he turned.

The sun rose through a perplexity of distance without cloud, the drainages flowing and angling into a maze of declines and mesas, the snow melted away not a mile or two down, long stripes of red earth, cuts of black, thin splinters of green, the speckle of brush, far ranges thrust like spines or broken ribs. Below him, in the swale, still in shadow, the odd small oblong pool of water centered a blue sky, and with the sky above and reflected below, with the plain falling toward the sun, with the early heat, it seemed to him that the surface of the earth there was as thin as the surface of the reflection.

He had walked farther than he'd thought. The horses were small, tied to the wagon. The men stood at the fire. The smoke looked dense in the shade, but when it rose into the light, it spread thin against the blue and dissipated. The morning was absolutely still. No movement of air or bird. The men's voices rose up.

"You sleep all right, Henry?"

"I always sleep all right. I told you."

"My hip is stiff. It cracks when I move."

"It was cold."

"Yes. But that's gone, or it's going, when the sun clears the ridge." Owen crouched, black against the fire, and fanned the flames with his hat. "I think we've got only a few miles to go today."

"Fort Washakie by noon, maybe?"

"Seems like it."

"Will we stay there for a day or two?"

"Just a few hours should do it. One night. We don't have time for visiting. There's plenty of time later."

"When we get to Cheyenne, we might stay there for a while, maybe?"

"What do you know about Cheyenne?"

"I don't know nothing. I just asked. I just said maybe. Maybe not."

"You don't know nothing about towns. There's not much you'd want to know, not about a town at the dead start of a territory."

"Then why'd you bring me? Seems like one of us should've stayed behind. Seems like the land ain't ours if one of us ain't standing on it."

"I wasn't going to leave you there." Owen stood, placed his hat back on his head, turned slowly and scanned the ridge, touched a finger to his brim when he came around to face Walker, and turned back to the fire. "That boy Avary. He's a sad little fellow, but he's got some skill."

"I could learn some things from him."

"Don't you go learning too much. We got the ranch. That's our business. There's room for his kind of business only so long."

"I know. I'd just learn what's useful." Henry looked back over his shoulder, up to Walker, looked back to his father. "You saw that girl of his, didn't you?"

"Pretty thing."

"We oughta known she was there all winter."

"It would've been our death to get up to his place."

"But she was pretty, you said?"

"Cute as a girl can be. Black as the devil."

"I would've seen her, if I could. See how she moves and all, you know. See what the men get out of her."

"A girl like that takes a bit of control. Any girl takes a bit."

"I wish I'd seen her. I been thinking about her, over and over. All I been seeing is those Illinois boys holding her, and her skin torn up."

"That's no good, son. I'm sorry if you got thoughts like that."

"Oh, I'm strong enough."

The sun angled down into the swale and caught them there. The snow was tracked all around the camp, centered on the fire circle, with the wagon tracks dragged through from the north, and muddy hoofprints, bootprints, and the snow stained where they'd thrown their refuse. Henry turned full-on to the sun, held his arms out, gathered the heat. Then he turned around, looked up toward Walker, and shouted, "You get down here. We got a ways to go."

"I'll be there directly," Walker said, no more than a plain voice, no shout.

Henry stood still a moment, then removed his hat and held it to his chest, seemed to look straight up into the open sky, looked again at Walker, said quietly, "All right," and turned away. The men crouched, poking around in the skillet. If they said anything else, Walker didn't hear them until he got all the way back down to the fire.

The road showed itself a half mile to the west, and they caught up to the twin lines. Two hours into morning the snow had mostly retreated, lingering in the shadows beneath the sage. Walker sat in the back of the wagon and watched the sun draw the snow away, the earth crack and curl. Sagebrush for miles. A snake slept in the sun, its shed skin a translucent crumple caught in the grass, its new skin as wet as drowned gems. And then they were beyond the snow altogether. East on the plain, a figure on horseback moved past recognition, and later another moved against the hills.

Walker watched how Owen's and Henry's coats steamed in the strong sun, or it was the dust the horses stirred that rose all around them. Finally both men took off their coats and dropped them into the back. Walker leaned forward and took the coats, folded each, stuffed them behind him, leaned against their cushion, protected his spine from the cut of the tailgate's edge. He smelled the smoke on the coats, the burned sage and pine worked right into the weave, and he thought of the fires in their cabins, the fires on the range, the stack of wood taking spark, the palms turned toward the flame, the crouch at the heat, the level of their shoulders, the distance that took the smoke.

"You boys watch yourselves when we get in at the fort,"

Owen said. "No telling what we might come up against. But it should be all right."

"We're set fine," Henry said.

"I don't see any problem," Walker said.

"That's all I want to hear," Owen said.

Long before they reached Fort Washakie they heard, buffeted on the wind, the discharge of a rifle, the crack of sharp objects, and, finally, shouts and horses. And then they came around a final steep hill, and, where just a year earlier there had been nothing, they saw the slow focus of activity, as if the dust of crushed leaves and the moulder of layered leaves along the river had taken to the air, taken life. There was a field of a hundred tipis, and the green clouds of cottonwoods along the Little Wind River, and the square whitewashed buildings, and lengths of unfinished fencing. The grass was thick and bunched.

They drove the wagon down the hill, forded a curve of the river, came up from the water with the horses prancing with the excitement of such a crowd. The road looped out among the tipis, crossed the river again, and headed back toward the fort. Children ran up naked, laughed, slapped the horses' flanks and sent road dust flying. South, at the settlement's fringe, a man in a fancy breechcloth and moccasins rode a tall black pony—against his thigh the man had planted a stick tall as a lance with a broad straw hat attached like a flag, a long yellow ribbon fluttering behind his gallop. Walker watched that man weave in among the tipis, his shoulders narrow and dark with sun, his grip on the pony no more than the shift of tendon beneath the skin, his lips pulled back from the intake of air, his eyes always focused just above or beyond whatever he saw. There were other men frozen in clusters, with their shadows converging behind them—some of them spoke softly, some of them seemed to sleep in the afternoon heat, some were nearly naked with their bare chests taut or slack, some were covered but for their arms and legs. There were necklaces, shells, metal rings, bear claws. There were beaded leggings, pouches, medicine bags, earrings. The women were off in the maze of shelters.

And then Owen pulled the wagon in toward the center of the fort, along the mowed parade ground, past the flagstaff with the flag loose in the breeze, down the line of warehouses, officers' and men's quarters, guardhouse, magazine, all in a state of construction, men working everywhere in blue uniforms or stripped to the waist. Square white headquarters tents on the lawn. The sounds of chopping, hammers, the whine of a horse-powered sawmill. Voices all in English, with a range of accents. Turkeys and chickens loose along the road and across the grounds. Owen stopped in front of the sutler's store. The cottonwoods reached high.

They all three climbed down from the wagon and stood in the brightness, Owen and Henry together, Walker around the back. Some men broke off from observing the nearest work and approached—the blue coats, the five bright buttons down the front to the U.S. buckle, a certain blankness to their attention, each man with a thick moustache carefully curled past the corners of his mouth, the ears prominent beneath the short-billed caps, a cream smoothness to the trousers as if each pair had been laundered and pressed. A few Indians waited in the nearest shade, watching. A sergeant stepped up, shook Owen's hand, saying, "What we got here, sir? You fellas starved to death?"

"We're down from the Wind River Valley."

"Ah, the cattlemen. Yes, sir. We been watching for you." He looked Owen and Henry over, looked past them at Walker leaning against the tailgate. "And what's with that prairie turnip?"

Walker looked down at his own limbs, at his deerskin, looked up at the sergeant, at his eyes small in their squint, at the round white slab of his face. He came around the back of the wagon, up to Owen's shoulder, up to the sergeant's shadow, almost reached a hand toward him but instead nodded, saying, "Avary."

"Eh?" The sergeant looked at Walker, tightened his squint, turned to Owen again. "Is he your scout or boy or what?"

"I got a lodge," Walker said, "up in the Wind Rivers."

"What's he saying?"

"This is Walker Avary," Owen said. "He's got a homestead started."

"You'll have to see the land office about that."

"Yes. We're headed to Cheyenne. He's helping us out."

"Well, that's friendly, ain't it?" The sergeant reached and brushed Walker lightly on the shoulder, saying, "Good for you, Avary," and took Owen by the elbow, started him toward the store. "Come on in. We'll get you comfortable, and I'll see if I can rustle the captain. We'll see how bad you're gonna treat us on this deal." The rest of the men split off, back to work.

Henry stood beside Walker, looked at Walker, said, "Go on in. Don't you want to?"

"You go on," Walker said.

"I gotta take care of the horses."

"No. I'll do that."

"You don't have to."

"Go on." He pushed at Henry. "I'll be along."

"You'll water them?"

"Sure."

"Brush them?"

"O.K."

"I wish you'd come in." Henry looked at the horses, looked into the wagon, looked at the sutler's store, the porch bare, looked past Walker to the Indians, took Walker around the shoulder. "The horses will be all right. Don't you want to come in?"

Walker ducked from under his arm, urged him on. "Follow your daddy. There's nothing out here I can't handle."

Henry said, "Sure," reached back and tapped Walker on the arm, said, "I'm just going to assure that we don't get took—we been made dumb by the wilds." He headed inside, in with the sergeant and Owen and the others.

Walker looked at that store, the planed whitewashed boards, the glass cut and fit, the porch smooth and still yellow, still not grayed by the weather, the sign above painted with neat black letters—GENERAL MERCHANDISE—and the walls around the windows painted with curling letters—Groceries, Fresh Lead, Hardware, Lumber, Spirits, Trade, Cigars & Tobacco, Flour & Feed, Furniture & Undertaking. Walker could enter across the porch, into the smell of sawdust, tin, leather. He listened. Nothing but the sound of construction, nothing in the windows but the reflection of the men far on the grounds. This building must have gone up quickly, it must be outfitted with shelves, cases, hooks in the rafters, a stove, a register, a safe. And the proprietor would be tapping at a ledger with a pen, the oil lamp slicing into the higher shadows, the creak of a chair settled beneath a man's weight, a drink to quench the miles, Owen's voice, a string of empty jokes about distance and trails and the welcome sight of such a wild profusion of goods, Henry taking hold of something—an apple, a spoon, a new hat unadorned—and testing its weight, stepping around behind Owen, watching Owen's hand on a glass of whiskey, the rise and tip of the liquid, looking across the store to the window and the day beyond, to the wagon, to Walker just now starting to attend the horses, Walker's head ducking behind the tall haunches, out of sight, leaving only the busy grounds and the store and Owen and the proprietor's voice working through the questions. How many head? Quality? The captain wants what you can give—I want what you can give. You're early. You're in time.

The Indians approached Walker from the shade, mostly older women and a few young men. Walker let them pass around him, concentrated only on the harness as he worked to loosen the buckles. They peered into the wagon, looking over the gear, as if there were anything worth trading for—rotten blankets, cups and plates, canvas—with the rifles secured in a latched box. Then they turned to Walker. The women came right up behind him, and he felt their fingers tracing his shirt seams. He looked down at the deerskin tanned and sewn by Mary, dark now with wear. The women's fingers came up his arms, across his shoulders, pressed at the base of his skull—he felt their blunt nails, the calloused fingertips. He turned to face them. They were around him, three of them, their eyes level with his. He looked into the wet blackness and saw only the reflected shape of the horses. Nodding, he brushed his palm down the front of his shirt. They spoke to him. They clicked their tongues against their teeth. They might have smiled, they might have frowned, but he could draw no emotion from their faces. He tried to separate words from the flow of sounds. Nothing. They pinched at his elbows, his chest, worked the hide between their fingers. They talked on. He watched their lips, the flat teeth, the nostrils calmly drawing air, the ears black with dirt, the hair too black and gray to reflect the afternoon heat, the great profusion of wrinkles multiplying with each move of the mouth or blink of the eyes, as if the women aged a year with each phrase uttered, the guttural singsong, as if they spoke right into him and stopped his blood. He turned away and released the harness.

He took a brush from the wagon and led the horses toward the Little Wind River in its tunnel of huge cottonwoods. When he came to the top of the bank, he looked down on an Indian boy standing naked and a knot of about a dozen ponies out in the water, lazing in the shallow flow about their legs. Walker led the two horses down, and the ponies looked at them nervously a moment before turning back to their own. He let out the leads and the horses stepped down and nuzzled the surface of the water, exhaled, throwing spray, and started to drink. He dropped the leads, backed away, and squatted on his haunches. The boy did likewise. They both crouched there with the mountain flow coming down through the channel and the horses calm and obedient.

Walker could see an edge of the Indian camp above the bank, the tipis tall and taut, with smoke hazing up through the bundles of peeled poles. Each tipi faced east, and Walker thought of what the entrances opened to each morning, the sun sweeping up from the horizon. Some of the hides were rolled up the poles to allow the afternoon to blow through. A woman fished hot stones from a fire pit, placed them down into a willow basket, and steam rose. Her tipi was painted with thick-necked horses circling endlessly, the men tiny on the horses' backs or falling beneath an attack.

Walker looked at the boy, nearly a young man. "You come in here from out there someplace?" Walker said, sweeping his arm east toward the plains. The boy looked at him—the dark flat face not yet worn by the sun—and nodded, remained silent, so that Walker couldn't know if the boy had understood. He looked at the boy's bare feet, his shoulders thin and a little hunched, his hair smooth and caught with thistles.

The boy could have been Mary's brother—the same small sad features, thin wrists, darkness of skin. Difficult to imagine the parents, difficult to translate the hardness of the adults in the camp into the delicate, unconcerned litheness of the boy or the girl. The boy's forearms crossed, his hands hung limp, his skin worked across his ribs with his breathing, his genitals loose in a shadow of fine black hair, his lips pursed and relaxed with thought and the slow shift of his eyes. If the boy had slept in a shelter with Mary, he would have heard the vague whistle of her breathing, and the same sound might have vibrated his own skull. If the boy had followed Mary through those mountains, she would have dressed him in hides, leggings, a breechcloth to contain him, the same hides she had tanned and sewn for Walker, the same soft warmth and even stitching. When had the boy left her? It could have been a year, it could have been five. Perhaps the boy had been taken with the sickness and left for dead. Perhaps he'd fled one way and Mary the other, and his final sight of her had been of a dark slash quick against snow, climbing to a pass. In any case, he had lost her. Maybe he had looked for her, listened for her, followed spring and summer to the camps at higher elevation, followed the trails along the highest ridges, followed the bighorn sheep to their farthest echo, the slippage of fresh-cut stone to a field of scree a thousand feet below, followed each ridge to its finality at the spine of the range, and from there the world circled in all directions and faded away into other ranges, rivers, barren plains, cloud.

The boy hurried down from that absolute view, descended through the defiles, left the trails he had learned without thought, left the last stark hopeful echo of Mary's voice, came out onto the plain, and found this tribe. There were battles. There was love. He wandered the plains east. And then he came back around to this fort, back to the shadow of the mountains again.

Walker pointed toward the mountains. "You know anything of that range?" No response. So he tried to use Mary's words. "You know Tukudeka?"

"Kucundika," the boy said, looking east.

"Engaa," Walker said, pointing again at the mountains.

The boy stood, came over to Walker, reached down and held Walker by the shoulder, gripped his shirt and tugged until it cut across Walker's throat. "Engaa?" the boy said. "Dayiane?"

Walker pulled his shirt back from the boy's grasp, but the boy stepped closer, his legs straddling Walker's shoulder, pinning him there in his crouch. The boy pinched Walker's ear, tipped his head to the side, his prick grazed Walker's chin and pressed there, the boy hunched toward Walker's ear and spoke in a sharp whisper. The sounds were Mary's, the flow of syllables, and he spoke for five minutes or more, the long flow of a story, it seemed, and through it, through the rise and fall, the kicks of consonant and the images vaguely rhythmic, unshaped blunt force and miles of ground without relief, without shade, Walker had the boy's skin wrapped around him, pressed against him, that scent a scent he knew, the body's oils sheening the dark skin, mixing with the pulverized dust of the territory.

And then the boy kicked back from Walker, and Walker caught his balance, stood up brushing pebbles from his palms, and the boy had climbed the bank, the sudden sloshing of his ponies in a slow move to follow. The boy entered into the willows, the branches long and sprung and orange and taking him against his sides, along his legs, snapping back with his passage, wriggling in his wake.

———

When Walker led the horses up from the river, he found a private sitting at the front of the wagon. The sutler's store was still blank, the door open to shadow. There was still the sound of hammering, and now the smell of cooking from somewhere across the parade ground.

The young man on the wagon tipped his hat to Walker and said, "Your friends have gone over to meet the captain. I chased those Indians for you. They was likely to make off with some of your gear."

"Maybe you ain't seen what gear I have in there."

"If those Indians was waiting for you, you could find them." He pointed toward the camp.

"Why would they be waiting for me?"

"I saw they was with you before you went off. They'll come back, I guess, or you could go looking, if you want them."

"If they want me, they can find me."

"All right. I just thought I should chase them." He climbed down from the wagon, took one of the horses' leads from Walker, and started into the trees. "This way. I got an order to corral 'em."

Walker followed with the other horse. They passed among the cottonwoods. There was a stretch of empty tins already deep in grass—rust, jagged edges, red and white and black labels—and green bottles, strips of cloth, leather, the broken hubs of wheels. Then wild roses, the dark leaves and pale spines, the new flowers starting pink. Magpies scared from the trees, swooped and dipped ahead through the shade, then found an opening to the sky, and their fretful aag-aag-aag circled above the leaves. Between the gray cottonwood trunks, a few empty hammocks strung, and, between the final trees, laundry lines with white sheets abandoned to the falling sun.

They came out from the grove, to a fence, a long paddock with a good fifty head of horses scattered, grazing. "In here," the private said, and he opened the gate, they led the horses in, set them loose, slapped their flanks, and left them to graze the slender wheat grass and brome. The private shut the gate, said, "Come on," and started along the line of the fence, toward the far corner, the shade of a broken stand of birch and silverberry in the middle of open green. Walker followed. "When you want your horses back, you tell me," the private said. "I'll get them for you."

As they made their way a good half mile down the side of the paddock, a quarter mile along the far end, the sounds of the fort faded, caught in the long strips of trees that cut the plain. Walker heard the private's boots creaking with each step, the rustle of grass, the give of the earth where the ground was wet. Slowly, Walker found focus on a man leaning against the fence at the corner, waiting there, smoking, watching the shadows stretch and swing behind the horses. Walker and the private came up to him.

The man nodded a greeting without hardly looking at Walker, and then he pulled a pouch from his jacket and took his time rolling a cigarette, sealing it with a dainty tip of his tongue and a quick slide of his thumb. He passed the cigarette to Walker, who took it, held it to his lips, leaned to accept the light. He inhaled and felt the smoke tingle the back of his neck. The private went around the man to the far angle of the fence, and they both faced Walker, hung their weight on the top pole, their arms up like wings. "I'm Hawkins," the private said. "And this is Mitchell."

Walker looked at the crumple of their collars, the loose dangle of their buttons. They were no older than he was, maybe younger, maybe Henry's age. Mitchell watched the distance, his rifle leaned against his leg, and his eyes roved and paused, roved and paused, bleared by the rise of smoke from his nostrils. Hawkins chewed the corner of his moustache.

Mitchell let his cigarette butt fall, and he raised onto his toes, looked down over the fence, watched the grass where the butt had fallen, saw no smoke, and relaxed. He rubbed his pursed lips with a fingertip, looked at Walker, and said, "We're stuck here. We don't want to be stuck here. We been thinking of all those empty miles north and west, but we ain't sure about safety." They both nodded at Walker, seeming to urge him to take another drag.

"You've been up in the Winds," Hawkins said. "You've been out there." He tipped his head back toward the mountains.

Walker squinted into the sunlight. Past the men, past the trees, the mountains were vague and flat—not much more than scenery, hazed blue for effect. "Yes. I've been."

"And you ain't been in any bad straits?" Hawkins said.

"From what?"

"Indians."

"Nope."

"So," Hawkins said, "you know Indians and trails and the mountains, is that right?"

"What I know about Indians you could put in one eye. But maybe I know something of the Winds. Or, more exactly, I know just one creek, straight up as far as you can go."

"Uh-huh," Mitchell said. He nodded and let his arm slowly stretch till his fingers grazed Walker's sleeve. "You're an Indian countryman, sure as shit," Mitchell said. "Hawkins spotted you from clear the other side of the grounds."

"I'm no special countryman. No more than anyone. No more than you boys, probably, with a little time. Where'd you boys come in here from, anyway?"

"I got on at Cedar Rapids," Hawkins said.

"Louisville."

"You got any kin?"

"I got a mama and three sisters and seven cousins and what all else," Mitchell said.

Hawkins shrugged. "I got 'em, but if I knowed 'em half way, do you think I'd be here?"

"What got you signed on?"

"I don't know," Mitchell said. "I was thinking of something else, I guess." He seemed to focus out into the paddock, stood up straight, pointed toward the herd. "I tell you, if any trouble stirred up around here, if there was some serious cover, I'd take that roan and be gone."

"Where to?"

"Aw." He scratched his head and settled again. "That's our problem."

"We've been thinking," Hawkins said. "If we get that chance to take a jaunt, we might go up into the Winds. There's got to be a path that wouldn't bring us back down here. And there's got to be a way to get something out of those mountains. Last month, we got a trapper came down out of Popo Agie, told us he saw gold and a diamond big as a cabbage."

"Oh, sure," Walker said. "And waltzing elk. And the squirrels play Shakespeare."

"Ha," Hawkins said. "Damn."

"We could pay you, maybe, or work something out," Mitchell said. "You could keep us safe, couldn't you?"

Owen neatened up the wagon. He piled in some new supplies, and he tossed on the ground the ruined clothes and whatever else looked beyond repair. He wore brown trousers tucked into tall black boots, and a striped shirt buttoned to the neck, and a wool vest, and a hat still stiff and unsettled. In the shade beside the store, as if the store's shadow were a curtain closing him against the white wall, Henry was naked, dancing around on the thistles, pulling on his new clothes. His shirt was plaid, and he buttoned it slowly, smoothing the cloth against his chest.

"You look at these," Owen said, handing Walker a stack of clothes topped with new boots.

Walker riffled through the stack, felt the fineness of the cloth, the plaid like Henry's, the weight of the leather, said, "Thank you, sir," and placed them down in the wagon.

"We got signed on to supply this post with beef," Owen said. "I took a draw on my roll, and I ordered a whole wagon of supplies sent up to the men. You can change into your clothes over there with Henry."

"No need for such nice clothes. I don't have any appointments or anything."

"I thought you might want something new before that deerskin crumbles away. That's all."

"Who'd know me?"

From beyond the barracks, from the edge of the trees, Owen and Henry and Walker were called to supper with the men —a meal of venison, turnips, potatoes, bullberry pie. And filtering in with the troops, from wherever they'd been hiding or trekking for the day, were more than a dozen travelers, trappers, a top-shelfer and his servants pausing on an expedition. As if they were at some odd male social, they all sat at long tables, the uniforms and the random others, all trying to engage each other in a laugh, passing the bowls and heavy platters.

These men were all on their way into something, or out of something, all new to the territory, and each had imagined Wyoming as no more than a series of points and names and ideas from a map—north and west, tribes, game, paper mountains, Chugwater, Pumpkin Butte, McDougall's Gap, Lead Creek, Murphy's Ranch. What else could they have known about Wyoming? They had sat in a chair at a window above a forest of elms and oaks and a sliced view of a lake and swans cruising the inlet, or they had sat in a chair at an inn where the low ceiling had accumulated two hundred years of rich brown glaze from pipe smoke and fire smoke and candle smoke and the roads had ground themselves so deep into the earth that you could scarcely miss them much less crawl up out of them over the well-fitted height of stone walls, or they had sat in a chair and listened to winter spark against the panes. They had dreamed. They had sketched their own trails across a map. They had scratched through a name like Lead Creek, obscuring it with their own details—gray water bubbled down a stone staircase, and then the grass and white-lace flowers filled in, and odd birds with sharp red beaks and wings that opened like huge hands, trees in perfect pine rows, mountains as steep and flat as a framed etching, buffalo on the ridge as dark as thunderheads. Then the final shift of thought into claim, purchase, walls constructed and sealed, seasons washing over a roof like time or music or the sweep of a hand, and the night silent and empty beyond the windowpanes. To all that world and dreaming they had now begun to attach distance and fear.

A few Indians strode through the dinner gathering, and they seemed to be on their way somewhere, but they always turned back in and crossed again. Walker saw the medals some of those Indian men wore—the profile of Jefferson or Jackson or Madison. Dark with handling, the medals hovered there on lengths of twine, glancing against the center of each chest.

Out in the evening sun, at the edge of the parade ground, a large white hospital tent had been erected, and its walls filled and strained with the breeze, the flaps on one side tied open. Inside was a long table draped with an American flag, with chairs arranged on one side and the other. The officers milled about in there. When a group of elders approached from the nearest tipis, the officers took their seats behind the table. The Indians entered, took their seats opposite the officers. The flap ties were loosened, and the entrance closed.

The evening lowered through the trees and stilled the breeze. When the meal was finished, the enlisted men moved off to their duties, and the rest of the men gathered toward one end of the tables, pulled out their flasks and bottles. Walker sat at the base of a cottonwood with Owen and shared his whiskey. Henry shared from the top-shelfer's silver flask, listening to the man's broken story, half German—a wrecked train, a nine-foot grizzly that took five shots, a tent that sailed far out over a ledge in a howling gust, and how that tent floated gently to the river below, the white canvas swallowed in the white rapids. The men drank until the day's lost heat settled in the gut.

The hospital tent glowed with lantern light. No one had entered or left for over an hour. They were talking in there, or translating something, or smoking, or eating whatever had been prepared, the venison, or a mash of roots, or potatoes, or cakes of fat, or dried berries, or bullberry pie.

Henry and the top-shelfer's servants built a fire at the edge

of the trees, and the flames darkened the sky, smoking out
the first stars. Up into the cottonwoods, shadows moved the
branches, the leaves fluttering.

Owen brought an envelope out from his shirt pocket and
handed it to Walker. "I've got ideas about our valley," he
said. "That's a letter for Sarah, to be posted directly from
Cheyenne, and maybe by this fall or next spring she can find
someone to bring her on around. You go on and read it, if
you want. Tell me what I left out."

Walker tipped open the crumpled envelope and pulled out
the letter. He held the pages up against the fire, and the light
leaked through the thin paper, setting out the words. The
handwriting was a straight scratching of ink without spatter.

*—with a spot for a decent house shaded from the summer heat,
although the heat might be welcome at this elevation, and the
sound of the creek. You will approve, I think, Sarah, of the plot
we have set out for the garden. The soil does not seem rich at
first, but it sustains already a great profusion of wildflowers and
thickets of shrubs heavy with berries. It will be no problem to put
up enough preserves just from what you can gather within a
stone's throw. Henry and I miss your handiwork. We get by
passably, and Henry has learned to bake a beautiful round loaf
of bread, but the service is lacking your niceties, as is all else in
our bachelor living.*

*There is nothing here yet, Sarah, although I have made it
sound as if we are settled. At the confluence of this creek and the
Wind River I would not be surprised to find a town in a few
years. The valley has much to offer a cattleman with a bit of
patience. At the moment, the only other white man within a hundred miles is a serious young man who has built a lodge up in
the Wind River Mountains. You would love the spot he has and
the job he has done with it, and the pretty Indian girl he has with
him. We are hoping that others of his mettle will take to the valley
soon.*

*It was a winter I could have used you, Sarah, although I
would not have put you through it. The wind sometimes blew for
a week straight, with the darkness thick from the storm clouds,
and it was all we could do to hold on to the bulk of what we had*

started. Our rations were low almost from the first day; I had misjudged how much food it would take to stay warm and working through such hardship. All that went wrong is my fault, of course, and I worry every day about what I might have done different. We have graves already. We have mounds of stone where the young cottonwoods circle and the grass is full of purple aster. That would be Grant and Mulford and Finn; perhaps you remember them hiring on. Grant was not yet nineteen, Henry's age, and he had the sweetest blue eyes and not much of a beard, he was scrawny and strong, and he was always taking his mama's name in vain. Finn had a way with a complaint, as if he were chewing on something sour. Mulford had come all the way around to these mountains, he had a wife and three girls left in some town where they had real civilization, he told us, and he had a thought in that gray head of his that he would get in on the beginning of something, but I do not know where to send his wages, and truth be told I do not even have his wages yet. At this point it is only the love of God and an idea of what we have learned that keeps me from falling into despair. But that is done, and we will not be surprised by this mountain winter again. The young man with the lodge saw himself and his girl through without even the succor of another Christian to share his prayers. I dread to imagine these mountains without a loved one near.

You will arrive, Sarah, and in no time, you will see, this empty territory will be bustling. Come with me, if you can, in your dreams, if I am still clear to you. We have finished our supper, it is the height of summer, the shade is cool beneath the trees, the creek is fast. You are wearing your pale yellow dress with the white buttons, and the hat with the black ribbon. You are younger than you have been in many years; it is the air here that freshens your step and your smile. We harness the team and take to the road, and in less than an hour we see the town spread along the river. And there will be the hotel, the saloon, the mercantile, and all the men and women we have come to know— you must place their faces and their names as you will, because I have been too long from a crowd to imagine the wonderful feel of a room full of laughter and women and smoke. But there will be a doctor, I guess, in his black suit-coat, and a banker with his *gold eye-glasses, and our son Henry with his new bride. It does not take a dream to guess that our fine boy will find himself a girl of great worth, and she will be lucky to awake to these mountains. There is music and dancing and then the long drive back to the ranch with your hand on my thigh and my hands on the reins.*

And one day, when the valley has changed and these times have moved on, I will take you to Walker Avary's lodge, the lodge of which I have spoken, and we will stay for a week with nothing but that lakeshore to wander. He will have cabins, I am sure, in against the trees, and at dusk the elk will descend from the aspens and pause at the water—

Walker folded the letter, turned it over in his hands, studied it for smudges and fingerprints, but it was clean. He replaced it in the envelope, held it up to the firelight again, saw how the thickness of the folded pages darkened the center of the flimsy envelope, and nothing of the words shone through. He handed the letter back, and Owen slid it into his shirt pocket and held his hand there, pressing at his chest.

"You think that will do, Walker?"

"It's all right, sir."

"I want you to know you're part of the valley."

"I know I am, sir."

Owen passed the whiskey. "Maybe you want that Indian girl of yours for your wife?"

"No, sir. I can't claim her."

"It seems that she'd be as good a wife as any. Then you'd be squarely settled. I've been thinking—maybe I didn't know what she was when you first showed her to us."

"No, sir. You knew. You knew better than me."

At that moment, an hour after sunset, Walker thought of his lodge in darkness with only the vague trail up from the Wind River. Would he find it again? He had thought once that he could almost smell his way into that valley with eyes closed. At that minute, in the mountains, did it rain? Did the wind cut from the peaks? Did a grizzly claw an aspen? Did Walker's mule sleep itself through dreams of desert? Did a mountain lion trace the ridge, pause and yowl at a scent?

From inside the lodge someone might stand at the window, hear that yowl, and wish the shutters were secured against that sound, against the void of the lake, against the way the stars dove deep through the water.

Walker laid out in his mind the maps he'd followed. The crinkle of charts. The Rockwell hold, the unfolding of the continent he held inside his shirt, against his skin. The railroad pamphlet, more advertisement than lore. The map the Chins had sketched and falsely annotated. His own maps spidered with bits of memory. The words of the Sheepeater girl stringing trails toward game, trails toward shelter, trails toward wildflower.

A man yelled. A rifle discharged somewhere out across the parade ground. A man grabbed a passing Shoshone girl by the ankle, she kicked him in the teeth and ran off, and he slumped, blood draining down his chin. "I got a woman," he said, dabbing at his mouth with the back of his hand. "That's not the girl I need. I don't want her."

Around the fire, one man and another took a story off toward its first interruption or challenge. They talked of the vacant miles covered, always veering off roads, away from forts, away from the certain and inevitable sight of pioneers with their tidy homes on wheels, their tablecloths, their frills in need of a good launder, their daughters staring mutely ahead. They veered toward the defiles and groves, the swamps of skunk cabbage, the water lilies dappling the black pond, the moon and lodgepole pine, the aspens gold and full of uncertain noise, the rivering lines and swirls in the gneiss, the columbine and bluebells in beds of fern, in beds of boulders crusted with yellow lichen, the tundra meadow stiff and undaunted beneath a summer storm, the prairie smoke, old man's whiskers, whitebark pine, primrose, sunflower, monkey flower, glacier lily, yellow-orange spikes of butter-and-eggs, clustered red berries of mountain ash, alpine laurel. A man was treed by a sow grizzly watching its cub, another was treed by a cow moose watching its calf. The moose grazed the willow breaks in widening circles. The grizzly stripped berries better left for a human's supper. The treed men thought of the creek where it soured from the heat of a spring, the lean of a rifle left in camp, the last hot shave, the smell of a barber's pomade, the cougar tracks lost that morning, the sage grouse stewed with onions and biscuits, the stack of stiff hides and severed trophies loaded onto a train with the boss's trunks, the elk's bugle. And they talked of a grass fire taking the miles to every side, ash in the sop, a corpse hooked in the shade of a tree-line fir, the night sounds of the wampus cat, a two-day sick on bad tulapai, devil visions from leopard sweat, a spring flood, a no-way treaty Indian making off with hoss and beaver.

And then a hunter named Cootie went on with a tale he'd started at dinner. "—over the pass into the Powder River, and we got a camp set, and our man is going over the outfit and asking things about woodcraft, and when he thinks he's got it all in mind he takes his skinny English stock of a rifle and goes off to test his bottom sand. Me and Edd sat a full day on our duffs, and then we went looking for elk."

"Hey, Coot, ain't that a English stock I seen sticking butt-end from your roll?"

"I come to own it, yes. It's a nice rifle. But, I tell you, some mean stuff camped on our man's trail." Cootie told how he and Edd came back into camp a few days later and saw that Englishman's horse loose among the trees, his rifle in the dirt, and there were tracks all through the camp, the horse was stiff with old caked sweat and cut on the forelocks and the blood was long dry. They studied the tracks close— they were wolf prints and their man's boots—and the tracks all went off into the trees and rocks. They searched awhile, they yelled out the man's name till it wouldn't echo no more, and then they cooked some supper. They built up the fire after dark and sang some songs loud, thinking how the man liked those sad songs they sang, and they waited for the moon.

A huge moon came into the pass, the globe squeezed between the sheer slopes, the moon's whiteness so clearly traced with gray that they could nearly discover the ranges and paths and canyons that wandered there, and the moon seemed to be trailing right down into the camp, and down with it came their man. He was naked and gray, his haunches low, his strides planted long and uncentered, he was running faster than they could grab, and then he was gone on by, and they didn't see him again.

With sunrise, they tried to follow his trail. They got only a mile of tracks and then he was onto the rocks and lost. Back up at the pass they found his shirt that he'd torn off, or it had been torn from him, and they figured he'd been bitten by a mad wolf.

"Look here," Cootie said. "Our Englishman saw himself ready. We was just his hunters, Edd and me, and we wasn't going to push him one way or the other."

"Ain't that what he paid you for, you and Edd, paid you for pushing him the right way?"

"We ain't promised the man a single thing."

"And you paid in full."

The men talked on about England and money, and Walker watched the way the teller always turned toward the fire, the light of the flames flashing across his teeth. He saw England with big rolling fields all mowed, and old stone walls swallowed up in hedges, and the forest like a garden, and white marble statues of maidens crouched by a pool, and nothing more fierce than a sparrow or a mole. And then the Englishman hops a ship with his trunk and his sporting rifle and he sees the white cliffs eaten by the sea, and then he sees nothing till New York, and then he takes to the plains. One day's horizon is more than he's traveled in a life. In Cheyenne or some such town he goes looking for a hunter, and they all come up to him to get a free drink and tell their story, and he tries to take their measure though he doesn't know enough to judge the wear of a man's boots much less judge the truth of battles with father grizzly or bare scrapes with the red man, so he chooses a hunter based on the ripe smell of the man or because of some lie.

"We all know you, Cootie—you ain't a bargain, but you talk good. And your Edd there seems a cute little chap."

So the Englishman took his jaunt from Cootie and Edd, built his fires, caught sight of a moose or an eagle, shot at whatever seemed edible, probably hit something, probably ate a bit of stringy charred squirrel, breathed the mountain air, felt the hollow of his stomach, and found his way back to camp thinking he'd got a start on the wilderness. The camp was empty. The fire pit was dead. He sat there with the cold evening whistling the trees and the ashes kicking up and the snapping of the tent flaps and the constructed solidity of the wagon with its rusty iron fittings and the crumple of tins with their peach-sugar innards crawling with ants and the dry scatter of paper trash and the kick-broken firewood stacked beside a boulder and the absence of any breathing thing but his horse and himself, and even then he could no longer hear his own breathing or feel his heart. He waited as the hills took the sun down into cloud and a high pink spread quickly and vanished. He waited as the stars fell through the gaps in the clouds. And then the clouds filled in.

He tried to separate out the darkness, but it seemed to come as much from his own sight as from the night. He couldn't get himself to light a fire. He couldn't get himself to light a candle and search for the stores, lay hands on his money, loose the soft folds of the map, palm his watch from its felt bag, find the ammunition—it might all be gone, spirited off. He tried to think his way on into the territory, but where he should have pictured the pattern of the map, the elevations and vistas each labeled and aligned, he saw only the weight of black night filling a blank square. He could not force an image of contour or river or evergreen. He tried. He found he could not even see his home or smell its woody dampness. Somewhere through the pass the moon rose, so padded in dense cloud that its light seemed no more than a slate tuft shifting through storm. Rain fell in misty drops.

Walker roused. Some of the men had wandered toward the sutler's store to find more drink. A man dropped an armload of sticks on the fire with a burst of sparks. A man rubbed his back against a tree trunk. A man gave his beard a fierce scratch.

The hospital tent flaps opened, a sudden flash of the white walls and the suspended globes of light. The elders and the officers all moved about for a minute, the faint voices, the stiff blue and the sashes and fringe and pale robes, and then they emerged in pairs, pursuing their own shadows. They split onto two paths and made for the fires in the camp or the buildings with their heat behind glass. In the tent, a man closed the flaps behind the last officer, and one by one the lanterns doused, leaving the tent gray and ungrounded.

The night was cold. Walker took the last swallow from Owen's bottle and stood, steadied himself against the tree, looked down at Owen, held the bottle down to him. Owen grasped it, tipped it against the firelight, tossed it away.

The talk went on at the fire. There was Henry, the light white against his teeth, and the stories he told, the drowned beaver den, the dead mother and kits as flat as the flat tail, and the northern sky glowing green, and the horned owl that clipped his hat. The men pushed him.

"Shit. That's all you got to tell?"

"What are you hunting?"

"I know about pasture," Henry said. "I know about grazing." His eyes were wide, almost blank, above his smile.

Off through the trees, with the firelight shadows lengthening, accumulating one across another, Walker headed for the river. Someone came in against him, a bottle pressed between them as the man took him around the shoulders and said, "I'm watching your horses for you." It was Hawkins, pulling Walker in a circle, and they stumbled against a tree. He brought the bottle to Walker's mouth and fed him a gulp.

Walker coughed through the burn, and another arm circled him, they all rolled around the tree, the roots lurching them shoulder to chin to brow. It was Mitchell. He said, "*I'm* watching your horses. Hawkins here is watching the road to the north."

Walker stopped them, held them to the tree with his arms

up across them, his head pressed into one chest or the other. In the darkness, he had only the smell of them, the wool, and the muscled bulk so much beyond him. "Shouldn't you get on back to your duty?" Walker said. "Didn't I see the brig they've started building?"

"Oh," Mitchell said, "we got the evening. Truly. We're making our own trouble. Nothing to worry." He slid down the tree, taking Hawkins and Walker with him, and in that shifting tangle Walker found himself pinned.

"I got a cache out here," Hawkins said.

"He can't find it, is all."

"No. I'm just not there yet. I'm on my way to get there. Gotta be sure I ain't giving it away to no one. Listen to this, Avary." He took Walker by the ear, pulled Walker's head up onto his chest, hugged him there, a brass button pressing a cold dent onto Walker's temple. "I got rope. I got tins of fruit. Tobacco. Socks. Bullets. What do you think of beads?"

"I don't think of beads."

"For the Indians."

"I think I could say for half-sure that if you're worried about hostile Indians, beads won't do it."

"I *told* him that." Mitchell laid his hand on Walker's back, and Walker felt nearly covered.

Hawkins stroked Walker's hair. "Don't you worry," he said. "I didn't take none of your gear."

"If he did," Mitchell said, "he'd be bringing it back to you. Ain't that right, Hawkins?"

"That's right, Mitchell."

They went silent, holding him.

Walker didn't move. He was woven with those two young men, his legs twisted, his arms caught. He opened his eyes. He closed them. He was unsure if he looked up or down, toward the river or away. He was unsure of the softness that pillowed him, of the knobs of bone that curved his spine, that splayed his legs. He thought his way along his limbs, found his left hand twisted against a rough surface, the palm tingling, the fingers curved or straight, no certain pain, found his feet stretched with the stretch of his legs, cold in the damp leather, tendons thick with night and drink, found his right hand warm with a pulse.

Hawkins and Mitchell were still now. Perhaps they saw the firelight far off through the trees. Perhaps they had been so long in the night that they saw the river where it cut the grove, saw stars in the water. Mitchell's hand was a weight on Walker's back, Hawkins's hand settled now on Walker's ear, closing Walker's hearing down into their bodies. Walker heard the cunning quaver of their blood, the hoarding of acid and bile, the pooling in vessels as opaque as etched glass, the percolation through shafts wreathed with muscle, airways varnished with old pollen, a drift of milt, a fossil pearl gathered on an irritation, a rub. And he heard them speak.

"I've been target shooting. I've got a steady shot that takes the center every time."

"I've been dressing the game the hunters bring. I've got a pile of antlers taller than my shoulder. Heavy, those branching spikes."

"I ride patrol, down as far as Camp Brown, out to sunrise, into salt flats and pools of oil. I've gone up into the hills, cut the trees, seen elk on the next ridge, always the next ridge."

"In the desert we got miles with nothing but riding and the dust, then the desert well, that rope cranked down into the hole, the splash and the bucket raised, and they fill the barrels before they let us drink, and then they fill the barrels again. Some poor soul dug that well. The red dirt is all stirred and mounded around the hole. No Indian dug it. I don't know if I saw a bit of surface water in a hundred miles—just saw the green way down a draw, a big shit cottonwood in the next valley over, an hour off trail, or the little drop of aspen far up a slope, and the aspen fringed with pine, and then stone and the barest scrub. There's water under that slope, under the dry layer, to feed those aspen, you know. You can feel the cold water in those white aspen trunks. You feel the water in the shade."

"I saw a wall of split rock above the Sweetwater, and the

river in pasture. I could've dove into the green. Sweet. I saw ice in a buried swampy creek, right into summer, ice right down in the grass."

"We sleep in the tent with no wall from the night but the flapping canvas. With that canvas noise you don't hear nothing else. Just the wind getting stronger or dying off."

"I don't want to hear the Indian camp out there. The voices. The babies. I'd just as soon hear the wind dying."

"I hear Hawkins turn on his cot. I know the weight of him on the frame. I know the time he takes from one turn to the next turn. I know how he holds the blanket in his fist."

"When there ain't a moon, Mitchell talks in his dreams. He saw a rock like a chimney. He saw a bear like a man."

"I hear Hawkins turn and try to get comfort. His joints pop. I know the heat on his skin when his joints have been working."

"Mitchell saw a lion swipe a buck out of the air. He saw a cliff of ice where the trail oughta be."

"We might get on from here."

"We might get up into the Winds."

"We might get so far into the Winds that there ain't a trail a man could find to bring us down."

"The Indians have a lace of trails down here. We have a full trace going on their trails."

"They have this whole plain tapped."

"They don't stop for water nowhere that I can see."

"Can you hear them?"

Silence again. Walker heard their breathing. His ear was cold. Hawkins's hand had slipped away.

Then he heard voices, the high laugh of breaking glass. Or it was nothing. Or it was something he'd heard before, and it had found him—a sound following from a thousand miles, ten thousand miles.

But he heard the settle of the birds, their heads tucked beneath the wing. He heard the cold dampened by the river. He heard the leaves waiting to shine in the sun, great rafts of light. He heard the plain's deep fissures, and the water caught in darkness, and the sigh where the water rose.

"What ideas do you have for leading us, Avary?"

He pulled himself up from them, he was out from their heat, he heard their voices follow him, saw the echo of their voices illuminate clearly for him each obstacle, each trunk and root, as if their voices were nothing but light shining. But then, beyond their sound, he still moved fast, safe, down to the river, along the bank. Through the willows the plain opened, the shelters, the white cones, the smoke in a hundred thin trails, and in the dark night the tipis seemed to float, seemed to rise or fall, the glow of each nearly amber, nearly quartz, nearly pure light and symmetry stretching away, without anchor.

He went along. Some shelters were sealed, some open. He saw flame. He saw a man preening, hunched over himself. He saw women asleep. He saw the horses fly on those white hides.

Then a man was against him, taking hold of him. He turned, tried to turn away, found himself far out in the camp, and each direction, each escape, seemed to trail deeper into the white constellations. The man smelled of smoke and sage. Walker spoke a string of sounds. Mary's sounds. The man's hair was plaited, long, woven with something brittle, grass or the spines of feathers. He touched the man's ear, ran a finger down the man's smooth chin, down the neck to the shoulders. The man's chest was lumped with scar. The man's legs were smooth and corded. The man held to Walker, held his ear to Walker's sounds. He nuzzled into Walker's long hair, seemed to chew, to taste. He fingered in through the gut-woven seams of Walker's shirt. He brushed at Walker's lips, at the stubble. He spoke back into Walker's mouth. He had hold of Walker's waist, and Walker was above the ground, the man's nails scraping at him, the sharp grip drawing blood. The tipis hovered and began to flow, back and away, and through the gaps in the hides Walker saw turtles and drums, a wing still muscled and tight with feather, shawls, skulls, patterns of diamond and cross and square, pouch and bone, bowls and robes, flame and skin, the link and thrust, the quiver, the anklet, the amulet, the shell and bead.

Walker imagined the Englishman flat on the rocks with his
clothes torn away, his fingernails burrowed into lichen, the
ache of the wolf's gash growing up his leg, conducted
through his bones. There was nothing in that night but the
memory of the pursuit, the blackness, the jaws, until he
caught the bristled trunk of a tree and felt its branches take
him under the arms and lift him, and finally the wolf abandoned him. Cootie gone. Edd gone. There had been another
day since then, his hands slowly drawing in tight until they
were as clenched as claws, the sun in hot streaks through the
clouds, the air seeming to burnish, to reflect finally only silver,
his vision so honed that he thought the edge of each tree and
stone and cloud might be sharp enough to cut. He thought
he could taste wolf on his tongue. His skin vibrated as if each
sound struck the head of a drum.

He was near the cottonwoods, almost beneath the high branches. He heard the overlap of the serrated leaves. The Little Wind River drew from the mountains' spine. He heard the stones grinding on the cold riverbed. He tested the scrape across his belly. He felt the blood's flow back through the branching veins, felt the valves opening, closing, felt the knobs of his spine against the ground, the weave of bone and pain. He rolled to his feet, cupped the pain against his belly. Toward the river, he slid down the bank, through the willows, held his shirt up, palmed water to the wound. It numbed. He held his hand against the current, felt the trail east toward a greater river, the rivers all meandering into one.

He remembered an old path through sumac, through spindled oaks, and a clanging church bell, and a rattling line of heavy wagons. The path crossed the fields, the fresh-turned ground waiting, and for the first time he thought to trace the prints, to see where they entered the path, see where they angled for another break. He fit his soles to those prints and squared himself to each direction they took, to the west, to the rising ground and the stone walls, toward the wooded spaces cut and grown again, and another village. He remembered the tight fit of his boots to those prints. The pressure of someone else's boots had already been given to the ground, the hollow had already been carved. He stepped into the waiting space. It was as if the ground had no need for his weight. Those tracks weren't always a perfect fit, but they were more of a fit than not—they were a man's boots, a man's tracks.

He headed on. The cottonwoods flowed around him, the black leaves too dark for stars. The trunks sliced his approach, splitting lantern from window, field from structure. He saw the shift of black where the men slept. The fire had gone to coals. Owen lay flat on his back, his nostrils whistling a dead song, his dreams locked toward Cheyenne and the land office and a clerk and a ledger. The top-shelfer slept on a cot, his servants on the ground beside him. Cootie and Edd curled with their gear, the slender English stock between them. And Henry slept in a line of men. He saw Henry's shoulder, the turn of the head, the shape of the legs. Henry shifted in his sleep, rolled onto his back. Walker crouched at the boy's feet. Henry's eyes opened, the whites like vague clouds. Henry might have seen him, might not have seen him, in the dark grove. Henry spoke, his voice a strange music, almost another language, and the words escaped with nothing to catch them, with nothing to hold them until they settled toward sense, if there was sense to be made.

Walker came onto the road that edged the parade ground, and the whole fort was laid out. The lanterns and windows lined one direction and another, each light anchoring a spike of refracted light, each spike twisting as Walker squinted and tried to focus. He saw no shape or shadow, no men, just the forms that contained the light—lanterns and windows. The night, without a moon, was dismissed by those lights.

Beside the darkened sutler's store he found the wagon. He took his rifle and the new ammunition. He found his knife, found a canteen, some jerky, a coiled rope. He slipped off his old boots and tossed them, slipped off his bloody trousers, pulled on the new trousers and boots that Owen had offered. He wrapped the goods in an old blanket, cut an end of the rope and tied the bundle, slung the rest of the rope and the bundle over his shoulder. He dug around and came up with a fresh wool blanket.

He let himself in at the paddock gate. The soldiers were asleep in the grass, or trying to place shapes against sounds, or watching the last coals in the fire ring sink to red, or there was no one. He continued, straight on toward the middle of the paddock. The horses lazed together, big bulks of heat breathing, shifting. He brushed among them, deep in among their walls. If they spooked, he would be caught up, trampled, abandoned. He ran a hand down their legs, tested their joints, cupped a hand beneath their mouths, and they turned in toward him, nibbled at his palm. Perhaps for them he was part of the soil, part of the night, an odd pocket of air drifting. He could walk upright beneath their necks, could duck between their legs. Which horse? Any would be fine, any would carry him farther that night than he could walk in a day or two, and the best might carry him direct to the Wind River by noon or earlier. He felt along flanks and found the U.S. scar on each. Owen's beautiful chestnut and bay were in there somewhere. The horses all milled about now, and he couldn't know if the horses that came against his touch weren't the horses he'd already explored. He felt their backs for the remnants of saddle marks, felt their chests for the remnants of harness marks, but he found them all clean and smooth, their histories washed away. He had brushed Owen's horses himself, leaving them blank and lost in the paddock, mixed with a good fifty head or more. He would have to choose a horse without benefit of color or shape or an idea of who had broken it, who had urged it off the plains and onto these uplands. When he noticed that one horse followed him, nuzzled at the back of his neck, he turned and captured it with a rope loop.

He fashioned a hackamore. He placed the fresh blanket on the horse's back. He led it to the gate and out, and he heard the other horses follow, a sleepy wandering from the paddock into grass no greener than the grass they left. He held the horse there beside the fence, climbed to the top rail, stepped out into the darkness, and the spine came up beneath him, and he laced the reins through his fingers. He twitched his heels and the horse leapt north, leaving behind the sudden rumble of the other horses and a human voice.

In the dark, he measured the horse's stride. The stars clustered and wheeled around the North Star, and he moved slightly to the west of north. Beneath the sound of digging hooves, the constant rhythmic battering, he heard the undertone of the moist prickly pear, the grass as faint as ruined paper, the sage with its brittle twisted branches and oiled leaves. He had left the fort, left the valley of the Little Wind River and the camp. He couldn't count the miles. He rose across shallow ridges and descended toward another rise. The night air lifted the heat from the surface of his skin, but the horse's heat and frothing sweat and his own heat and the headlong dazzling blindness of his speed kept him warm. He rushed somewhere between the plain and the mountains, above the miles without break where a man could be seen from twenty miles distant, below the steepness where a horse could founder, where he might sink into false perspectives and dead alleys. He held to the horse's neck when the going was rough. He tensed when it seemed they might have drifted from their trail, and the horse responded. He spoke to the horse, a steady whisper as constant as their speed, his words as much to urge the horse as to distract his ears from any sound that might follow. "Easy. You know this territory. Easy."

And then the horse slowed to a rocking lope, and Walker heard the ground soften, he smelled water, and the horse came to a stop with its hooves down in a pond or slow creek. They stood there a long while after the horse had drunk its fill. The horse was tall. The insects seemed to noise far below in the grass and brush or whatever lined this space. The stars wavered deep in the water, snaking away in each direction. Walker smelled antelope, somewhere to the east. He smelled flowers, a scarlet scent. He smelled pine, distant and elevated.

He slid to the ground, pulled the blanket down with him, smelled the damp heat of the wool, the horse's sweat and his own. Leaving the horse to graze, he fought into the brush, felt his way along the bank. The cool settled close over the dark water, tangled with the roots that reached from the bank, the branches that closed the sky over the channel. He heard the water's slow movement. He dropped his bundle and rifle, pulled off his boots, smoothing the dust from the tooled black leather, pulled off his trousers and draped them in a willow. He stepped down into the creek.

Through yesterday's long clear sky, the water had flowed down its channel, and it still carried an edge of the stark mountain sun. He crouched, felt for the bottom stones, held his balance, and lowered himself into the water. His hair slicked and flowed. His deerskin shirt clung to him. He drifted and rolled. The stars reached down through the willows. He removed his shirt and held it in the creek—the flow filled it, billowed the torso and arms—and then he dragged it heavy and limp from the water and let it drain, shook it, hung it with the trousers. Drops pattered the ground.

He sank into the creek again. Already the water had lost its trace of him, the smoke and sweat gone. He brushed his wound, let the water enter around the edges and carry away the leaves and soil and remnants of another man's skin and strength. He held the water on his tongue, let it close his eyes and silence his ears. He tasted meadows and rot and old ice and musk. And deep beneath the water he heard the dissolved echo of water threading the cliffs, water breaking through a rock slide, breaking white against fallen logs. He stood. Quickly the air dried him. He heard the wide sky, the moonless terrain.

Near dawn, miles north, he followed a trail that ran along the base of the foothills. It was Owen's horse he rode, the tall chestnut, Shell. He saw above the hills the first gray light on the lower forest, the first high hint of granite. He looked back. For as far as the light allowed, no one followed. In the hush before the clatter of sunrise, he scanned the plain. He caught no movement out there.

The sun rose, a white blaze so instantly hot and huge that the horizon might have been no more than a mile away. And

then, ahead, with the sun, Indians swept up onto the trail
from a downhill ravine. They came straight on in a single
line, and for a moment it seemed to be one pony with a
swarm of legs, one man with his own image splitting and
hazing in his wake. Then they kicked their ponies to the left
and right, the stiff bristle of manes, and they continued in a
fast wall.

Walker balanced his rifle on his lap, adjusted the bundle
on his shoulders. Dust smoked up from the ponies' hooves.
Keeping his hands casual on the rifle, he leaned forward, and
he might have prepared to speak, but all he heard was the
thud of Shell's hooves and the powerful smooth silence of all
those Indian mounts. He tried to see the men's focus—they
had no squint against the sudden brightness, as if the sun had
been up for hours or days or had never set.

The Indians would see Walker on Shell, with the hackamore and the blanket, Walker hunched at his travel, his black
hair long to his shoulders, skin dark with sun and the road,
his hands playing the rifle. They would see a short man in a
deerskin shirt, high on the back of a horse clearly too handsome for him, even with the white ripples of dried sweat on
the neck. That shirt—the work of the seams could not be his.
It was trade. Or he'd stolen it. It was ruined. They might
guess that he'd known Tukudeka, that he would know an
escape to the lambing of mountain sheep, to the white lakes.
He might lead them to fresh game, cached valleys, root fields.
They approached.

They had caught the same trail he had found. How many
other trails flowed into that trail? The men rode the trails their
fathers had ridden, the lines of the years running through a
thousand parallel years. They closed their eyes to the sky and
saw their blood in a map of veins branching and joining.
They quartered the plain by heat and game, a scent on the
air, their homes forever shifting, taken along, dragged behind.
They were drawn by the hot flame of buffalo dung and dry
sticks, the deep pools of spring, the thatched willow and the
fallen cottonwood, the topography of skin. Perhaps for them
the hills did not rise and recede, the mountains did not loom

and fade, the rivers did not leak to a final faint reflection in the distance, the plain did not shift between lush and desert. Perhaps for them the whole range of the world was constant, always fully formed, carried with them—sun and moon and dark moon and clouded sun and the last sharp sliver moon and the red sun forever eclipsed and returned and eclipsed. The plain tilted toward the rising sun, always washed toward that light, always shifted from night.

Walker prepared to speak. They rushed past. He turned. They were already beyond recognition—what tribe?—their dark backs, the crease of each spine, the black hair, the flow of each pony's tail.

He lost the trail. He crossed no water. The slopes folded one against another, ribbed with bits of animal trail, remnant terraces that started and quickly broke away. The wind buffeted the grass, filled his clothes, dried him and left his skin smooth. He watched the distance. In the rising heat the plain was a botch of color. No way to know if anything moved out there—everything swept along in purled waves. At his left hand, the hills were speckled with boulders exposed from their ancient settle, junipers with their stunted dark-green needles and blue berries, and then the sky, parched without sounding, no clouds or more solid heights.

He looked back. Hoofprints trailed him like a string of shadowed code. Along the seam between the plain and the foothills, the light seemed calmer, as if the fold captured the light and heat and held it still. He watched that fold. It was crossed by vague gaps where the dry creeks cut through. He thought there might be a band of antelope a few hills back, their black horns sharp with movement, but then they were gone. He kept watching, trying to determine the distance. He saw the band again, rising clearly. Not antelope—he'd seen it wrong, thought it was closer. A few miles back, men on horses came along, maybe ten of them in uniforms. They had followed. He urged Shell into a trot. He kept on straight. There was no cover on the plain, no way to know how precarious an entry into the foothills might turn out to be.

He kicked Shell into a canter, gripped him, his feet barely hooking the lower barrel curve, but he was secure. With the crush of sagebrush and grass, Shell took great long strides, tossed his head and accelerated, as if he was fresh, as if he saw a green distance. Walker didn't think of how high above the ground he traveled, of how boldly they stirred the dust they abandoned, of how his small fist of a heart paced Shell's stone muscle. This was pure speed, this was miles covered. The land rose, the slope cut to sky ahead, that northern sky with clouds starting far behind the blue, and then they leapt the ridge's spine and a hollow opened directly, and Shell rocked back and caught his momentum on his hind legs and slid and jumped and the slope crumbled. With each jolt Walker remembered the wound across his belly. He held his hand there. He held the rope and Shell's mane. A mile ahead, from a split in the foothills, a creek flowed through a strip of willows.

Quickly they were down the slope, and then the going was easier, the land nearly flat and free from sage. Shell crossed trail after trail, the bare dirt scratchings that traced among the grass toward the willows or toward the plain or up toward the hills. And then Walker pulled Shell up slightly and they crashed in among the willows, the branches whipping and snapping around them, against Walker's legs, against Shell's chest and flanks, and a dozen bluebirds scared up, circled around, dove out of sight, and a flicker flashed its huge speckled shape and drove for the canyon and the pines above. Walker pulled Shell to a stop. Shell stood tall, ears erect, looking forward toward the sound of the creek, looking back toward the ridge left behind, his ribs expanding around his excitement.

"That's all right," Walker said. "I'll stop here."

He slid to the ground, deep beneath the branches. Shell still rose up into the blue, and the path behind was wide and trampled and cracked. Walker watched the ridge—Shell's hooves had gouged long slashes down the slope. Walker counted a minute, counted two. He turned and led Shell deeper, to the creek, and they both drank. The water was fast and cold on its scoured bed, the stones small and green, black, white, gold. In the evening, the sun would fall behind the hills and the shadows would be huge and still and settled. He crossed through the creek, took Shell along, and they rose slightly through the brush, toward a single dead cottonwood. The wind had fallen, dampened by the heat.

He tied Shell to the cottonwood, testing the knot to assure that it would come loose with a tug. He lifted his shirt. The jolts had opened his wound, and fresh blood drooled down his belly. He pulled the blanket from Shell's back and used it to dab at the blood—the brown wool darkened and matted. He dropped the blanket against the cottonwood, kicked dirt on it, took out his knife and sliced the blanket clean through the bloodstains. Then he scuffed around, breaking sticks, digging out roots and leaving their bare white tendrils in the air.

He gave Shell a long scratch on the chest, said, "You're a good boy, you're a strong boy, and Owen'll want you back," and left him there. He angled off into the willows, upstream, careful to leave no trace. The branches slid around him. Birds stirred beyond sight. Large black flies circled in the hot shadows, and dragonflies hovered above.

He stopped where he could look up from the willows and see both the southern ridge and the crown of the dead cottonwood. He dropped his bundle and loaded his rifle, looked along the sights, swung around, focusing on the ridge, on the tree, on the northern slope, on the hills where the creek emerged. He watched the ridge. The men had been a few miles back. He estimated their travel, their hoof falls. When he calculated them close, he said, "Easy, boy, Shell," and he fired the rifle a few times straight into the sky. Shell, out of sight beneath the tree, shook himself and exhaled loudly. "Good," Walker said. He reloaded the rifle.

He watched the ridge. The men came up in a line, paused a moment, rushed on down the slope, out of sight. He heard their approach. He turned, aimed at the cottonwood branches, brittle gray against the sky. He listened. The creek was buried in its channel. He bore the gun against his shoulder, holding the aim. The men were close. He pulled the trigger. The cottonwood's top branch shattered and fell. Shell whinnied and stamped, and then he was galloping back through the willows, across the creek. Walker loaded and shot at the northern ridge, hit a rock, started a few yards of dirt sliding. The echo circled. The men shouted. Walker loaded and shot at the hills, at the mouth of the canyon. The sound entered the hills and returned. He heard hooves and rattling gear. He took up his bundle and ducked through the willows, wove deep into the branches. He shouted north, letting his voice catch among the boulders and junipers, his voice a string of sounds, the Shoshone man's sounds, a quick burst. Then he fell silent.

He heard someone chase down Shell. He heard a crash along the edge of the brush. The men spoke tight among themselves, their voices traveling far above the willows.

"You heard them?"

"Get down."

"I ain't seen them."

"No way to know."

"Up there, I guess."

"You go on in. See what you can find."

"I'm not going in there."

"We'll keep an eye on you."

"So will they, I think."

"Go on. Can't no one see you in this brush."

"Not till I step on them."

The sound of a man walking and a horse following. They sloshed through the creek. After a few minutes, Walker heard only the horse—the man had mounted up—crashing back through the creek.

"See here."

"Looks like a dead man's blanket."

After a long silence, someone shouted into the afternoon heat. "Walker Avary."

"You crazy?"

"Shut up."

"We're as good as hidden in here."

"Hard to figure that boy."

"If he got in trouble with the Shoshones—"

"Those bloody trousers we found—"

"Stolen horse. That's enough."

"We should look for him."

"Who knows who else we'd find?"

"Just settle yourself down."

Walker heard the long wait. Someone shouted his name
again. The horses chewed their bits. The afternoon went on.
He was wedged deep in the half-dead, half-cold branches. He
backed out, stretched flat on his back, his bundle propping
his head. Through the leaves, he watched the clouds sail
down from the peaks. The sun drifted west. The air cooled.

When the light had faded from yellow to thick green, he
stood. He could still see the southern ridge, the slope cut with
hundreds of churned hoofprints. He kept himself low. He
could see the cottonwood, the northern ridge with the little
scar of the slide he'd started, the hills. Birds passed around,
fluttered, settled in. There was movement out there, the
horses slow toward the hills, or down the line of the creek.
He heard no voices, saw nothing, until two men rode to the
southern ridge, dismounted, sat and watched. And at the
northern ridge two more men came into view, and they sat
on their horses and watched. No way to know where the
others had stationed themselves.

Walker sat again and waited until full darkness. Then he
stood, strapped his gear tighter to keep it silent. He moved
through the willows, back toward the creek, sank his bottle
into the cold water. Then north. He threaded his way between sounds.

Along the foothills, hours north into night, he passed through
long stretches of grass, where his steps were hushed, and then
he smelled sage, adjusted his stride, entered in among the
tough brush for a mile or more. He made good time.

He watched the stars. They cut along the ridges and kept
his trail straight. He felt the faint depressions of paths
underfoot—a path opened by a daily trek toward water, or

the path of a seasonal migration, or a path carving an ideal transition from gully to field—paths dug by antelope or deer or coyote.

If he looked far behind the darkness, far to the north and northeast, he could see flecks of firelight on the plain, two fires, he was sure. Could be twenty or thirty miles to those tall fires, each centering some unknown activity—flames to center a circle of tents, flames to ward off the black and the stars. He couldn't tell if those two camps could see each other—he was above, they were out in the corrugations of the plain. He walked on for hours without much altering the angles toward those fires. Only the vastness of the dark allowed him to find those white points, and with dawn he might not see anything out there, no movement, no focus.

Before first light, the stars started to drift from the black, falling like sparks to ash. He was moving fast down a slope. He heard how the night air had accumulated in a stand of trees, how the birds had already stirred and expanded their feathers and looked toward the east, how the antelope beyond the trees waited to hear how close he would come, his steps too conspicuous to signal danger. Then he was into the trees, he found standing water in long pools in a creekbed, he drank and saw reflected the last stars and dawn's first rushlight. He curled in an elbow where trees had fallen and crossed. He awoke once to find the cottonwood leaves bright.

In his dream, he approached one of the fires on the plain. It was a party of surveyors, the hot roar of sagebrush lighting their sleep in their two-man dog-tents, the bell-horse hobbled nearby and the other mules and horses grazing within the sound of that constant metal tang, waiting to be rounded in the morning. In with their supplies, the flour and dried fruit and coffee, tobacco, baking powder, salt, and maple sugar, they had packed into canvas cylinders and pannier boxes their instruments, writing kits, old trousers, flannel shirts, crumpled felt hats, California blankets, waterproof ducking, dry woolen socks, spades, hatchets, matches, the camera.

Walker unrolled their charts—contours half discovered, unnamed or neatly labeled, and the calculated elevations, the
waterways that slowly betrayed their pattern, the passages
and deserts and buttes, the exclamations of highest peak, low-
est sink, the settlements no more than a distant reference,
the warnings and fords and vain hatchings of timberline and
gold, the black granite, the quartz veins, the layers of broken
earth. He took his time with their journals—sketches of birds,
guesses at classification, the patterns of leaves, roots, clusters of fungus, spikes of flower, the burrowing mammals,
snakes, owls, the herds, the skulls and spore, the tracks and
nests. And he found packed in envelopes, carefully numbered
and named, a blue feather, flowering sage, claws and teeth
plucked from a carcass, hooves and horns. And he found in
boxes, packed in straw, blown eggs—one off-red and spotted,
one white and speckled, one pale blue, one blotched green,
one pure white.

With night he continued. No firelight to the east. The fire to
the north burned again, but it had moved, or it was different
altogether, smaller or farther away. Every few miles he paused
and took a swig from his water bottle, filled from the pools,
and he tasted the settled run-off and clay and mixed slough
of land and animal.

Slowly he turned toward that firelight. He thought the fire
might be on the road where he and Owen and Henry had
passed. He might find himself there, still traveling south, that
night and every night accumulated on the plain. He might
see how he sat his haunches, how he looked past the fire, how
he listened.

The range here angled toward the northwest—he left the
hills and moved more directly north. It would be no great
diversion in the greater scheme of his trail. He would get far
enough from the hills to gain a perspective on what he faced,
to see the peaks and trace their snow and granite. Through
the hours the flame grew, and then something passed across
it or it was beaten down a moment by the wind, and finally

it died away completely or he had lost sight as he headed among the eroded folds. But he'd set his direction, attached to the center of the spiraling constellations.

The warm breeze passed him and moved on ahead. He heard the miles. He heard antelope sprint far below on the flats, perhaps on the wagon road, moving south, or it was horses and men.

As the horizon reached up through the stars, he found the firelight again, not a mile distant.

Walker sat where the ground was soft, the dirt nearly powdered among the brush. The fire was still a ways off. He tried
to catch movement or something of the camp's shape, but he
saw only the white flames, the light rising and shifting
through the smoke, and then the flames dampened beneath
a burst of sparks and billowed again. He rested his chin on
his knees and stared at the light. The stars directly above the
camp wavered and flowed. He stared without blinking. The
fire might have been just another star, and as it fell through
the darkness, the heat of its slow descent unsettled the stars
in its wake.

When he awoke, the sun was a quarter up from the horizon.
The ground was scattered with parched grass and clots of
sagebrush. Lines of antelope prints trailed north, but he could
see no animals in any direction. No horses or mules or oxen.
He was more than a mile out from the foothills, and he could
now see the high peaks and snow, and he remembered how
each granite bulk stole from the blue, and he studied the pattern of the peaks for a while and took his bearings and then
he knew how far he'd traveled and when he would reach the
next running water, many miles north toward the Wind
River.

Straight ahead, down a slight decline, the camp was set on a crease of thickets and stunted trees, a green stroke that ran from the foothills and on out toward the plain. A wagon lay on its side, its axles exposed, canvas loose and flapping. Walker stood, adjusted his bundle across his shoulders, hefted the rifle, and approached. His boots dug into the dry ground.

He came to a blackened fire circle without flame or smoke, a pile of gray ash stirred against the stones. At the tipped wagon, he tested the broken wheels—they each spun a half turn before a spoke or strip of iron caught. He came around the wagon, looked into the tunnel of arched hickory stays and the shredded canvas—in that space, the bottom of the wagon was a wall, the wagon's sides were a brief ceiling and floor— it was a tight vessel, no light leaking through.

Walker reached in among the broken cases and crates, found a scrap of jerky, brushed away the ants, let it soften on his tongue, and chewed it to a sweet, spicy pulp. He washed it down with a swallow of yesterday's dense mineral water from the pools. In the meat he tasted the grass and pollen from a richer plain. In the water he tasted a buried sea bed, the tiny husks of the creatures that glow at the sea's surface in waves of luminescence.

He heard a song whispered—a voice too round for a bird, too shaped for an animal—forced air and changing rhythm. He backed out from the wagon. The voice stopped.

The camp was strewn with litter—a pair of socks fuzzed with burrs, a girl's white woolen mitten, three spoons bent and blackened, shards of a blue-and-white china plate that pictured bridges and steep hills, soft trees. A black enamel kettle sat beside the fire circle. Some tins had been stacked in the shade—fruit, hash, stew. And through it all were foot-prints, hoofprints, and a mash of trampled branches and leaves.

Walker followed the prints out and around, tried to judge the number and direction. There had been at least a dozen animals, probably more, horses and oxen, come in from the plain, returned to the plain. He trailed the prints for a while east along the edge of the thickets. What had been wild and deeply slashed prints, twirling here and there and back on themselves, gradually settled into a more contained flow, with less force behind each step. He stopped and watched the prints continue through the sage, over the next hill. They would hit the wagon road down there, somewhere invisible in the heat. He turned back.

At the fire circle, he tried to reconstruct the voice he'd heard, if there had been a voice, and guess at its origin. He watched the air, started forward, into the thickets, through the openings, the bunch grasses and penstemon and licorice, shooting star, Solomon plume. He came to a bank of rose and gooseberry woven in drooping arches, the small white gooseberry blossoms mostly gone by and the fruit started, the rose blossoms beginning, the large petals crinkled and quiet pink. He knelt and reached in among the branches, looking for berries and rose hips. The gooseberry thorns, the long dense hairs, burned his fingers. He found only a meager palmful of remnant fruit from the past season, no new fruit ready yet. Here, in the under-arch of the brambles, a gooseberry branch had drooped straight to the ground, and where it touched it had sent down roots and sent up a spike with fresh green leaves and transparent thorns.

He circled past the brambles, pushed through the ten-foot willows—the old branches cracked, the young orange whips traced his sides and then snapped back. On his hands and knees, he crawled through a wall of silverberry, paused and rolled onto his back, struggled with his rifle and bundle, reached among the soft silver leaves, tipped up one leaf after another, found the yellow dot of blossoms between stem and branch, found last year's gray olives. The musty sweetness of the flowers coated his skin.

There were red birches ahead. He heard a flutter—not a bird. The birches sprouted in bundles from their roots, the trunks splayed out and up. Within each bundle was a basket of shade. He came on through willow weeds, horsetails, comandra, and entered into the birches. His bundle caught, his rifle thumped against the trunks.

Deep in a nest of shade and litter—leaves, cloth, tins,

branches—a girl sat on her folded legs, her face toward Walker, and, behind her, a boy lay asleep. The sunlight was high in the leaves where the branches thinned and laced. He watched that light as it filtered, tried to see the girl's face, saw a pattern to her white skin—veins of sweat run through grime, or the translucent veins of the leaves shadowed, or her own buried blue veins. Her face was long, a smart square jut to her jaw, her black hair curled around her ears. A spot of light caught her cheek, beneath her eye. The light was an odd-shaped opening down through a shift of leaves, and the shape stretched and diffused. How many layers? A dozen or a hundred leaves had settled and aligned with the sun's angle. She looked up into the leaves, the light shone directly into her eye, she winced and looked down, rubbed her eye with her blackened palm, brushed her skirt square over her knees.

From her lap she took up a broken arrow shaft and touched the bristled feathers to her chin. "See here," she said, and she held the arrow toward Walker. There was carving on the wood, zigzag grooves that started halfway down from the feathers and ended where the shaft had broken. "The grooves are blood seams. They drew out the blood. I've learned about these things. I knew some Paiutes. We crossed—" She turned, pressed at the boy's chest. His shirt was open. Her hand flattened, covering the wound. "I broke off the shaft," she said. "I couldn't pull out the point. I couldn't bear to have these sage-hen feathers sticking up in the air. Do you have any water?"

"A bit."

"I need some." He reached his canteen to her through the branches, and she shook it, held it close to her ear, judging the slosh. She unscrewed the top, smelled the water, drank down the swallows that remained. "I used up the last of my water last night. I'll need some more. I made tea from willow bark." She returned the canteen and handed him a tin cup.

Walker wound himself back through the branches, made his way past the birches, through willows and big sagebrush, to the dry creek. There were long crescents of white sand set in eddies of red clay, stretches of mixed gray and green river rock. He stood on the bank a moment, looking east and west—the creek cut from sight in both directions. He stepped in and headed uphill. Where the willows and sagebrush took both banks and blocked the mountains, he found the creekbed dampened to rusty brown, and he stopped, knelt there, put down the cup and the canteen and pulled a kerchief from his bundle.

He pressed his fingers into the clay and dug out cool, slick handfuls. Slowly he opened a conical hole, heaving the clay to the side, smoothing the edges of his progress. Two feet down, the bottom of the hole began to seep around his fingers. He dug a few inches deeper, pressed the cup into the bottom of the hole, secured the kerchief tight across the cup's top. He watched the cotton soak, filtering the clay. He extracted the cup, poured the dark water into the canteen, and set the cup again.

He could have covered miles already that day, or he could have slept below the foothills in another shimmering sun-filter of cottonwood. From the creekbed he could see nothing of the mountains or the nearest hills. He turned toward the north, toward the west. Nothing but the thin willow leaves on the whip branches, the gray catkins, the bitter bark. Nothing but the sagebrush grown to giants here, the branches swirled and shedding, the leaves silver and barely furred, waiting for the end of summer to spike its yellow flowers. The sky was unruffled, no bird or cloud moving through.

He had traveled this way before. With his back against the Wind River, in the constant sound of the river's flow, he had watched the sun explore the surface of the range, toy with steepness, each new angle of the sun flattening the slopes or turning them abruptly sheer, massive, ashen. With his head pillowed on stone, he had watched a waterfall enter white into a long lake, the water carrying sound with it, voices torn and swallowed with the destruction of the lake's morning reflection, the cliffs and trees mixed and rippled until bark and stone and cloud were a single uniform skin. With his shoulder squared in Captain Avary's window, he had watched the Pacific's valleys and plains, had observed the currents, the shift of color and the bare white froth at the boundaries, white as a thin line of sand or shell or clay or pulverized mountain— what silver schools traveled those currents, felt the heat and tug and the sweep toward shore and the reckless turn of wind and weather and the calming dissipation of the doldrums and the acceleration again?

He climbed to a better vantage. The plain rolled north, the mountains shifted slowly toward the sun. The traceries of water were everywhere—high snow, grassy slopes, far green depressions snaking. Had the Circassian girl followed water down from the range when the days had passed, when the only sounds she heard were her own breath and the heavy gait of the gold horse and the weave of echo and night? These waters could submerge for miles at a stretch. Had the Sheepeater girl found ice, slept in the blue-white, melting the range's first drops with the heat of her shoulder and hip, her arm cradling her cheek? Even through summer the highest snowfields would melt only at the edges, only on the surface.

He knew that he could continue, walk on without return-ing to the girl, leave the cup buried in the clay, take the miles without worry, dig himself back to his lodge, listen to the waterfall and the slow stout wandering mule. He knew that he could take the miles without a voice near, spend the years without a guest to attend, without a story to remember, with no girl to follow, no boy to know, no claim to secure. But, perhaps, every possibility of water now held a girl or man or cabin or ruin or abandoned wagon. Perhaps he had walked into another territory, left behind an old emptiness.

Through the noon heat, he followed his own tracks back from the dry creek. The thickets blocked his passage, and he turned left and right, drawn by the shape of the brush against sky and distance, and then that particular break of red birches which already held for him a scent, a sound. He climbed in through the branches, smelled the fear long dry, the wound ripped close to the heart, the end of that boy. The girl reached for Walker's hand, he felt the cool fingers grip, she

helped him balance, took the canteen. She drank a few long
swallows, holding the weight of the canteen on the up-angle
of her thin arms. Water ate through the darkness on her chin,
washed the color from her lips and left the faint rust blush
of the soil. He heard her throat work to draw the liquid down
to her center. He heard her dry round nostrils whistle, almost
heard the dirt crinkle in the creases of her small gray eyes.
He heard the rush of her eyelids as they tried to moisten that
gray, as they tried to clear her sight. The boy was not going
to move. She looked at him, slowly screwed the top back on
the canteen. The boy seemed to have flushed blue around
the eyes, as if night had settled there.

"Thank you, sir," she said. She touched Walker's wrist,
and he felt her pads raise his pulse to the surface—she pulled
her hand back, and his pulse disappeared, far below the skin
and tendons. "I'm Eugenia, if you wanted to know. My
brother is dead."

"Yes, ma'am. I'm sorry." He introduced himself, tipped
his hat and replaced it.

"Avary. That's good." She pulled a tin and an opener
from the roots and leaves, pried the tin open. "It's nice to
have a full canteen, Mr. Avary. There isn't any water in that
creek—I've been up and down it a quarter mile."

"There's water under the surface."

"I didn't look." With a spoon, she dug into the halved
apricots, the slick orange domes, the rough blemishes, cut the
apricots and ate a few pieces, then passed the tin to Walker.
"You'll like these, Mr. Avary. Have you ever seen an apricot
tree? They have thin branches and ribbed leaves, like a plum.
They wouldn't grow here."

"I've seen an apricot tree." He took a bite and let the sweet
smoothness slide down his throat.

She raised the canteen again, tested its weight, opened it
and drank. "This water is a little strong," she said, "but I'm
not going to complain. It's wet. Later, you'll show me how
to find water myself."

They finished the apricots. Walker settled back, and Eugenia settled too. The three of them were lined tightly in the hold of the tree. No air moved through, just green shade, the sunlight prying through the canopy.

A summer yellowbird dove in, grabbed hold of a branch and swayed wildly with the sudden arrest of flight. It held cottonwood fluff in its beak. There was a nest there, woven of grass and leaf and cotton. The bird glanced down and moved on.

It wasn't a month ago, she told him, we heard a river from ten miles across the grassland. Think of a river that big. We came to it and found a torrent—it was too wide and high to cross safely. We were in a line of wagons then. Fifty people. Fifty. I couldn't know all the names. Some of the men rode along the river, looking for a ford, but there was no better crossing within a day's ride. So we waited. We hoped the flood would subside, but it never changed. We waited almost a week.

I was at the river, in the cattails. I was splashing water on my arms and neck. Five men rode up, they were young men driving a herd of unbroken horses, carrying a new colt, and they had to fight to keep their string together. They came right past the camp, they almost drove the horses straight into the river, but I heard them and I startled up and the horses shied and scattered.

Here on my shoulder I was caught by a flying stirrup and the heel of a boot. I bled. My sleeve was wet, so the red blood feathered. It took the young men an hour to gather the horses again. They were very sorry for the blood and my pain, though I couldn't really feel it. They didn't care at all about the work I'd caused them, that hour of hard riding. One of them, a boy named John William from Dakota, offered me a shirt from his sorry roll of gear. I didn't want his shirt—I held it only a moment, smelled him on it, smelled Dakota dust, and handed it back. He wanted to stop the bleeding, he tried to press the shirt against my blood, he tried to wrap the shirt around my shoulder, but the bleeding had already stopped. He said that he and the others would help us cross the river.

The boys pushed us. We had been sleeping and listening to the river and digging roots for roasting. The men took the wagons apart, removed the wheels and poles and axles. Then they sent a man across, and with ropes they ferried the goods and the women across in the wagon boxes. I sat in a wagon box with sacks of flour and sugar and salt and tins of baking soda. They pushed me off from the bank. I swung out fast to where the water was black and noisy—it smelled like cold stone. Then the man on the far shore pulled the second rope and the box dipped and almost swamped and I felt how heavy and fast the water was, and then the man pulled me past the center and I drifted to the bank. I sat with the other women. I wouldn't have crossed back.

Once they had ferried the stores and the wagon parts, they had to get the animals across. The oxen didn't seem hardly bothered at all—they were so heavy that they just opened their eyes a little wider when the riverbed fell away beneath them, and they looked at the sky and at the others around them and they just kept moving until they dug into the sand and came out wet and went right to the next field to graze. Then there were the unbroken horses to get across— two dozen. Almost all of the men, even my brother, were mounted up. The horses were ready to bolt again. When they entered the water, the lead horses tried to make a break up-river, but they were cut off, and in a few strides they all sank into deeper water and struggled to swim and to hold themselves against the current. They all moved slowly downriver. One of the young men had tied the colt's legs together and slung the colt over his shoulders and held him above the water while his mount struggled beneath him, and the mare followed close. The men's shouting was just part of the river's roar.

My brother wasn't used to the tack. They had given him a horse with a Mexican curb. When he was first into the deepest water, the horses tried another break, and he pulled

up on the reins to hold control. He watched the horses ahead
and yelled back at someone coming up behind. He didn't
know that his constant pull on the reins forced the horse's
mouth open. The river went straight into that horse's mouth.
I saw his horse go under. The break came around him and I
thought it passed right over him and my brother was gone.

The river curved. We all ran and watched the water and
came to the bend. The loose stock was out and circling
among the trees. The colt was down and loose and stamping
its legs. I saw my brother wet and vomiting and wringing his
hat. His horse had drowned. It wasn't even his horse—it belonged to another man—but no one said anything.

Eugenia and Walker pulled the body out from the red birches
and laid the boy flat in the sun. On the bunch grass and red
paintbrush, Eugenia tipped the boy to one side and the other
and drew his shirt off his arms. "Mr. Avary," she said, "I'll
need the water again."

She tipped the canteen and wet a corner of her long skirt.
Shifting closer to her brother, she dabbed at his wound,
smoothing away the dry blood. The arrow shaft was hard in
the center of a swirled bruise. "I'll leave that in there. I won't
disturb him." She pulled his boots and trousers off and piled
them to the side. Then she stood and unfastened her skirt,
dropped it, laid it out on the grass, and rolled her brother
onto it. Against the grayed cloth, the boy's legs contorted.
His bloodless shoulder rose into the air. Eugenia removed her
blouse, wet a sleeve, worked at the body, behind the ears,
across the brow. She rolled him again. His nipples, two shadows. His crotch, buoyed and bare pink. In the full sunlight,
against the boy's white skin, only the faint mottled freckles
on his shoulders were distinct, only the shadows tracing the
joints. Young boy—very young—no edge to him. He might
have continued to soak up the sunlight until he faded completely into the cloth that held him, the cloth itself bleached
white.

Eugenia was bare now but for her bloomers and her boots
and green socks. She was young herself, no more than fifteen

or so. Her breasts and shoulders and belly would burn in the sunlight. But she was quick about her work. When she needed better vantage, she held the boy by an arm or cupped his head or shifted his legs. She handled the body squarely, brushing at each blemish. She never looked up, not at Walker or at the distance. Soon the boy was washed—she'd used only the minimum water. She laid him out straight, arms at his sides, hair slick, eyes closed. His wound floated on his whiteness.

Eugenia took up her brother's shirt, shook the dust from it, and pulled it on herself, buttoned it to her throat. She dropped her bloomers, toed off her boots, and put on her brother's trousers, pulled on her boots again and laced them. The clothes fit her snugly. "These are better for this country," she said, rolling her shoulders, smoothing the pants over her hips.

She wrapped the boy in her skirt. His head lay on the dirt, his legs exposed from the knees. She lifted him and turned slowly, holding him, scanning. "Follow me."

She started along the birches, found a spot where the grass opened against willows. There was squaw currant with its sprays of pink flowers, the flaring tubes. Eugenia stopped in the shade of a short cottonwood with a thick, gray trunk. She looked up into the leaves. "Hear that?" she said. Walker listened. The breeze caught in the leaves and branches. "It'll bring the sky down," she said. "There won't be such a big sky." She sat against the trunk, with her brother in her lap. "Please dig here, Mr. Avary."

Walker yanked out the grass and flowers, piled it all to the side—the green blades, the leaves and purple heads, the shed brown, the white roots. Then he dug with a fallen branch. It was slow work. Near the surface the ground was dry and dense with clay and sand and gravel and the cottonwood roots. A few inches down the soil was moist, easier to dislodge and crumble, but with the meager stick he could only scoop a handful at a time. He found old burrows, spiders, deeper roots, stones with the crushed edges of gravel, and stones as smooth as marble. The breeze didn't carry off any of the heat, and the sun swung beyond the tree and left Walker knee-deep and sweating, the sweat drying white on his arms. He squared the hole to no great depth.

"That will do," Eugenia said.

Walker stepped from the hole and helped her with the body. They laid her brother down in, cradled in her skirt. Beneath the sun, he was bright. Eugenia stepped in beside the boy, tucked the edges of her skirt around him, covered him, wrapped him away. Then she climbed out and stood beside Walker.

"You should say something, Mr. Avary. I've been talking and singing to him for two days."

He looked at the boy's feet, the bruised toes, the pink nails. "I think he must have been a good boy."

"Amen."

"I think you'll miss him."

She took up the stick and started working the soil back into the grave, and the boy's wrapping dampened the sound. Quickly he was gone. Eugenia and Walker filled in the dirt, broke the clumps and sifted, ran their hands over the top, patting, leveling.

"Do you want a marker?" Walker said.

"No road passes here."

Eugenia found a hat in the broken crates and tucked her black hair up under. None of that first view of her remained, none of that calm turn in the shade, none of that brief unconcerned exposure to the sun before she'd buttoned herself tight again. She sorted through the tins. "There isn't much left," she said.

"You've used it all?"

"I haven't used hardly anything."

He knelt beside her, watched her shadow, counted the tins. "We can leave when you're ready," he said. "We'll pack whatever we can carry. This ain't much of a hiding place."

"I'm not hiding. I'm waiting. I've been left. My brother and I were left."

"When did you last see your mama and daddy?"

"Same time I first took to that brush."

"Two days waiting is enough."

"Not even a full two days yet. I wouldn't be much of a daughter if I ran off."

"You can't just wait."

"I know how long they'd look for me."

"They must know where they left you."

"Take a look out there, Mr. Avary. Can you tell one hill from the next?"

"I can."

"Well, that's good to know for when I'm ready to leave."

"We should start packing up."

He judged the weight of the supplies, considered what they might carry and what they might leave behind, all dependent on which direction they headed and how long they would travel. He unwrapped his bundle and laid out his gear. Eugenia added a few items—socks, scarf, fork, cup, matches. She fashioned a slicker from a square of canvas. With two duffel bags and rope, they made packs, padding the straps with ruined clothes.

Then they righted the wagon. It was basically intact and strong. A few of the bent hickory stays still curved nicely, and Eugenia found enough canvas to pull tight over one end. In that curving shade, she laid a bed of grass. They lazed in there, listening to the afternoon. With the heat rising from the ground, no sound traveled cleanly. Insects buzzed and clacked in bursts and fell silent and started again.

A thunderstorm advanced from the mountains, pushing ahead of it the cold smell of rain, and they stashed the packs beneath the wagon and climbed back up to their canvas room. The rain came at a slant, and they held the openings closed, sat still as the roar passed over. With the first close lightning strike, Eugenia reached for Walker, and he felt her hand holding tight to his trousers at the knee. He turned. The light wavered with the flow of the water over the canvas. She was shaking. The wind gapped the canvas and the big drops struck her and she released him and fought to close the canvas. Then she curled there, her arms raised and hands clutching the seam, her head resting on her shoulder, lips wincing to a near-smile with each lightning flash and boom. The storm moved on quickly, the canvas brightened, and they opened the shelter, lay there with the smell of wet canvas, looking out at the fresh sky and the green steaming thicket.

"I've always known summer air like this," she said. "Wet. But this territory will be dry soon enough. I've never felt such empty air. And the ground. It takes everything in and sends up these scattered little twisted plants. We must have traveled fifty miles of that plain without a tree."

"You had the sagebrush."

"Trees for ants. At home you could hardly find the ground for all the green and the fallen leaves and fungus and rotted logs. In ground like that you could grow a tree almost without a seed."

"I knew that kind of land. You couldn't see a mile without climbing on top of something. You couldn't see where you were going."

"Not if you hadn't already been there. I used to trail off through the back fields, into the woods, across the creek. The neighbor's farm was older. I went on through the corn and sunflowers, the stalks with the tassels shaking loose their dust, and the huge plates of the sunflowers turning with the day. I could hardly see the sun. The farmhouse there was tall and plain, with shutters and a porch and honeysuckle and bees. Lazy bees. A road passed in front of the house, and when I came out of the fields I almost always saw traffic—a loaded wagon, or a man on a horse, or sometimes a boy walking and singing, or a girl alone, but I was alone, too. Those travelers were on their way somewhere—I couldn't tell where they were going. The road branched ten times before the next town, if you didn't get lost first."

"You could follow the roads?"

"I knew the pattern of turns for a few miles in each direction. But it was the farmhouse I was after. I lifted the cellar door and stepped into the cool air. I thought I might catch a fever from the damp, but then my brother would have to press cold rags to my neck, and that didn't seem awful. I always went to the same corner. There was a doll house in a

style I had never seen in a real house, with pillars and railings
and velvet, and the dust on its roof seemed like city snow. I
could loosen a clasp and the whole front side of the house
opened. I held my hand inside the rooms, and the air in there
was as cool as the air in the cellar. Of course."

"You slept there."

"Sometimes. I heard the voices from above."

"And you took something."

"I'm not a thief."

"No."

"But, yes, I took a painting from the parlor wall. I tied it
in my hair with a ribbon, and I went back through the fields,
and I took the painting out when I was safe, far in the trees,
where the creek sound was louder than the sound of insects.
The painting was so small, Mr. Avary, that I held it on my
palm. The paintbrush must have been a single horsehair. It
was a night scene or a dark storm scene. A small boat was in
trouble, with some men upright in the boat, and in the water,
in the waves, where there should have been just sharks or
whales or some other fishes, I remember pink and gray people, all muscled. I had not imagined that painting before. A
man floated with his arms stretched over his head and his
mouth open and his eyes closed, and there was a light on his
chest that didn't seem to come from the sun or the moon,
and that beautiful light faded only where his waist sank into
the green waves. And a man curled like a newborn baby,
holding to the side of the boat, trying to climb in, and his
head was buried beneath his arm as he heaved himself from
the water, but the water still had him. And a woman held
herself back against the boat, her head turned so sharp against
her shoulder that it seemed her neck was broken, and that
beautiful light was on her chest also, and the light was clear
even where her hip sank, and her eyes were half closed with
something like pain, and her mouth was a smear."

"What did you do with that painting?"

"I buried it near the creek. The wet ground was as dark
as shade. In the autumn, that ground was like a bed of cinders
with gold coins fallen across."

"I knew those fallen leaves. But they were red and orange. They were like overlapped hands. In spring, after a whole winter under the snow, they had no color at all."

"In spring, I watched the snow melt back from the fields. There was the black soil steaming at the center, and the white fringe, and then the tall bare woods like a broken fence. The ground was pure mud, and I thought it would never dry. But soon the sun was drawing the water up from the ground and filling the air, and the woods leafed out as solid as a dam. And then the men started turning the soil."

"I've never worked the fields, but I've seen the fields worked. They dragged out whole crops of stone before anything green sprouted. They built walls with the stones."

Walker followed Eugenia through the thickets. She climbed to the lower branch of a dead cottonwood and looked out.

"What do you see?" he said.

"There's something moving, it must be twenty miles out there."

He climbed up beside her, followed her direction northeast. "You have a good eye. That's twenty miles at least."

"What is it?"

He held to the limb, tight against Eugenia, watching. "It's moving directly, so there are probably men involved."

"They're coming this way?"

"Maybe. Maybe not. These trails swing around."

He awoke to the smell of woodsmoke. Eugenia had returned. The breeze carried sparks from the flames, high icy clouds skimmed fast from sunset. Walker lay there awhile, closed his eyes, and listened to her move. A cup clanked on a stone. A branch snapped, consumed by the heat. He opened his eyes. Beside the crates, Eugenia held a chip of something white, turned it over, tested the edge against her tongue, dropped it.

"Do you think that fire should be so high?" Walker said. He climbed down from the wagon. "It's a beacon."

"It brought *you*."

He moved past the fire a hundred yards. His own shallow prints, coming in from the southwest, had been wiped away by the rain, and the trail was filling with night. No sign of a road out there, no fires or smoke. He turned back. Eugenia poked at the flames. He came up behind her, touched her on the shoulder. Rising beneath his fingers, she twisted to face him, the firelight threading the hairs that escaped her hat.

"We can put a few miles under us tonight," he said. "I'll lead you out of here."

"Not yet." She moved to the far side of the fire, settled down into a nest she'd gathered. "Here."

He joined her.

"Where would you take me, Mr. Avary? You can find a road?"

"Yes, I can find a road."

"A fort?"

"If you want."

"A town?"

"I haven't seen a town for a long time. But I know where to find a town."

"What town?"

"It's just some dry hills all dug up and turned inside out."

"Is there a hotel?"

"Yes. A square hotel with a balcony over the boardwalk."

"How many rooms?"

"Maybe four or six. I saw it from far off."

"Curtains in the windows?"

"I don't know why not."

"Does the town have houses?"

"Of course. Some were whitewashed, with good roofs. Some others were almost fallen in. No care to the construction. Abandoned, I guess."

"And your house?"

"Square. Plain. With windows."

"In that town?"

"No, ma'am."

"Curtains?"

"Shutters."

"That might be good enough. What do you look out on?"

He closed his eyes a moment, watched the heat through his lids. "Gold aspen in the fall."

"How far is the place?"

"On foot, it's a long way."

"And where were you going out here?"

"I was going to sign a claim, but I got off the trail."

"No. You were on a fine trail."

Eugenia fed sagebrush and dry willow into the fire. She smelled of the young boy's sweat and blood, the half-formed skin and age. She draped their legs with cotton and knit wool, pulled stiff canvas around their shoulders, formed a shell that cupped the heat. She tilted the canvas to thwart the breeze. The heat built and wouldn't escape.

Walker felt the heat across his brow, down his arms, felt the cold night behind his ears, at the back of his neck. He loosened his shirt, pulled off his boots and watched his black toes curl and grip and relax. They ate dried beef and drank the dense water. There was no sound beyond the breeze carrying the fire's heat, no sound but the night shifting the thicket, the firelight leaking into the brush.

"This is where I sat when I first saw you," she said.

He saw nothing but the sagebrush fading in ranks beyond the flames.

"I was brewing willow-bark tea for my brother's fever. I saw your eyes out there. I thought you were a coyote or a wolf, because the eyes were square to the front. I piled on more wood. I thought I needed a rifle. Your eyes didn't wander from that spot where you sat. I watched until you fell asleep—the eyes didn't turn away, they just closed. I thought that you could hear the fire and the night through your sleep, and you could hear the animals moving and smell their movements before you heard them, and I knew that, whatever animal you were, sleeping out there, as soon as your eyes opened again I would have to be alert. So I watched the space where you slept. I thought of the way the ribs hold the heart and lungs, and what a solid wall the bones make, but the wall is thin, and I thought of the channels of the ear and of how

I'd seen white bugs living in my dog's ears and of how those bugs must swim in sound, and I thought of the cold night beyond the fire and of how we keep ourselves safe from the cold with fur or skins or a burrow, and I thought of how, if I were you, whatever animal you were, I would be able to follow me, no matter where I ran, with no water to drown my scent, with no door to block my back, and I thought that you, whatever animal you were, must be able to smell my brother and know he'd been hurt and know what taste his flesh would have, something like red salt and string. I didn't sleep. Before dawn I saw your black hair over your knees in your slump there, and I took my brother away, not because I thought we could hide, but because I thought you might not bother if we weren't right out there, if I wasn't offered, or you might be frightened by our absence, wondering who I was and where I'd gone and what weapon I held. It took you a good long while. After a few hours of waiting, I wanted you to come. You were slow, Mr. Avary. But you surely aren't dangerous. Not that I can tell."

She stood up. "Come with me," she said. He pulled on his boots, and they left the tall fire and its smoky heat, walked out past the light, into the sagebrush, up the nearest hill to the south. Turning back, they faced the stars that seeped right down into the earth, seeped straight to their small white flame against the brush. "Out there," she said, and her hands on his shoulders turned him northeast toward the plain. "They came closer, but then I lost them. They were swallowed up. But now—" What seemed far below, in some vast depression, a flame burned, and farther on, somewhat more to the east, another flame burned.

Walker and Eugenia stood there a long while. She leaned against his back, rested her chin on his shoulder, and her hat bumped his brim. The fire they'd left behind in the camp faded to red, was lost to sight—a memory of heat. The night dampened, the sky lowered, the stars wrapped around them, or the ground was rising.

"Tell me how well you see," Walker said, and he felt the heat of his breath escaping.

She released him, stood beside him. "All afternoon, I kept seeing something."

"You made out what it was?"

"Fourteen men."

"You saw that?"

"I kept seeing. Each man with a horse, strong horses, a roan and some bays and two buckskins taller than most horses I can remember, and one with a bobbed tail. The hooves didn't seem to make any sound. No kicking stones or breaking through brush. As if the ground had been cleared for them. Or as if they were not on this same plain. Very fast and smooth, when they're urged on. But I didn't hear any urging."

"They're too far off for sound."

"There were four whites and ten Indians, and they had weapons, of course, I know that. I don't like the idea of arrows. I prefer bullets. The whites were all the same, with straight faces that got narrow at the chin and moustaches that flared wide and then drooped, and their hats were turned brim-down, as if they'd been sat on or drenched or worn out, with leather straps woven tight around the crown and black with sweat. The Indians all had strings of white beads that looped and looped down their chests until it looked like armor, and they had black hair that rose straight up from their brows and fell down in stiff thatches, and they didn't seem stirred by speed. Their lips were each a different closed shape."

"You couldn't see that."

"That's what I remember, Mr. Avary."

He watched, but if someone passed across those flames, if someone added fuel, it was far too distant. Fresh stars inched through the thick air at the horizon.

There was water moving—Walker could feel it in his lungs, on his hands, at his collar and cuffs—the water was wicked by the darkness, drawn up from the riddled ground, the tunnels and burrows, the sinks and openings, the sands that swallowed rivers, the mounds that crawled with insects, the dens curtained with roots. Perhaps, on that hill, the pocked surface of the earth would collapse under their weight, fall to a slurry of leaf and claw and crumbled stone and deep ice. He placed his palm on Eugenia's face, and she was damp. He felt for her hand, and she was as cold as he was.

"What else do you remember of those men?" he said.

"They killed a sage hen."

John William was meeting a brother in Jackson's Hole, she told Walker. The young men were taking their unbroken horses up the Wind River and over Union Pass. John William said the land was good along the Snake, and my daddy asked questions and liked the answers and it was decided. We would miss Fort Laramie altogether, but the young men said that was fine, they'd take us by a better route. The other wagons kept on toward the fort and the Sweetwater and South Pass.

It was a bad road we followed into Wyoming. We stopped an afternoon for repairs. The heat was sharp. The air was so dry it seemed to kill the scent of things and left only the bright edges. The men let my daddy finish the work and hiked off to bathe in a creek. They dragged their clothes through the water and then wrung them all out and threw them on the rocks to dry. I saw how the sleeves were twisted and how the cloth stiffened in the bright sun and formed to the rocks, and I thought of how much force it would take to push an arm through one of those sleeves. John William used palmfuls of the creekbed sand to scrub the black from his neck, scrub the dark V that arrowed down his chest, scrub the lines on his legs where the tops of his boots rubbed. They all laid out in the sun beyond the cottonwoods. The grass was straight between their legs and arms and against their necks. I was near. I saw the leaves layering up through the heat, and mag-pies came dipping through and stopped to sharpen their beaks. I chewed on white grass stems and listened. They talked a long streak.

We'll get them on to the Snake.

Far enough.

Kaz got his eye on some mules back with those—

We ain't going back for no mules. We got enough trouble with these horses.

You still going to the Sweetwater Mines when we get done, John William?

I might. I might not.

You'll find shit in those mines. Might as well dig the dirt right here.

A boy needs money for love, don't he?

She's a sweet thing.

What kind of house you got planned?

Double cabin, with a breezeway.

We won't have nothing if our Paiutes don't catch up with us. We need their help. I don't know what use a wagon is for cover.

We'll be seeing them Indians today, I'm sure. They won't let us get ahead too far. They won't let us go alone.

I heard their voices continue—I didn't put much meaning to the sounds, not then, but when they spoke of love their voices were soft as the warm drifting shallows of the creek. When I awoke, the men had dressed and headed on. I followed. There was nothing for a while, just the tall grass and animal trails and trees. Then I saw that one of the young men had gone on ahead, and he came out of the trees and waved back at the others, and behind him some Indians were deep in the shade.

I watched the young men enter into the trees. They all stood in there talking. One of them saw me out in the grass, and he waved at me, and I stood still and waited. They all came out in a line, came up to me, gave me a greeting, and I followed them back along the creek. I watched how the whites and the Indians planted their feet, how the grass crushed beneath each sole.

The Indians had come down from Dakota, and they were on their way back to the Great Basin, and they told a story of how they didn't want to cross the Wyoming Indian territory alone or go around by the north, so they would be joining up. I listened to them. I knew they were Paiutes. The young men made it clear that the Indians were to be trusted. I had not seen Indians before. I wanted them with us. And the young men wouldn't go on without them. I didn't say anything as my daddy asked questions, and so we all traveled on together—we had the wagon, the five white men and their horses, and the three Indians with their gear and their extra horses.

Two days later we drove into a whole world of mauvaises terres—the wheels sank into the spongy clay and left long grooves across the ground. With the hoofprints and the lines of the wheels, it looked like music printed on the ground, but all I heard was the wheels and the creaking tack and the crush of sagebrush. And then we came to a badland river without much flow. It had dug itself deep into the soft ground, and the banks nearly hung out over the channel, and the water was brown and sour.

John William climbed down to the water. The bank was thick with red mud, and John William sank to his waist. We had to pull him out. He was coated with red. The clay dried on him, and when he moved the clay broke away in long thin pieces. I picked the pieces up. They held the pattern of the weave of his trousers and the shape of his legs.

We spent a day cutting a ramp down the banks, another day walking far out across those bare hills to cut sagebrush and rabbitbrush. The surface of the ground was sometimes like wet ashes that had dried and hardened, sometimes like stripes of solid rust. I could see how the wind moved the ground, I could see the fine grains skimming from the walls into the gullies. Rocks lay half exposed. There were round rocks crusted with lichen, tables of green rock, chunks of agate with the old woodgrain in tiny columns and swirls. And out on the soil I found, held by some invisible root, lichen like rolls of pale green paper scrap. One of the young men or another or a Paiute pointed to the birds that sat the spines and flew the currents of the eroded hills, and I looked to the ravens and buzzards and eagles and prairie falcons and horned larks and nighthawks.

They handed me the brush they cut, and I turned back

toward the wagon. Across the hills and the carved shadows, the wagon sat in the anchor of its own shade, the tallest, squarest thing for as many miles as I could see, but it was nothing and the canvas shook in the wind. John William passed me and handed me his hat. The felt was soaked with sweat. The brim cooled my neck and ears. I looked back at his tracks, and they were clean across the surface.

I dropped the armload of brush beyond the wagon and returned, following his prints. He had crushed a wild onion's lilies. Farther along, I found a mat of roundish leaves—each leaf was slick green on top and white and soft underneath, and above were stalks of little yellow flowers. John William was talking to a Paiute, and his voice skimmed clearly like a voice across water. The Paiute didn't answer—just bent and hacked the rabbitbrush at the root. John William's hair had dried, and it stuck up in blond curls and horns. And then I found other yellow flowers. In the spaces between the rocks and in the crushed boulders, there were masses of plump green and violet leaves in the shade of yellow stars. On the flats and near the brush there were prickly bunches of cactus with tough flowers yellow as lemon and white as butter. On the banks of a gully, there were taller plants with the flowers closed tight, but in the cooling evening just before dark I found them open in wide yellow blazes. A Paiute found me there. He reached past me, cupped the flowers, tasted the pollen. John William followed. We three climbed a jut. Though the sun had set, the horizon was still lined with silver light, and the hills and valleys were cut sharp. The Paiute spoke a long string of words. He was naming things, I think. John William put his own words against the Paiute's sounds. River. Wind. Cold. Star.

The next morning, we built a dam with the brush. The water flowed through our work, the mud rose and thickened, the branches soaked, but soon the crossing was dense enough to support weight. They sent the wagon first. I sat at the back and watched the water rush into our tracks, the brush woven tight beneath our progress, and then we were up the far bank and I saw our camp and the marks we'd left and the men and the horses coming fast and the sudden splash and then the miles and miles of dry.

We kept on, found a better road. We passed Poison Creek. We followed the Bad Water. The next night we saw a fire back along the road—whoever it was made no effort to conceal the fire, so it didn't seem dangerous, and I even thought it would be pleasant if they came into view and I could watch them slowly catch up and guess at who they were by their shape and the dust they stirred. But the second night, when we saw a fire again, one of the Paiutes rode back with one of the men, and they returned before dawn and roused us all.

We headed off in the dark, left the road, moved southwest, fast when we could, flying quick enough through the creeks that we couldn't sink. At dawn, I looked back, and that music still followed us wherever we went, the lines and the notes on the ground. We could only push so fast, and without a road to follow we had only the horizon to shape our direction, the Granite Ridges and the Big Horn Mountains and the Wind River Mountains. We were in a bowl. There was no real hiding.

It was a two-day run. We tried to stay at the bottom of each fold of the plain, but every few miles we had to dash up and over to the next fold. I would look back and see the Rattlesnake Hills going gray, but I never saw a soul that I would recognize as human. Each night there was a fire behind, where we could see it clearly. We lit no fires ourselves.

Then the mountains were coming up, and we were near to this place. I saw the openings in the hills and the dark trees and the cliffs and the peaks far above. I had seen snow on these hills, cold snow, but now it was gone. We crossed a road, far down there—I couldn't see it today, I can't remember it. My mama and daddy were on horses now, and all the whites and the Indians were right with us, not going to leave us, though they could have moved faster, but they never veered off, and John William kept circling us to drive the oxen straight though they were near to going over. My brother held the reins and whipped and tried to steer around rocks and ditches to keep the wagon upright, but we were moving slower, and he shouted at me, and I couldn't hear his words over the wagon.

We came up along the brush here. I leaned out from the wagon and held on and I saw the four whites and ten Indians a mile behind. They were at no more than a trot. Then they were moving faster.

Our young men and Paiutes and Mama and Daddy were all churning now, crashing into the edge of the willows, going on ahead, rushing back. Then they stopped the wagon, John William pulled me from my seat, my mama came around and told me to go, the oxen were already loose and I jumped from their hooves, my brother followed, John William pushed me deep into the thickets, I lost my brother, and I didn't find him till long past the last sound I heard.

Walker and Eugenia found the cinders still red, and with grass and splinters of sage they started a flame. They kept the fire low, just enough to send shadows around the camp and against the wagon. Under their canvas ceiling, they arranged the blankets, watched the stars and the firelight on the canvas. Walker worked her buttons free as if they were his own. She tried to kick off her boots. The breeze was slow, constant. Walker felt the dampness in her hair, the dampness in his own hair, smelled the smoke, almost liquid smoke.

"I haven't looked as far as I could, Mr. Avary. I've hardly looked for them at all. I don't want to look."

"You don't have to look."

A bird squawked, a night startle, and fought among the branches, the hard quick sound of air battered by the wings, and then the bird passed directly overhead and moved to the south, blind.

"Eugenia. I know this territory."

Eugenia rolled with the blankets. She was warmer now. She was tight in those boy's clothes, loosening them, and it seemed that Walker's deerskin thongs had looped her buttons, and he felt where the dry grass mattress had scratched her wrists and belly—hot, vague imperfections. As she held her hand to the wound on his belly, he felt the scabs crack.

Another bird passed overhead, leaving the brush for the open.

It was snowing. The flakes melted into their skin, their brows, their shoulders, hands. They saw the snow descend through the stars. They saw the firelight against the canvas.

An animal came through the brush. They heard its breath whistle, its hooves clip the fallen branches, and it broke through the last wall and they heard it shy at the scents of their camp, heard it stamp and jump to the side, and then they heard it leap and accelerate, incredible speed, chasing its own sound to the south.

The snow fell harder. They smelled the smoke. Walker tasted the snow and smoke on Eugenia's brow, and it seemed to have substance, it was gritty. The snow came down through the firelight.

More birds. More antelope.

They sat up in their vessel, crawled through the canvas room, looked out into the camp, to the fire they had left—it had died away. They stood up on the bench, looked for the source of the firelight. A long line of red flame approached from the north. The snowfall was ash. Soon the fire would reach the far side of the thicket.

They found the packs, they pulled them on, and Walker spun a quick moment, judging his own speed and the girl's and the fire's. They started toward the foothills. They weren't moving fast enough. They dropped a tin, another, until they were running faster than the smoke.

They reached the pines, the arched ceiling, the complex of limbs and fallen trunks and the creaking lean against the breeze. Walker stopped—no way to know how far he would dive before he came out to sky again. He turned back. Eugenia turned with him. Their view of the plain was cut by the canyon walls. Red crescents flowed south from the thickets and took the hills and shrank and broke again and died away or moved beyond sight.

"Come with me," he said.

"Where else would I go?"

"Hold on to me. You won't be able to see." But he didn't know what she could see.

He felt the tug of her hand on his pack. Testing the incline, he palmed the air, stepped forward into the trees, navigated without stars. As the ground rose, he found the way opening. The pine branches raked far above, the pitch locked insects and darkness. There might have been mice in the roots, beetles at the bark. There might have been catamount or grizzly or wolf.

Her voice followed him, a whisper dicing the unknown gaps. What did she say? He kept walking. He passed through each word. Nothing held still. But it was not her voice—it was their footsteps in the sheets of needles and the ferns and shed feathers.

Then the trees diluted, stalled, the last of the eaves washed away, the night stretched across meanders and marsh, stars now in standing water, sinking away, and a mile farther the water flowed and the stars swam and broke. No sound of animal or bird. Eugenia was silent.

At dawn, the rocky slopes were pink. They found on a boulder the scratched image of an elk, the legs sticks, the belly full, the antlers a long backward curve above the slender neck. And farther on they found boulders stained dark and clouded with pale green lichen, and within all that color and shade, mountain sheep climbed and a man held aloft a mysterious half-hoop. And they found on a sheer wall a creature with eight eyes, clawed arms winged at the shoulder, sinew of a mouth, and across the bulk of its square body there clustered circles like lakes, dots in groups and alone, snaking lines like rivers and roads, mazes woven against the neck, and hatch marks that counted something across the belly.

They slept through the day and the night. The valley was orange with fireweed, streaked with forest. Eugenia moved up along the edge of the trees, her pack settled on her back. Walker followed. He felt the sun catch and release him beneath the boughs, felt the air sharp with liquefied pitch. He turned in among the trunks, came to a fresh oozing gash, yellow and shredded, where a bear had clawed away the bark. He held his palm to the pitch, pressed it there, watched the amber thickness well around his pressure, thought that if he remained there, if darkness came, if coolness sank from the ice fields far above the valley and followed the course of the creek and flooded the woods, this stickiness would harden, hold him within the tree's pulse.

Eugenia came around the trunk. He peeled his hand away, held it up for inspection—smears of thick yellow. He smiled, knelt and pressed his hand to the ground. She took his wrist, held his hand close—it was scaled with needles, sloughed chips of bark, lichen. "Move," she said. He flexed his fingers. The scales shifted and crunched. "It looks like armor," she said.

Turning, she was already through the trees, into the sun, and he followed to the creek where the boulders held an edge of cool, a rush of cool sound. She took off her pack, he dropped his, and she pulled him in through a depression of willow, propped him at the edge above the noisy creek, nestled him there with his head rested on his outstretched arm, his hand down in the flow. She lay beside him, nose to nose, knee to knee, ran her hand out along his arm and held his wrist, kept his hand down in the water. "We'll stay until it's all washed off."

With the coldness, soon he felt no hand, no tugging at the chips of bark. He closed his eyes. He smelled her, or it was the willow he smelled, the fine smooth orange branches, sharp leaves. Or it was himself. She exhaled, he inhaled, cradled in that ball of green shade, his hand gone. He heard the water. With a quick pain he felt his bones bare to that glacier melt, that erosion, as if the mix of dissolved granite flowed into his open veins.

He saw himself floating in cold water. A woman leaned over him, her hair black against the sun. She pushed at his chest. He felt the sharpness of her nails in the gaps between his ribs. The water flowed over him, in through the seams of his tight eyelids, in finally through the seam of his pressed lips, down through the bare dark channel to his lungs. The trees were above the water. He began to move. Long soft waving tendrils of green scum traced his fingers, his shoulders, and let him pass. Fingerlings skimmed from beneath his shadow. Then with a final moment of steep acceleration he was out into a wide calmness with nothing but the sun high above the surface of the water. Slowly the sun shrank to nothing but a star, and the water became heavy around him. The lake was deep. How old were the rainbows and brooks and browns that cruised there, how hooked their jaws? The sun was joined by others, the black sky streaked with the circling stars. He settled onto a bed so soft and smooth it might have been nothing, slick, thoughts, and a cloud puffed around his weight, and for hours, days perhaps, he waited for the cloud to settle again, to clear his view of those circling stars, but the cloud held around him, coated him, and he tasted what had been deposited there. *Ten thousand nights of fallen star-light. Sounds that echoed, drifted, took with them bits of the cliffs. Footfalls on the web of trails, footfalls up the drainage, up from the lowlands, footfalls high as the bighorn curl, too high for an enemy to follow. Lichen. Roots. Flesh. Bone.* The woman took him up and smoothed away the darkness from his skin, he saw her dark hands on the roundness of his belly, he saw his skin too white for a newborn boy whose mother was already dead—he should have been grayed with ash, red with ocher, slathered with mourning—but the woman held him in her darkness, held him to nurse, and he tasted granite at the teat, spruce, long nights with the sound of wolves, sound of bear, sound of waiting, hiding.

Eugenia pulled his hand back from the water. His hand was clean and white, without feeling. Huddling with him, she pressed his hand between her thighs, and slowly he felt heat begin to jitter along his nerves.

"Have we left any tracks to follow?" she said.

"Very hard to follow."

"I know we crossed rock. We crossed through those fallen needles. I watched the valley this morning while you slept. I didn't see anything. What do you hear?"

He listened, and for a while he heard only the passage of the creek, its force chipping at the boulders, and the sound of Eugenia close, her breath, the weight of her settle moving the branches, crushing the leaves and blades. Then he heard the dry breeze above the branches, the air stripping moisture from its low lie and burning it to nothing, the air on its way to something else, unseen. He heard the gray jay, heard it lift itself through the empty bright air, heard its feathers brush and catch and spread, its claws grip a branch, head twitching, eyes back along its line of flight. He heard the scrabble of animals, the collection of grass, seeds, fluff. He heard the wandering, far up the valley, of a bull elk, heard the animal

move on through the towering shade. He heard the pressure
of broad pads on a trail, the leap over a fallen tree, the edging
along the creek—a cougar drawn by a scent. He heard the
way these sounds spun among the valley walls. As the day
drew moisture from the land and took it up into a sky too
dry for clouds, the sounds also rose and dissipated. He tried
to place other sounds against the day—a horse's hoof catching on a downed log, the groan of tack, the crack of stone on
stone—but there was nothing.

"We're deep in," he said.

"I don't want to go back down there."

"We won't."

"Can you take me home this way?"

"I can take you home."

The tins lasted almost two weeks. They ate the sweet fruit at
dusk as they kindled the fire. They heated the stew. They
carried a few of the empty tins, boiled water in them, drank
from them. The tins blackened, but they held their shape.

In their slow wander through the summer weeks, they
found abandoned wickiups, the cones of aspen poles, and
they slept inside, in the cached skins. The shelter was placed
in deep woods, with the sound of the thick pine trunks holding against the air above. Or the shelter was at the edge of a
grove, with the water breaking close, the gurgle of a brief fall
into a deep cauldron pool, and the higher sound of water
brimming and taking to the channel. Or the shelter was at
the bottom of a steep canyon, with lines of aspen following
the springs, and at night the weather seemed to move high
above the cliffs, only the afterthoughts of wind and rain drifting down.

In the evening, they might walk to the creek, they might
listen to the water, wash their arms. When the clouds cleared,
the stars were caught in the trees—the Milky Way braided,
the loose branches swayed. They returned to the fire, ate a
full belly of the fish they caught, of the meat they dried. Near
sleep, Walker heard the shape of the water and the shape
of the things it flowed around. An ankle might break the flow

the same as a branch, twigs might sweep through the water the same as fingers.

In the marshy sinks, in the old beaver ponds, he found arrowhead, skunk cabbage, lilies. Perched on solid ground, he reached out with a long stick, dug into the bottom mud, and roots and tubers floated to the surface. She watched him from across the water. *Roast the lily tubers. Pound the lily seeds, boil them or grind them. Roast the arrowhead tubers. Cook and dry the skunk cabbage roots, grind them into flour.* Eugenia worked at the fire's edge. *The orange fruit of the mountain ash, boiled to a sweet mash. Oregon grape. Dandelion root charred for coffee.*

Walker followed the traces. A creek entered into ferns and white flowers, and, in the stillness of early morning, the fronds themselves seemed to sound with buried movement. In a pocket where elk had slept, the grass was pushed over in dense swirls, and the trail was lost where the rocks took the ridge. In a stand of spruce, old and heavy and tight against boulders, he found a mat of bones. He came around the edges, held to the trees and roots, and leaned out over. He found skulls. Bits of hide. Shreds of sole with the black claws curving from the small bones, dangled at the full reach of the leg. And in with the bones, there were straps, bags, decorations, and in the bags he found remnant feathers, grain, crushed leaf, seed, root. They had been dogs, twenty or thirty as large as Russian hounds, each able to carry a good weight, each killed with a sharp blow and left behind.

There were days when Walker and Eugenia didn't speak. He purposely lost her, let her go on ahead or fall behind. She didn't call for him. Hiding in a shaft of sunlight, he slept deep among rocks or trees, and awoke, listened to the pause of late afternoon—the air had balanced between elevations, the sun an even blanket. He climbed out. Each direction, the light slanted and found its way. He saw the heavy-headed wild-flowers, the red dappled petals shot through with bright heat. He saw the aspen's black wrinkles on white, and he looked at his own wrists. He saw fingers—she reached down between rocks and let the columbine's bleached violet soften the back of her hand. He saw black hair—she stooped through the fallen branches, and they caught at her long tangles, clearing them back from her shoulders. He saw lips—a gray jay paced her, looking for scraps, and she turned, shaped an opening, and exhaled—jay sound, a whistled note, the same note rushing above, diving for the next hold.

Walker found the trails, heard the animals shift their ears to follow his passage, smelled old smoke on the air, and he took to that scent, to the next shelter. They passed a trail that circled a pond, a trail that lined toward a creek, a trail through the youngest aspen fluttering at their knees, a trail that headed straight down out of that place through woods and huge boulders. The sounds went on—wind, rain, the cold woodpecker tap. Eugenia listened for the rifle shot, joined him. Their knife wore down through constant sharpening. At the obsidian cliffs, they sifted the chips, struck stone to stone, came away with slick, sharp scrapers and blades. He was behind her, and his hand, bare in the cold, ran the line of her chin. He smelled the soot, the trout, the unwashed work. He felt the shape of each stand of spruce or pine, the black masses.

Walker pressed his fingers into the elk prints, the deer prints. Along the water, he found his own prints from a day ago or a week ago, found smaller prints and looked up for Eugenia. Her boots were crumbling. Her prints held only part of the sole, and through that cut-leather print he found the creases of her skin pressed into mud and sand. And then he might find a bare foot, a print with the toes distinct, the print shallow and quick, and again he looked up for Eugenia, saw her far at the trees, tried to remember if she had walked there, if she had bathed there, if she had left her boots in camp, if this print would fit her print.

Eugenia ducked into the shelter, he ducked after her, they crouched and turned together to secure a skin across the opening. She lit a fire in the stone hollow at the center, and with the smoke the small flames took the darkness. They settled across the fire from each other, waiting for the warmth to fill. She placed more wood on the flames. The space brightened.

They disrobed, an awkward bit of shuffling about and rolling onto haunches, and then they were naked, still across the fire. Walker looked at the sticks blackening toward red. He saw her narrow face, the barest fringe of lashes, the slash of eyebrows, the crease on her forehead where her hat would sit. He lowered himself onto his side—firelight on his full pale length. She also lowered onto her side. Her muscles were distinct beneath the skin, as if the muscle were barely covered, as if it was only the brightness of the light in that cone of heat that gave whiteness to her surface. She was too pale, as if she had been freshly dug from a richness of loam, far away, washed and dried, laid out to be tasted as an exotic is tasted, a moment of pleasure, an adjunct to nourishment. He saw the folds like the folds of cabbage leaves deep in the folds of a valley, the fingernails honed sharp with work, the strength clear beneath the whole construction of softness as if to say I have no care for what I might have been.

Eugenia told Walker of crossing Nebraska, traveling through the first high country. The trees had died or been cut or never were. A woman waited at the horizon, and when they came near, she turned and walked up the road, and they followed in the wagon, and after a quarter mile she veered north onto a track vague in the tall grass. Eugenia's daddy stood high on the wagon, judged the way, and then followed the woman. The track strung across the round hills. The woman stopped at the crest of the final hill, turned and waited, and they came up to her. They saw beyond her a few trees, a creek running, two adobe huts, some corrals. No one was about. "Don't go any farther," the woman said, looking at Eugenia and her brother in the wagon, "not with those children. The men are off collecting the herd, so I need you, sir, just you."

Her daddy climbed down, and he and the woman went on toward the ranch, went into one of the huts, and he came right back out and walked around the yard for a minute, and then he squared his trousers on his hips and returned inside. After a while, he and the woman emerged and walked to the shed at the far corral, came out with some tools, and went on into the cottonwoods where the shade and the under-growth took them from view.

Eugenia watched the north. Small birds flew up from the cottonwoods, against the farthest hills, but they weren't hills, they were clouds darkening. She closed the flap at the back and at the front. The rain came on, but she and her brother and mama were dry, and the lightning strikes weren't close. They sat together on the crates, they ate shortbread, they sang rounds, they brushed her mama's hair.

They waited in there for more than an hour. When her daddy returned, he didn't look in to see that they were all right. He just sat at the front in the rain and turned the wagon back and finally they felt the main road smooth out beneath the wheels. He drove on till well after dark. A woman and three children gone to diphtheria, her daddy said.

Walker told Eugenia of the bowl of the white valley, black ice stretching away, the snow blowing in tangled streaks across the surface. He stood with Mary at the lip of the promontory, near the piled logs, looking at that flow across the black ice— it was as though the falling snow were caught on that long gap of nothing, afraid to fall into the void, rushing toward the solid edges. The lake was without plumb, without color.

Mary held her lips to his skin and steamed him warm. Taking his hand, she stepped over the edge of the promon-tory. They fell into a wall of fluff, slid to the edge of the ice, walked out onto the surface. They saw how the ice was cracked, the cracks like fine crumpled ribbons of foil laced three feet down to the trapped water. The wind tried to slide them back as they moved forward. The blowing snow cut around their ankles and left shadows of open ice in their wakes. They kept on out from the shore, straight up the lake, and stopped at the middle.

For hours there on the ice, Mary hugged him against the wind, held him in the cross of her legs. They pulled at their collars, retracted their chins into warmth, tugged their hats low across their brows.

They saw the shore, the darkness of the woods, and they saw up through the underside of the clouds the white accumulating, weighing the cliffs. They heard nothing but the bare scrape of crystals rushing across the ice. No voices. Straight up, they searched for a brighter glow in the thick cover, searched for the sun, but they were cold and too far beneath it.

"There's no one here," Walker said. "We're alone."

They continued up the lake. Soon they neared the falls churning over the boulders—the force of the water kept a large half-circle of the lake clear of ice. They veered off, came to the upper shore, climbed from the crunchy ice at the edge, and followed around to the boulders, found the falls, headed up along the creek. Soon the valley leveled, and the creek was nothing but a silent depression in the unbroken snow. They walked up the center of the depression, heard nothing of the flow beneath. The going was open, the surface hardened enough to hold them from plunging to their knees.

They lay on the sandy bottom of the dead geyser pool. Floating heat. They were beneath the surface of the valley. Above them, icicles spiked the whole circle of crusted snow. The steam rose, and the snowflakes hissed in that gray uprush. The sand had chipped from the mountains, the grains had welled from the roots of the range. He tasted the depth of the fissure to the core of flame far below. He floated himself to the log that lay abandoned in that hole, climbed out along its white reach toward the darkness where the pool dove deep. The sun brightened through the crystallized clouds. If the final edge of the storm shredded away, the light would swirl down the rock walls to the surface of the pool, reach beneath the overhang and illuminate that descent of ancient geyser, that tube, that artery, soft with mineral, folded and gray and alive with the rise of bubbles.

Eugenia told Walker of a house with dark, slender rooms. The windows rose past her reach—high glass and deep sky.

A woman lowered her into a long ocean of warm water in a claw-foot tub. Eugenia saw the woman lean over her, and she saw, far above the woman's round face and frizz of dry hair, the sky in a great blue pane toward the ceiling. She floated like a chip in all that warm water. The woman fingered her to and fro, tipped her to rinse the soap away. It must have been her mother.

Walker told Eugenia of the first sunlight in clouds and sloping peaks, and the snow backlit, and the trees fogged and unfocused, and the stiff willows as encrusted as white coral, and the path tamped and the snow squealing underfoot with the cold, and the creek melted free, the thinnest layer of steam drifting down with the flow, the softened snowbanks lined with bare shadow, and the under-rocks buried in that clear cold water and seeming out of reach and lost. Then the voice ahead, the smoke, the flames yellow in the gathered sticks.

Eugenia told Walker of the hour before dawn. They all packed what little had been unpacked for the night. She wandered away across the open. There was sage, wet and dense. The cactus needled through her boots. Yucca dragged at her dress. The light was too gray to betray her, but the east would pinken eventually, a pure line, the color resting there a long, cold time before warming. For now, though, she saw only silhouettes, and the edges of the world seemed distant—the buttes flat and eroded, the peaks rising in brief serrations. She stopped. She heard someone damn the horses. She heard the oxen fight the harness. Even if she were to continue into the morning, she could not walk far enough—the light would soon rise, and she would be as clear as distance in the empty air. Someone approached. She waited for the shape to rise above the horizon. She saw the solid block of shoulders, the familiar crush of his hat.

"John William," she said.

"We have to move. I'm sorry to have brought this on. I'm sorry, Eugenia. Let's go."

———

Walker told Eugenia of Henry and Owen, and their ranch on the northern creek, and of their trail to Cheyenne to lay claim, and of his own claim yet unsigned. Four hundred miles to Cheyenne from these mountains. He had imagined the land office, the table and the stack of large maps, the white creased sheet of paper that set out the Wind River Valley, the line of river and its tributaries, the ridges and peaks to each side, the shard of memory triangulated, and in there Walker might find an approximation of his creek and follow it up to the sketch of his valley, his lake, no more than a snaking scratch of ink, a crosshatching of slope, an oblong of gathered water. And beyond the edge of the map, beyond the edge of the range, lay the stacked and layered bits of other maps buried beneath, and the grain of the dark-stained land-office table, and the tight fit of the floorboards, and the counter with its ornate molding, and the clock preparing to chime, and the windows opening out into the streets. In the land-office ledger offered by the clerk, each page would be lined with faint blue and fainter red and entered with square letters and numbers until it was nothing but a solid block of symbols with blotches of open where only paper showed, where ink had not dripped and scratched, where the whiteness was already complete and correct, or where the whiteness waited for something yet un-imagined to be added and totaled and made right.

And after signing for the claim, there would be a mercantile to visit, to stock up on supplies. Walker knew the shelves, the goods, the walls lined clear up to the pressed-zinc ceiling—the scents of wool, spice, the faint acrid of metal, sweets, salted meat, lilac water, and the labels with their ornate green ovals, swirls of red letter, fat faces of blond babies. Walker knew the people, the voices, the bulk of them, the accents, the variety—men who traveled in sealed compartments, men whose legs carried the sweat of horse or mule, men who contained their effort in a jacket too thick for summer. Some of the men gathered goods to be taken back through the streets and stacked in pantry or closet or drawer. Some of the men gathered the whole range of living to be bundled and loaded onto horse or into wagon and transported far beyond town. A young man placed on a counter the ingredients for bread, the ammunition for a rifle, his long thin fingers brushing nervously over each. Another man pulled on a wool pile jacket, tugged at the lapels, inhaled, smoothed the warmth over the barrel of his ribs. Another counted out a pile of white candles. There would be ladies unraveling bolts of cloth so fine it would melt in full sunlight. There would be girls scooping themselves a weight of lemon sugar. Walker knew the clerk, the way he glanced to the door each time it opened, not to see the new arrivals but to judge the quality of the afternoon. "I'll tell you what I need," Walker said. "A pair of overalls, some shirts and drawers, two pairs of trousers, a new hat, socks, boots, overcoat, a ducking coat, a brass lamp, a draw knife, an ax, hardware, and all manner of food." He recited the goods, the labels, the origins—how many of the tins would line the trails and lose their words to storm and wind and fire?

On the dirt floor of the wickiup, in the firelight, he shaped his lodge for her—the windows and hinges, the seams of the logs, the suspended candles, the flames on the hearth. Then he shaped the valley, the lake, slopes, cliffs, empty.

"Is there business in the place?" she said. "Travelers?"

"There will be."

"How did you find it?"

He marked the farthest corner of the open dirt. "Here is where I was born," he said. Then he scratched a thin line, drew it far south, far west, north again, east, into the territory, to the valley. "And here is the lodge." He went back to the beginning and started embellishing the dirt to each side of his line, naming each new scratch and pebble, adding earth and water. Here a sprinkling of needles made a forest. Here a cinder made a wharf. The ocean with its great distance between each carved wave. A jumble of islands no more than a gapped wall to each side of the passage, the shape of each island hidden, unseen, incomprehensible. A bit of coast, a stream, a pool, a trail. Here a thatch of bark made a city, a scoop made a bay. Here a rail line, a desert, a river, a peak. He told her of Green River City and the fire, of the approach of the Circassian girl and her loss, of the lake and the long sound of the waterfall, of the Sheepeater girl and her run into darkness across a field of shattered cliff. He laid his hand across his lake, the range, the territory, and told her that here the winter had been far deeper than he was tall, that the world had gone to snow and night, and that only the fire had given them color. Then he removed his hand and looked at the sooted blister on his palm. The tracings in the dirt curled in on themselves, and only a narrow swath to each side of the trail was illuminated, a useless language of the hemisphere, no legend attached. "Does this tell you?"

She touched a finger to the dirt and firelight at the open center. "I came from here, through here, straight west," she said, "and I don't see why I should stop."

Walker led Eugenia up through the drainage, crossed to the next, more direct now, rose through thinning forest, toward the mountain sheep, until they found the higher lakes, the granite. They slept in a crevice of open rock, where the purple elephant's head and laurel padded their shoulders and hips, where their tiny fire seemed no more than a single flame. The moon was large, making its quick arc from cliff to cliff —they could almost feel the heat of its brightness. Water as cold as winter dripped from the snowfields and springs above. At night, the lakes took a skin of ice at the edge, but when the sun came into the valley each morning, the ice melted. The valley swerved west.

They followed a string of lakes below the spine. Walker dozed on the rocks. He heard Eugenia at the edge of the water, across the lake. He heard her pile her clothes on the rocks and take her first steps in. She waded out. The water was cold enough to split a skull. He opened his eyes as she sank into her own reflection—a floating head and trailing ripples. Her hands reached out and cupped the water. She kept her chin clear, her mouth open, sucking the thin air. She slowed and her strokes cut and she felt beneath her on the rocks to find a place to land her feet. Then she was standing. The water gave up its waves and lay still around her.

He remembered—mountain sheep trail close to the edge to see the world below. Far above the last tree, he found a hunter's blind at the lip of the cliff. He and Eugenia crouched together in the semicircle of fitted rock. Clouds rose through the day and passed out to the plain. Then they heard the sheep approach, those sharp hooves rattling the loose granite. Walker held the rifle. Eugenia watched him. The bulk of those rams, the horns a dense ridged curl too heavy for an earthbound creature. Walker shot. The meat would give them another week.

They came through a pass. Ahead, the land scooped in great broken fields, old stunted forest, snow, shattered peaks. They slowed, stopped in the matted growth, rolled onto their backs when the sun was highest. They crossed one cold creek and the next, and for a numb hour after each dunking they felt nothing of the boulders beneath their feet, nothing of the sharp mica. The light dazzled from each foothold. They scrabbled up incredible steepness, found chimneys and steps. The snow clung in dirty shadows.

He led her along the highest ridges, followed the bighorn trails, no real trail. The tufts of shed fur. A line of ewes and lambs a mile below. A ram beyond the next wall.

The earth opened out into hazy blue. They could hardly breathe, the air blowing away before they could catch it in their lungs. For hours Walker sat and watched the land below. He saw cliffs descend from the highest broken plain, and then he saw the pools nestled in the walls, the white glacial water, and the forest took hold far below, where the water flowed with greater noise.

They followed a long diagonal split down a wall, with a thousand winters' damage the only stop between sky and a sheer drop. And then they were on the shore of a tiny lake. A ram's horned skull sat in the center of the white water. Old litter had soaked down between the rocks, and Eugenia picked through it all, came up with a stone blade.

"Leave that," Walker said.

"These stone bowls?"

"Too heavy."

He was already down over the ledge, and she followed into evening. They passed around each lake. With dark, they found a stone shelter, rock walls and a doorway and shaped beams. Piled sheep skulls. He knew this shelter. They sat in there, drank water, ate strips of dry meat, covered their legs with a blanket.

"How soon?" Eugenia said.

"Tomorrow."

"Your lodge?"

"Yes."

"That's good. I didn't think this range would end."

The night was cold. The matted roofing had partly given way. He lay on his back and watched the stars appear and swim the gaps, and new stars came along, and the first clouds could not fully obscure the stars. He felt the skulls stacked at his feet, the horns looping and hooking each other. The sky thickened and it rained long and steady. They moved into the corner, where the dryness was still secure. He listened to her breathe, as soft as the rain. He listened to the slickness of the stones, to the lichen and alpine primrose absorb the storm. He heard the wind sound the shelter, bring out the deepest tones, deeper than thunder, more faint than memory.

He thought someone might stand at the shelter door and look inside. Someone might stand there and listen. Stand there a long while and then turn away. No light leaked through the storm. If someone were out there, in the bowl of the valley, she would hear the rain driving darkness and thought and cold against the earth, carrying it all down through the scree. She would remember those cliffs when they held the remnant snow and the open sky, when the sun blazed through the fast clouds, but that could never have been, there could never have been sun, no memory of sun, not with this rain, not with the thousand-thousand sounds— water breaking on stone, breaking on plant, breaking through the spider webs that strung the boulders, water on the black rosy finch, on the nest, the cup of grass in the deep crevice, water on the three white eggs. There would be no moving through such a dark storm. She would hear the shelter, the two together. She would hear the altitude. The storm rumbled. The surface of the cold lakes roared. The clouds lowered, the mountains rose into the underside of that dark wave, the mountains sailed on across another plain.

He held Eugenia in the wrap of skins. He felt the lines of her shoulders, the small pooch of her belly. He heard the second heart beating inside. In another day or another week, the rain would turn to snow. Eugenia lay still. Walker waited for morning, for the gray view to open down the valley.

The afternoon was warm and still. Far down the valley, trout cruised in the clear water. A pond with old beaver sign—gnawed aspen, a broken dam. Then steep banks, fallen spruce. Walker took to one of the logs, spanned the creek, stepped down. Eugenia came along, passed him, moved on, quick toward the dull sound of the waterfall. Walker fell behind.

From the edge of woods he came out above the waterfall and the lake. The cliffs had been struck white with heat, the sky ran blank across the surface of the lake, and there was Eugenia angling down to the shore. The sound of her footsteps, the stumbling skids on gravel, and the waterfall spilling.

He watched Eugenia follow an animal trail. The path had been taken from water's edge to the cover of woods and back a million times through the slow destruction of the mountains, the slow carving of the valley, the gradual sift of sediment and accumulation of water. Nothing moved but Eugenia and the reflected light on the water. She was not much of a girl, a small thing—beautiful, yes, fast, slender wrists—and he wondered how she'd suddenly gotten so far ahead, passing among aspen, the white trunks, and into the last of the wildflowers. He thought she'd take the reach of the valley before he'd catch her up, take her arm, pull her slower.

But someone else had taken her. A man on horseback met her, reached down for her pack, pulled her up, returned along the lake. It could be Charlie. Deep inside the high clear afternoon sunlight, Eugenia and the man rode out of sight behind the lodge, and then the man rode on alone, into the woods.

In the empty valley, the lodge rose like a ghost, like the frame of a dream, the logs as dark and solid as living trees. He saw how the lodge commanded the valley, how its squareness gave scale to the parallel flights of the ridges, how its bulk saved the lake from being nothing but gathered water. He moved down the lakeshore. The lodge seemed taller now. He came close, onto the promontory. He saw the weight of the stones that held the logs safe from the ground, the stones chipped and cleanly fitted and the same gray as the cliffs above, the stones no more than gathered flecks of those mountains. He circled around, felt the heat gathered in the walls. Weathering box of spiked and split and hefted logs.

And across the outlet, a small barn and round corrals and a shed and his mule and the horses. The mule seemed to have driven the horses to a far corner. The whole arrangement was fresh and planned, not what he would have constructed, but useful. Along the narrow meadow, cattle grazed and dozed. And down through the woods, the thump of an ax driven into a log, the snap of wood taking flame. He felt each sound hollow his stomach, tighten his hands, and he turned away, turned toward the lodge.

Behind the glass, in the backlight of the far window, was a border of red curtain. He opened the door, stepped inside, onto the dirt floor, dropped his pack.

Eugenia crouched at the edge of a bunk. He reached up toward the ceiling, where the light wheel dripped with old wax. He ran his hand along the side wall where someone had started gluing newsprint in layers—the black-and-white faces, the fancy dresses, the guns and saws and brick buildings and ships. On the new shelves, on the table top, there were ceramic containers, metal pots and utensils, a stone bowl, tins, baskets, fishing pole, dry flowers in a cup, leggings, socks and longjohns, shirts, skins. On a peg, a quilled tunic, Mary's tunic, the fine dyed patterns draped under their own puzzled weight.

He came around to the bunk. She was settled, a bowl in her lap, working at a ball of dough. She stood, moved to the hearth, worked at the ashes and raised a flame, found a Dutch oven.

He crawled deep into the bunk. The logs were damp with condensation—the mountains had seeped in through the wood's veins. It seemed that for years, perhaps all his life, he had lain in a space like that, with Mary, against the wall.

Mary had burned sage in an earthen mug, burned twisted strands of grass, dry flower, twigs, until Walker said, "Put that out. We don't need the heat. Where do you think that smoke is going but into our lungs?" Mary added more fuel, and the light set the walls to moving. The walls always seemed to rise with the upward drift, always seemed near to rising into the night and leaving them without shelter.

Eugenia, at the edge of the mattress, removed her clothes, pushed the buttons through the gapped holes. Walker climbed forward, touched her ears, tapped at the ridges of her brow and cheeks. Then she was naked, beside the hearth. She reached into a steaming bucket of water. Slowly she scrubbed a rag down an arm. The water carved the grit from her, left her not white but red, her hands brown, her neck brown below the chin. She washed her breasts, her hips, poured water through her hair. She was clearly round now, oddly shaped, the vague sway of her back, the child small and nestled. She softened her calloused feet, dug the soil from her nails with the tip of a knife. As she tracked mud from the floor, she tried to step around, to clean and dry each foot and place it beyond the mess. Then she stood in the heat. The drops of water and the light they held faded one by one until she was plain, dull, without reflection. She took from a shelf a plaid shirt and pulled it on. She took from a peg a pair of trousers, secured them with a length of rope. She rummaged for boots but found only her ruined pair and some fresh socks. "These won't do at all," she said, folding the socks back onto the shelf. "I need some decent footwear." She turned, opened the door. The afternoon lay quiet in the trees. He saw birds swoop and dive. She stepped outside. "Maybe Charlie," she said, holding the shirt closed at the neck. She glanced back. "Look in on those biscuits, please." She walked away, took to the trail, toward the creek.

He listened to her footsteps. No real silence in the valley. For him, the waterfall would have been silence. The cattle kicked stones and called dumbly. The horses whinnied with every new sight or vague approach.

He stood up from the bunk, tipped the lid from the Dutch oven and saw the white lumps beginning to harden. He opened the door on the lake side, stepped out, watched the valley. A few minutes, and he saw someone ride down through the aspen, descend into open sunlight. It was Owen. Riding Shell. No sound from him, no footsteps, no crush of grass and the browning wildflowers. Owen moved his hand, Shell turned, they headed straight to the shore. The steady, slow, heavy steps. He knew that stride. He almost felt the horse beneath the spring of his own thighs, the grip of his calves, the drive simple and direct.

Owen dismounted at the shore and dropped the reins. He undressed, folded his clothes, stepped into the lake, lowered himself beneath the water. His body wavered there, his limbs arching, propelling through the shallows. The bottom was sandy, skittery, with broad flat stones. Then he sloshed to the surface, let out a hoot, stood up onto the shore, his skin red from the cold, wings of hair along his collarbones, fur on his belly, the thick hair almost a shadow wet and slick on his legs. Owen looked far down the length of the lake, looked to the lodge with its seams and panes and stone chimney. He raised a hand and called out. Walker heard his name pass and circle round the cliffs and come back to him again. He had not heard that voice for a long while, and he took a moment to sort the sound—had he just heard it, had he always heard it, was it the voice of more than just someone he'd known on a trail? Owen waved again, then turned toward the sun, tipped his head back to take the full straight angle, a small figure far

on the shore, feet planted on the beach, not father, not
brother, just Owen from down the valley, across the Wind
River. That was all. No more than a surprise. No more than
a visit. Business.

Walker backed away, tested the biscuits, pulled the Dutch
oven from the fire. And then Owen came up against the light,
high on horseback in the doorway, and he swung down, left
Shell to wander, came in, dropped a leader with three small
trout on the table.

"We thought you were dead, Mr. Avary."

"I'm not."

"Good to see you alive. Very good. I'm glad I caught you.
I just rode up for the day. We've got plenty of work up here.
I could use your skill. I can use all I can hold on to. You can
see I got Shell back."

"I'm sorry about Shell."

"That's all right, Walker. Things work themselves out. We
only lost two days on the way to Cheyenne. You must have
some sort of story to tell, son. The story itself would be worth
the trouble you caused."

"No story. I had a different way to go. That's all. I've got
a girl now."

"A girl? Another girl?"

"She went down to see Charlie. She needs some boots."

"Is it that Indian of yours?"

"No. It's not her."

"We ain't seen that Indian girl. What, it's been three or
four months since we lost you?"

"That might be. If you say so. I don't know."

"We went ahead and laid claim to this valley. We already
had our cattle here, you know, and Charlie, and now the
improvements."

"My claim?"

"You wasn't at the land office with us, Walker."

"No. That's right."

"We got all this work done on corrals and a barn and shed.
You seen it? A cozy set-up. I got some work done on this
lodge to make it more like a place to live. That old shelter of

yours wasn't much but an Indian burrow." Owen walked through the room, tested the windowpanes, tested the mattresses. "You can stay here, if you want. Charlie's got a tent down at the creek. He don't use this lodge much. He says the wind is too noisy. I don't hear any wind, do you?"

There was just the lake's brightness uphill and the solid woods downhill, beyond the open doors. "There isn't any wind," Walker said. "Not now. I don't hear anything." He tried to hear the constant falls, to hear the funnel of the valley, but Owen was shuffling around the room.

"Let's get these fish going," Owen said, and he scooped them from the table and handed them to Walker.

Walker found a skillet, some grease, put the skillet on the flames. He pressed the trout down against the heated grease. They sizzled, and a spatter caught the back of his hand. He sucked at the burn.

Owen stood at the window, looked out at the lake. Walker stood at the door, looked at the same view. A crow came down from the upper woods, gave the lake a quick look, and kept moving. The crow could be down at the Wind River in a few minutes, it could find the fields rising toward the northern range, could find cottonwoods and carrion.

"Two days after we lost you, Walker," Owen said, "when we was trying to catch up to where we would have been, we rode right into dusk. Henry was at the reins with the carriage lamp lit. The horses' hooves threw echoes back from rocks, or there were no echoes, just nothing at all out there. I saw some thicker sage and outcroppings ahead, and it looked like a spot for us to camp, so I gave Henry an elbow and he flicked the reins and readied the turn. Then a broad bright bird flashed up into the beam of our lantern and Shell startled and caught it with a toss of his head and it lifted above us and its wings spread and it hit the tailgate and released. Henry pulled the wagon on into the sage. We climbed down and took the lantern and shined the light back at the road. We found some feathers on the ground. There was no sound from the road. There was no squawk or flapping."

"You killed it?" Walker said.

"I don't even know what it was," Owen said. "The darkness of that road never came clear. No sense of the road even. The stars filled solid to the horizon. We built a fire. We grilled cuts of the antelope we'd shot that afternoon. The day's heat disappeared. There were sounds far off. I'd say the wind was a solid creature. It left traces. In the morning, the dust on the road was rippled, and the sage leaves were torn."

Walker returned to the fire. The trout were browning. He tipped them, looked at the flesh inside. Owen laid two plates on the table, two forks, two cups of lake water, and sat waiting. Walker took the skillet from the fire, slid a fish onto each plate, set the extra aside. He pried two biscuits from the oven and placed them beside the fish. Then he sat across from Owen and they started eating. Owen dug the flesh from the cheek.

"Do you know how many miles we traveled?" Owen said.

"I don't know."

"I have a map in the barn—I'll show you later. There's a good wagon road all the way below Fort Washakie. Then you come along the railroad. I tell you, the noise of that machine—it's a beautiful thing when it passes out of hearing. Then we came on into Cheyenne at dawn. You missed that city, Walker. There were hundreds of miles of grass and scrub and strings of fence, and then of a sudden there were full-blown streets and puddles and yards. And already there were people out and about. Ahead we saw a crowd of men and children looking at something. We came on and saw three poles angled together tall, and a rope hanging down from the join, and a body hanging there from the neck. There was a sign inked on paper, pinned to him. It said, 'This man was hung by the Vigilance Committee for stealing mules.' The dead man was young enough, not even as old as you. His cheeks were all black with bloody scratches. His neck was blue with the throttle of the rope. A man in uniform was working on the rope with a knife. He was sawing and trying to keep from touching the body. It was not a good sight, not for our first sight of the city. You ain't planning on stealing any mules, are you, Walker?"

"I already got a mule."

"It's a good mule all right."

"I'm not stealing anything."

"No."

"Not stealing anything for keeps."

"No." Owen tapped his fingers on the table, scratched his chin. He looked at the fire already gone to ash. He looked at Walker, reached across and tapped the back of Walker's hand—the sharp crescent nail dug into a blue vein—retracted his hand.

"At the land office," Owen said, "we found our sections on the charts—this high country is not hardly mapped at all—we had to fill in the details and draw the roads we've been using to drive up and down our valley and up to here. We signed the books and papers and paid our fee and stepped out to our wagon. I liked the Wyoming dust that coated my horses and everything I carried, liked it better then. Shit, I would've rolled in it, I was feeling so good and content and ready to start right back. But Henry wanted to have a time in Cheyenne. You should've come along, Mr. Avary."

Owen drank the water down, tapped the empty cup. He ate the biscuit, finished his fish, stepped to the downhill door and flung the bones and skin off into the grass. He stood there, looking toward the creek. "I want you to build a decent cabin for me, sheltered, but in the sunlight. There. Near the trees. I'll pace it out for you."

Walker looked past Owen, through the door, looked toward the creek and the boulders, to the spaces he had long plotted for cabins, three or four at least, the lights squared beneath the spruce eaves.

"I'll tell Charlie," Owen said. "You can work with him. I know you can skid logs. A winter job for you. And we'll see what work we can find for your new girl."

"Work?"

"See what her skills are. See how she matches with the chores. Make sure she shares in the operation. We got a list of possibles I can think of."

"A list?"

"Something fair. Passable. A modest job to keep her place here, if she wants to stay."

"Listen, Owen."

"Walker?"

"Listen. You don't know—"

"Oh, son, we'll work it out. You've got your place here again. We'll make this whole high country something, won't we? I told you my wife, Sarah, has come around from Montana? And Henry met a girl in Cheyenne—I wouldn't be half surprised if the girl showed up before winter. A sweet girl. No doubt. Walker, there's already a better road digging through. No time for business that doesn't pay in the long run. I'll keep you busy. I'll be fair. I've already been fair, haven't I?"

Walker looked out at the afternoon lowering, the fish bones in the grass, the horses and mule in the corral, the cattle lining toward the creek, and Shell too lined toward the creek, empty stirrups swaying, reins trailing underfoot. How far up the valley had the cattle wandered through the summer? How many head? How many men had built the barn, the shed, the fences? Good fences, buck-and-pole, and the barn squat and square and shingled, and a log bridge across the creek, the logs chipped flat on the top, and the trails trampled to bare dirt. If the Sheepeater girl crept finally to the ridge and looked down, if she had found her way from the high skyline domes and back through the defiles and across the drainages, if she hadn't shied from the scents, if she hadn't found another trail, followed another creek to another river, if she hadn't moved out onto the plain, if she hadn't found her sweet brother or ridden fast on a bareback horse or folded the hides, packed the tipi, if she hadn't fit her language to another, her voice taking them all back into the range, her story rising past the swallowed rivers, past the sagebrush on ground black with rain, past the glacier lilies in the summer snow melts, the marsh marigolds, the whitebark pine fallen and bleached hard and unlikely to rot, the stone valleys sheened with fast water, blotched with lichen, the lakes pure as sky and jumbled with islands of boulder and cut with jumping trout and their growing circles, the bighorn, the midnight shelters, if she waited, if she had returned, what would she see? A man working, or men working. She knew the sounds. She had followed him through the whole construction of the lodge, followed him through whatever he desired. But the men she saw weren't him—she knew his small shoulders, his hunch of concentration, his voice, his eyes, his black hair grown long, his hands. The lodge, its windows newly curtained—red eyes at night. And the other buildings, the world sprouting new trails and smoke. Why would she find her way down from the ridge? Why would she let those new voices wash around her? She would see Eugenia walking up from the woods now, Eugenia wallowing along in huge boots, Eugenia looking up, stepping into the lodge. "Owen?" she said.

"Yes, ma'am." He backed out of her way, watched her pass, nodded, stooped a bit to see up under her wild hair.

"I'm Eugenia. Walker's wife. Good of you to visit." She lifted the lid from the oven and tested the biscuits. "These'll do. I was helping Charlie get his stores organized." She slid the last trout onto a plate and sat at the table. "I'm going to eat this fish, if that's all right."

"That's all right," Walker said, watching her break through the crisp scales.

"Yes," Owen said.

"Good." She smiled, chewing, and motioned for them to join her. Walker sat on the bench beside her, and Owen sat across. She rubbed Walker's knee, her touch clear through the tattered cloth, fingered the deerskin at his elbow, ran a finger across his brow and hooked his hair behind his ear. "This place is pure luxury," she said. "This place is all I want. We're early in the territory, so we can shape it, build on it. Isn't that right, Owen?"

"Yes, ma'am." He smiled, looked at her dark hands, her white brow. "That's what I'm thinking."

"And Charlie says your wife has arrived."

"Yes. She has. Sarah. Last month."

"She'll be wanting to come up and see what a nice claim Walker and I have here, what nice work Walker has done. All settled. All square. All secure. She'll want to see our child when it comes. She'll want to visit. She'll want to walk with me around Walker's beautiful lake. I can't wait to meet her. I'm sure she's a fine lady. I'm sure she'll want to share my hospitality. She'll want to hear the story of how Walker saved me. As fine a young man as she could want to know. How he brought me the long way through the range and found his home."

The advancing clouds were high above the valley, the last of the evening in the treetops, the stars beginning to leak through. No wind. Not even a breeze. Soon a crescent moon would clear the ridge. From off through the woods Walker heard the shifting of the tall dark trunks, the snap of something broken or falling, but the sounds were slow, without direction, and each seemed to have traveled a long wandering path before finding him.

He found the trail along the creek, followed the rolling passage of the water, and he paused where the view opened back through the woods to the corrals and shed and barn. In the gray light, the horses stood together, head to tail. The buckskin mare. The monster black. Shell, waiting to take another trail. And Walker's mule in its own corner, asleep or listening, sure to know every sound.

He walked on, stopped when the low angle of Charlie's tent came in among the trees. Firelight on the canvas. The woodsmoke drifted, the woods smothered and dim. Charlie and Owen shuffled about, tending to chores. Charlie, a big man, a head taller than Walker, the broad brim of his hat, his shirt pockets full of paper, snuff, pebbles, nails, his boots sharp and neat. And Owen, heavier now, the paunch of a rich summer. Their supper was settling in their guts, Eugenia's cooking, enough food to slow any man, a warm weight toward sleep. And they were quiet, after the hours of Eugenia's voice, the songs she'd led them through, a whole string of tunes. She could have kept them singing on into the night, but they were tired, and they'd excused themselves.

They pulled off their socks and boots and trousers and shirts, hobbled about on the littered ground—cones, sticks, sharp rocks. Each washed his face and hands with water from a cold bucket. They pissed against a rock, a tree. Then they reached into the tent, came out with longjohns, dry socks, dressed themselves in the soft clothes, warmed their hands at the flames.

"Your wife don't expect you, does she?" Charlie said.

"She's too busy to expect anything."

"You got her running?"

"No. She has her own ideas. I'm glad for anything she can do. She's better at most things."

"It's lucky, I guess, that you got her to come into this territory."

"I know. She's a good gal."

They ducked into the tent, one after the other, their voices cut with the groan of the cots, voices half lost.

"—smoke the meat we got, the moose—"

"—all's fair, and a start—"

Then they were silent, deep beneath the blankets. As well as anyone who had slept these mountains, summer and winter, Walker knew the long fall into sleep, the weight of blankets and the thought of morning, the grip of darkness and the way sound carries through a cold dawn, trapped between the sky and the frosted earth, the sound of something unseen hurrying, something digging through a tunnel to a dark burrow lined with shed fur, grass, dry flowers, or something weaving the air among the crowning branches, catching hold of a branch in the thickest burst of branches, sidling against the trunk, looking up into the clouds that afforded no access to a high escape, looking down at the earth for the movement of something small and hot blooded. On the coldest mornings, you dare not move an inch—any movement might take your warm skin onto a cold expanse of bedding, might open the covers to a draft. You barely breathe. You listen far beyond the walls, through the woods, and sink deeper.

Walker continued, from trail to trail. There was nothing left of evening. He stepped over the fallen logs, beneath the low branches and leaning trunks, ran his hands along the skin of fat boulders.

His shelter was slumped into the mountain. The men had taken parts of it to burn—one wall was gone. The structure might stand for a few years, or it might moulder away beneath the weight of the coming snow and the warm spring mud. Eugenia had already been through whatever was left in there. She'd come back to the lodge with an armload, saying, "It was all dry. All stored. Look at this."

He ducked in against the roof beam, as if he held the roof with the shrug of his shoulder. He smelled the remnants of fire, the dust of beetles, frail glue of broken webs. He couldn't reach the floor, couldn't bring himself to release his hold on the beam and slide fully beneath the roof. But he knew what he would see—what he would feel—the stones black with soot, the stones lining the storage pits, the smooth spaces against the walls where they would lie, the cold translucent shards of obsidian, scraps of horn. All picked through. The useful bits taken. He stepped away.

He caught the trail that rose among the spruce, came to the buried end of an old rock fall or avalanche, and, uphill, the ground was open, a slash cleared through the forest, open nearly to the ridge, rimmed with aspen, white trunks, grown with snowberry, yarrow, aster, cinquefoil. The moon shone now, in a scrap of open sky. Around him, the light was caught by the boughs, suspended.

Far up the slope, almost into the first stars, a dense clump of trees anchored a moonlight shadow. He saw the wolves running from around that darkness, a dozen at least, bounding. They would catch him. Beautiful, the strength of them, the leaping and the teeth, the tails out behind. They were almost at him, they would carry him off. But they spread out,

swift as the moonlight they carried—they were coyotes, marauders—and passed on. Long gone. Not to be followed.

He turned, faster now, found another trail toward the shelter, on toward the lodge. The going was smooth, curving
through a tall corridor among the trees, and then he stopped
at the edge of the woods.

The lodge, perched on the promontory, lamplight red in
the curtains. Inside, between the panes, the space was bright.
He approached. It seemed a long rise from the trees, with the
valley huge around him, the moon slow through the clouds.

Then he saw the lake. The long flat gap gathered whatever
moonlight hadn't already been trapped by the ridges and
cliffs. The light sank into the water and shaped another night
without limit, as deep as the sky, dense with lazy currents,
dense with old rain.

And the lodge towered. The smoke gave cleanly from the
chimney. There was nothing else for this space. And he heard
Eugenia—she crossed the light, opened the door. The sharp
sound of the hinges lined straight away and didn't return.
Then the sound of the fire on the hearth, the stones he had
fit, and the sound almost of the light in its endless echo from
wall to wall, a welling into the rafters, and the dark logs holding what light they could on their dusty curves, their knots,
remnant bark. Eugenia's trousers were tucked into her boots.
She held an empty plate, a knife. She squinted, looked toward
him.

"I wish you'd come inside."

At the table, Walker spread the maps—the Chin brothers' map with its false markings, the railroad pamphlet with the Pullman cars like palaces and the snakes of tiny names, and the map Owen had brought from the barn, the claims laid over the terrain. He marked himself in Wyoming Territory, reached west and marked the bay, reached south beyond the paper and marked the inland passage, reached east onto the table and marked another bay, triangulating his years. Leaning over the skein of rivers and mountains, he counted the turns and miles from each border—an impossible stretch of land, rising to these peaks.

Beside the maps, Eugenia laid the quilled tunic, the deerskin clothing dug from Walker's shelter, the skins. She leaned there in the failing lantern light, working her hands over the surfaces. The skins were worn, darkened by wear and oil and dirt, stiff and flaking. He smelled something dense—age, filth.

He remembered the Sheepeater girl squatting over her work, scraping at the backside of a hide with a flat sharpened stone the size of her palm, a stone from the obsidian cliffs. Bits of stringy matter curled against the blade's advance. She brushed a pile of scrapings into the fire, and the flame sizzled and spit.

The lantern died out. He could no longer see much of

Eugenia beside him at the table, just her shape, just the flat silver windows. He heard the falls. He heard the night hum the chimney, stir the last coals toward ash. The smell of those hides. He felt for her hand—her fingers rested on the quilled patterns.

"Walker," she said. "How soon?"

"The child?"

"The winter."

"Could be tomorrow, or a week, or a month or two."

"So we might not see any traffic till spring. I have time to get my mind straight. You think Owen and Charlie enjoyed the supper?"

"It was good."

"All I had was their dry stock and tins. I can do better. There's so much out there. I'll have to talk to Sarah."

"She's only been here a month."

"And how long have you been here?"

"I can't remember when I first arrived. Or if I ever left."

"We'll have to start marking the days." She stood up from the table. He heard her lift the skins, and then she was at the bunk. He heard the rustle of her clothes, the noise of the mattress as she settled. She was against the wall, her voice boxed in deep. "I'd like you to point the way to the road down at the Wind River."

"It's not a road. It's hardly a trail."

"We would have followed that trail, my family and the others. I want to see it. I've just had the notion that if I went down there I'd see us pass. Is that a crazy idea?"

"You want to know."

"What's the land like down there?"

"There are tall spruces leaning out over the long river-bends, and big striped badlands, and thick grass, and eagles, ravens, antelope, and mountains to each side."

"I could watch the trail. I might just hear the river and the wind in the spruces, but after days or years I might hear the wagon wheels and the horses. Which side of the river does the trail take?"

"The near side."

"So they could come up to me without trouble, if they saw me?"

"Yes."

"Do you think they'd know me, my brother and mama and daddy and John William and the Paiutes and the other men?"

"They might."

"Or they'd look at me and keep going?"

"Up the trail to Union Pass and on to the Snake River."

"Yes." She shifted. He heard the skins slide across her shoulders and neck, catch against her hair. "Somewhere toward the pass, the river thins to nothing. I've seen the places where the rivers start—you showed me."

He lit the lantern, lowered the wick until a broad flame flickered orange. He ate a spoonful of the canned stew and a biscuit. He stoked the fire, worked it until it burned tall. The room was a tight box of heat. In the bunk, she was rolled beneath the skins, silent now, buried. He stripped off his clothes and stood at the hearth, felt his skin dry and tighten.

He smelled the acid beneath his arms, musty as decay. He filled a pot from a bucket, water so cold it might have been ice, and heated it at the fire. Steam rose and drew the scent of old forest from the walls. He wet a rag and smoothed his face. Palming a scrap of soap, he worked up a tiny lather beneath his arms and at his crotch. He dabbed at the soap bubbles, pushed them into swirls, a fleeting, airy decoration. He continued with the rag, dipping and wringing and working with the soap. He traced his toes, his fingers, his bony shoulders, his neck, his lips. He tasted himself on the cloth —the same taste he had always known, or known for years —if he had ever tasted any other way, he had forgotten—the soil of sweat, the soil of granite and sap. He poured hot water through the cloth, rinsed the soap from where it clung, and wrung the water onto the floor beside the hearth. It pooled there, the milky water, unlikely to evaporate cleanly, so he soaked it up with another rag—a muddy mistake.

He held still beside the fire, ran his hands lightly over his skin to spread the dampness thin and let it draw away. Then, with the fire's heat still strong behind him, he stood at the window and edged the curtains farther back. The glass was cold.

The night was far dimmer than the lamplight, the sliver moon deep in cloud. He saw how his hip bones had risen, how his hands had reddened and thickened at the joints. He thought of Captain Avary's hips and joints and the loose muscle of it all. He couldn't see anything passing in the night—the lake was blank. He crossed to the other window. Outside, his shadow blocked a lit square of ground. Nothing moved. No sign of fire or lantern. No doubt Owen and Charlie were long asleep, drawn into dreams, wrapped from the cold.

The lantern sputtered out again. He touched the windowpane—he was gone. He wondered if he would see an animal if it passed. He watched long enough for the darkness to open. He saw the trails dug by the men's summer passage, the footprints and hoofprints and the bare hollows where the prints had filled with dust and spruce needles and flower scrap. He saw the edge of the trees. He knew the splay of the roots. He saw the limbs and their droop, and he knew the angle of those branches when they were weighted with snow or disturbed only by the breeze. He saw how the ranks of dark trunks slowly filled each gap into the distance, how the passage of any man or animal would be a series of separate moments of passage cut by the straight blackness of the heavy trees. Only the woods themselves held the complete arc of movement.